and racism in our collective backyard. This powerful novel shows us the true meaning of, 'it takes a village,' and that doing the right thing should be color blind."

—**KAREN WHITE**, *New York Times*
bestselling author of *The House on Prytania*

"*Mr. Jimmy From Around the Way* is a thoughtfully written, thought-provoking, complacency-smashing novel of redemption and restoration, and a testament to the truth that it is in lifting up others that we ourselves are lifted up."

—**MARIE BOSTWICK**, *New York Times* and *USA Today*
bestselling author of *Esme Cahill Fails Spectacularly*

"In Jeffrey Blount's poignant novel, *Mr. Jimmy from Around the Way*, James Ferguson must lose his life to gain one worth living. The catalyst for his awakening is found in Ham, Mississippi, a community of systemic racism, poverty, and violence. This is where Blount's writing shines. With a true sense of place and authentic dialogue, the author introduces characters not easily forgotten. I found myself crying and cheering for those characters, lost in their pain and ultimately, joy. *Mr. Jimmy from Around the Way* is a heartwarming story with the emotional depth of an important read."

—**JOHNNIE BERNHARD**, author of *Hannah and Ariela*, winner
of the National Federation of Press Women, Novel Award 2023

"A feat of beauty and cultural significance, *Mr. Jimmy From Around the Way* is at once heartbreaking and defiantly hopeful, a work of force that illuminates the human condition. Written with amazing grace, the novel immerses us in the life of unforgettable billionaire James Henry Ferguson who struggles to keep his faith in his darkest hours, putting the very fate of his community at stake. Packed with tension, hard-won wisdom, surprising twists, and shattering emotional power, it's a testament to the infinite possibilities of good will and personal transformation. Jeffrey Blount has delivered a vivid portrait of love, race, redemption, and the American dream. It reaches into your heart, twists it, breaks it, mends it, and ultimately transforms it—it doesn't let you go. An instant classic."

—PAMELA HAMILTON, author of
Lady Be Good: The Life and Times of Dorothy Hale.

"African American billionaire James Henry Ferguson had it all—a successful career in Washington, D.C. and a beautiful and loving wife and daughters. And then he lost it. His fall from grace landed him in the small, segregated town of Ham, Mississippi, where he hoped to hide from the world, and his own moral failure. Settling into the poverty-stricken neighborhood known as 'around the way,'—long abandoned by the powerful White forces that be—he falls in love with the people—especially the children—who affectionately call him, 'Mr. Jimmy.' Blount balances page-turning plot twists and turns with elegant literary prose and emotional integrity in this amazing novel. Fans of the 1970 movie, *They Call Me Mister Tibbs!* and the 1974 memoir (and movie) *The Water is Wide* by Pat Conroy will love *Mr. Jimmy From Around the Way.*"

—SUSAN CUSHMAN, author of *John and Mary Margaret* and
the editor of the anthology *Southern Writers on Writing*

"A moving novel with richly drawn characters and sharp prose. Author Jeffrey Blount explores what happens when a mistake causes one man's family, friends, and strangers on the internet to challenge his integrity and make him doubt his own worth in the world. *Mr. Jimmy From Around the Way* teaches us that every journey to redemption ultimately must involve a painful reckoning with your true self."

—STEVE MAJORS, author of *High Yella: A Modern Family Memoir*

"A crime of the heart draws a devastating sentence. Can James Henry Ferguson find his way back? Is redemption even on the table? Using a deft hand, Jeffrey Blount takes us behind 'Mr. Jimmy's' agonizing journey, where black and white figure prominently, and yet—as in the lives we all lead—everything is a thousand shades of gray."

—**STEVE PIACENTE,** author, life coach and communications trainer

"Jeffrey Blount's *Mr. Jimmy From Around the Way* is a compelling narrative of a man's search for the meaning of goodness in his life and the world around him. By dynamic use of flashbacks, he allows his readers to live in the tension between the values espoused by James Henry Ferguson's Black Baptist parents and the ethical standards rampant in the-get-rich-quick culture in which he has become a billionaire. While James's life is shaped by a social mission to alleviate the effects of extreme poverty, the book is not a homily. Rather, the intersecting life stories of all Blount's characters raise questions for his readers. How do we determine if a person is a 'good man' or 'good woman?'—or simply a good human?

Blount implies how we might heal the fractured world around us. James, a leading Black businessman, must listen to the ideas and hopes of individuals within one impoverished community before developing a plan for deploying his philanthropy. It is clear James did not become a billionaire businessman without supportive family members and mentors and friends during his education. Similarly, he cannot become a 'good' philanthropist without the collaboration of the community members whom he is trying to help.

These questions are embedded in a graceful narrative with sparkling and witty dialogue. You will find yourself smiling, even laughing, as you journey along with Blount's characters. But you will, by the end, find yourself moved to tears by what abject poverty does to human beings. At least, I was."

—**LARRY I. PALMER** is the author of the memoir, *Scholarship Boy: Meditations on Family and Race*, and professor of law emeritus at Cornell University.

MR. JIMMY
from **AROUND**
the **WAY**

ALSO BY JEFFREY BLOUNT

The Emancipation of Evan Walls
Hating Heidi Foster
Almost Snow White

Susan,
May you find meaning in this journey. *Blessings!*

MR. JIMMY

from AROUND

the WAY

a novel

JEFFREY BLOUNT

BEAUFORT BOOKS

Hardcover: 9780825310324
Ebook: 9780825309106

For inquiries about volume orders, please contact:
Beaufort Books
sales@beaufortbooks.com

Published in the United States by Beaufort Books www.beaufortbooks.com
Distributed by Midpoint Trade Books, a division of Independent
Publishers Group
www.ipgbook.com

Interior design and cover design by Mimi Bark
Cover image by © Yolande de Kort/Trevillion Images

For my children,
Julia and Jake

All slave rolls and sea glass
And love

"Mercy, be kind in this moment
and come to my aid,
before I make a wreckage of
myself again."

—S.A. Borders-Shoemaker

––––––––––

"Each of us is more than
the worst thing we've ever done."

—Bryan Stevenson

1984
Washington, DC

PROLOGUE

She and her quiet sorrow were the beginning of his giving, nudging him quietly yet powerfully from his youthful preoccupations and awakening a long-forgotten oath. When he exited the post office, breathlessly late for work, he saw her leaning against the wall, her poverty starkly evident in her threadbare dress and the frayed pocketbook she tightly held. He forgot about his job.

His minister father lived for one thing—to feed his flock both literally and figuratively. As a child at the dinner table, he had felt the gravity of his father's sincerity as he praised God and ended each day's grace with a line from The Lord's Prayer.

Give us this day our daily bread.

Each night, for all of his childhood, he knew his father's hope was for everyone to be fed. His father hated the idea that anyone, particularly children, should finish the day kneeling before the Heavenly Father with an empty belly. As his father fastidiously ended each night's grace, he'd promise himself that he would follow his father's lead. But in the passage of time and the messy fog of life, he had forgotten. And now she'd soundlessly called him out.

She stood stiffly, her back pressed hard against the cement. Looking straight ahead, she refused to see him as he slowly walked toward her. As he got closer, tears pushed aside the dust on her face, floodwaters of relief announcing an end to that morning's drought. As he stopped at her side, because he knew he shouldn't force her to look head-on at his prosperity, he longed to take his hand and wipe away her tears. Instead, he opened his wallet and looked at the only bill he had. A twenty. He held it near her hands. Looking briefly out of the corner of her eye, she snatched it and quickly crumpled it up in a fist. He turned away when she began to tremble, visibly struggling with her poverty, his gift, and how they both now defined her.

Blocks away, in the quiet of his car, he cried. Why hadn't he had a thousand dollars in his wallet? He would have given her that in a heartbeat. To prove it, for the next month, he went to the post office every day, carrying one thousand dollars in cash, hoping that he would see her. He never did, but he promised that the moment they shared would shape him as an individual and guide him as his father's daily grace once had.

2016

Washington, DC

Lady Nymph
@lnymph

Trippin!! Old brother paying for the booknerds to go to college. Yo I fucked this dude! A desperate frantic fuck too. Money large though! 😆

2017

Ham, Mississippi

ONE

No good deed goes unpunished. If he'd said it one time, he'd said it a thousand times. He said it in his dreams. He said it on long, lonely, introspective walks. He said it in his mind when he should have been thinking of other things. He whispered it to himself in the midst of crowds, and he screamed it aloud as he stood in front of his new home, which was about fifty feet from a dusty, dirt road, overlooking acres upon acres of overgrown field, desperate for the attention of a good farmer.

"NO GOOD DEED GOES UNPUNISHED!"

When he stopped yelling, he looked down the road to his left. Maybe fifty or sixty yards away, a woman stood with a hand against her forehead, shading her eyes from the sun as she tried to see what all the screaming was about. He ignored her and walked up the steps, took the keys out of the mailbox, and opened the door to his new life.

He bought the little house after seeing its picture on the internet. He called the real estate office and asked for Olivia Fey Carol. She sold him the house without him ever setting foot in it, and for an extra sum, she put him in touch with a contractor who was shocked but pleased by the opportunity to turn an old eyesore into a house once again.

When he found it, the house had long been a fine example of rural decay. Resting on crumbling brick columns for a foundation, it had settled into an awkward lean with only a few pieces of the tin remaining for its roof. Its clapboard outerwear was holey and dry, gray with age. Every window and door had been boarded up for years. It looked like he felt.

Now though, the house had been revitalized. All four rooms. Bedroom, kitchen, small storage room, combination dining, living and family room, plus one bathroom. In what he would grow to facetiously call his great room, there was a couch, a coffee table, a Barcalounger, and a large flat screen TV on one wall. It was the one extravagance retained from his old life. Satellite television with the NFL package so that he could watch whatever game he was inclined to.

He, however, had not been revitalized. Not even close. He settled into the lounge chair, folded his hands in his lap, and stared into the blank TV.

He *was* James Henry Ferguson. He *had* a wonderful life.

That life started with Rebecca Harrell, his most amazing wife. He leaned back and stretched out in his new recliner. He closed his eyes and concentrated as he sought to discover her once again. It was thirty years ago when they met. There was nothing special about the day. He was a young, ambitious 25-year-old in the big city, which is what he considered Washington, DC, to be. She was waiting at a bus stop, a brown paper bag full of groceries in her lap. She was quiet and peaceful, staring in the direction from which her bus would be coming. She wasn't even smiling, yet she seemed radiant. Her countenance moved him deeply, and as he changed direction to walk to her, he desperately hoped that she would be someone with whom he could immediately connect.

She turned when she felt him coming toward her. What she did next sealed the deal for him. It was simple. She looked up at him and smiled. She didn't even know him, but her first reaction was to display kindness. Her face didn't curl into a mask of rejection for just one more hungry male armed with his latest pickup line. It said something about the kind of woman she was. Open. Gracious. Tenderhearted and humane. He wanted to be with her.

"Hello," he'd said, holding out his hand. "My name is James Henry Ferguson."

She took his hand and held it. "Rebecca Gale Harrell. I don't usually give out my middle name at the first meeting," she said with a little laugh.

He was embarrassed. "I'm sorry. It's how I was trained to formally introduce myself back home."

"And where exactly was that?"

"A small town in Virginia."

"Good manners in small-town Virginia, I guess?"

He smiled. "Yes, ma'am."

She slid over on the bench, and he sat down. The bus came and went as they spoke, and eventually, he gave her a ride home. That night, he took her out to dinner, where everything he thought she was as he'd walked toward her earlier in the day turned out to be true. He was swept off his feet.

His cell phone ringing brought an abrupt halt to his reminiscing. He scrambled to get it out of his pocket.

"Hello."

"Hello, Mr. Ferguson. This is Olivia Fey Carol."

James sat up in his chair. "Oh, hi. Nice of you to call."

"Have you arrived?"

"I have. I'm sitting in the living room."

"Great. Should I come over? Is there anything I can do for you today?"

"No, I'm good, thank you. You guys did a great job. Everything is here, and the place is clean and comfortable."

"Well, good then. It's the first time I sold a house to someone and then had it fixed up for them before they even set foot in the place."

"I imagine my request was an odd one indeed, but as I said, you've handled it well."

"Well then, I'll let you continue to get acquainted, and I'll stop by sometime later in the week. And oh, before I forget, I left something special for you on the counter next to the fridge."

James twisted around in his seat and took note of the black, rectangular box wrapped in a sky-blue ribbon.

"I see it. Thank you very much, and I look forward to meeting you sometime in the next week or so."

"Bye now."

"Bye."

Reminiscing was painful, and James decided he needed a distraction. He'd try sitting on the front porch for a change in scenery. Maybe it would inspire his mind to wander some place different. Some place less complicated. Some place less painful. He opened the screen door and walked out onto the front porch. An old woman stood at the bottom of his steps, waiting and staring. Her hands were resting in the pockets of her faded, blue housecoat. She had loose, thinning, white curls about her head. Walnut skin and feisty eyes. Skinny but tough-looking, reminding him of a description he'd heard a Texas football player give about himself—a thin piece of leather, well put together.

"I guess you done screaming for today," she said dispassionately. "That be right?"

It was the woman who'd been watching him yell at the house when he first arrived.

"Yes, ma'am," he replied. "I do believe I'm done."

"What's your name, son?"

"James Henry Ferguson, ma'am."

"What your peoples call you?"

"Jimmy."

"Why you here, in . . . in this here particular house?"

"Seeking shelter."

"From?"

"My sins."

She looked around at the cracked and parched dirt road in the direction from which she'd come. He could see her face settle into something disagreeable and hard. She turned back to the field across the road with the big, worn and half collapsed For Sale sign.

"Ain't hell a funny place to come to, to *hide* from your sins?" she asked.

James followed her gaze, nodded, and frowned.

"Well then," he said. "I guess the joke's on me."

"I reckon most folks around here be laughing at you rather than with you," she replied. "Where you coming from anyway?"

"A northern city."

"That's all I get."

"Yes, ma'am."

Her eyes met his, colored in skepticism.

"Why come to this here part of the country?"

"I grew up in a rural area like this. My daddy is a country preacher. I needed to get away from the city and back to my roots."

"The city turn you into something you don't like?"

"No, ma'am. It had nothing to do with the city. Just life taking an unexpected turn."

She nodded as if she understood and held out her hand, which he took, and they shook on their uneasy meeting.

"My name is Miss Septima. I'm your next-door neighbor," she said, nodding in the direction from which she'd come. "I'm round about 92-year-old I reckon, and I ain't afraid of nothing but artificial flowers on my grave."

James had no idea how to respond, so he just nodded and kindly smiled.

"I'll be seeing you, I guess," she said as she turned to walk away.

"Yes, ma'am," he replied. "I suspect so."

And as Miss Septima slowly made her way down the dirt road, James Henry Ferguson took a seat on his new front porch and wondered why he told her anything at all before turning his gaze skyward to consider whether or not his life was over.

He was awakened by a persistent summer breeze, opening his eyes in time to witness the setting sun. He had been asleep for hours, and he wished for more because he hated waking to more nothing to do and more nothing to be. He missed his family so much. He guessed that with all that had come to pass, they still missed him too. Or at least the man he used to be.

In the kitchen, he stood looking at the gift box on the counter. Given the size and shape, he thought it had to be a bottle of wine or maybe champagne. He chuckled. She thought he should be celebrating. He opened the box anyway and was shocked when he saw the $1,400 bottle of wine. It was a 2009 Lafite-Roth-schild, and without touching it, he could sense the taste, born of an elegant blend of 82.5% Cabernet Sauvignon, 17% Merlot, and 0.5% Petit Verdot. James had only one real vice. Olivia Fey Carol had done her homework well. Out of all the things that had been written about him, only one obscure blogger had written about his love of wine and this brand in particular. There was an envelope, which he lifted from the box, opened, and pulled out the note.

I know that you are far away from home in several ways.
I'd hoped that something familiar would
help to ease your transition.
OFC

She knew everything.

There was also a glossy, black corkscrew in the box. He picked it up and rolled it around in the palm of his hand as he scanned the familiar label. He could use it. He could open the bottle, let it breathe for a time, and then come back to its familiar comfort. But in the end, he wistfully placed it back in the box. He took his time wrapping the ribbon around the box, transferring the well-intended gift to the back of the highest cabinet, knowing all along that it wouldn't have contributed to his well-being. In fact, in reminding him of one of his worst moments in life, it would have accomplished just the opposite.

The last time he'd tasted it, he was alone in a lovely four-room suite at the Willard Hotel in downtown DC, banished, flipping from channel to channel, trying to catch a glimpse of his story on the local news. What he eventually saw caused the very next beat of his heart to thump so hard that he had to deeply rub his chest with the heel of his hand, hoping to massage away his sudden discomfort. He had been sipping his Lafite-Rothschild, chatting with his lawyer, Mason Easton, when he stopped his channel surfing at a local news station broadcasting live from the front of his home. Or what had been his home. He sat up sharply in his chair. There was a cluster of microphones at the end of the walkway, waiting to greet whoever would be coming out of his front door. His head became abruptly cavernous. He suddenly felt lightheaded, and the sound of a strong, raging wind blew through leaving behind a dull and pulsating echo. His phone slipped through his hands as they rose to grip the sides of his head. Mason Easton called to him from the floor.

"James! James! Pick up the phone, man. Are you okay? You have to talk to me . . . "

It faded.

All he could hear now was the thumping inside his chest. All he could see was his girls coming through the front door.

Katherine, 24, and Lillian, 19. Both tall, lithe, and in his mind, still innocent. Why would Rebecca feed them to the wolves?

They came out walking hand in hand, and the still cameras began a furious racket, clicking, and clacking. A harsh and angry dialect. But then everything softened when he saw the tissues in Lillian's right hand. It even made him smile a little because it was just so her. If they scolded her, they would later find her in her room, tissues in her hands, preparing to wipe her eyes and blow her nose. They knew when she'd had a bad day at school because she would come to the car with tissues in her hand. They knew when she broke up with her first boyfriend because on one Saturday, their usual date night, Rebecca passed her door and saw her on the bed with tissues scattered about.

She was a step behind her steadier, older sister. Katherine was like his mother, strong and willful. She didn't suffer fools lightly, and she spoke her mind always with force, armed with a formidable intellect. As she got closer to the microphones, she reached into the hip pocket of her jeans and pulled out an index card. She let go of Lillian's hand and began to read.

"We are here because our mother is unable to be. We are here because we would like our privacy returned. What our father did was unconscionable, and it has destroyed our family. Our mother has been a loving, faithful partner, and he broke her trust. He broke our trust too. You all know the sordid details, and we don't know why you keep coming back to us, especially when you know much more than we do. We have nothing more to say. We will never speak publicly about this again. Neither will our mother. So there is no need for you to return looking for any information. Nothing sensational here. Just broken hearts. If you want sensational, talk to his girlfriend, Lady Nymph."

Lillian unintentionally dropped a tissue as they turned to walk back to the house. Katherine slipped the card back into her pocket, and the picture switched to the next news story. But just before, had he caught a glimpse of Rebecca at the door, waiting on the girls to start their lives without him?

Mason Easton called once again from the floor and James picked up the phone.

"Hey, James. I'm sorry. I caught that."

James took a sip of his wine, which for the first time, tasted like something wrong. Like failure. He threw his glass into the next room of his suite. It made a thud when it hit the carpeted floor. He hung up on Mason.

Now, it had gotten dark. He'd made it through his first full day in his new life without *taking* his life. Briefly, he considered food, but his stomach was unsettled. Maybe there would come a day when he would not be held captive by these agonizing memories, even though there were some he couldn't imagine being without.

In his new bed, sleep escaped him. Thinking of Rebecca kept it at bay. Her best smile was her softest smile. He lived for it. Often at dinner parties, he fell out of the conversation and watched her even as he pretended to listen. Sometimes, she would catch him, blush, and smile before giving him the mini nod to pay attention. But that wasn't the one. Sometimes she would laugh hysterically, and he would wait for the moment just as the laughter ended, receding into the briefest of smiles. But that wasn't the one either. *The smile* first happened on a stroll through Dumbarton Oaks Garden. They'd stopped for a rest, and James decided to take a picture. He fumbled with the camera, checking the film and settings. She sat waiting. When he looked up, there it was. She had been watching him, and rather than laugh at his histrionics, she had the softest smile on her face, which was full of everything that had become them. It took him by surprise, and he was overcome with indescribable emotion. He kept it a secret, only telling her about it on their thirtieth wedding anniversary. He'd never wanted her to try to produce it for him. It didn't happen all the time, but when it did, he liked that it was unplanned, unencumbered, honest, and utterly sincere. It told him that there was one thing he could be sure about. He could be sure that he had been loved. Completely.

TWO

James Henry Ferguson grew a beard. His first ever. Not a full-on James Harden, which he concluded must have taken the NBA star many months, if not years to cultivate. His three weeks of growth was infantile by comparison. Each morning, he rose intending to shave, but each day's sprouting was the only indicator that his life was actually moving forward. It was the only consistent momentum present during this period of self-imposed solitude. A period he felt he sorely needed to gather himself before stepping out and into his new world order, which is why he ignored any attempt made to contact him. Now, he stood in front of his bathroom mirror, rubbing his beard, reflecting, and contemplating a clean-shaven new beginning.

During his weeks of seclusion, Miss Septima was the first to disrupt his quiet by shouting his name from the bottom of his steps, two days in a row. He paid her no mind. Olivia Fey Carol must have called a dozen times. A few times he answered, but he put her off. *Call me in two days.* Other times, he let the calls go to voicemail, which he never retrieved. On his second day in Ham, he drove an hour away to shop for groceries so that he wouldn't create any *it's that stranger* noise by shopping locally. He was an excellent cook, but he didn't have the desire or the energy. So he bought easy—eggs, bread, milk, sweet tea, and cereal. He bought lunch meats, frozen chicken tenders, breaded shrimp, and french fries. He bought Jack Daniels St. Louis Style pork ribs, packaged, already cooked. And Hormel meat loaf with tomato sauce. Anything that he could shove in the oven and heat quickly or microwave. But his past life continued to haunt him, scattering his emotions, and blunting his appetite. So much so that when the first knock to greet his front door sounded throughout his home, he was ten pounds lighter than when he arrived. This time he welcomed the interruption.

Two young boys stood on the other side of his screen door. One of them held a box of Hershey's chocolate bars. In DC, he would have smiled nicely and said that they didn't welcome solicitations and to have a nice day. But this was different. This was reminiscent of the woman from the post office long ago, and he never forgot his pledge.

Their clothes looked washed, but there were holes in their Fruit of the Loom undershirts, which stood in for real t-shirts. Their shorts were worn, the colors faded and stained. No socks. He could smell their body odor from three feet away, and some toes and sides of feet peeked out of the tears in their well-worn sneakers. James opened the screen door.

"You boys want to come in?"

"Uh-un," one said, shaking his head.

So James stepped out onto the porch to meet them on as equal footing as possible.

"You Mr. Jimmy?" asked the same boy.

For a second, James was stumped but then remembered he'd told Miss Septima that his family called him Jimmy. He nodded to the young man.

"What's your name?"

"Beech. That's it. They named me after a tree my granddaddy liked in his backyard."

"My name is Juba," said the second boy. "It's a African king name."

James nodded, raising an eyebrow so that he might seem impressed. "It's a pleasure to meet you, young men."

They looked at each other and giggled, struck by his fancy tone and choice of words. He understood and let it go.

"Can I help you?"

They continued to stare at him.

"Miss Septima ain't said you had no beard," Beech finally said.

"I grew it since I last saw her. What's with the candy bars?"

Juba held the box out to him. "We selling candy bars to raise some money for materials for our class. We got a new teacher. She say if we raise enough money, we can get supplies and have a pizza party."

Beech jumped in. "My mama say she got them new stars in her eyes, thinking she can change something with her Teach for America self. She gone run away before too long. Just like all of them."

"Who bought the candy bars so you could sell them?"

"I think she did," Beech said.

"Well," James said, "how have your sales been?"

"Huh?" Juba asked.

"How many candy bars did you sell?"

"Bruh, the real deal is, ain't nobody got no money for these things. That teacher don't know what's what yet. Miss Septima the only one bought one. You want one? You look like you can buy one."

"That depends," James answered, ignoring the comment on his obvious wealth. "How much are you charging?"

"One dollar for one candy," Beech answered.

"How many are in the box?"

"I don't know. You?" Juba asked looking at Beech, who shook his head.

"Read it," James said. "It's right there on the corner of the box."

Beech stared at the box and haltingly read.

"Thirty-six c-c-count. It say thirty-six."

James looked at Juba. "If there are thirty-five left, since Miss Septima bought one and each one costs a dollar, how much is the entire box worth?"

They both just stared.

"What grade are you boys in?

"We in the sixth grade," Juba replied.

"And how old are you?"

"Eleven," Beech answered.

James nodded thoughtfully. He left the boys out on the porch for a moment and came back with cash in his hand.

"If each one is worth one dollar and there are thirty-five left, then the whole box is worth thirty-five dollars."

"That's a lot of money," Beech said, amazed at the final calculations.

"Here's thirty-five dollars," James said.

"You gone buy the whole dang thing?" Juba asked.

"That's right."

James could see that the boys were taken aback. Beech might have been handling a million dollars the way he looked at the money now in his hands.

"Thank you, Mr. Jimmy," he said, as Juba handed over the candy, but James waved him off.

"It's yours. My gift to you both. Divide them up. Break the odd one in half. Or share them with your friends. Whatever you like."

"Aww, Mr. Jimmy! Bruh, you all right!" Beech said, and the boys energetically waved as they walked away. Waiting for them along the road was Miss Septima. She spoke with them for a minute and then looked toward James as the boys continued on their way. She waved, and he returned it in kind before stepping back into the house.

Word got around. In the next four days, James bought six more boxes of candy.

He shaved.

As he often did, James woke in the middle of the night to find himself disoriented, desperate, and alone. In these moments, his life with Rebecca easily razed his newly erected emotional walls. Some nights, he wrapped his pillow around his head, squinted and yelled, as if that would help him block out the memories rapidly filling his head and bruising his heart. Other nights, he cried softly, haunted even by the very best memories. He wanted nothing to do with them because, in truth, they were the most painful. Sometimes, he found himself rocking on his front porch, hoping for distractions. But it was pitch-black, and he couldn't see a damned thing. The only diversion offered came from the field across the road, the sound of the half collapsed For Sale sign flapping in the breeze. In the end, he always gave in.

Once, he closed his eyes and surrendered his heart, recalling what it was like to be awakened from a peaceful slumber by the profound affection in Rebecca's whisper.

"James Henry Ferguson . . . "

He would wake up yearning for the acute tenderness he knew he would find in her touch, always reminding himself to pay attention to the warm sensation created throughout his body when her skin met his. When she seemed to give of herself in a way that could not be recreated in a dimly lit room or in the light of day. These were the only times that his love was so intensely draining that he couldn't even speak her whole name. He only had breath enough to whisper *Becca* . . . just before they would make soft, passionate love and fall back to sleep in each other's arms. Later, he might wake up and glimpse the shape of her body in the moonlight and be moved to pray, thanking God for the most important blessing of his life.

Another night, he woke up thinking how much he loved just being in the car with Rebecca. It's why he was always suggesting that they take long weekend rides. They talked and talked and talked. They weren't big on playing music loudly or dancing in their seats. They weren't inclined to sing because neither of them had a good voice. Sometimes though, if the right song came on, he might hear her softly, almost whispering the words. Her jeans usually rolled up above the ankles. Her feet on the dashboard, her painted toes wiggling now and then.

THREE

Reverend Ferguson stood on the dirt road in his preaching shoes. Every Sunday, fresh from the pulpit and after blessing the faithful as they passed from his sanctuary into the corrupt world, he gathered Sister Ferguson and little Jimmy. They took a long, reflective walk along Route 674, the country road that passed in front of their home. But before they could start, he would reach down and take some dirt from the road and spread it over his Florsheim Imperial Wingtips. On windy days, he'd let Mother Nature handle the job for him. Either way, he dusted his best shoes.

"I have done this all of your life, Jimmy," he said one Sunday. "Yet, you have never asked me why."

"Sundays are 'don't speak until spoken to' days," Jimmy replied.

Sister Ferguson's laughter was unrestrained. Even the Reverend had to join her.

"My son," he continued. "I have been the beneficiary of God's great love. He has held me above the flock so that I might see and feel their needs. He has made me a pillar of the community. But I will never say anything like this in front of anyone but you and your mother. And I hesitate to do that, but this is a teaching moment. Otherwise, we must be humble at all times."

Jimmy nodded.

"You know that your grandparents were sharecroppers. By the fruit of their exhaustion, they sent me to college. Virginia Union University and Seminary. This dust is a symbol of my birth and my growth. Every Sunday, I spread it on one of my best symbols of success, and it ties me to where I came from. It takes me back in my mind and my heart to who I am at the core. Do you understand, son?"

"Yes, Daddy. I do," Jimmy said.

"Thus endeth the lesson," Reverend Ferguson said, nodding.

Some years later, Department of Transportation workers paved the road. The Sunday walks ended. James missed them dearly, but he never forgot his father's lesson. So when he stepped off the bottom step of his new house, he thought he would remind himself. Even though his father and mother now refused to speak to him, siding with Rebecca and the girls. He stepped onto the dirt road facing Miss Septima's. He knelt down and spread dust over his canvas Vans, which were not his best shoes. But the counsel remained the same. He must be humble. With that in mind, he began his walk.

A deep, full breath accompanied his first steps. Country air seemed to be the same everywhere, he thought. *Lung candy*, his mother sometimes called it—fresh and sweet. The soft crunching sound of his shoes in the unsophisticated dirt also brought him comfort. Even the old For Sale sign added to his rustic, bucolic sensibility. His eyes smiled. The grasses in the field were beginning to show the first signs of their autumn browning. Soon, the leaves would be turning, boasting a palette of gold, brown and orange. This is why he came here. To hear nothing but birds and the rooster's morning call. To be in a space that reminded him of a simpler time in his life, where good, kind people were living good, decent lives, striving to better themselves in a less complicated world. But the joke *really was* on him. Fully. Because Ham, Mississippi, was not the world James Henry Ferguson had in mind.

As he neared Miss Septima's, the air turned quickly from sweet to rot. His stride slowed as he began to see what he apparently couldn't or wouldn't see before. Back in Washington, when he first sat down at his computer to look for refuge from the misery he had created, did he not look at the Google Street View? Was there one? Did he not take a virtual walk through this place that was now his community? Was he so enamored of the little house, sitting at the edge, off by itself, that he just couldn't see the forest for the trees? *What were you thinking?* This, as he began to witness the tragedy of poverty unfolding before his eyes.

Miss Septima's was the first of a long row of houses, most of them shotgun. Many looked like the exhausted shacks of the enslaved that he had seen in books. Miss Septima's was reminiscent of a Praise House, with two slumping box-like rooms on either side. Over the first weeks in Ham, in passing glances, he had noticed that her house, a little more than a football field away from his home, seemed old and gray. But he never imagined that this would be the close-up view. There were three steps up to the porch, which was all fractured wood. Old, uneven, splitting and bowing. One would always have to watch where he stepped. How does she manage at 92? The walls were weathered and broken like his house had been. There were gaps where the walls met the porch floor and at the roofline. The porch was populated by four less than stable plastic chairs. Three two-by-fours held up its roof. One was shorter than the others, resting on two bricks, which almost evened things out. The roof itself was one layer of tin, rusty and with holes at the edges. As he looked ahead, down the row of houses, nothing seemed to be whole.

Passing Miss Septima's, he heard laughter or tears. He couldn't decide which. He didn't know what he'd do anyway if they were tears. He didn't know the woman and didn't want to go where and when he might not be appreciated. And shouldn't he have learned by now? No good deed goes unpunished. He kept moving.

Unkempt bushes and trees lined the yards. The houses all resembling Miss Septima's in their upkeep. In his world, they would have all been condemned, and the residents would have been forced to evacuate for their safety. But not here, and he understood why, which added an intense anger to the emotions now rushing through him.

Everyone seemed to have electricity or at least an attached meter. A couple of homes had old cars out front. Some had air-conditioners propped up in windows by two-by-fours. But there were gaps around the window frames. How did they pay the electric bill?

Every house had substantial siding missing. The foundations were in serious disrepair. He stopped walking and slowly shook his head. He wouldn't find any of his authentic youth in this place.

He was so thankful for the diversion when Juba, the king, ran up to him.

"Mr. Jimmy, Mr. Jimmy! You taking a walk?"

James smiled, warmed by the boy's excitement at seeing him.

"I am, Juba. What's up for you on this beautiful Saturday afternoon?"

"I been over to the pond trying to get a catch. Ain't caught none though. I need to go back, 'cause that's supposed to be dinner. We ate your candy for a couple of nights. That was good too!"

James nodded. When Juba and Beech had come to his front door selling candy, he knew their educations were lacking. He knew that they'd come to his porch from poor families. But he had those families in his hometown. So he didn't think anything was out of the ordinary. He didn't think they were representative of an entire neighborhood or larger community. He didn't understand that they were the embodiment of a section of Ham, Mississippi, society languishing in abject poverty.

"You wanna meet my mama?"

"Oh," James replied, not at all ready for that step. "Maybe another time."

"Please! She know all about you."

"Well, okay," James said, feeling sorry for the boy.

He gave in and followed Juba into a situation he'd only seen in movies. Or in the commercials for emaciated Black and Brown children with distended abdomens. Children from other lands, where White workers pushed meal into their mouths while flies landed on their faces and in their food. Where it only cost fifty cents a day to change their world. *Not here*, he thought.

Patrice was his mother's name. She was sweet and, as James could tell, kind and open to a fault. She welcomed him, attempting to profusely thank him for the Hershey bars, but Juba did most of the talking because she wasn't fluent in English and struggled to speak even in broken sentences. Or maybe she had special needs that had never been identified. There were three other children in various stages of undress. They stared at him, tall, straight, and skinny. They didn't know what to make of him. And he didn't know how to be with them. Juba's mom was missing most of her teeth and coughed consistently and deeply. She was a single mother.

"Mama twenty-seven years old," he said. "All of us got daddies, you know. We just don't know who they is."

The house was in shambles. Uneven floors. In some places, you could see through to the ground. There were wide gaps around the doors and windows, some of which had paper towels stuffed in them. The smell of dirt and dampness filled the house. And maybe mold? He couldn't be sure. He felt as if he needed to sneeze. In the kitchen, dishes were piled in the sink that had water dripping into it from a nasty leak in the roof. It had rained heavily during the night, James remembered. The walls were all black, black. *What the hell?*

"Why are the walls this black, Patrice?" he asked.

She tried to answer, but when it seemed to be taking too long, Juba jumped in to fill the blank spaces. James learned that they had no natural gas in the house. Juba said that nobody in this part of Ham had gas. And they couldn't afford an electric oven. So Patrice cooked in the house with butane, and the black, sticky walls were the result of that. And maybe the reason she coughed so much, he wondered. Sometimes when the two old hotplates, presently on the floor, tucked in between a cabinet and the rusting refrigerator, would work, they cooked that way.

Juba's family and the rest of their immediate neighbors didn't have water heaters. They bathed in cold water or heated it on a hotplate. No one had a shower. He thought back to the boys' body odor when they first came to his front door. When he passed the bathroom, he nearly fainted. *I have to go . . . .*

He was thankful to his hosts and said he would be stopping by again soon, but in the moment, he couldn't really imagine it. He couldn't believe what he'd seen was real. He wanted to get home in the worst way.

As he passed by Miss Septima's, the noises he had heard before were now easily discernible, and they did not constitute laughter. Her cries were louder, more guttural, punctuated by her helpless and dependent calls for her God. Briefly, he thought about Patrice, but could she be of any help? He looked at the house next door, listing and seemingly abandoned. He really wanted to go home. He wanted to shut out the noise of this poverty he'd planted himself next to, but he couldn't ignore her cries. Still, as he started toward her house, he felt he would regret this good deed as well.

"My Jesus, my Jesus! Please, please somebody, my Lawd!"

He took his time walking up the steps, unsure if he should be approaching, not knowing what was causing her pain. He decided to look in a window, but it was covered with a heavy plastic that painters used to cover floors, and it had clouded over. He pushed open the door, which didn't have a lock. Miss Septima was on the floor, crumpled, blood running from her head and face. She didn't seem to be able to move from the waist down, twisting her upper body in obvious pain and flailing her arms. She was delirious. When she was able to focus on him, to see that someone had actually come to her aid, she began to cry. He knelt by her side, her bloody, trembling hand now pulling at his shirt.

James spoke softly to her. He held her head in his hands and told her that he was there for her. He talked her down a bit before trying to figure out what had happened.

"You fell?" he asked.

She nodded, still grimacing from the pain. He touched her housecoat as he sought to comfort her further. It was wet, and it stank of urine. He looked her in the eye without flinching to show her that he didn't care.

"When did you fall?"

She fought hard to answer. "It was dark."

"Oh my God, you've been here all day," he said, angry with himself for earlier—for walking past her cries. "I'll get my phone. We have to call an ambulance."

"Slow to come round here," she managed.

"Okay," he replied. "I understand. I have to get you to a hospital though."

"Ain't got no insurance."

"You won't need it. But you have to trust me. I have to leave for five minutes."

"Lawd Jesus! Why you gone do that?"

"I will be back, Miss Septima. I will be back."

James rushed out of the house, breaking through one of the rickety porch steps as he did. He sprinted to his house with everything he had, so happy that he had decided to shave. He changed into slacks, a nice shirt, and his suit jacket. He dampened a couple of towels and took a couple of dry ones as well. He rushed out to his car.

When he leaned down to wipe the blood from her face, she calmed down a little. She looked at his suit but didn't bother to ask why he'd changed. She understood. In the midst of hurrying, she cautioned him.

"Don't you get no blood on your Sunday best, now."

James smiled as he continued to wipe the blood from her face and hands. After he'd cleaned her up, he went into her bedroom and grabbed a dry housecoat in the hopes that a nurse could change her at the hospital. Then he knelt by her again and prepared her to be moved. In the process, he knocked over a bucket of buttons, and Miss Septima screamed. She reached for them as if they were her children he'd hurt. He pulled her hands together and looked her in the eye.

"Okay now, Miss Septima. I need you to look me in the eye and stay with me. I'm going to lift you. It might hurt badly, now. I can't tell if you broke a hip or something else. You ready?"

The tough old lady who questioned him on the day he arrived fearfully nodded. She was like paper. Her big housecoat had hidden the thin undernourished old woman from him.

He carried her to the car, making sure not to trip on the step he'd broken earlier.

He put her in the passenger seat and leaned it back.

"How are you doing?" he asked as he put on her seatbelt and then his own.

She nodded.

"Okay. That's good," James replied as he saw her face turn sad, her eyes taking in the interior of his BMW M760i.

"This car is prettier than any house I ever set foot in. You got a TV in here."

He started touching the dashboard monitor, choosing to ignore her comment.

"Lawd, what you doing now? Ain't we better get going?" she asked as he typed the hospital address into the car's navigation program. He told her he was setting up the GPS.

"The what?"

"It's like a map inside the monitor here. It will show me how to get to the hospital."

"Have mercy," she said, as he sped out onto the dirt road. "The things White folks can come up with these days."

James felt sad for her. "No, Miss Septima. Actually, a Black woman named Gladys West is largely responsible for this."

"Get on outta here!"

"Yes, ma'am."

"My Lawd."

James was never so happy to see a hospital emergency room. With Miss Septima in his arms, he burst through the automatic doors almost knocking over a maintenance worker mopping up some sort of spill. He had tried to keep her in conversation as he drove along the winding, unfamiliar roads. But she started fading, dipping in and out of consciousness. He became anxious because he couldn't remember if a concussion patient should be kept awake. He reached over and shook her just in case. Her head wound began to bleed again. He gave her a towel, but she couldn't hold it to her head. By the time they arrived, her face was a bloody mess, as was her housecoat. Blood and urine. And she was clearly in pain from something other than her head.

"I need help! Right away!" he yelled as he cleared the doorway into the hospital, carrying Miss Septima. James realized a feeling that he'd had tens of thousands of times in his life. A Black man of obvious status in a room full of White people drawing a contrast between him and the Black help—the Black man with a mop whom he'd almost knocked over and Miss Septima.

"Can I help you?" a young, thirtyish woman behind a counter asked.

"What kind of question is that?" James asked, with blood now running onto his shirt and suit coat.

"Are you next of kin?" the woman asked, nonchalantly.

"What! No, I am a neighbor," James responded.

"Do you know what kind of insurance she has?"

"She doesn't need insurance."

"What?" the woman asked, beginning to laugh.

"I'll pay for whatever she needs."

"And what are you going to do, break open your piggy bank? Maybe you should take her to the colored hospital over in Thompson."

Now there was laughter from the White people in the adjoining waiting area, but James was not about to be distracted by them.

"I know," he said. "Insurance or not, you are required by law to help her. Now, we need to see a doctor, damnit! You call someone and right now!"

The woman responded angrily, "Boy, you can't talk to me like that. I'm not having it."

As her face reddened, the automatic doors behind Mr. Jimmy opened, and a young doctor walked in with a backpack casually hanging off one shoulder. When he saw Miss Septima in Mr. Jimmy's arms, he let the backpack drop. "What happened?" he asked, reaching for her.

"Doctor," the receptionist called. "Doctor!"

But the young doctor ignored her and kept his attention on Miss Septima. The receptionist picked up a phone, angrily speaking to someone about the situation.

"Follow me," the doctor said to James.

The doctor, assisted by the maintenance worker, pushed opened the large double doors. James followed, and just as they were all inside, they were met by another doctor and several nurses. This doctor was older and had the aura of a man used to being in charge.

"What's going on? We just got a call about someone creating chaos."

"I don't know about that, Martin," the young doctor said. "But we have a patient here to see."

"Do we?" Martin asked.

"Excuse me! Look at her," the young doctor responded incredulously.

"This hardly looks like an emergency to me," Martin said.

"How do we know? We should be looking at her now! Why are we just standing here?" he asked, before turning to James. "This way, please."

But Martin stepped in their way. "I'll just take a brief look here," he said, reaching out to Miss Septima, but James pulled her away. He handed her to the young doctor, who pushed through the small crowd to a bed, the older doctor yelling at him all the while.

James pulled out his cell phone.

"Put that away," Martin shouted at him.

"Who do you think you're talking to?" James asked. "I'm calling my attorney."

Martin started to laugh.

"Mason."

"James. I didn't expect to hear from you for another couple of weeks."

"Mason, I don't have time to talk or explain. I just need this. Just north of Ham, Mississippi, there is a hospital, Merrimack General. Buy it."

"Just like that."

"Yes, buy it."

He hung up the phone and looked at the arrogant doctor. "I moved here a few weeks back. I did my homework to make sure I was near a good hospital. This one. In the process, I learned that there had been some administrative problems that left the hospital fighting its way out of a financial problem. Well, I'm going to fix that. I'm buying it, and you should start looking for a job."

Martin continued to laugh. "I should be asking you who you think you are?"

The young doctor turned away from Miss Septima and looked at his colleagues. "How can you guys not recognize this man? This is James Henry Ferguson. He's a billionaire. Like ten times over. He used to be on television all the time."

His colleagues began typing James's name into their cell phones. One by one, they began to look up at him with shock on their faces.

"That's who I think I am, Martin," James said to the doctor.

James looked at the name tag on the young doctor's white coat. "Dr. Longford, thank you for taking us seriously. You keep your job, and if the sale doesn't work out, I will make sure you get the job of your dreams."

Dr. Longford nodded. "Let me take care of her now."

James nodded and started to back away.

"Wait," Miss Septima said.

With coagulated blood on her face, still smelling of urine, she reached out for James's coat as he moved to her.

"You got blood all on you," she struggled to say.

"Oh, it's okay, Miss Septima. I have plenty of suits."

She looked at him, so tired but she had one more thing she wanted to say. She made him lean closer. "Well, now," she said. "Don't get carried away with yourself. You ain't no Jesus. But I do believe he sent you. Give us a kiss."

James laughed and kissed the top of her head. He walked out of the emergency room and stopped for a moment, glaring at the woman behind the counter. He gave a fist bump to the maintenance man who was now mopping up Miss Septima's blood from the entry way.

"You," he said. "You get a promotion."

James left him leaning on his mop, grinning from ear to ear.

FOUR

James Henry Ferguson was pleased. So far, his good deed had not come back to haunt him. He wished more than anything that he could be on the phone with Rebecca Gale Harrell in that moment. There was no one he wanted to run to more when positive things had occurred in his life. She would have been proud of him and pleased for him. If only . . .

It took some time, but he eventually shook off his longing and smiled as he watched Miss Septima sleep. She slept deeply, aided by painkillers. And, he thought, by the comfort of a sealed room without the damp night air seeping in through cracks and crevasses to wreak havoc on her aged joints. Aided by the opportunity to rest in a comfortable bed. Even a hospital bed. He had seen hers as he searched for a dry housecoat, the edges collapsed, leaving a small uneven space in the middle for a troublesome rest. And at 92, she wasn't alone for at least one night. He was there for her. A small piece of that lost man come back to offer company and comfort.

After she'd been moved to a private room in the hospital, James drove home to change his clothes before returning. He felt relieved that she hadn't broken any bones. She did have a concussion, and her cut required quite a few stitches. She had severe bruising on one side, and she'd pulled some leg muscles, making her think she had broken something and making it difficult for her to stand. So she just lay there most of the day in her urine.

The young Dr. Longford had come by to check on them before leaving. James was appreciative. He only left Miss Septima's side to go stretch his legs now and then. Or to get some junk food from the vending machine in the waiting area. He could tell then that he was a great subject of discussion. Maybe they wondered if he really would buy the hospital. If he really could. Maybe they were deep into their research, sharing the details of his fall from grace.

Back at her side, he thought about so many things. But mostly about how the day's events had shaken him. He hadn't felt so deeply unmoored since the night Rebecca changed their lives. Earlier, he'd left his new house, for the first time feeling somewhat hopeful, only to be met with horribly debilitating poverty and Miss Septima's accident. With Rebecca, he'd come home from a successful day at work, ready to share with her the news that they had finally acquired that restaurant group headquartered in Playa Vista, California. He found her sitting quietly with her hands in her lap, in the living room, which was a room they never used except for company and holidays. He knew that it must be serious. He dropped his shoulder bag.

"It's really a very normal thing, James," she said, her hands shaking, her eyes slowly filling and reflecting like sparkling new, golden cat's eye marbles. When they spilled over into tears, he reached out and brushed them away. He kissed her on the forehead and the tip of her nose. It made her smile.

"I want to say before going forward. I am not unique in this. In any way."

"Okay," James said as he sat across from her.

"I went to see Dr. Larus today."

That made James smile. They all loved Dr. Larus. She'd delivered both girls and had taken such amazing care of the family.

She was the OB/GYN for the girls now too and a close family friend. He nodded.

Rebecca took a deep breath, her hands continuing to tremble. This made James's heart hurt. He hated to see her in any kind of distress.

"James, it's about our sex life," she said.

"Okay," he replied. "What about it exactly?"

"I'm not comfortable right now. Having sex, that is."

"Physically?"

"Yes, and emotionally as well."

James was stunned. Where had this come from? What did it mean? Had he done something? There was so much to unravel in the moment. He could only shake his head in wonder.

"I'm just . . . I'm just trying to figure out what you're actually saying. Our sex life has always been great. Have I been missing something? I mean, what's happening here? What did I do?"

"It isn't about you, James."

Now, he cocked his head in skepticism. "You know that there are a thousand memes online using that 'it isn't you, it's me' line. You need to protect my weak male ego? Is that what's happening?"

"No, James," she answered, throwing up her hands. Then, she put her head in her hands for a moment. "This is really difficult for me. I have so dreaded this moment. But you have to hear me. It really isn't you. It really is me. I am having trouble even approaching the desire to have sex. I just don't have the urge to."

"You used to," he said, understanding that this was at best a very weak rebuttal, but everything seemed to be slipping away so quickly. It was all he had in the moment.

James remembered well the first time they had made love. It was two weeks after they met. They took a picnic to a park. They drank wine, had bread and good smoked gouda. Maybe it was being outside in the fresh air underneath a clear, spring sky.

Maybe it was the smell from the field of azaleas, heavy in the air, all around them. Whatever it was moved Rebecca to lay back on the soft plaid blanket, one hand brushing the length of his arm, finally resting on his thigh. He felt a rush of emotion as she slowly began unbuttoning her blouse. James looked around. He couldn't believe this. It was a Saturday afternoon and people were walking throughout the park. Even so, he didn't want her to stop.

She let her blouse fall aside, exposing her sheer bra, and she pulled him down to her. She unsnapped the bra as they kissed and placed his hand on her breast. After a long and passionate kiss, she suggested that they play it safe and go back to her place. They both laughed and he agreed. In the car, she left her blouse open so that he could see her as they drove. They were both swept away with desire for each other, and their lovemaking that day set a tone for their relationship going forward. Rebecca was often the initiator and often, as he liked to say, the aggressor. Certainly, their opportunities for such impromptu moments decreased as they both got deeper into their careers and when Katherine and Lillian arrived. But they always made time. Unless one of them was traveling, they never let a week go by without making time to make love. What did it mean that he didn't see she was losing her desire for him?

"How long have you been feeling this way?" he asked.

"It's been a year now."

"A whole year!"

"Yes."

"And you have been pretending all of this time?"

"No. Not at all. I mean yes, but not all the time. It's been a gradual thing."

"What did Dr. Larus say?"

Rebecca leaned forward and took James's hands into hers. "She's been helping me work through this. About a year ago, I began to feel depressed."

"Why didn't you tell me?"

"I did, sweetie, and you were great about it. Maybe you remember that I told you that you couldn't fix what I was feeling. That I wasn't sure what was going on with me. You may remember setting the hammock out in the yard with a pillow and a book for me. Underneath the dogwood and the pines. You might remember, I lay there all day and never touched the book. You made pork chops, fried corn, baked sweet potatoes, and sweet tea. You remember?"

"Yes, I remember," James replied.

"The days around that day. They were horrible for me. That's when I started to not feel like myself. When I started to feel uncomfortable around you."

"Me?" James said as his eyes now began to well.

"Imagine one day you woke up and you didn't want me to touch you. Even more, you knew it would be upsetting if I touched you. Imagine feeling that way about the love of your life. Imagine that you had no idea where the feelings came from. Like you woke up one morning with a cold, and you couldn't figure out where you'd picked it up. I just didn't know what to do with it all, so I called Dr. Larus. She recommended a woman. A psychologist. I started seeing her then. While you were at work."

"Why didn't you tell me how you felt? I feel terrible that I didn't know. I don't know what that says about me."

"You know that you can't know everything about me, even though I know you would like to think you can. I love you, James," she said, trying to reassure him.

"I know," he said, lowering his head.

Rebecca kissed the backs of his hands. "I had to work on some things for myself. At first, I didn't recognize that it had anything to do with sex. That was a recent discovery during the therapy process. It took most of the year for me to get there. I began to pinpoint the issue, and I found out that I was not alone. I found out that it happens to so many women. Some are worn down by having children and the life that follows. For some it's purely physical. I mean, it causes them great pain. Or hormonal. For some, like me, it's a lack of emotion. I don't love you any less. I still believe I need the physical intimacy. I just can't get there in my head."

"Am I . . . what? Disgusting to you?"

"No, you're not disgusting. I know you feel like I am rejecting you, and I hate that you're feeling that way. I really, really do. It took me a year of therapy to come to grips with the fact that often, having sex leaves me feeling desperate and sad. I don't like feeling that. It's disturbing to my core. I've been trying to manage it. Recently, my therapist suggested that it might be time to tell you because I was losing myself. I felt as if I was teetering on the edge of an emotional abyss. I needed to stop the fall."

James loved Rebecca more than anything in the world, but he thought she should understand that in the moment, he was the lost one. He had no idea how to understand, to put in context what she was telling him. What was this going to be like? He was going to want her. And it seemed as though that was going to make her an emotional wreck. He couldn't force her. He'd never be that man. However, he was still a man. A man who wanted to make love to his wife.

"So what are we doing, then? How do we handle making love?"

"For right now, for my mental health, I need a break. And I'm continuing to get help because there is so much I still don't understand. I'm still working through things. I'm sorry, but I can't answer that question now."

"I just wait until what?"

"Until I say I'm okay to try. I will try. I promise you that."

"How long will that be?"

"How can I tell you that, James? I just don't know. But I promise you that I will try and try again until I get it worked out."

"And what if you can't work it out?"

"I don't want to think that way."

"Well, should I join in the therapy?"

"Oh, James," she said. "I know you're scared. I am too. Really, I am. I find myself wondering how I could be in this great love and wake up one day feeling so off about such a special part of it. I still don't understand it. But my therapist reminded me that life throws all kinds of challenges at people. Completely unexpected challenges. But we will get through it together. I promise you that. But right now, I am at such a confused and fragile point. I need to find out more about myself first. I think I need to be more stable before I could think of adding you to my sessions, but I am willing to consider it. Just not yet. So, for now, I need to do this by myself. I'm not saying it will be forever. I hope you can understand."

Rebecca left him there, leaning into his confusion. He heard the warmly familiar, but in this moment, aching sounds of the staircase as she made her way upstairs. He felt he could not follow. So he picked up his bag and went downstairs to the basement. To his home office, their former playroom, renovated just after Lillian left for Princeton. He fell into what would normally be the comfort of his Barcalounger, rubbing his hands along the worn green leather of the arm rests. But it offered nothing to block his confusion and fear.

Was he a bad lover? He hadn't asked her recently if he had been pleasing her. He always felt he could tell. She seemed happy. She hadn't asked him if he was being pleased by her. Certainly, she could tell that he was. What happened? What couldn't she tell him? What had she said to the therapist or, more importantly, to Dr. Larus? He didn't want the doctor to think he was a bad lover or an inconsiderate husband. He didn't think he could ever look at her again.

James became overwhelmed by the notion that, despite her promise to work through this, Rebecca might never want to have sex with him again. It scared him. He pulled out his cell phone and reclined in his chair. He searched for *women who no longer want to have sexual intercourse with their husbands.* He was surprised to see how many pages of articles populated his screen. They had headlines like:

"I Love My Partner –
But I don't Want to Have Sex Any More"

"Wifely Duty" and Why So Many Married
Women Eventually Prefer No Sex"

"I'm Turned Off by My Husband
and Don't Know Why"

"After 23 Years of Marriage, I'm Over It"

He read for a couple of hours, forgetting to go up for dinner. But then, he hadn't heard Rebecca above him in the kitchen either. They'd always made dinner together, both of them loving to cook and the feel of their comradery as they did so. He stopped reading, laying the phone on his chest as he wondered if after all of this time, if after all of the special moments in their life together, if after always carrying the deep love he still had for her, his marriage to Rebecca Gale Harrell might be in real trouble.

It seemed like yesterday that they were young, so in love and bringing home their first child from the hospital. After six years of just the two of them, all of a sudden, he was riding lonely in the front of the car and accepting the fact that he needed to get used to a new way of doing things. Now, he had to turn his head quickly or glance in the rearview mirror to catch a glimpse of Rebecca. She was in the back now, next to Katherine and smiling for all she was worth. Even though he was beside her as she delivered, he couldn't imagine her feelings of accomplishment and delight at the ability to bring a life into the world. He felt all of it in her smile. She had a hand inside the car seat; maybe resting on Katherine's little feet or cupping her tiny hands. Either way, the two of them brought him immense joy. His girls.

They brought Katherine home from the hospital in a fog of contentment. They were dizzy with love. She had become their sole focus, and everything around them suffered because of her arrival. They didn't pick up the paper for days. Dishes were left unwashed in the sink after they'd filled up the dishwasher. Trash bags piled up on the back porch because it might take too much time away from Katherine to walk them out to the alley. Their bed remained unmade, and the mail piled up at the foot of the front door. One day James was coming down the front staircase with Katherine in his arms as the mailman shoved more letters and magazines through the slot in the door. He looked at James and the pile of mail that had fanned out across the floor of the front hall, shook his head, and chuckled as he turned away.

Rebecca and James warred for Katherine's attention and then laughed at each other. They drew lots to decide who would stay up late with her. They spent hours beside her on their bed, listening as she made her baby noises, watching as she scratched her cheeks while attempting to put her thumb in her mouth. They changed her and bathed her. They read to her and played music for her. James napped when Rebecca fed her, and she napped just afterward. Days went by with hardly a notice. By the time Rebecca's parents showed up, their world, other than Katherine, was a complete mess.

Mrs. Harrell, James's mother-in-law, was an elegant woman, but she did not let that get in the way of her feistiness or razor-sharp wit. James grew to love her dearly, and she was determined to get their train back on the track. "You two have lost your minds," she said laughing. "I know you just had a baby, but this whole thing is hardly normal."

She and Mr. Harrell got busy. They cleaned the house while calling the new parents various names that came down to them being slobs. They shopped for groceries and cooked, and most importantly, they stole their granddaughter from them.

Mrs. Harrell looked at James as he stood holding Katherine after dinner one evening. She held out her hands. "Give her to me. Come on now. Hand her over."

James was reluctant to give up his time.

"If I don't have my granddaughter in my arms in thirty seconds, I'm going to have you committed, because you two are off your rockers."

She tilted her head at James the way mothers do when they mean business, and over her shoulder, Rebecca looked at him and winked. James smiled at them both, thinking just how much he loved his life. He gave Katherine to her grandmother, and Mr. Harrell handed him tickets to go hear some jazz.

"Fatherhood isn't going anywhere," he said. "You go be a husband and wine and dine your wife."

"Yes, sir," James said, and that is how he and Rebecca got their first night out after Katherine's birth.

They ate dinner at Giovanni's Trattu, downtown on Jefferson Place, where they had their favorite Italian dishes. James had spaghetti carbonara. Rebecca had spaghetti alla puttanesca.

An hour after dinner they were at One Step Down, a rather intimate club on Pennsylvania Avenue. They watched and listened as Sonny Rollins played alone for an hour. James became fond of saying that this was the night he learned that a saxophone could be made to laugh and cry; to tell a story without words. It had been magical. Later, they found an equally intimate bar with a quiet corner table and toasted Mr. Harrell for his choice of musical talent.

They stayed there, laughing, talking, and unraveling new spaces in their love until it closed. When they arrived home, Mrs. Harrell, who'd been up with Katherine, met them at the door. She took one look at them, gave them both long, loving hugs and sent them to bed. They slept until dinner.

Rebecca had always been his rock as he had tried to be hers, giving everything he had to her and taking everything he truly needed from her. He had always confided his deepest fears and his strongest desires to her. Now, he'd learned that for a year, she had been hiding some of hers from him. That realization forced him forward in his chair, his mouth abruptly open, grimacing in response to his pain, his chest rapidly expanding, swelling with the sudden and unfamiliar infection of doubt. With regard to Rebecca, it was an illness he'd never known. How would he ever exist if she had stepped onto the slow road to leaving him? This kind of love would haunt him forever. There was far too much of it to ever pretend that it had never existed.

FIVE

When James's cousin Malcom got chicken pox at the age of six, Mrs. Ferguson set up a playdate between the two boys. When his cousin Tippy got the mumps, she set up a playdate for her and James. Mrs. Ferguson, like a lot of parents, believed in exposing their children to those and other juvenile viruses as soon as possible. They could get them out of the way early in childhood and make sure they wouldn't get them as adults when many of the viruses were more dangerous. Reverend Ferguson and James always teased her that with the mumps, she only half succeeded. The virus had only affected one side of his face. He could remember the pictures of him at age five, strolling around with his unbalanced face. Now, at 56, here he was with an unbalanced face once again.

He stood at the entry of the dining room of the rehabilitation center, the low-grade pain on the left side of his face ever present. He watched Miss Septima, who was eating lunch with three elderly Black women. By now, he knew them as members of the Missionary Circle from her church. Before her accident, he had begun to think of her as a lonely old woman who lived in a shack, whose only purpose was to study him from the middle of their dirt road. But during her recovery period, he'd seen her church community consistently come to her emotional aid. Even now, they had her laughing. It made him happy to see that, and he held back from walking to her table, allowing her the time she needed to enjoy her friends. He made his way back outside and took a seat on a bench in the garden just beyond the entrance.

Much had happened in the two weeks since she'd left the hospital. When he wasn't at her side, he was busy preparing for her return home and beginning to find a space of comfort within his new community. After spending the first night in the hospital with her, he bought himself an old pickup truck. He drove it to the nearest Lowes and bought wood, saws, hammers, and other tools. He bought a microwave, a toaster oven, and a triple burner hotplate for Patrice so that she wouldn't have to burn butane for cooking. He stopped at a mattress store for the best mattress set he could find. Back at Miss Septima's he lowered the new box spring and mattress onto the bed frame and dragged the old set outside. He tossed it on the truck and smiled, thinking about Miss Septima peacefully and comfortably sleeping in her new bed. He would shop the next day for some neutral bedding, and when she was better, he'd take her shopping so she could pick something that better reflected her taste.

He then went to work reviving Miss Septima's porch. As he yanked up broken and rotten boards, he thanked his father and grandfather for teaching him the art of carpentry as a young man. And he entertained the seemingly nonstop chatter from his new best friend, Juba.

"Mama fried up some eggs this morning. And some sausage. And Bruh, we even had some biscuits. I can't wait for dinner."

"Oh, yeah," James said, laughing. "What's for dinner?"

"Don't know. She said it's a surprise."

"Do you like surprises?"

"I don't know. Ain't never had a good kind."

James stopped prying up boards for a moment, looked at him, and sadly smiled.

"I reckon I will though. And Mama said it's all 'cause of you. She said you give her some money to buy groceries. She said you something special."

James rubbed Juba's head. "If my father were here, he would tell you that we all are something special, Juba. I say, especially you," he said. "Why don't you give me a hand? All of this talking when there's work to be done."

"What you want me to do?"

"How about I give you this crowbar and you yank up the porch boards?"

"Bruh, that's easy as pie. I got this," he said, reaching out to take the crowbar, but James held onto it.

"I thought you wanted me to help," Juba said.

"I offered you work," James said.

"That's what I'm gone do soon as you let me go."

James laughed loudly. "Juba, you don't work for free. You are worth something. If a man offers you a job, you take it if you want it. But you deserve to get paid."

Juba looked shocked and a bit confused.

"Listen to me, little man. You have worth. Never work for free. This isn't chores at home. This is a J.O.B."

Juba smiled and nodded.

"Well," James said.

"Well what?" Juba asked, beginning to laugh. "What I'm supposed to do?"

"Negotiate."

"What's that mean?"

"You tell me how much money you want for the work you'll be doing. If I don't agree, I will give you a number that I want to pay. We go back and forth until we agree on how much you get paid."

Juba took a minute to think. "Can I work every day after school?"

"If I'm working, yes."

"Then a dollar a day," Juba said proudly.

"You are worth more," James said.

"One fifty?"

"More."

Juba started to laugh. "Two dollars a day."

James smiled. "It's a deal. Let's bump on it," he said holding out his fist. Juba returned the gesture, and the two of them went back to work.

Over the next few days, Juba warmed to James. They worked. They laughed. They talked. And Juba laid out his life story easily. James felt rewarded by the boy's growing trust in him, and he loved learning about Juba, his family, and his community, even if most of his stories were difficult to hear, leading James to think about his parents, who would have nothing to do with him now. Still, he felt blessed to have been raised in their care, blessed to have been given an easier start in life.

Often, they sat for a while after work, and Juba began to show his comfort in casual but meaningful contact. He leaned against James, shoulder to shoulder, as they talked. Sometimes, they sat back-to-back, and James felt Juba's head rest with all of its weight between his shoulder blades. At the end of their fifth day together, which was a Friday, Juba surprised him with a long and firm hug. As he turned to walk away, James considered this growing friendship, with its bittersweet education, a new and heartwarming blessing in his life.

The next day, James went to work early. Talking so much with Juba also had its downside. It put him behind schedule. He wanted the porch to be finished by the time Miss Septima came home. After an hour or so of working as quickly as he could, Juba showed up, but not alone. He brought Beech with him and six other boys. Juba negotiated work contracts for them all at two dollars a day, and they worked all day long, hauling wood, handing him nails, measuring incorrectly, and making him laugh.

At the end of the day, James walked back to his house and came back with a bottle of Pure Leaf extra sweet tea for each of them.

As they sat, enjoying each other's company, Beech got serious. "Ya'll know things gone be different around here tomorrow. I might not come back, Mr. Jimmy."

"Tomorrow is Sunday," James replied. "No working tomorrow. Tomorrow is for football."

"Can we come watch?"

"Not without your parents' permission."

"Can you ask them?" a boy called Rube asked.

"No," James replied. "That's on you. But back to you, Beech. You seem nervous about tomorrow. What's happening?"

Beech looked around at the other boys, nervously calculating who else might want to be delivering this bad news. Finally, he decided it had to be him.

"Fountain Hughes coming home tomorrow, they say."

"Who is that, and why do you all seem to be afraid of him?"

"He Miss Septima's great-grandson. He lives right there," Juba said, pointing to the house next door. "He got a wife and a baby."

"Huh," James said. "I thought that place was abandoned. Where's he been?"

"Bruh, he was locked up," Beech said. "He beat up this White dude. He only got one year though. My daddy said because he was a football star. They took it easy on him, or he woulda been gone for a long time."

"But why are you all so afraid of him," James asked again.

"Because," Rube spoke up, "he a big man. He got muscles on top of muscles, and he mean. Miss Septima only one got some pull over him. He just mad all the time."

"Yeah," Beech said. "Beating folks up. Drinking, drugs. You name it."

"Did he have a job?"

"Drugs," Juba replied.

"I mean a legal job."

Juba said that he came from a long line of sharecroppers. "He grew up working that field over yonder," he continued, pointing at the land in front of James's house, with the broken For Sale sign.

"What happened to the farm?"

None of the boys knew. They suggested he ask Miss Septima, and they suggested he stay away from Fountain Hughes.

The door to the rehabilitation center opened, and Miss Septima's friends walked out. They looked at him knowingly, which made him uncomfortable. He had been so lost in thought that he hadn't seen the rusty old van from Christ Our Lord Church pull up in front of him. A man got out to help the ladies into the van, and soon they were gone. Miss Septima would be waiting for him inside. She was to be discharged, and he was her ride home. But instead of going inside immediately, he sat back in his chair because he didn't know how to explain his face and what had happened to him in front of her house.

Saturday night, after having such a nice day with the neighborhood boys, he felt alive in a way he hadn't felt in over a year. He felt like happy food—a burger and fries. So he got in his pickup and followed his GPS to the nearest Five Guys. He ordered at the drive thru. He ate a comforting meal in his great room overlooking the land between his house and Miss Septima's.

Despite all of the good feelings, he later found himself, as usual, haunted in the night by his past life. He did what he could to put his memories aside, but eventually he was overwhelmed. When he did finally fall asleep, it was not from the exhaustion of a day's hard work, but from the emotional stress of the arduous night.

On Sunday, he watched football nonstop. In fact, he watched football whenever it was on television. High school, college, and the pros. Women's professional football. Australian Rules Football. Aside from too much wine, it was the only thing that brought him peace inside his little home. The only thing that kept Rebecca and the girls out of his head.

So he was happy when Monday came, knowing that there was work to be done outside of the house. He made another trip to the hardware store, buying some porch chairs and tin for the porch roof. He worked steadily through the afternoon. After school, the boys joined him and renegotiated for three dollars a day. Toward the end of the afternoon, Patrice, her other kids, and two other mothers came by to see James and to pick up their sons. At the same time, a car drove up, and two people got out, the woman holding a girl toddler on her hip. As the car drove away, James, on his knees, stopped working. Through the settling dust, he laid eyes on Fountain Hughes and his family.

Bess, his wife, was as tiny as Fountain was large. James thought them to be an odd pair physically. Bess may have been five feet five, barely over one hundred pounds, her face resting in melancholy. Fountain looked to be at least six feet five, maybe two hundred sixty pounds. All of it muscle, deliberately on display in his wifebeater and largely covered in tattoos.

"Told you," Rube said, as he watched James watch Fountain.

Fountain walked over to James, who rose to meet him. Fountain looked around and considered James's work. The floor of the porch had been rebuilt. So had the roof and its support beams. Juba had just unwrapped and carefully placed four new wooden rocking chairs on the porch. He had been standing by, proudly observing them as if he he'd bought them himself.

"Hmmm," said Fountain as he turned his focus to James. "Seem like to me you just put lipstick on a pig."

Now, it was James's turn to consider his work. Until this moment, he had been quite proud of it. He had thought it would make Miss Septima happy. And there was the new bed inside as well. But the truth was Fountain had a point. The rest of the house was still crooked, broken, and porous. What had he been thinking? That she would be satisfied with his partial effort? Was this like only having the twenty-dollar bill when he should have had a thousand dollars?

"It's possible that you're right," James said, softly nodding. "More like a new bill on a dead duck."

Fountain seemed startled by James's tone and pattern of speech. Even though he was conceding to a failure of sorts, his voice carried the diction and confidence of a man who had failed many times but had always come back to succeed. A man who occupied a space of intellect and power wrapped in a counte- nance that Fountain had only seen worn by White men. Even though Fountain was bigger, stronger, and younger, James could tell that he was now the one intimidated. The wind had shifted with a sentence.

Here was James, in cargo shorts covered with tattered spots, a couple of them worn completely through. A t-shirt that was, in his mind, broken-in to the point of ultimate comfort, the collar partially separated from the shirt. He wore old socks and grubby old boots from LL Bean. Still, he knew himself to be much more than his comfortable old clothing.

He sighed, looking around at his team of young workers. If any of the boys were wearing his clothes, he would see pov- erty before anything else. And at first glance, they would appear overripe with a lack of self-esteem. A Trojan horse internalized before they knew they were even affected. He would see their shame because they, like him, were taught that the clothes made the man rather than the opposite. All of that would be reflected in their carriage, unconsciously demonstrating to the world that they believed they were less than. But James had been lucky in life, raised with enough hope for change and opportunity that he had been able to see that particular countenance. He grew to believe that he could have at least some of it. The kind he witnessed as a freshman at Princeton University. The kind he reached for and acquired over time.

The campus seemed to be inundated with White kids wearing ancient and ripped clothing. Wearing his freshly ironed jeans and button-down shirt, he had been stunned. His parents would have never let him out of the house dressed in such a manner. But the White kids, most of them from families with very deep pockets, strolled around campus and the town of Princeton like millionaires in their charmingly ragged clothing. His father had noticed it too, whispering to him and his mother, "These children even smell like old money. They may not look like it, but you can *feel* that they are dripping in it."

James used his academic prowess to make them see him, working his way into that community as far as he could being African American. Once inside, he worked hard at pretending. In time, he walked with a similar kind of overt confidence. The money dripping would come later.

The question was how Fountain would react to this overt confidence. They stood face-to-face, each in his own way, in conflict with the burden of being Black in the United States. Over the years, James had felt this strand of the race noose many times. So had other highly successful Blacks he'd known. To stand across from a much less successful African American with two possible outcomes, both of which James had experienced. One afternoon, before his fall from grace, he stood just inside his front door, looking out on his neighborhood. It was one of the city's finest and most sought-after. It was also predominantly professional and predominantly White. He was following an Uber Black car on his cell phone. When the car rolled to a stop in front of his house, he saw the Black female driver. As he approached the car, the look on her face told him that this would be a positive encounter. As he settled into the back seat, she turned to him with a smile.

"I have to tell you," she said. "When you walked out of that front door, I was so proud of you."

But there had also been the incident from their first week in the house. James hadn't known what day to put out his trash container. On Thursday morning, he and Rebecca were in the kitchen when she heard the hydraulic sound of the city garbage truck.

"James," she called. "The trash can is full. Can you put it out quickly? I hear the truck."

James ran outside in his suit. He looked like a billion dollars with his cuff links, his loudly expensive watch, and his Allen Edmonds Oxford wingtip shoes. He began rolling the container to the street. The Black woman driver pretended she hadn't seen him. He had to yell twice for her to stop as he made his way to the street.

"Why you late, mutherfucker?" she yelled.

This would be the unpleasant encounter. In addition to her profane greeting, he could tell by the set of her face. It could be problematic for many blue-collar Blacks to witness extreme success in another Black person. They saw great success as selling out or just felt the pain of knowing that level of success had forever passed them by. James would always be rich, and she would always be driving a garbage truck or laboring in some similar job.

"I just moved here. I didn't know what day to put the garbage out. Or I forgot. I'm sorry to make you back up."

As her coworker jumped down from the truck to grab the container, she continued her assault on James.

"You should know, damnit! You think I got time to waste on your coon ass? Next time I'm gone leave your ass out here in the street holding onto your rich trash. Don't think you got nothing on me!"

James had met his next-door neighbors only days before. They were a lovely White couple, he a lawyer and she a surgeon. She was also late, grabbing her container at the last possible moment. She, also wearing her office best, ran it down her driveway to the truck, followed by her little dog. The truck driver stopped the truck and patiently waited. When his neighbor handed off the container, she apologized for being late and holding things up.

"Oh, you good," the driver said with a smile. "Take your time. I love that little dog of yours."

They chatted for a bit as James turned to walk back to his house, slowly shaking his head.

Now, he stood looking at Fountain Hughes wondering which way this would play out. A hint of distrust in the air caused James to consider being proactive. He attempted to set the tone for the moment by offering his hand. "It's nice to meet you."

Fountain refused the gesture. It was not a promising beginning. Bess must have sensed it as well because she moved as casually as she could between the two of them. She kept their daughter on her hip.

"I'm sure you're happy to be home," James continued.

"What you know about anything?" Fountain asked, angrily. "You don't know nothing about me. You think you something better because I was inside. That was some bullshit. You don't get to hold that over me. You don't know my story."

Not knowing how to respond, James stood still. Juba walked over and stood beside him.

"I heard about you," Fountain continued. "Gone buy the hospital. Save the poor Aff-free-can 'mericans!" He paused for effect. "Ain't nobody want you around here."

Juba wrapped his arm around James's waist, indicating that Fountain hadn't spoken for everyone. Bess backed herself into her husband, as if she could hold him and the situation in place.

"Ain't nobody ask you to do nothing," Fountain continued, waving his hand toward Miss Septima's porch. "What you think? Miss Septima gone owe you something? She ain't got nothin' to give you."

"I have grown fond of your great-grandmother. I just wanted

to help. The boards were broken and uneven. I was afraid she was going to fall."

"Oh, you have grown fond," Fountain replied, mimicking James. "You nicing up so you can get her land and then you be after ours. Use all your ill-gotten gains on us. I ain't gone let you take advantage of her or us neither."

James was quickly getting tired of where the conversation was going. He thought he should just call it a day. He turned his back on the situation and he began to collect his tools. The boys moved to help him, but Fountain Hughes wasn't having it.

"Where you going?" He pushed Bess aside and James stopped to look at him again.

"Fountain," she said. "Let's us just go in the house. We got to keep airing it out anyways." She looked to James. "Me and Essie been living with my mama while Fountain was inside."

Because she had been a protector of sorts, James wanted to respond. "I wondered why the house was empty. I thought it might have been abandoned."

"We in it," she replied.

James picked up some boards, and the boys began to do the same, but Fountain knocked them out of his hands. "People say you got a billion dollars."

"I do," James replied. "I worked hard for it," he continued, trying to indicate that nothing had been given to him.

"Oh, I bet you worked hard all right."

"I don't know what you're getting at. Let's just walk away and try this again tomorrow."

"A good night sleep ain't gone make me change my mind about what I see. I know men like you. You get rich being a stooge for the White man. And just like the White man, you make it off our backs."

"That's just not true," James shouted back. He'd had enough and began putting things in the truck again.

"Then how it happen? Ain't no White people help you get it then?"

"Of course, I worked with White people," he said while continuing to load up. "Yes, many have helped me."

"There you go then," Fountain said, opening his arms and turning to his gathered neighbors. "This fool ain't getting over on me. He here to take something from us. He just told you the White man made him."

"I didn't say that!" James shouted a little louder than he had intended.

"Shut the fuck up," Fountain said, shoving James, almost knocking him down. James was rattled as the shove signaled Fountain's significant strength. Now he was once again the intimidated one.

"Fountain! Let's get on in the house, now," Bess shouted, but he was lost in his anger.

"Yeah, they made you," Fountain said as he walked toward James. "I know how the White man do. I know better than most. And I know how fools like you get on their good sides. How many White dicks you suck? That's the only way you get anything. You suck and suck til you lose your mind?"

"This is crazy nonsense," James said. "I'm sorry that things are bad for you right now, but that's not my fault. I'm trying to do a little good here. Just a little go—."

Fountain could no longer contain his distaste. The blow was swift and so powerful that James saw black, his body frozen, hands up defensively, eyes closed, his head turned away from everyone by the muscularity of Fountain's effort. He didn't feel the second blow as sharply. It was more of a thud that rumbled through his body. His vision returned but it was blurry. He heard Juba scream and Patrice haltingly call to her boy. James was suspended in pain. Something shifted. He might have stepped backward. The third blow was so hard he lost control of his limbs. He began to urinate on himself as he collapsed all akimbo into the dust. On the ground he felt Fountain's foot against his head, and he lost consciousness.

When he woke, Juba was lying across him, protecting him. He was yelling at Fountain as he cried, but James could not make out what he was saying. James began to cry when he realized that he had lost control of his bowel. He could smell himself.

"Go. Go on, now," he moaned to Juba. Someone pulled the boy away, and Fountain Hughes laughed. It rang out around and through James, like a crack of prodigious and unnatural thunder that made houses rumble for miles and miles and miles.

James did what he could do to escape his pain and shame. He crawled. In his thoughts, he considered what he might look like to the boys who were beginning to like him. To respect him. He considered the adults who, besides Patrice, would have him on the grapevine in no time. Some distance away from Miss Septima's, he stopped crawling. He dropped his head and laid in the dirt road, considering how he had run to Ham, Mississippi, to escape extreme shame. He considered that it had found him anyway.

James wiped his eyes. He really had to go inside to get Miss Septima, but he decided to give himself five more minutes to let his eyes dry and clear. He didn't want them to be red. He didn't want her to see that he had been crying.

His jaw, though it was much better, still looked swollen. It had been a complete mess after Fountain had nearly killed him. He had no idea how long he laid in the dirt before he began crawling again. At some point, he felt he could sit up. He was dizzy and he stumbled home as if he had been drinking. He stood as best he could, naked in his backyard, washing his foul clothing with the water hose before putting them in the washer. Throughout the night, his head hurt, and his limbs shook involuntarily. Fountain seemed to be still hitting him. The inside of his cheek was chewed up and bloody. So much so that he was surprised some teeth hadn't come through his skin. It was hard to open his mouth wide enough to drink water. His breathing was rapid and shallow, but he thought that might be anxiety.

In the night, when the pain became too much, he called the hospital and asked for Dr. Longford, who had gone home. About 20 minutes later, he returned James's call anyway. He told James that everyone recognized his name and they wanted to know why he might be calling. Maybe he had already bought the hospital. So they called Dr. Longford and told him to return the call and gather information. He was shocked to hear James's story.

By the time Dr. Longford got to his home, James was delirious from exhaustion. It didn't take the doctor long to conclude that he had a severe concussion.

"I'm worried," he said. "About the loss of control of the bowel. It could mean a brain or spinal cord injury. It doesn't look like it, but I want to make sure you don't have a broken jaw."

"I don't want to be seen in the hospital," James said. "I'm sure you can understand."

Dr. Longford nodded. "I thought as much. I've got you covered. We can do an MRI tomorrow at a private facility. I know two of the owners."

But before Dr. Longford came by to pick him up, James was surprised to find the local police at his front door. A man and a woman, both White. The looks on the faces of both officers confirmed that he looked like someone who had been brutally harmed. As he let them in, he noticed that his pickup was parked in front of his house. His tools and excess wood were neatly laid out in the truck bed.

"Mr. Ferguson," the female officer said. "We received an anonymous call. We were told that you had been attacked by Fountain Hughes. Is that so?"

"Yes, it's true," James said.

"You know he just got out of jail," the male officer said. James nodded.

"He can't stay out of trouble, that guy. People have given him a break more than once. He ran out of goodwill finally."

"Mr. Ferguson," the female officer continued. "We are here to get your side of the story and to assist you in pressing charges. We would need you to come to the station so we could have some pictures taken, et cetera, et cetera."

James sat down at his kitchen table. He looked through the window at Miss Septima's house and contemplated his options. After a moment of quiet in which he reflected on the vision of his father at the dinner table in prayer, he looked back at the young officer. She seemed sincere in her effort to put him on the path to justice. She went about her job in a kindly manner, which he appreciated.

"Thank you," James said. "But I won't be pressing charges."

"Are you sure?" the male officer said. "I mean you're badly hurt. He should pay for this."

"I am hurt, but I'm not pressing charges."

"Well, okay," the female officer said. "It's possible that the prosecutors will press charges without you. It is a parole violation as well."

"Then I will hire the best possible lawyer for Mr. Hughes. I will pay his bail. Do whatever I need to do to keep him out of jail."

Now their expressions changed. They looked at each other, the male hunching his shoulders in disbelief. James ushered them to the door and waited for Dr. Longford, who drove him to get his MRI. In the end, there didn't seem to be any brain or spinal cord damage. Luckily, his jaw was not broken. He was given medicine for his pain and told to rest. Dr. Longford said he would check in each day.

Other than the trip for his MRI, James did not leave his house. He did sit on the porch every now and then. The autumn breezes were comforting. One day he woke up from a nap, staring at the ragged For Sale sign across the field. As he gathered himself, he noticed that Juba was sitting on the floor next to his chair. James was still embarrassed by how he looked. He remembered his condition the last time Juba had seen him, and he felt deeply ashamed. He hadn't taken the time to consider how he would reenter his new relationships or if he even wanted to. Or, frankly, if they would have him back. But the concern on Juba's face told him otherwise. It warmed his heart. His eyes welled. His lips trembled.

"It's okay, Mr. Jimmy," Juba said. "You ain't got to say nothing. I'm just gone sit here. Don't worry about nothing. I got you."

James cried anyway.

Despite his best effort, his eyes were still red when he entered Miss Septima's room. She sat in her wheelchair, cradling her belongings in her lap. New clothes he'd purchased and that she'd refused to wear. She preferred her housecoat until it needed to be cleaned and she was forced to wear what he'd bought for her. Once she put on the expensive, soft, and comfortable clothing, she hardly ever wore housecoats. All of it in the new duffel bag he'd bought her.

A young, blond woman sat beside her.

"Well, you late," Miss Septima said, a wry smile on her face.

"I know," he said.

"Man ain't never supposed to be late to pick up his best girl."

"I'm so sorry. It won't happen again."

"Better not if you want me to stay your best girl."

They all laughed, and the young caretaker stood, introduced herself as Carol, and walked to the door.

"I'll see you both on the way out," she said.

"Thank you, darling."

Miss Septima put out a hand, curling her fingers, waving him closer. James walked over and leaned forward toward her hand. She placed it softly against his swollen cheek.

"I know why you ain't been here in a week. I know it all," she said. "My church sisters told me."

James nodded.

"That boy always been troubled. Always! Lost, like a June bug born in July."

"Yes, ma'am."

"I heard they come get him."

"Yes, they did."

"But you got him out of it. Why you do that?"

"He's not out of it altogether. My lawyer hired a lawyer here and we are working it out. He's at home with Bess though. I can tell you more later."

"Okay," she said. "Let's get on home then."

James pushed her out into the hallway, and Carol took over. Outside, James drove up in the pickup to get Miss Septima. When he came to help her get in, she refused.

"Uh unn," she said. "I ain't riding in no dirty pickup truck. Where is my chariot?"

"I thought you didn't like my car. You didn't seem comfortable with it."

"Well, it is a highfalutin thing. But I got to thinking. Back when I had a TV, there was this commercial. White girl talking about how expensive her shampoo was. She say she was worth it. I reckon I am thinking the same thing about your car."

"That you're worth it?" James, said smiling, on the verge of laughter.

"Damn skippy!" She replied.

Now, he did laugh. Out loud. She was, as they say, something else.

"It will take me forty minutes. Can you wait that long?"

"Patience is a virtue," she replied. "I'm full of virtues. You'll see before too long."

James looked to Carol, who assured him that she would be fine waiting. She said she would put her in the common living room until he returned.

James drove home quickly and changed vehicles. As he drove down the road past the twenty-two shacks, all in a row, Juba, his siblings, and Patrice waved him down.

Patrice started the question and Juba finished.

"Where's Miss Septima?"

James answered as he started to drive off. "She wanted the car. Back in forty minutes."

Miss Septima was pleased. "I got GPS in this thing," she told Carol.

Carol chuckled. "Do tell."

"She's my girl," Miss Septima said, smiling as Carol closed her door.

On the way home, they kept up their light banter. Both laughing as she regaled him with stories of the old folks' rehabilitation facility. James took notice of her fine storytelling abilities. He was surprised at how good she was making him feel. In the moment, she had made him quite happy.

As he returned to pick her up, he had the radio on a 70s station, and it had been playing at a low volume beneath their conversation. Then James noticed the beginning of one of his favorite songs. It was Groove Line by the band Heatwave. James turned it up loud so that the bass was vibrating the doors.

"What in the world," Miss Septima shouted.

"It's one of my all-time favorite songs," he yelled. He continued singing along, at the top of his lungs. Then, he surprised her.

"I'm sorry, Miss Septima," he said, pulling over to the side of the road.

"Well, what in the hell is happening?"

James rolled down the windows, setting the music free. He then got out of the car, went around to the shoulder of the highway, and began dancing to the song as he sang.

"Boy, what in the hell is wrong with you?" She yelled out the window. She twisted in her seat as he danced. She looked behind and to the front. "Well, ain't nobody coming. Go on and get it out of your system then. Child, I ain't never!"

James danced for the remainder of the song. When he got into the car, Miss Septima was laughing and shaking her head. When they arrived at her house, a crowd was waiting. There were folks James hadn't met before. Beech and Juba were putting the wheelchair ramp in place over the steps. They had built it with James.

James put Miss Septima in the wheelchair, and her neighbors came to greet her. Over the group, he saw Bess next door, standing just outside her house, her daughter wrapped around one leg. She looked as if she wanted to be a part of the homecoming but was afraid to do so.

James was touched. People came up to meet him. They thanked him for taking care of Miss Septima, who was loudly drawing attention to her new porch.

"Get me on inside now," she said to James.

He turned to greet one last neighbor. A woman who thanked him for giving her son a job.

"I never seen my boy proud before," she said.

"You're welcome," he said. "My name is James." He reached out to shake her hand.

"No, no, no," Miss Septima said. "You got to leave that fellow, James, back in the big city with all the big city noise. Around here you Mr. Jimmy. That's all. That's how I like it."

"Yes, ma'am," Mr. Jimmy replied.

SIX

The day after Rebecca put a temporary hold on their sexual relations, James tried again to speak to her about what it all meant for them long term. And what her struggle said about him. Rebecca, already weakened by the emotional stress brought on by the first conversation, was not interested.

"I told you, sweetie," she said. I can't have that conversation now, and I don't know when I will be ready. Please don't pressure me. We have to move forward this way."

This was atypical of Rebecca. It was unlike her to present such a hard façade to him. They had always talked. About everything, well, as far as he now knew. In the moment, he hadn't known how to respond to her sharp rejection. When she left the room, she'd left him feeling as if there were no options at all to be discussed regarding their sex life. He felt sad, wondering what if and what now.

Two things he did not wonder about were his love for his wife and his dedication to his vows—for better or for worse. Things had always been so wonderful in their marriage that he had forgotten worse was a possibility. Now, it was staring him in the face. He was looking at the certainty of temporarily losing the sensual touch of his wife. And, in his mind, he was looking at the very real possibility that she might not want him again, ever. *I mean, that's a possibility now, right?* he asked himself.

The daylight hours found them living much the same. He went off to work and came home. She, having long ago left her marketing career to raise the girls, went about her daily routines. James's business dealings and very public lifestyle still made for great dinner conversation. Together, they continued to find the same incredible joy in working together on their philanthropic projects. They still watched evening television together and cuddled up on the living room couch to read the latest bestsellers. Bedtime, however, proved to be a different story.

There was something about crossing the threshold into the bedroom. Their moods soured. A couple who had always found it easy to talk struggled to find the right words that could distract them from the mammoth in the room. They were awkward. Their nightly routine with its unconscious consistency and timing was disrupted. They began to find reasons not to look at each other, to be busy with some thing or other. To James, Rebecca seemed shy and vulnerable undressing in front of him. Maybe he sensed a restrained fear on her part as well, which wounded him. He started turning away and averting his eyes, but the moment the light was turned off, he kept that flash of her body captive in his short-term memory. It was the last thing he thought of before falling asleep.

A month after their conversation, Rebecca tried. James had been wandering about the first floor, eating junk food, and talking to himself, working up the nerve to go into their bedroom for another night of unease. When he finally walked into the room, she was standing by the bed, naked, seemingly physically and emotionally open to him. He offered a soft smile in recognition of her effort, and he felt the moment overtake him, arousing him as in happier times.

They were no longer young, but she still excited James in ways he could not describe. She had aged so beautifully. Still upright, curvy, and elegant. Still, in his eyes, extraordinarily sexy. He took his time walking to her. With each step, she seemed to get more nervous. When he let his hands run around her bare waist, he could feel her body tighten as she inhaled quickly and then could not release the breath. He stepped away so that she could breathe. She walked to the bed while James undressed. They successfully managed to begin sex with James trying his best to be attentive. To never let his eyes leave hers, but Rebecca became uncomfortable anyway and he began to feel like some horrible monster. He quickly moved away from her, and she rolled over, away from him. He turned out the light and got back in bed. *Such a bad omen,* he thought. He stared at his alarm clock, watching the numbers change until he drifted off to sleep.

In the months to follow, they would try and try again. Each time was reminiscent of their first failed attempt. Rebecca claimed to see progress. All James could see were the numbers on the clock as he fell asleep in fear of what might come. In fear of what he might lose.

After each of those efforts, Rebecca would ask for a break, but she assured him that she was making progress in therapy. She asked him to have patience, but eventually, it became too much for James to handle. Watching her walk nude through the bedroom brought feelings to the fore that only intensified as the weeks came and went. He started staying in his basement office at bedtime. He watched television or went over work details until he felt she was fully asleep. One night he quietly slipped into bed with her and in the morning, she got up wearing a nightgown. Another way of reminding him that life had changed, because the two of them had always slept in the nude.

Mason Easton was James's best friend. He had been since they were put together as freshman roommates at Princeton University. They both had come from middle-class families of similar values and financial status. Mason's being White had been James's only concern. Within the first week, that was put to rest by Mason's obvious respect for him and by the genuine kindness he offered to everyone he met, no matter who they were or what they looked like. This impressed James immensely. It wasn't long before they both knew that the other would be a great friend. They fit together perfectly and remained roommates for the entirety of their college career. In long dorm room conversations, they laid out their life goals to each other, James to be a successful businessman and Mason to be a successful attorney. They vowed to help each other achieve their dreams. Now, James was a rarity, an African American billionaire, and Mason was a rich, nationally regarded corporate attorney. And because he wanted to be, he was James's personal attorney. Only Rebecca knew the adult James better.

By month five, James could no longer contain the emotions that warred within him. He had to speak about it or go crazy, and Mason was his only trustworthy option. They met at the bar section of the restaurant Salt & Pepper in the Palisades neighborhood. After James dropped his bomb, they sat silently beside each other staring at the televisions lined up above the bar.

"I don't know what to say, brother," Mason said.

"I know," James replied, putting his hand on Mason's shoulder. "Neither do I, really. I just needed to say it out loud to someone."

Mason nodded. "I'm sure you never thought you'd have to work through anything like this?"

"No. Not at all."

Mason leaned back, taking a long drink of his beer. "I'm trying to think about how I would be handling this if it were me and Aubrey."

"Don't even imagine it. Don't do that to yourself."

Mason allowed for some quiet before asking James the tough question. "But do you think she still loves you? I mean, she went a whole year talking about you to a therapist but never talking to you."

"That definitely has been haunting me since the day she told me about this. I do think she loves me though, and I don't want to just walk away from everything we built just because we're having trouble in the bedroom. You know how much I love her, Mason. She's my whole world. Of course, I have the girls, but they are moving on and living their own lives. She's my everything, my soulmate. I can't imagine a life without her."

"So that settles it, then. You wait it out and hope for the best. That's your only option."

"I know, and I am trying, but I am having real trouble containing my confusion and frustration about why we are where we are in the first place. We don't really talk about it. We exist around it. I think I should be the one in therapy."

"Maybe you *should* be talking to someone. On your own."

"Could be. I don't know. What I'm sure I have to do is to force myself to trust her. She says she's saving herself. It's all about her mental health. Still, I ask myself that question every day. Does she still love me?"

"Well, then," Mason said. "While you're waiting, I guess it's you, Mrs. Palm, and her five daughters."

"Oh my God," James replied. "That's a sad and tragic solution."

"Just saying," Mason said before waving down the bartender for another beer.

But back in his home office, James seriously considered Mason's conclusion. He had come home from the bar with such an urge to be with her. Such an urge to make love and fall into each other's arms afterward. To prove that this was all a bad dream. That he didn't need any other kind of release. Now though, he wondered, was he searching for the deep feelings attached to lovemaking or just the basic need for physical release? Had it come down to that? Was it that primal urge and not the romance denied? He pulled out his cell phone and took a deep breath and considered the risk of climbing over this new wall. The risk he set aside the moment he searched for and found some porn sites, which he spent significant time looking at.

Later, he went upstairs and crawled into bed beside Rebecca. His online world hadn't changed a thing. He was still needy. He wanted his wife, and he wanted her to want him. He wanted them to be able to complete the act of lovemaking and come away from it snuggling and blissfully satisfied. Their failure to do so gnawed at him in the deepest places. He rolled over to look at her. She was turned away from him, lying on her side. He could see the lines of her body, her shoulder to her waist. Up and over the curve of her hip and down her leg. So beautifully alluring. So not his to have.

SEVEN

The morning after his conversation with Mason, James walked into his favorite coffee shop on K Street, underneath the Whitehurst Freeway. The same time every day he opened the door expecting to hear the attached little bell ring, signaling to the staff that a new customer had arrived. Or in his case, an old customer who had, travel notwithstanding, appeared every morning at the same time for years. He'd been through many young baristas in that time, all of them getting to know him in their own way. Quentin, with the hi-top fade haircut and tattoo sleeves on both arms, was a stickler for routine, and James happily followed suit.

"What's up, Mr. Ferguson?"

"Another morning, more problems to solve," James would respond.

"I hear you. Same, same?"

"Yes, sir."

Some days, Quentin would go through the routine of asking even though he'd just finished making the latte as James entered the shop. But James didn't mind. He liked the routine, and he liked the young man.

Outside, he continued his morning ritual. He took his coffee to the park across the street, where he sat on one of three benches and looked out over the Potomac River. It was a good way to meditate before the business day began. As he sipped, he stared at the water. He preferred the ocean by far, but this would do for a city. In the distance, he heard seagulls racing, and he watched them diving just above the shore. When the noise of the Georgetown neighborhood waking up quieted now and then, he would listen for the call of the mourning doves, his favorite singing bird. Listening to them created the feeling of meditation, which was good for him and centered him for better decision-making when he walked up the street to start the business day.

On this morning, however, he was distracted. Although he heard the gulls and the mourning doves, he was thinking of the email he'd received that morning from Mason. The alarm had gone off, and he'd waited to see if Rebecca would do what she'd normally do before all of this confusion had started—roll over and kiss him before falling back to sleep. She did not. Did she actually sleep through the moment or was she just refusing to engage, hoping he'd get on with the morning and leave? He shook his head as he walked into the bathroom, closing the door behind him.

He took his cell phone with him, as usual, to do a quick check of the news and his email, noting in his mind what he had to deal with first. As he turned on the shower water to let it warm, he saw an email from Mason, with FYI as the subject line.

> Just thought you should know that I came home last night and sat down with Aubrey. I was so stunned by what you told me that I wanted to share it with her for some perspective. It turns out she already knew. She's known since Rebecca started having problems. Rebecca's mother knows all about it too. I did NOT know anything. I want you to understand that. If they thought I'd blab, they were right. I would have told you. Call me if you need to, brother.

James did adore Rebecca's mother. They had a wonderful relationship, but he had trouble with the fact that Rebecca had discussed their sex life with her. He had trouble with the fact that she'd shared this information with Aubrey as well. Why would she go to them to discuss the intimacies of their marriage and not him, the man she called the love of her life? This was confusing to him, as was the way she'd shut him down the day after she first told him about her issue. When he'd wanted to talk again. Now in the park, her refusal felt harsh. Even mean. This was so unlike his Rebecca. She had to know she was hurting him, and it was not like her at all to be so unkind to him or anyone else for that matter.

In fact, Katherine and Lillian would often refer to her as the *Queen of Kind* or the *Duchess of Nice*. In those moments, he would smile and remember the moment he met her at the bus stop, the very second he understood her innate benevolence. It was her mother who had confirmed she had been that way since an early age.

One day, a couple of months before their wedding, James and Rebecca visited her parents. It was early morning, and her childhood home was quiet. He tip-toed down to the kitchen, toasted an English muffin, and made some tea. He sat at the table on the side porch that provided access to the morning sun. It wasn't long before Mrs. Harrell surprised him and took a seat across from him.

"Are you sure," she said, "you want to be married to my little sloth child? One who would sleep the day away, every day?"

James had laughed. "She only sleeps late on the weekends."

"You mean every day she doesn't work."

"Okay, you're right, but that's all right with me. I can get some work done, and when she wakes up, I'm all hers."

Mrs. Harrell had smiled. "Oh, I think my girl hit the jackpot!"

Again, they laughed.

"Your daughter is special," he said. "She has such a good heart, and it sort of inspires the best of my nature to come out."

She smiled, reached out, and patted his hand.

"I remember the first time she showed us how truly big her heart was. We knew she was a good child and cared for others, but we didn't know that she would risk herself in any way for another person. But one night I got a call from the mother of a boy in her first-grade class. She was in tears and calling to thank Rebecca for standing up for her son. It seems this boy had a bully who picked on him every day at recess. It had been going on for some time, and apparently teachers couldn't be bothered to do anything about the situation. Rebecca, though, had gotten tired of it, and that afternoon she'd strolled over and pulled the bully off this little boy and put him in a headlock and wouldn't let go even after he started crying. The teachers eventually pulled her off. She was sent to the principal's office, but we never heard about it because the boy's mom raised hell at the school about the bully and that they'd better not punish Rebecca or she'd sue the school, the head of school, and the teachers who'd been letting the bullying persist."

"I never heard that story," James said.

"It's a favorite of mine. And we learned something else about Rebecca in the aftermath of that incident. She didn't tell us about the headlock because she knew she had really been wrong to attack the boy. She knew she should have gone to the teachers or to the principal's office. And she had been frightened by her actions. Your girl will withdraw into herself when she's frightened, feels confused, or feels she was significantly wrong about something. Even if hurting someone was maybe the right thing to do. I'm glad the mother called us. Otherwise, we wouldn't have known. Even after the call, it took us a week to get the story from Rebecca's point of view. She doesn't like to talk about her failures to maintain her good character and kind heart. She doesn't like to talk about things when she's scared. Just so you know."

James had nodded at the time and thanked his soon-to-be mother-in-law for the heads up. But all he took from the moment was that it had been a cute story about his fiancée. Now, in the park, he stood up, tossed his empty coffee cup in the trash, and walked over to the water's edge. He leaned on the railing and watched the water ripple. And he thought, *well, that must be it.*

It had to be. Whatever was going on was so traumatic she had been retreating, going into a shell. *Maybe she hasn't spoken to me because she's afraid. Like her mother said.* He hoped that was the case, that things were too confusing for her. That she got really scared about whatever this was. That's what she'd indicated in their first talk, he remembered. Maybe she even feels she knew she was wrong for shutting him out, but she couldn't get out of herself far enough to tell him. It has to be it, because how could a woman so good and by her account, so in love with him keep him in the dark? But by the time he'd left the park and found himself halfway to work, he began to feel like he was just trying to make the best of a bad situation. Making excuses for her. Yes, she was a good person, and yes, she did get scared and retreat at times. And certainly, she was going through some kind of personal terror, which only served to remind him that the best person he had ever known had found him unworthy when she found herself in need. She found her mother worthy. For God's sake, she found Aubrey worthy. But it took a year and the urging of her therapist to tell him. As he opened the door to his office building and spoke to the security guard, he knew that this fact would always be there for him to wrestle with. Always hard for him to shake. It continued to eat at him as he sat behind his desk.

By month seven of their ordeal, James was spending a part of the night in his home office at least twice a week, looking at porn on his phone. Afterward, he would crawl into bed beside Rebecca and conclude that he was losing himself.

EIGHT

Mr. Jimmy was sitting on the front porch with a bottle of sweet tea when the Honda Civic slowed to a stop next to his pickup truck. She got out of her car and began walking toward him, her long, full, red hair, her blouse and her multi-colored peasant skirt blowing in the wind. In total, she moved like fire, forcefully, pieces of her popping and moving here and there but with a graceful rhythm, nonetheless. At the top of the steps, she stopped, her hair and clothing settling. Her green eyes sparkled; her face evenly dusted in freckles. She smiled. Mr. Jimmy took his time rising from the rocker, taking in the length and breadth of her. He crossed the porch and held out his hand, which she firmly grasped. She felt dangerous.

"Are you," he asked, "a good witch or a bad witch?"

"Everything I feel like I know about you calls for more originality."

"I hope you're right about me. Still, the question fits the moment."

"Well," she replied, smiling. "Might depend on the time of day."

He chuckled. "Olivia Fey Carol. It's nice to finally meet you."

"Is it?" she asked. "It kind of felt like you were hiding from me."

"I'm sorry. I guess I have a lot of explaining to do."

She stepped up on the porch, and Mr. Jimmy offered her a seat in the second rocker.

"You know," he said as they sat down, "you weren't what I expected to find on your company's website, and you aren't what I expected in person."

"No?"

"Let's say you're a little less buttoned down. A little less . . . Junior League."

"You should put that broad brush back on the shelf," she said.

He laughed. "Duly noted."

He took a sip of his tea and realized that he was being a poor host. "Would you like something to drink?"

"I'm a fan of sweet tea," she replied, nodding toward his. "Mind if I come in with you for the nickel tour?"

He chuckled. "The penny tour, you mean. It isn't big enough to charge a nickel."

As he moved toward the refrigerator, she stuck her head in the bedroom and bathroom. "You're awfully neat for a guy living alone."

"That's a young man's problem. Or at least one who hasn't been married long."

"Blaming it on the wife. So typical."

"I see you brought your broad brush with you as well."

"I did, and it's hot pink!" she said with a wry smile that he would come to treasure.

He unscrewed the top and offered her a glass with ice, but she refused.

"Cheers," he said.

They tapped the necks of their bottles, and she looked at his counter. "I gather you drank the wine?"

"No, I haven't. The right moment has yet to present itself, so I put it away for safekeeping."

She nodded, but he could see that she recognized the bit of sadness her question brought to his face. He moved past her.

Back on the porch, they rocked and talked, getting to know each other. She was relaxed and easygoing. Mr. Jimmy appreciated that and her ability, as a woman who knew about his downfall, to apparently reserve judgment pending her own assessment.

"So," he said. "I know because of the wine that you did some extensive research on me."

"Guilty," she replied. "You would too if some dude offered you money for a house he'd never seen, in the poorest section of the county, and then asked for help getting it refurbished. Especially with the quick turnaround you asked for. There were two contractors working together around the clock to get this little mansion done in time for you. Of course, I was curious."

"Understandable," Mr. Jimmy replied, nodding. "I googled you as well. I don't know how you managed it, but you don't have an online profile. Only what's on your office website."

"It's very easy. No Facebook, Twitter, or Instagram. Or the fad sites that the kids love. None of that makes me comfortable."

"Well, at least I found out that you have a family. Tell me about them."

"Robert is my husband, but you can call him Yankee."

"Why? Is he from New England?"

"No, Austin, Texas."

"But that's further south than we are here," he said, surprised.

"Yes, but Austin is like, well, OZ—since we're using movie references. Lots of odd people and horses that change color."

Mr. Jimmy laughed.

"His parents are professors at the University. And he is, as they like to say here, of a liberal mindset. So in the middle of a heated political argument a few years back, he was given the nickname, and he pridefully adopted it. The kids even call him that."

"How old are the kids?"

"Bea is thirteen and Walt is ten. They are really good kids."

Mr. Jimmy looked at her and smiled.

"What is it?" she asked.

"I'm trying to get around the broad brush. You show up looking like you're right out of the 60s and you're married to a southern liberal. You are not the Mississippi White woman I expected. You wouldn't even belong in my hometown in Virginia."

"Well, I was on my way to being that woman you seem so afraid of. I guess I was her until after I graduated from Ole Miss and flew off with the Peace Corps. Much to my parents' horror, it changed everything for me."

"How so?"

"Ghana opened my eyes, my heart, and my mind. I learned that there are different worldviews. Legitimately different from my own. Those lovely people became part of my story, and I became a part of theirs. I met so many people from so many countries. I found a universal humanity, you know?"

Mr. Jimmy nodded. "I believe I felt all of that in your picture on your company's website. Saw it in your eyes. That's why I chose to call you."

Olivia smiled and continued. "Well, I brought all of that home with me. My family wasn't too pleased to see me all of a sudden making small talk with Black folks. Their reactions were completely strange, given that I'd just spent two years in a country full of Black people. But you know the deal. This is Mississippi, and these Blacks are the sons and daughters of American slaves. Also, they weren't too happy that I fell into non-profit work to fight poverty and to find some economic equity for people who grew up absolutely dirt-poor just miles away from me. People that I never learned to see. So I moved to Austin for a breather from my folks. I ended up meeting Yankee. I came back when my mother got sick. Eventually that brought the whole family here. I got into real estate because it was flexible while taking care of Mama, and I stayed with it after she got better. Yankee is a partner in a law firm here."

"A lawyer, huh? Well at least there is something typical about you."

"Touché."

"But back to real estate. That isn't the real you, then?"

She shook her head. "Not even close."

"What is? What would you be?"

"I studied history in college, and I love it, but in my heart I'm an artist. I paint. Several years ago, Yankee built a separate tiny house in our backyard. It's my studio."

"Ever make any money at it?"

"Oh, look at you. Attaching dollars to missions of the heart."

"I am a billionaire."

"Oh my God! Can you say that again? Because you just don't hear people say that to you very often in your life."

They both laughed a little harder, truly beginning to enjoy each other's company.

"Every now and then I get asked to paint a mural in office buildings. I make some cash doing that. Is that sufficient?"

He feigned a yawn. "I guess so."

"Okay," she said. "That truly is enough of me for today. Now onto you."

"But you know everything already."

"I don't know how you got to be Mr. Billionaire. I know your path of education, but I don't know the particulars."

"It's a long story as you might imagine."

"Can I get the elevator version?"

Mr. Jimmy chuckled at her persistence. "Sure," he said. "I think I can manage that. As you know, I did my undergraduate work at Princeton. Afterward, I went to the Wharton School. As one can do in places like that, I made friends in high places. Really good friends. I travelled with them to their homes. I met their families, and some of the parents grew to like me. A couple of the fathers took me under their wings."

"Why?"

"They wanted to help me succeed. They wanted to lend a hand to an African American student. So, they taught me alongside what I got in the classroom. Just as they did for their sons—my friends. As I was getting close to getting my MBA, I was asked what I wanted to do. I'd done a paper on a couple of men who had some success in the restaurant area, and I liked the things I uncovered in my research. One of my mentors got me started, investing in my first restaurant. In time, I was very successful. I paid him back with interest, and I bought more. I invited other classmates to go into a business with me where we bought restaurants around the country. We then created chains that turned out to be outrageously successful, and I kept the controlling interest in our company. We repeated this multiple times, creating several chains that you would recognize. In time, we sold them for a lot of money. Then I became the investor in other restaurants and then mall projects. I continued to diversify into real estate keeping my hand in the restaurant business. In time, I became a billionaire. That's the short version."

"Well, that's quite impressive."

"I couldn't have done it without my friends and their families."

"Are they still your friends? I mean, after everything?"

"After some discussion. Yes. Because they stuck their necks out for me, they faced some backlash. You know, for helping a Black guy get to this level only to see him do what Black men do, fuck things up."

"Oh, come on! White men don't fuck up relationships?"

"All the time, but as you said earlier. You know the deal."

"Yes," she replied, nodding. "Unfortunately, I do. Did you have to tell your friends why you went with that woman?"

"I didn't have to. I just did because they deserved to know.

They do love me."

"Can you tell me? The *why* had to be something extraordinary. It eventually had you calling me and escaping your life. And yes, I have wondered about it over and over."

"It's not extraordinary. I'm told it's a fairly regular occurrence. And I didn't have to escape my life. It collapsed on top of me. There was no life left. It burned down to the ground. There was no reason to hang around crying over the ashes. And I will tell you anything else about me today because after the fall I have had, not much about my life feels like it is still mine alone. So it's just easier to be open about everything. What else can I lose? But I can't tell you that yet. Because I am afraid I wouldn't get through the story without too much obvious pain. If you get my meaning."

Olivia nodded and gently smiled. She slowly turned away from the tenderness he was already beginning to show because she understood. For a time, she looked over the acres of land across from his house. She drank some tea.

"I probably should get going and give you a break from the inquisition. But before I do, I think I should tell you that people are talking about you again. Here in Ham this time and, of course, for different reasons."

Mr. Jimmy sat up in his rocking chair and looked toward her. "Who is talking?"

"The better question is who isn't talking?"

"What's being said?"

"The hospital. The word is that you threatened to buy the hospital. That has some people wondering because, well, you can. Are you?"

"Yes, I am in the process now."

"I'll be damned. Let's just say there are people who don't want that. Local officials can make it hard on you. The planning board, county Board of Supervisors?"

"Why do these officials care so much? The company that owns the hospital isn't from Mississippi."

"Because you are a Black carpetbagger of considerable ill-repute."

Mr. Jimmy stared, unmoved and unsurprised.

"Ever see a cowboy movie where there is one wealthy rancher who runs the local town and everybody in it? He has his gun hands, as they say, to keep everybody in line."

"Yes, I have."

"It's sort of like that here. There are approximately twenty-five thousand people in the surrounding county. Eight thousand in Ham. Google the president of the Board of Supervisors. He's rich and powerful too. Not in your league, but you are on his turf, and he runs it like he owns all of it. He didn't appreciate the scene you made or the threats and veiled accusations."

"Hmmmm," Mr. Jimmy said, slowly nodding his head. "The scene *I* made?"

"What will you do?"

"Buy the hospital."

"Okay," she replied. "I will do what I can to help you."

"Why?"

"Because being a real estate agent keeps you in everybody's business. I hear a lot of things. I could write one helluva gossip column if I wanted to. As I said, I know about the hospital and Septima Ruffin. And Dr. Longford, who is in a bit of a pickle at the hospital because of you. I knew what kind of pickup you bought not long after you purchased it. And I know about you and Fountain Hughes. I know that Black folks are whispering about a certain Mr. Jimmy from the neighborhood around the way. I know that you are creating hope in places that didn't exist before you came. That's what I wanted to do after the Peace Corps. I still want it. I'm sure you know it's dangerous. Building hope, I mean. Especially in this area of Ham."

Mr. Jimmy leaned back with a sigh. "Yes, no good deed goes unpunished."

Oliva Fay Carol nodded, staring at him seriously. "I think you're a good man, James Henry Ferguson."

"But you know the truth."

"I know a piece of the truth. Yes, I saw a lot of the horrible online conversations about you. I know many of the things you were labeled. I know that you have been lumped in with some pretty shady people. But I know that before your issue, you were tremendously well-loved. I also know from my research that by the goodness of your heart so many people have better lives. That feels a lot like kindness to me. I think you might just be a regular guy with a big heart and quite an interesting story. I like good, complicated stories. I work hard at being complicated myself, you know?"

He smiled. "Oh really?"

"Yes, really!"

His smile grew wider. "I had a feeling that I would like you."

"I definitely have to look at that online photo. I think I need to put one up that isn't so personally transparent."

"I'm not sure you could. You are who you are, and it just jumps out."

"Will you come to dinner sometime? Yankee makes a mean carbonara," she said again with that wry smile.

"Wow! You can leave now. You are scary. You're no artist. You're FBI."

"With this hairstyle? Hardly."

"Yes, I will come to dinner. I'd like to meet your family."

Olivia stood up to leave. They offered pleasant goodbyes, and as she got to her car door, Mr. Jimmy called to her.

"Yes," she replied.

He was looking past her, at the farmland across the road.

"Would you represent me in purchasing that land?"

"All of it? It's a hundred acres going back over the curve of the land."

"All of it."

She smiled and nodded. "I'll be in touch."

NINE

It was the last time that James Henry Ferguson would see his office, high above the Georgetown skyline, overlooking the Potomac River. Had he known what was about to happen, of course, he would have lingered in the doorway, enjoying a lengthy and contemplative moment. A moment that would have included memories from so much of his professional and personal history. A moment for the room that provided so much of the space and time in which he found and grew into himself.

He might well have remembered the first time he brought Rebecca to see it. He had blindfolded her in the outer office in front of his assistant's desk. He'd held her hands and guided her inside the special place, which he alone had decorated and of which he was extremely proud.

Rebecca had laughed. "Oh, James," she said as he stood behind her, removing the blindfold. "This is so . . . so . . . I'm not sure. Manly?"

James laughed too because she was correct. Manly, in his own way, was what he had been reaching for.

"I suppose you need some antlers and stuffed animal heads to make it all come together?"

He smiled in response to her making fun, wrapped an arm over her shoulder, and took a deep and prideful breath. "Sit down," he said. "Let me tell you how we arrived at this moment."

He had her sit on the heavy, dark brown, leather couch. He sat across from her on one of the two matching leather chairs facing the couch, on the other side of the coffee table covered with large, bulky picture books of Washington, DC. He gave her a minute to take it all in. The dark green color of the walls and the dark cherry–stained wood trim. The high-back brown leather chair behind a large wooden desk that might have put the president's to shame. Just below the windows, now hidden by heavy wooden shutters, was his mahogany conference table, which sat 14. Across the room from the wall of shuttered windows was a wall of empty bookshelves. Over the years, they would become full of the ghost-written books of his business colleagues and friends. On the walls were pictures of his young family, in heavy, ornate frames.

"What, no chandelier?" she teased.

He smiled. "I have dreamed of this all of my life," he replied, spreading his arms wide and looking about the room. "When I was a kid watching old movies, all the successful men, be they lawyers, doctors, hunters, or mob bosses, had offices of this color. In my head, it was all synonymous with success. Year after year, show after show, it grew on me. I thought one day I will have an office like this. And it would be a sign that I had reached a base camp from which I could ascend the mountain of achievement and prosperity. I have waited and waited to build it. Until I could look in a mirror and know that I was worthy of this notion that is purely mine, but nonetheless a laudable goal and landmark. With your help, Rebecca, I am sitting inside one of my lifelong dreams. I have carried it for so long that at some level, it's difficult to believe I'm actually here."

On the following weekend, they went to dinner, and for dessert Rebecca suggested that they take some Lafite-Rothschild to the office.

"We have to christen it," she said.

They each raised a glass and toasted to continued success. When the bottle was near empty, they made love. The only time they would do so in his office. Often, when he was having a bad day or a deal had fallen through, he would think of that night and the generous and gentle lovemaking. It refocused him and reset his priorities. It warmed his heart and settled his mind. It always brightened his mood.

The office also brought warmth to Lillian. When he could, before she got involved in afterschool sports, he would wait for her in the carpool line. She would burst through the doors when her number was called, running as fast as she could with her backpack flopping and weighing her down. Her braids swinging and her grin growing. He was always overwhelmed to see how happy she was just to know that he was there.

They would head to the office, and if the shutters were open, she would close them, blocking out the sun.

"I like it, Daddy, when it's just the lamps."

"So be it, my love."

"That way," she continued. "It's so comfy in here, it's like being wrapped in a blanket."

She would throw herself onto the couch with a book. She would remain curled up and reading until it was time to go home for dinner. Not long after this ritual began, he bought her an afghan, dark green and soft. If she was in the office, she had it wrapped around her, and no one else dared use it. She often fell asleep while he worked and even when there were meetings at the conference table. His partners and employees watched her grow up in that office. And when they dropped her off at Holder Hall for her freshman year at Princeton, the last thing James did before leaving was to wrap the afghan around her shoulders so she could remember the comfort she had always received in her father's office.

Katherine enjoyed her time in the office as well. James often went into work on Saturday mornings, and this was her time. They stopped for donuts, bagels, or waffles and ate them at the conference table while they chatted about life. Afterward, he worked, and Katherine, who preferred the windows to be uncovered, looked out over the river, watching the collegiate rowing competitions or the people leisurely strolling along the waterfront. She would also drop by sometimes during the week, and he would stop working and put a hold on his calls because an afterschool visit from Katherine usually meant there was something serious to discuss—from classroom subjects to political affairs. When she was in 8th grade, she wrote her first significant school paper. It was an argument in favor of right to die legislation. She wrote it at his desk. He'd moved to the conference table where he often glanced at her focus and persistence. She got an A+, and she proudly handed it to him as a gift. He had it framed, and it hung above the couch in a place that was hard to miss as you entered the office.

This very special room was where he sat alone and in reflection the moment he learned that he had become a billionaire. He could barely speak when Rebecca answered his phone call. It was, as she told him, a remarkable achievement for any person but particularly an African American boy from the rural South.

"You were blessed to be born into such a loving and supportive family. They gave you the space and freedom to dream the biggest dreams."

James agreed and called his parents to tell them so.

"I wanted you both to know that just moments ago, I became one of the few Black billionaires in the United States."

"Do me a favor," his father said.

"Yes, Daddy. Of course."

"Hang up the phone. Go straight outside and throw some dirt on your shoes."

James nodded and replied. "I will, and thank you."

But at the end of that working day, he closed the door to his office without looking back or thinking twice. Alone in the elevator, he called his favorite Uber driver and then called home.

"Hey, sweetie, what should we cook tonight?" He asked, trying to set a positive tone for their evening.

"I am not in the mood to cook."

"I'm sorry. Is everything okay?"

"Yes. I'm just in a lazy mood. That's all. Me and my early glass of wine."

He chuckled. "My favorite way to be. How about we go out?"

"What do you have in mind?"

"Soul food! How about Georgia Brown's?"

"Oh, you know I'm always up for that!"

"Deal. I'll make a reservation from the car. Be home shortly," he said as he walked out of the elevator.

As he approached the exit of his office building, he saw a young woman with a microphone and a legal pad in her hands. Beside her was a man with a video camera, which he raised to his shoulder as James neared the door. He walked out onto the sidewalk, and she called to him.

"Mr. Ferguson, I'd like to ask you a couple of questions."

She was hyped up. The expression on her face told him that her adrenaline was pumping. She was excited, and there was a knowing kind of confidence in her posture. He understood that seeing this in a reporter who wanted to talk to him could not be a good thing. On the other hand, he hadn't done anything wrong. James was an up-and-up businessman. No shady deals, and he'd never had to look over his shoulder.

She pushed the microphone into his personal space. "I'd like to show you something."

"Okay," James replied, trying to get over being caught off guard.

She turned her cell phone around so that he could see the screen and she pushed it closed to his face. It was a tweet.

Lady Nymph
@lnymph

Trippin!! Old brother paying for the booknerds to go to college. Yo I fucked this dude! A desperate frantic fuck too. Money large though! 😆

"Do you recognize this tweet?" she asked.

"No," James said as he studied it.

"Do you know the person who tweeted it, Lady Nymph?"

"Yes," he replied, almost under his breath.

Mason later told him that his face changed in such a way that anyone watching the resulting video clip could see that his life had shifted beyond repair. He morphed into shock. He could barely feel his body, but the sense of dread and immediate shame was palpable. The reporter became his father, questioning him about committing a most unforgivable sin.

"Were you having an affair with this woman?"

"No. It was only one time. Less than a half hour of my life."

"You cheated on your wife, Mr. Ferguson?

James, staring straight ahead, did not answer.

"Are you going to tell us that it was all a mistake?"

"There was no mistake. I did what I did. I made a choice."

"But why, Mr. Ferguson? Is your marriage in trouble?"

James began to come to his senses, and over her shoulder, he saw his Uber waiting.

"When did this happen?" he asked.

"She tweeted an hour ago. She must have seen our story on you providing free college for every senior at the high school where you delivered the commencement address."

"Well, no good deed goes unpunished, I guess. I really have to go now," he said.

"Can you tell us why you did it? Why would you make a choice you knew was wrong to begin with?"

James brushed past her. They followed him to the car, still asking questions, attempting to get the best shot of his agony. He closed the door, and his driver pulled away, leaving the reporter and videographer in the street, where they would soon be joined by others. The media stakeouts in front of his office got bigger day by day, which is why he would never return. The driver sensed that James was in a crisis that required silence. He rolled up the windows, turned off the radio and kept his eyes on the road. James looked outside, watching the houses along Foxhall Road pass in a sickening blur. Soon he would be home. Soon he would know if he had destroyed everything he had ever lived for.

When James opened the front door, he felt the house had changed. The tension that had been reserved for the bedroom had become a low-hanging fog throughout the entire home. And it wasn't the anxiety he'd brought with him from his time with the reporter. It was a blanket of hurt and despair that originated in and belonged to the house. It was Rebecca.

He stood still for a time because he didn't know how to keep walking toward the unfolding tragedy of his life, a life he'd left wavering but intact that morning. But he got moving, albeit slowly and cautiously. She was not in the dining room or the family room or the kitchen. He found her standing on their back porch, arms folded across her chest, staring through the screen at her flower garden below.

"Rebecca," he softly said. Her name. One word which, in the moment, he imbued with pleading, desperation, hope, and a cry for forgiveness. When she turned, he could see that she had felt none of that.

"Let's go inside," she said. "I am sure that what we have to say is not for the neighbors to hear."

They sat down across from each other in the living room. James couldn't help thinking that this was where they sat when she first told him that sex had become difficult for her.

They sat quietly for a moment, too old and too far along in their marriage for any kind of histrionics. There was no screaming or breaking of furniture or shattering of precious, antique glassware and fine china. The emotional wealth of years together tempered the flames of hysteria.

"How could you?" she asked.

James, incredulous that she would have to ask, responded. "Anger. Frustration. But, I guess, mostly anger."

"But we were working on it, James."

"Were we? We tried to have sex, and we kept failing and then not talking about it. I didn't feel we were fully working on it together."

"We were definitely getting somewhere. I was getting somewhere. You didn't have to do this to us."

"How can you say that? The last time we tried was months ago. I've been so frustrated, and I felt like I was being purposely starved. I wanted to feel wanted. I wanted to . . . to just have sex! I guess I just got desperate, and the opportunity presented itself."

"We resist all types of temptations all the time. Like me, right now, not cutting your heart out."

James looked up at her, surprised. She'd never said anything like that to him before.

"And it was more than just the sex," he continued. "All of this was so painful for you for quite some time. Yet you kept it all from me. You chose to open your heart to a therapist and our doctor but never to me. The one you called your soulmate. I felt cheated on. I felt unsettled, wondering if you really loved me. If you did, wouldn't you have talked to me? For a year, you lied to me. In and out of the bed."

"That is true," she continued matter-of-factly.

"And then after you dropped the bomb, you continued not to fully discuss it with me. You left me to wander through this maze all alone. And with each step, I just got more and more angry. You should be able to understand my frustration."

"It isn't that I don't understand your frustration. I do. But understanding you going so far as to share your body with another woman is something I just can't do."

"I was feeling desperate and unloved."

He reached out to hold her hands, but she pulled them onto her lap and sat back in her chair.

"Enough that you would ruin everything? We had it all, James. We had it all. Now, even if we were to stay together, our relationship would be forever tainted. Every time we walked into a room full of people, I would feel dirty."

"Rebecca, I am truly sorry. I deserve your anger. But we can beat this. People make it past these things all the time."

"I'm not just any people," she said, the hurt rising in her voice for the first time. "I had a standard for our love. One that you agreed to keep at the altar. You failed."

James dropped his head and spoke to the floor. "I did."

"And your failure is now all over the television and the internet. Aubrey has called already. Outside these doors and windows, people are picking apart our lives. They are looking down on our love. A love that many of them dreamed of having. You killed that. Do you hear me, James?"

He looked up from the floor to meet her eyes. He nodded.

"You killed that."

He nodded again. "Still, I'm begging you, Rebecca. Don't end all that we have. We can make it. No love is stronger than ours."

"Maybe you are right. Maybe what you did isn't that big in the scheme of things. After all the years together. Maybe I could get over the sting every time you hugged me going forward. Maybe I could handle it inside this house. But you and I both know that the fire has only just started. We are about to be burned badly, and while I might be able to get over your fling, I don't think I can deal with the public ridicule of being another woman who has to put up with the nonsense from her man and publicly suffer the shame. I don't want to be called out like Hillary Clinton for sticking with my man. And our daughters. I have to teach them that they deserve better than this. You have failed them too."

James sat quietly without an answer.

"What happened to you, James?" she asked, pleadingly. "I don't understand how you could make such a choice. You were the ideal man. You were kind and thoughtful. You were loyal and trustworthy. You never let your anger get the best of you. You operated within reason. Your parents taught you that, and now you so easily succumb and forget what we built together over so many years. It was just selfish. Extremely selfish. I was trying, James. I really was."

James knew. He had been in many arguments in his life. There was a moment in each when he understood that it had run its course and the issue had settled itself. He was losing the love of his life. He got up to make a drink. He saw neighbors slowly walking past his house, pointing, and speaking. Had they seen the tweet? Had they seen his interview? Or were they just noticing the landscaping?

When the phone rang, he knew it was the girls. When Rebecca began to cry into the receiver, he headed down into his basement room, closing the door at the top of the stairs. He threw himself down on his knees his face in his hands, pushed into the seat of his recliner. He screamed with everything he had. His tears soaked the leather, and although he wanted to keep that day out of his head, he could not.

That day.

James Henry Ferguson had never—not at any time in his life—been so angry. It had been just under a year since Rebecca announced her struggle with their sex life. While his emotional stability drastically wavered, life seemed the same for her, if not better. She went on with the family charity work. She gardened and played tennis. She had her book club. She was a reading tutor for the non-profit she loved—Reading Partners. She tutored several afternoons every week at an inner-city school. She was living a good life, productive and giving.

He, on the other hand, was working overtime to remain the man she loved. To remain the kind, thoughtful and giving husband. To hold onto the special feeling of love that had been the foundation of their life together. As the months went by, that affection grew more and more difficult to retain. His need for the portion of their love lost grew more difficult to ignore. He spent more and more time alone at night, angry, pining for the old Rebecca and losing himself in imprudent websites.

In time, he became numb to the basic pornography, and he searched beyond his gateway drug for something even more inelegant. When he discovered it, he gave it serious consideration. Continually, he found himself drawn to it. Alongside the typical scenes of loveless sex on his phone, there were flashing offers of supposedly needy women who were just around the corner from his home, desperately waiting for his particular touch. Flashing fonts and photos from milfs to gilfs, all in various stages of undress. What would it be like, he constantly wondered? He knew that their hands on his body could never bring to him what Rebecca's touch always had. But would it be enough to quench this desire to have what had been taken from him? Could he get away with it? Night after night, he pondered. That day, he gave in.

At a traffic light, he sat nestled in his anger, giving himself permission to do something that he knew was beneath him, that he knew went against every good thing about him. How many times had the notion of being able to look at oneself in the mirror without shame been a part of his father's sermons? How many times had his mother asked him to think about what he could live with when confronted by a choice that didn't seem quite right? Yet, he pressed the gas pedal anyway, moving forward, toward the shame, like Adam to the serpent's apple.

He had left his office midday while Rebecca was on the tennis court. There would be no reason for her to call him and no reason for him to answer for his whereabouts. As he rang the buzzer to enter the apartment building, he felt sure he would get away with his crime.

Lady Nymph was young and pretty. Medium height, medium build. Light brown eyes, coffee-colored skin, and a cascade of braids falling across her breasts. Her online biography said she was twenty-four, falling between the ages of Lillian and Katherine. She wore black heels. Her white jumper was formfitting. *She had to have poured herself into it, he thought.* It strained to stay buttoned from her cleavage to her waist. She smiled and stepped aside to let him in.

Lady Nymph was nothing like the sleazy pictures on his phone, advertising down and dirty sex. She seemed to be quite a clean kid. Happy even. Her apartment was quite nice.

"Why do you do this?" he asked, unintentionally, as he followed her casual sway down a short hallway, presumably to her bedroom.

"Money, Pops. Why else?"

That made him feel worse. "I'm not your Pops," he said.

"You're old enough to be," she replied. "I hope you are . . . fit."

James didn't answer. He just followed her into the bedroom. Once inside, he handed her an envelope. She opened it and took her time counting the money. He took the moment to look around, settling on the photographs on her bureau. There was one of a little girl, which he assumed was her, standing alone in front of Charles R. Drew Elementary School.

"This is a mistake, or it's one helluva tip," she said, looking up at him. "The price was clear, right?"

"Just take it," he responded.

"Okay, okay," she said, pressing her palms downward. "Let's chill out. Maybe we can enjoy this May-December whatever it is."

James watched her undress, and when she was before him in nothing but heels, he did not feel what he thought he would. However, he did not put a stop to the momentum underway because what he needed had to be there somewhere. Or so he thought.

When they were finished, she saw him to the door, where they matter-of-factly exchanged goodbyes, never expecting to see or hear of the other again. He slapped himself hard across the face and the sound of his epic moral failure echoed off the tile floor and walls. He took a deep breath and shook his head as he solemnly began the long wandering back to his car, understanding that he was leaving no better off emotionally than when he arrived. He had found nothing in that shameless moment to take the edge off his need. Maybe he only made things worse. Time would tell. At least it was over, and he would build a wall around it in his mind, and no one would ever know of his failed attempt to find what had been lost inside his marriage. In the moment though, he could not have understood the graveness of the interlude he had just experienced. In the moment, he was simply too hobbled by his pain and confusion to see the hurricane forming just beyond the horizon.

Two days earlier, he sat on stage at a suburban high school, just north of Washington, DC. The student body was 95 percent African American and 5 percent Latino. He had entered like the celebrity that he was. Everyone was atwitter when he walked into

the auditorium, hand-in-hand with Rebecca. They were royalty
in so many ways.

Months earlier, they sat with the principal, superintendent of
schools, and the graduation committee in charge of planning the
event. James and Rebecca had offered through their foundation
to pay for the college education of every graduate accepted by
a college or university. The school officials wanted James and
Rebecca to extend their gifts to the other graduates as well so
that everyone would have a gift to start their lives with. It could
be seen as a funding of the foundations of all of our young lives
just stepping into adulthood, they offered.

"Will every student be valedictorian?" James asked.

"Well, no," the principal responded.

"So," Rebecca said. "She will be given the special honor
of addressing her classmates and their families because of her
hard work?"

"Yes, that's right," the principal continued.

"No one gets to just join in on her moment. She earned it and
is deserving of significant and special recognition."

"That's right, Mrs. Ferguson. And I see what you're getting
at. It's just that graduation in and of itself around here is quite
an achievement."

"We understand that," James continued. "However, the kids
going on to college worked harder to achieve something greater.
That's what we want to reward. We are big believers in education
and its ability to change lives. We want to promote that idea.
There are those who don't feel so strongly about higher education, but we do. So this is our offer."

They all looked at each other for a moment, and the superintendent nodded. "Well then, we accept."

At the graduation, James rose just after the valedictorian's
speech. He shook her hand as she headed back to her seat. After
he had delivered a short but inspirational speech, applause filled

the room, and he asked the valedictorian to come back on stage. She was surprised but rose to join him. James handed her a card and asked her if she would please read it to her classmates.

The young woman stepped up to the podium. She opened the card and briefly scanned it and before she could read the first word, her eyes welled and began to overflow. She looked to her side at James, who nodded with a smile. She looked down at Rebecca, who sat in the front row, next to the principal. Rebecca gave her a big smile, blew her a kiss, and began to tear up as well. The young woman began to read.

"Would every graduate here who is attending a college or university in the fall please stand?"

The students stood, and for a moment there was quiet as the valedictorian gathered herself. "Rebecca and James Ferguson will be paying your tuition, room and board, and all classroom-related expenses for the entirety of your undergraduate education."

The room erupted in cheers and applause. Parents and students alike hugged and cried, the auditorium overwhelmed by a tsunami of joy. Some people knelt to pray. The valedictorian took off her mortarboard and flung it into the audience. Others followed and a photographer's picture of that moment ran large and above the fold on the front page of the next morning's paper.

By the time James and Rebecca arrived at Bistro Lepic for their post-speech dinner, the news had taken Washington, DC, by storm. President Jonathan Walker even spoke of it as he walked to Marine One on the south lawn.

"I am not surprised by this expression and gift of hope by James and Rebecca. They are wonderful people. They have always led with their philanthropic hearts as long as I have known them."

They received applause as they took their seats in the restaurant and the owner greeted them, pulling out a chair for Rebecca at their favorite table in a cozy, back corner. James ordered the beef medallions and Rebecca the calf liver with capers, garlic, black olives, and Jerez vinegar. They washed it all down between bites and laughs with a bottle of Lafite-Rothschild.

Two days later, he left his office without looking back and found out that Lady Nymph had tweeted about his episode in her apartment. That same day, unbeknownst to him, Ham, Mississippi, began quietly calling.

It had taken him quite some time to wander through that fateful day and its aftermath in his mind. Certainly, Rebecca had finished the call with the girls. But she did not come down to talk more about what they could do to fix the situation—how they could move forward. He had hoped that once she spoke to the girls, even after his dalliance, she would have thought twice about allowing the family they worked so hard on to wither and turn to dust.

It was quiet when he reached the first floor. The lights were out. He walked upstairs to find the second floor dark and quiet as well. He eased open their bedroom door to find Rebecca in the middle of the bed, wrapped up tightly in the linen, either asleep or pretending to be. Either way, she was delivering a message to him.

Although he wanted to, he could not lay down on one of the girls' beds for comfort, knowing that they were likely alone and in pain because of him. So he stretched out on a guest bed and hoped to fall asleep. But he could only stare out of the window, catching the moonlight on the pine trees that grew along the property line behind the house, hoping that Rebecca would see differently in the light of day.

TEN

James woke up to the buzzing of his phone. It was Mason.

"Morning, brother," he answered.

"Hey, brother. How are you doing?"

"Not so good," he replied. "I believe my life is over."

"I'm sure it feels that way."

"No, I really mean it is. I am only good here until the girls get home. When they all finish with me, I will be exiled. Tossed out on my ass. To what and to where, I don't know."

"I'm so sorry, James. I wanted to get to you last night. I tried calling several times."

"I know. I wasn't in the mood to admit to you what I'd done. I didn't want to say it to you because I still didn't want it all to be real."

"I think I can understand that. I was going to drive over, but Aubrey thought it wouldn't be appropriate."

"She was right. She didn't tell you to stay away from the bad influence?"

"Of course not, James. You're my best friend. I'm not going to walk away from you."

"You have no idea how much I needed to hear that."

"Take it to heart. Okay?"

"Okay."

"Listen, man. You're all over morning television. You're front page, top of the fold in *The Ledger*."

"I suspected that."

"With my crisis management lawyer hat on, I'm going to tell you that you at least need to read the newspaper article. Get a look at what you are up against. Then we can discuss how to fight back and change the narrative a bit."

"I don't want to fight back."

"What?"

"Mason, I did what I did. It was wrong. I don't want to pretend anything else."

"It was more than just wrong. This is solicitation of a prostitute. It's a misdemeanor here, but it's still a crime."

"So let it come. I did it."

"Think about what you're saying. It's not going to help the situation with Rebecca and the girls. I could make a phone call."

"No, I don't want that."

"Okay, we'll hope for the best, I guess."

"And what's the best?"

"With a man of your prominence, the DA could just decide not to prosecute given your good works in the community and that it's a first-time offense. That's what I would argue for if you would let me. I think that's what's likely to happen."

"I'm good. Let whatever happens happen."

"Okay, then. Just know I'm shaking my head over here. In the meantime, just tell me what I can do to help you right now."

"You did it already. You didn't let me go. I know Aubrey. She can't be happy with me and how what I did will bleed over into your lives."

"That's true. She's not at all happy with you right now, but I hope time will take care of that. It's you, Rebecca, Katherine, and Lillian that we need to protect right now."

"Okay, let me get the paper, and give me some time with Rebecca, and I will call you later."

"Sure. Call me anytime. I will drop anything."

"I know. I appreciate you, my brother."

James stood at the front door, searching as far as he could to his left and right, trying to see if anyone was about to walk past the house. When it looked as if he could make it out to the sidewalk and back, he made his move. It was barely light when he walked outside, wrinkled, disheveled, and unchanged from the previous night. While it was quiet, he noticed more cars than normal. On a usually quiet street, the only cars parked overnight typically belonged to his neighbors. But on this morning, there were extra. As he picked up the paper, the reason became clear as reporters and photographers launched from their unmarked vehicles, yelling his name and shouting questions for all the neighborhood to hear. The videographers began jockeying for the best position to record him turning away from accountability for his deeds and quickly walking into hiding.

Why did you do it?

Is your marriage over?

Will you continue to advise your former board?

Was it worth it?

Did you actually like it?

Wasn't the young woman your daughters' age? How do they feel about that?

Lady Nymph says she'll do it again. Are you going back to her?

How did you find Lady Nymph?

Is your wife still in the house with you?

Is she kicking you out?

They continued to yell as the door shut and even after as long as they could see him standing in the doorway. They took their positions on the street and on the sidewalk in front of his house. By late morning, when Rebecca came down, the street was full. Neighbors began calling to complain. Rebecca refused to handle any of the calls. James explained that he had no control over the media and strongly referred them to the First Amendment.

If you could keep your dirty old-man dick in your pants, none of this would be happening.

The awkwardness that used to be confined to their bedroom followed Rebecca from the second floor that morning. She had entered the family room hesitantly. In the kitchen, she poured her coffee stealing glances over her shoulder. Everywhere James moved found her moving to the opposite side of a room or to the next room. She looked ashen and disturbingly weak. It was as if she were suffering from a serious illness, her eyes presenting a frailty that he had never seen before. She looked afraid. Of what, he didn't know. Maybe, like him, afraid of an uncertainty that she never ever expected to carry. He felt more awful with each fleeting glimpse, and he was decidedly thankful when a call came that she could finally take. It was from Aubrey. As Rebecca spoke her first words of the day, he walked out on the back porch and sat with the paper. He looked at his picture with the valedictorian from the podium at the high school commencement, fully one half of the top of the front page. Of course, when he became a billionaire, he graced the front page as well. And many other times he had been in newspapers. But never like this. The worst of him from the woman's apartment, to social media, to the scrutiny of his city and beyond.

The Washington Ledger

A Goliath Falls

By Claire Simpson

Washington, DC - Just three days ago, James Henry Ferguson, a member of the Black Billionaires club, a Washington resident and a distinguished philanthropist, was on top of the world. Yesterday, he suffered an abrupt and stunning fall from grace. Even as President Walker sang his praises for providing a college education to an entire high school senior class, evidence of a possible double life was making its way onto social media. A 24-year-old woman, known as Lady Nymph on internet porn sites, tweeted in a very descriptive manner that she had engaged in sexual intercourse with Mr. Ferguson, who is married to former marketing executive, Rebecca Ferguson. The couple has two adult daughters, Katherine and Lillian. Immediately, the internet, which heretofore had been a great fan of Mr. Ferguson's, brutally turned against him, labeling him a womanizer and bedswerver, among other colorful names.

Ferguson completed his undergraduate work at Princeton University and continued his studies at the Wharton School of Business at the University of Pennsylvania. After graduating from Wharton, he received financial backing and purchased his first restaurant. Early on, he was known to have a great feel for the business and quickly became a remarkable success. A dozen highly successful national restaurant chains began under his leadership. From there, he continued his success in real estate. He was one of the first Black American billionaires and is currently the richest with an estimated wealth of ten billion.

Mr. Ferguson was also a megastar in the business world, making regular appearances on CNBC, Bloomberg and FBN. He also often appeared in this paper and others globally. Shortly after he married in 1986, he and his wife quietly began their philanthropic mission. In a 60 Minutes interview, she described how it all began. "When I met James, he already had such a beautiful heart," Mrs. Ferguson said. "It hurt him to see people in need and the idea that he couldn't help them often made him physically ill. So, one night we are watching the news and he sees a grandmother in a one-bedroom apartment trying to raise the four children of her daughter who had died. The father was nowhere to be found. The story was about landlords and how they didn't take care of the homes of their poor residents. When James saw how they were struggling to live on her small social security check in such conditions, we managed through friends to get a hold of the reporter and from there, we put them in a house and James got jobs for the kids old enough to work and for a time, he carried the family. The next was a family with kids without the ability to have a proper Christmas. James stepped in. We started an organization basically to watch the news and read reports to find families. Both of our daughters' first jobs were with this organization. This kind of giving has long been a family effort of love." Mr. Ferguson would continue this for decades. He was one of the first businessmen to show up at department stores before Christmas to pay off all layaways for families. Mr. and Mrs. Ferguson have been honored repeatedly for their goodwill, all of which, may be tainted beyond repair at this time.

Late last night, returning from Joint Andrew's Air Force Base, President Walker was asked about Mr. Ferguson's downfall. "James and Rebecca Ferguson are good people and amazing Americans. This kind of tragedy has befallen families for forever, and I am sorry for them. The First Lady's and my heart goes out to their entire family," he said.

Mr. Ferguson's lawyer, Princeton roommate and long-time friend, Mason Easton said that Mr. Ferguson would not be giving any more interviews. "The family requests privacy at this very difficult time."

Mr. Ferguson stepped down last year as the CEO of his corporation but remained as an advisor to the Board. There has been no word on whether or not that relationship will continue.

The article continued on page A10, but James did not turn to it. He decided that he had read enough. He folded the paper gently, although part of him wanted to rip it to shreds. In the kitchen, Rebecca sat at the table still talking to Aubrey. She had been crying. James placed the paper in front of her and made his way down to his office, where he thought he would stay until the girls came home. Until it would be time for him to leave them and to fashion some new sort of existence. At least they were both out of the house. He wouldn't have to come here to see them. He could travel to Princeton to see Lillian and eat at Teresa's, their favorite Italian place. He could go to Brooklyn to visit Katherine and maybe finally meet that new boyfriend they had been hearing so much about.

His phone vibrated. It was an email from Mason with a link to a YouTube video. "You need to see this too," he wrote. "This is going to hit extremely hard. There is a tricky revelation in this for you and Rebecca. I know she and Aubrey are talking now, so you have some time to prepare for what this will mean to her.

Call me afterward. We do have to talk about this."

James clicked on the link. He recognized the music from commercials for a tabloid television show. A vehicle for trashy celebrity stories that they loosely referred to as news. He certainly thought of himself as better than any situation that would appeal to that show or its viewers. Yet there he was. Stock news photos of him quicky interspersed between video clips seemingly going through a day in the life of Lady Nymph.

Then she was sitting on a set with one of the anchors who began her questioning as the theme music died down.

Anchor: Do you want to tell us your real name?

Lady Nymph: No.

Anchor: Oh, okay. Why not?

Lady Nymph: This is the only persona you need to know.

Anchor: Okay, Lady Nymph it is then. Your tweet was quite tantalizing. I guess I would say a kind of tease about what went on with you and Mr. Ferguson.

Lady Nymph: If you say so.

Anchor: You really had no idea who he was when he entered your apartment.

Lady Nymph: (Shaking her head) Not even when he entered me.

Anchor: Would you tell our audience how you found out who he was?

Lady Nymph: A TV report about him giving money to all those book fairies to go to college. But I just found out something else in the video you used at the beginning of this show.

Anchor: Oh, do you have some breaking news for us?

Lady Nymph: I guess so. I just figured it out.

Anchor: Please, do share.

Lady Nymph: I know his wife.

Anchor: Personally?

Lady Nymph: I went to Charles R. Drew Elementary School. She used to be a reading tutor there. She tutored me for a couple of years.

Anchor: So you had sex with a man who is married to a woman who used to tutor you in elementary school?

Lady Nymph: I know what I saw. That was her.

Anchor: Wow! That's an incredible coincidence.

Lady Nymph: Maybe, but I bet she tutored hundreds of knuckleheads over the years. But, hey, it is what it is. That lady was my tutor.

Anchor: Curious, once you found out who he was, why did you tweet about it?

Lady Nymph: Not every day you (bleep) a billionaire.

Anchor: Ah . . . true. Did you give any thought to what tweeting it would mean? That you could be destroying someone's life. A family? Now you know it's the family too of a woman who mentored you.

Lady Nymph: Look, He came to me. He paid me. That's on him. I tweet about a lot of my dicks.

Anchor: You say he was desperate and frantic?

Lady Nymph: Yeah.

Anchor: How do you mean?

Lady Nymph: I mean it was like the dude had been in jail for years and the first thing he saw when he walked off the yard was a naked woman. All of those years caught up with him. You know what I mean?

Anchor: (Nodded).

Lady Nymph: He was all over me. Hands everywhere. Breathing hard. I tried to talk him down. I wasn't looking for no heart attack sex (laughing). He was desperate for it.

Anchor: Was he out of control? Angry?

Lady Nymph: There was a touch of anger in his frantic thing. Little hot sauce from somewhere.

Anchor: Were you afraid for your safety? Did he try to hurt you?

Lady Nymph: No. No. It didn't go nothing like that. It was more sad angry, if that makes any sense.

Anchor: And finally, you say he paid you well.

Lady Nymph: Yeah. Like I said, the money was large. Way more than I was supposed to get.

Anchor: Did you ruin future pay dates by going public with this?

Lady Nymph: I guess, but I'm on national television with you. Getting my fifteen, yo (laughter).

James left his phone on the recliner. He stopped at the top of the stairs to listen for Rebecca, who was still on the phone. He wondered what they could still be talking about as he passed the front door, taking a long look at the growing crowd of media. Upstairs, he closed the door to his closet behind him. Inside, he pulled down two large suitcases and started to pack.

ELEVEN

As a child, it was always breathtaking. That moment when the leaves, dry, brittle, and weakened by age, abandoned their branches on a bracing autumn breeze. With just the right wind, strong and consistent, it would rain leaves for minutes at a time. The colors of his crayon box floated about him, overwhelming the sky as he ran in circles, twisting, laughing, and chasing. There were times his parents watched from the porch and laughed along with him.

"Fall is my favorite season!" he shouted once as the wind ceased and he turned to his parents to find his joy reflected in their faces.

"Is that so?" his mother had asked.

"Yes, ma'am."

"I would have thought it was the summer," his father said. "No school, lots of free time."

"Yes," his mother interrupted. "Shorts and t-shirts. Late sunsets and ice cream."

"That's true," Jimmy had replied. "But sometimes summer gets too hot. You feel lazy, and you don't want to do much. Things feel heavy. Summer is like eating molasses cake. You know what I mean?"

His parents had laughed. "Not really," his mother had said. "What's autumn like?"

Jimmy gave the question a moment of consideration. Then he said, "It's like the sound of ginger ale being poured on ice cubes in a glass. It's like feeling the bubbles popping in your mouth."

"Crisp, you mean?"

"Yes, ma'am. That's it. Crisp!"

Young Jimmy believed that autumn was like a cold splash of water on a person's face. While many thought of it as the dying season for Mother Earth, Jimmy contemplated the new beginnings, which, in his mind, overshadowed the pensiveness. For him, there was always a feeling of something special starting right after Labor Day. A kind of renewed productivity. All around his hometown, the fields bustled with activity, extra hands hired to take in the many harvests, silos being filled to the top. Trucks full of crops on their way to market. Kids got excited about school, if only for the first two happy weeks. Football started, which meant Friday night town celebrations even if the team lost. And community dances in the high school gymnasium. The World Series kept folks up late on school nights. There was an Octoberfest with a parade, including several marching bands, making its way down Main Street past his father's church, where they watched from the parking lot. There was just too much activity to be sad about the change in the weather.

This is what Mr. Jimmy thought about as he sat watching the late fall activity outside his house. He'd set his small dinner table lengthwise, underneath the window overlooking the land between his and Miss Septima's houses. He did it to provide more space in his great room for the kids when they came over after school. But he also loved being able to sit at the window, quietly by himself, looking out on the recently busy neighborhood of around the way. It got busy because Fountain Hughes left home without a word to Bess or Miss Septima. Bess worried, but no one else did. His return from jail had been like a dark cloud over the little houses, all in a row. His leaving after his most recent collision with Mr. Jimmy and the law, wherever he had gone, had brought back the sun.

Juba ushered Mr. Jimmy back into the neighborhood, where he was promptly and happily greeted. After smoothing out community relations, Juba along with Beech negotiated for more work. Mr. Jimmy bought a prefab shed and had it put up next to his house, where he could see it from his window. He bought lawnmowers and edgers. He bought hedge clippers, shovels, rakes, and three wheelbarrows. He put a padlock on the door to the shed and gave Juba the key. He was named foreman, and he ran a tight ship. Every day after school, he brought kids over to work. Mr. Jimmy hired whomever he brought. He kept a lockbox full of cash behind the shoes in his closet.

In the early fall, he worked with the kids. They cut lawns for the twenty-two shacks bordering the land that he was attempting to buy. The neighborhood bushes and hedges were scattered about without uniformity of any kind. He taught them how to trim them up. He watched the kids begin to feel good about themselves. They worked and laughed, and he watched the pride and self-worth begin to grow. They began to own responsibilities that should not have been theirs, leaving money in the purses of their mothers, who repaid them with good meals and loving hugs. In the afternoons, he found himself looking at his watch, waiting for them to arrive, longing for the sounds of a school playground outside his window. How he wished Rebecca could have seen it.

The yard work would soon be done for the season. Maybe one or two more days of raking leaves, but that would be it. He would have to find other ways for them to earn their pay. In the meantime, he would continue their schooling. While he recovered from Fountain's assault, he thought a lot about the day he'd met Juba and Beech. He thought about how much trouble they had reading and with simple arithmetic. He wanted to help, and he was quite happy with his plan of action. He laid it out for approval by Miss Septima and Patrice.

"The children got teachers," Miss Septima said.

"Yes, and so did my girls," Mr. Jimmy replied. "But we helped them at home too. To reinforce what happens in the classroom. These children. Your amazing son, Patrice. They are all so far behind kids their ages where I come from. They are capable of doing more than cutting grass when they grow up. But they have to learn to read. It expands the mind. Teaches them how to reason. It's the foundation for everything."

"This how you get all that money?" Miss Septima asked. "Just by reading?"

"It was the first building block on the road to the money. What do you think?"

Patrice smiled and nodded her head. "Yup," she said.

"Well, I guess so then," Miss Septima added. "Let us talk to the rest of the folks. See if their kids want to come."

Miss Septima and Patrice became his neighborhood marketing team. They convinced about half of the families, and Mr. Jimmy's house soon became a hot bed of activity. Juba, not one to ignore an angle, bargained for more. "You said one time that we could watch football at your house if our mothers say we could. Mine say yes. I'll come to read if I can watch football."

Mr. Jimmy said yes. On the weekdays, the kids came over right after school to read and then work. On Sundays, his great room was filled with boys and girls. They voted on which early afternoon game to watch. Mr. Jimmy sat behind them at his table, watching and enjoying the fun they were having. Sometimes on Friday nights, kids would come with their parents. And they would all squeeze into the great room, and they would watch movies. They watched *The Learning Tree, Sounder, Akeelah and the Bee,* and others. They were often so captivated that they would forget to eat their pizza. They heated it up in the microwave afterward and ate under the stars on Mr. Jimmy's porch and laughed at Miss Septima's stories.

Mr. Jimmy had enlisted Mason's help with the afterschool reading material. "I need the Bob Books," he'd said.

Mason had laughed. "The what?"

"Bob Books. They are these tiny little books that you can use to help kids learn to read. It's a lot of very basic drawings of characters doing normal things and the easy, descriptive words to build on. Phonics based. We taught Katherine and Lillian to read with them. Had them ahead of their reading level early on, and they never looked back."

"Okay. I'll try. But I warn you not to get your hopes up too high. It's been just under three months and Rebecca hasn't spoken a word to me. You ruined my reputation with her too!"

"What are best friends for? Mr. Jimmy asked.

"Yeah, right! It's okay. I still hold hope that she'll give in one day. I think I will ask Aubrey to call about the books though."

Four days later, the books arrived in the original boxes that the girls had used. The corners were crumpled, and some of the books had lost pages. Many of the characters had been colored in with colored pencils and given pet names. They touched Mr. Jimmy's heart in an unexpected way. He had to put them on the kitchen table and retire to the porch to ride out the wave of melancholy they had created in him. Created in part because there wasn't an inkling that Rebecca had cared to ask why he wanted them.

Mr. Jimmy taught via the Bob Books in a circle on his floor. The kids liked it even though some posited that learning wasn't supposed to be so informal.

"Mr. Jimmy, you crazy," a girl named Reenie told him. "You can't do your schooling on the floor."

"They did at the school my girls went to. And they learned to read very well."

In the beginning, their feelings had been hurt. Mr. Jimmy started with book set one for beginning readers. When they saw the simple pencil-like drawn characters on the pages, they asked with bruised pride in their voices, "Ain't these for little kids?"

"Not if you have trouble reading them," he answered softly, reaching out to hold Marquetta's hand.

She looked at the page and then at him, her eyes welling because despite her questioning of the material, she knew she would struggle. And she did. The sentence read:

Sam had a cat.

She took her time and managed to get through it, though haltingly. No one laughed the way they might have in school. They knew Mr. Jimmy wouldn't stand for it. They followed his lead when he clapped for her. The room filled with applause, and this time Mr. Jimmy's eyes welled.

"Along the way," he told them. "Some adults were unable to help you. Some adults, and this makes me really mad, failed you. If I fail you, it won't be because I didn't try my hardest. Pass the book around now and let everyone have a chance."

There was more struggling as the book made its way around the circle. There was more applause. Kids held the hand of kids next to them as they worked through the three-word pages. And in time, like with his girls, there was growth. They didn't say it to him, but he felt it in the way they looked at him. *We just needed to have someone who believed in us. Who believed we could earn it. We needed to feel loved. We needed to hear it from someone who made it doing it this way. We needed the road map from someone who had already arrived.* And this is what he felt when one or two lingered for long hugs before taking the dirt road home.

Their time wasn't all spent in struggle. Sometimes they told jokes and enjoyed a good laugh. Sometimes they just talked about what was on their minds in the moment. Sometimes they had questions. Especially about Mr. Jimmy's family, but he would only go so far as to say that he had been married. He had two adult daughters. He was getting a divorce. They eventually got the message with regard to his family, but they continued at every moment possible to question him about other things in his life.

"How did you get your money?"

"I worked for it. In the restaurant business."

"Where did you grow up?"

"Virginia. My daddy is a preacher. My mama is the church's first lady."

"Did you have a bicycle?"

"Yes, I had several."

"What kind of games did you play?"

"We played checkers and chess when I got a little older. My mama and I did puzzles and played board games, which my daddy hated."

"That's all? That sounds boring."

"It wasn't for me."

"What was a special place that you liked?"

"I liked going to Philadelphia, where my grandmother lived. She was the best grandmother in the world. I liked going for long drives in the country. And a real special treat was to spend a weekend in a cottage by the ocean that a friend of my father owned. We would put these chairs called Adirondack chairs right by the water and read our favorite books."

"You just sat there. You ain't even go in the water?"

"No, I went swimming too," he replied, laughing.

"What's a cottage?"

"A pretty little house."

"Can we go to that pretty little house?"

"No. I'm sorry to say that I can't either anymore. It was sold when my father's friend died. But all of you should go to the ocean at some point in your life. Everyone should put their toes in the ocean sometime."

"That ain't gone happen," Rube said, which took the adventure out of the room and ended the conversation in a quiet sadness.

Mr. Jimmy noticed that the kids had gathered around the door of the shed. The tools had been put away, and they should have been on their way home. But they were standing in a cluster, staring at the road, nervously whispering, and pointing. On it, three people made their way toward his house. Miss Septima, Bess, and Fountain Hughes. The last time he saw Fountain, it had not been a pleasant experience, even though he had tried to make it so.

As a young boy, Mr. Jimmy knew the expectations his parents had for him. One of the most important was the idea that he would be a law-abiding citizen. That he would never lose focus on how he should behave and do something to break the law.

"If you do something wrong and end up in jail, we will always love you," his father had said. "But we will let you do your time. Don't expect us to be trying to get you out when you've done wrong. So just do right. It's not that hard."

The lecture had been clear to young Jimmy, and whenever the desire to loosen the reins of behavioral norms occurred to him, it sounded loudly and firmly in his mind. He knew his parents were not trying to be unreasonable. He knew they feared for him, as a Black boy in the South, in any conflict with the law, and their best hope was to frighten him into good behavior. It worked extremely well, and because of it he had never even been close to a police station. So it was a strange thing indeed to find himself alone in an empty room, sitting at a metal table with a bar built into it, awaiting the prisoner, Fountain Hughes.

He came into the room shackled, hands and feet. He was, as

the old folks would say, "seeing red." With more effort than neces-
sary, they wrestled him into the chair. They hooked his handcuffs
to the bar on the table, announced a 20-minute time limit, and
closed the door behind them.

"Man, what the fuck do you want?" Fountain asked. He held
up his hands and the cuffs that bound them. "You come to see
what your massa done to me? You come to tell me to kiss his
White ass?"

"I don't have a master."

"Man, you should say that nonsense in the mirror so you can
see how stupid you look saying it. You just a rich-assed fool. You
think the White man can't take your shit whenever he wants to.
I got news for your Black ass. I seen it. All. My. Life!"

He pounded the table, his chains rattling.

"I know what my limits are as a Black man," Mr. Jimmy
replied. "You are right. I have had people remind me of the
place they believe I should live in."

"So why you here spouting this bullshit?"

"Because even as a Black man, I have had success. You've
seen it. The first thing you asked me before knocking me out was
if I had a billion dollars. If people are talking about me, then
you know it's true. Black people all over this country are having
success stories every day. Historically Black colleges are full of
Black people dreaming the good dreams. You can do something
positive. You can be better than what's happening in your life."

Fountain was incredulous. "Bruh, you just be happy living in
the Matrix and leave me the fuck alone."

"Okay," Mr. Jimmy said. "I didn't really come here today to
have that conversation. I came to tell you that I am not going to
press charges."

"Oh, so that's what's up. You want to show me that you got
some pull with Massa? I'm supposed to bend over for you now
too?" Fountain laughed loudly and angrily. "I already showed

you what I think of you. Take these off, and I'll show you the same damned thing. Fuck these honkies and their jail. And fuck you too!"

Mr. Jimmy sat quietly and measured the emotion in Fountain's face, in particular his eyes. He had never seen rage like this up close. It was at another level from the day that Fountain had attacked him, and he was happy that the handcuffs kept him on the other side of the table. Of course, in his childhood Virginia town, he had witnessed the pain of having suffered at the hands of a racist society. Many members of his father's church showed up at odd hours escaping the wrath of Whites, some intending to do them real harm, others engaging in fun-for-them bullying. Mr. Jimmy was aware of what those confrontations could do to the minds of Black folk.

"I didn't want to see you go back to jail again."

"Why you care? Wait, wait, I know. Man, you think we don't know your story. We know what you done. It's been going around. White folks spreading it like seeds in the field, sowing bad feelings about you all around Ham. I know what it's really all about. You just trying to use me to make up for the shit you did just to make yourself feel better. This ain't got nothing to do with me."

"If that's so, you still ought to be smart enough to take me up on it and get out of here."

"Now you calling me stupid. Man, you so lucky I got these chains on me. This time, boy," he said, slowly twisting his head from side to side, his mouth tight as he wished for the ability to commit the crime he was imagining.

"For whatever reason, I didn't want to be a part of putting another Black man in jail if I could help it. But the real reason I did this—or at least why I think I did it—is for Essie, your daughter. You remember her? There are too many Black children growing up without fathers these days. Sometimes the system takes them away in ways we can't fight, but there are times when the choice is up to us. You are going to get out of here. Accept the blessing, and make the choice to be a good husband and a good father. The quality of Essie's life depends on it."

Briefly, Fountain's façade cracked. Just the tiniest bit but enough to let Mr. Jimmy know that he had indeed touched a nerve. Just like him, above all things, Fountain did not want to be a failure in the eyes of his daughter.

"Yo! Yo, come and get me, man! Fuck this dude!" Fountain yelled half upset and half angry. He rattled his chains. He wanted to leave, and Mr. Jimmy decided not to argue. Nothing good was being accomplished. He had quickly and summarily failed.

Fountain turned to the side in his chair. He turned his head completely away from Mr. Jimmy, looking at the door, awaiting the guards and the freedom of his cell. The sound of the lock being opened echoed in the room. As the door began to open, Mr. Jimmy had his last say in the matter.

"No matter what," he said as the guards began to unhook him from the table. "It comes down to this, Fountain. You will be out of here soon. When you wake up every morning after, the first step you take is a choice you make. No one else makes it for you. Every day you choose the direction you will take mentally and physically. It's all on you in that moment. Make good choices from now on," he yelled just as Fountain disappeared from sight.

There was a moment of silence before he heard Fountain yell from a distance. "Hey, Massa Jimmy," he called derisively. "You ever march for Black folk?"

Mr. Jimmy had not, and he let the emptiness in the air answer for him. The last thing he heard was Fountain's laughter. The door closed, and Mr. Jimmy left, vowing never to set foot in a police station again. It had made him sick to his stomach.

Now, here he was again, Fountain Hughes, walking up to the edge of his porch, led by Miss Septima and Bess. When they stopped, he looked at the ground. It had a been a few weeks since he'd left. Except for Juba, the kids gathered at a distance. Juba stood beside Mr. Jimmy, his arms crossed in defiance. It even made Fountain smile, but Mr. Jimmy was in no mood to recognize his five-second display of humanity.

"Hello, Bess," he said.

She nodded. "Mr. Jimmy, thank you. I don't know how you done it."

"Well, first they needed me to press charges. I refused. Then they decided to charge him anyway, which they can do. I asked Miss Septima to tell everybody not to talk to the police. To say they hadn't seen anything. They had no witnesses, and finally, I told them that I started the fight. It was all on me. I know they knew that I wasn't telling the truth, but I knew it really wouldn't be worth it for them. I know a lot of lawyers. I was well instructed."

"That's something," Bess said. "Ain't it, Fountain?"

But he was not ready to speak, so Mr. Jimmy continued to carry the conversational baton.

"Miss Septima. I watched you all walk here. You were leading them. You sure have come a long way since the hospital."

"Child, I had to get myself back into shape so I could get outside. I was afraid of catching the house poisoning, you know."

"Yes, ma'am. I do."

The For Sale sign rattled in the wind. The small talk ended in waiting. In the uncomfortable quiet that ensued, Mr. Jimmy could feel the atmosphere change. The expectation that it was Fountain's time to speak hung heavily in the air. Finally, while looking at the ground he rose to the moment.

"I hit that White man because there wasn't nothing left to do," he said. "He was drunk and I shoulda thought about that. But he didn't have no respect in him. He told me I was a has been and that my life was over. Told me all I ever was was a colored buck to entertain good White folks on a Friday night. To carry that football. But it turned out I was just a small-time buck with small-time ability, and now I was just gone do what the rest do. Sit on the porch of that raggedy-assed thing I call a house and drink corn liquor all day, existing on his tax dollars. His face in the beer and that foam all over his beard. He was laughing. When the rest of them started laughing, I could feel it building up in me. My heart got hot, hot and to hurting. Hurt so much I felt like it was either die or explode. I exploded all over him. It won't nothing left to do."

He took the air right out of the sky. No one expected anything like that from a man like Fountain Hughes. Mr. Jimmy could see that the expressions of apprehension and fear on the faces of his neighbors had melted away into concern for a man carrying the weight of a shared abomination. Fountain looked around to see this, which, Mr. Jimmy thought, gave him the strength to dig deeper.

"My daddy and his daddy and his daddy. They were share-croppers," Fountain continued. "Always owing the man. Always afraid of getting sick, 'cause you know, if they did and couldn't work, they kick your ass out. The man owned the house. If you didn't work, you lost everything. He took it. The men in my family wanted better," he said. "Just ain't happen though. I thought I was going to make it playing football. I thought I could fix life for us. Mama gone on over to the other side now. Got sick and died from living in that," he said, pointing back down the road to the house next to Miss Septima. "She was sick for years."

"What exactly happened with football?" Mr. Jimmy asked.

"Sometimes, you can be good enough in high school, but that don't cut it in college. On the field or in the classroom. I couldn't cut it in college."

"He can't read right," Bess shouted and quickly retreated into her quiet. She turned her eyes away from everyone.

"I'll teach him," Juba said, his arms now at his side, his defensive posture gone.

Mr. Jimmy looked down at him and smiled. He put his arm around Juba's shoulder and pulled him closer. Fountain looked up and met Mr. Jimmy's eyes.

"While I was gone, I tried to kill myself drinking and staying all hopped-up. But all that time, I couldn't get what you said about Essie out of my mind. You said I needed to be better for Essie. For her life to be something. Man, I ain't want to be no failure. But when the game was over, you know, I didn't see a way to be nothing except collecting for the brothers selling. I didn't have nothing to work with." He seemed to be pleading now for everyone in hearing distance to understand.

"I didn't see a way to be what she needed me to be. Or Bess neither. And when there ain't no way, man, you feel it way deep down inside. You gotta run from it or it'll eat you alive like some acid."

Bess turned to him and then Mr. Jimmy. She took a deep breath and began to softly cry. Fountain put his hand on her shoulder. Her cry got louder.

"I don't know," Fountain continued. "I think it's too much to live with. Too much."

"But I can't run," Bess said. "I stay. I stay in that filthy house. I don't get no break. You took after your daddy good all right."

"The good Lord knows I'm sorry, Bess. She got word to me," Fountain said, looking at Bess. "She said she was going to you to help her and Essie leave me. Between what you said to me in the jailhouse about Essie and the thought of losing Bess too. Man, that would mean everything in this world that mean anything gone. So I changed up. I came back. We gone ride it out. Whatever it gets to be."

Mr. Jimmy looked at Fountain. "Didn't you ever think of just getting a job? Even at McDonalds or something?"

"No."

"Why not?"

"'Cause that seem worse than nothing. Seems final. You ain't going nowhere for sure. If I'm running, I never know what I might run up on."

"You ain't run up on nothing yet, have you?" Miss Septima asked.

"No, ma'am."

"That's a empty road you been traveling, son," she continued. "For you and the family."

"Well, I put all the eggs in the one basket. I don't have nothing else to bring to the table."

"Anyway, he sorry, Mr. Jimmy," Bess said.

Mr. Jimmy looked at Fountain, who sheepishly nodded. "I am that."

"Fountain," he said. "You were a good high school player. You learned how to play the game and the other players to be successful. The same thing happens out here in the real world. Black men like me—we can't change everything. That's for sure. But we learn to play the game. Some say that's selling out. I disagree. I studied the game. I studied the opponents. I learned what I needed to bring to the table to succeed. I learned to play the game better than many of them. And because of that, I won. Think of it that way. What do you bring to the table that can get you back in the game of life?"

"I'm on empty, Mr. Jimmy."

"When we parted at the jail, the last thing you asked me was if I ever marched for Black folks. I have not. And I know that looks bad on me, but I want to tell you a story. Not long ago, I was working out on my elliptical, watching a documentary about the integration of college football. There was this guy from the University of Maryland. His name was Darryl Hill. He was a running back and the first to integrate the ACC. One day, some very famous, young Civil Rights leaders, Stokely Carmichael and H. Rap Brown, came to him and demanded that he march with them. It wasn't his thing. Rap Brown called him a punk, and things got physical. After things calmed down and they got themselves together, Hill let them know that there was more than one way to fight the beast. He just wanted to play football and for the pleasure of doing that, he got death threats, and he took all kinds of disgusting abuse. But he kept running, doing it his way. He opened that door for others who ran through it and are now signing ninety-million-dollar contracts. So no, I never marched, but like Darryl Hill, I do what I do best with the same goal in mind. You understand?"

Fountain nodded slowly. "I understand, but I ain't got football no more."

"Who is talking about you playing football. Juba here told me before I first met you that you were descended from sharecroppers. He said you grew up working in that field right there. Are you a good farmer?"

"I can be, but that land ain't ours. Belong to a White man. Like everything else."

"You let me worry about that. I have a plan. In the meantime, you be a father and a husband. That's your job. Every day you get up and choose to be that and let me see you doing it well. We will, all of us, take care of each other until my plan gets underway."

Fountain and Bess looked at each other and for a moment, Mr. Jimmy could see what they were like when they fell in love. When that love gave them hope. He wanted to bring that back for them more than anything. He stepped forward and let everyone see him give Fountain Hughes a long and firm hug. "Thank you for coming," he said.

"Oh, he was coming," Miss Septima said. "I told him I whip his behind like my Jesus did the money changers if he didn't."

Juba led in the laughter.

TWELVE

Katherine raged.
James withdrew.

She was a whirlwind of contempt. She was a tempest of hurt and tears. She paced before the three of them, her eyes puffy, wet, and red. Her face was riddled with tension. She was often doubled over in screams of profane disappointment. She might well have been experiencing withdrawal, he thought. From the insidious drugs of love and trust that he had been giving her since the day she was born. Now, she had all but come undone in front of them. He had brought his little girl to this.

On his desk, in his office, there was a picture of the two of them. She could have only been weeks old. He sat with her on the couch in their first home, Katherine a cuddle ball on his chest, her head sweetly tucked into his neck and shoulder. She was asleep, and he was quietly looking into Rebecca's camera with a soft and loving smile on his face as she took their picture. Of course, he understood that at that age his baby girl had no idea what she was doing. But to him, it felt like she understood that he was her father and that she could lay her weight, her love, and her burdens on his shoulders. That she instinctively knew her love, and her need to trust were not only safe with him but absolutely treasured by him. He would give his life to protect them. That is what she had grown up believing. And behind her, Lillian.

James so loved his time with the girls as they grew. He endeavored to make himself as indispensable as Rebecca. He wanted them to be able to share their emotional needs with him as easily as they might with Rebecca. He worked hard to be at their medical checkups. He went on school field trips. He knelt beside them and guided them through their prayers. They read together. They sang together and played games together. They sat and talked about life. When they were little, they loved to have him brush and braid their hair after their baths. By the time they had reached middle school, they knew their daddy was undeniably dependable. And that is what they believed until he proved himself to be anything but.

Winding down from a good 20 minutes of exasperation, Katherine sighed deeply. Looking up to the ceiling, she said, "Truly. I just . . . I just cannot believe that we are here."

Here . . .

Sitting with, but apart from his family, James let the word seep into him and sit with him so that he could fully acknowledge the damage that rested in its meaning. Here represented the absolute worst moment of existence for him and his family. Here was their lives turned inside out. Here was the inability to defend himself or his family as the world came crashing down upon them.

It took Katherine and Lillian four days to get to them. They had to adjust to the hell in their lives, protect themselves, and then make a plan to get to DC. Shortly after *The Ledger's* article, their social media pages turned against them.

Ooops! Daddy is a whoremonger!

Daddy is just like every Black male, football, basketball, business. They can't handle it!

Sad, mad, horny Dad! You must be proud!

Bet you won't tell him what an ass he is!

Don't throw out the money with the bathwater!

Ask your daddy for me. Why can't Black men keep anything good in their lives?

Katherine and Lillian's pictures were in the paper along with James's and Rebecca's. They were plastered online across many different news and celebrity outlets. Katherine's work address was posted as was Lillian's dorm. Lillian was lucky in that she was on Princeton's campus, and she was protected by her friends who escorted her to class. The school's administration offered temporary security. But Katherine found the streets of New York City to be an uncomfortable place as she was constantly harassed by many who recognized her. She retreated into her apartment and the arms of her boyfriend, whose car she finally borrowed, driving to Princeton to pick up Lillian. There was no way they would get on a train or a plane.

While waiting for the girls to arrive, life for Rebecca was not much better. Against James's wishes, she decided to keep a doctor's appointment that she'd made months ago. Aubrey came through the adjoining backyard of neighbors and dear friends to get to their house. She refused to come inside because she didn't want to encounter James. Rebecca put on sunglasses and a big floppy hat and left with her. When she returned, she was shaken and angry. They had been able to get to the doctor's office without problems. Rebecca, feeling better about being away from James and their house, and fooled by how easy it had been to get to the doctor without issue, decided to take a walk along the Georgetown waterfront. They took precautions, staying away from the restaurant area. They walked to the opposite side of the park, to the far corner on the waterfront where there were fewer people, but it didn't help. They had judged the situation incorrectly. Maybe, she later told the girls with James sitting alone in the next room, the floppy hat and sunglasses drew attention instead of hiding her from recognition. It only took one loud woman who seemed to feel Rebecca was somehow at fault if she didn't shoot James and put him in a grave. She made such a racket, others eventually joined in and followed them across the street to the parking garage, shouting all the way.

> What are you going to do? Just stand by your man and your money? Why don't you be a soldier for women and take everything he has? Don't let us see another strong woman let a man take her heart and get away with it.

So many of the taunts and comments followed the lead of this woman. There were a few who argued to leave her alone because none of this was her fault, but she couldn't appreciate them because they were all just a part of the total disconcerting noise. It was shocking, unsettling, and an indication of what James had brought down upon them all.

Within two days of the newspaper article, per Mason's advice, James and Rebecca shut down their social media accounts. The deluge of hate toward both of them was unbearable. James had been sitting in his home office, reading hate-filled post after hate-filled post. He would ask himself why he was doing so, but he could not break away.

> James Henry Ferguson, joining the rich Black sex fiend club!
>
> Yes, right alongside R. Kelly and Bill Cosby!
>
> Cosby, Kelly, Ferguson!
>
> Next, we're gonna find out he beats his wife too!
>
> I feel a Ray Rice moment coming!

Being associated with R. Kelly and Bill Cosby made James physically ill. After throwing up, he lingered above the toilet, breathing hard and not understanding. R. Kelly had been charged with sexual assault and abuse of a minor, as well as making indecent images of minors. Bill Cosby had been accused of rape, sexual battery, and of drugging women in order to have sex with them. *I am not them*, he shouted inside his head. *This just can't be . . . .*

James tried to resist these associations. He had gone onto Twitter and Instagram. He posted a family picture with the caption, *This is who I am! I am not those men. Please offer us a bit of kindness.*

It only made things worse.

Luckily for James, he had shut it all down before a follow-up article in the paper questioned why he had not been charged with the crime of solicitation. Now, the District Attorney's office was publicly involved, and the story grew and became inflamed. James never asked, but he assumed that Mason had made the call he asked him not to. When the DA's office finally publicly acknowledged the issue, they spoke about James's gifts to the city and the country at large. They said what occurred, given that it was a first offense, would be a misdemeanor and that James would not be incarcerated. It wasn't worth their time or the taxpayer dollars to move forward. Still, more significant damage had been done.

Katherine, now exhausted, took a seat on the floor. There seemed to be nothing left to say. Lillian was on the couch on her knees next to Rebecca. She had an arm around her mother's shoulder, and she had been cradling her and kissing her head while Katherine raged. Rebecca was as she had been most of the time since the Lady Nymph tweet, silent or in tears. Lillian had tissues for them both.

Neither of the girls had been able to sit and quietly talk to him since they came home. He might as well have been a repairman who seemed a little off and they'd understood instinctively that they should move around him with great care for their safety. Humor him from a distance until they could get him out of the house. They were constantly at their mother's side, reminding her that they loved her and were there for her. They never once said that they loved him.

"I am sorry," James said when the quiet became too uncomfortable for him and he feared what his family was thinking.

Katherine threw back her head and laughed until she cried.

"You see, Daddy," Lillian said. "Just look at us. You see how that apology is no good? It doesn't mean a thing! People think you are a horrible person, and right now, I have to agree, and I don't know if I can overcome that feeling."

"Daddy," Katherine added. "Don't you see? You have made it impossible for us to go on with our regular lives, much less emotionally deal with what you have done. And look at what you have done to yourself and Mom. You ruined your reputation and made Mom look bad and almost laughable for all of the years she publicly called you the perfect husband and father. You've taken her credibility too. In that moment, did you even consider what the ripple effects might be? You betrayed her, Daddy. You betrayed Mom in a very public and sickening way, with a woman who Mom had actually tutored as a child. Think about that vision people have in their heads, Daddy. I mean it's all so incredibly fucked up! After all the times we heard you talk about that special moment when you and Mom traded vows and how important a contract that was. One you could never break. But here we are, Daddy. Here we are."

James looked at Rebecca. Maybe the girls thought he was looking for sympathy from their mother, but he was asking with his eyes, *Aren't you going to tell them how it all began?* Rebecca remained stoic. *Aren't you going to tell them that both of us are this mess? That you didn't know why you didn't want me anymore? That I had been devastated?*

Rebecca gathered herself and broke her silence. But when she spoke, her words were not what he had wished for.

"What happened to the young man who introduced himself to me with his middle name? I know we've come forward many,

many years, but I never ever thought you could lose track of your most sacred values. I look at you now, and I don't recognize a thing about you. Who are you?"

In that moment, James Henry Ferguson was broken. He watched the infrastructure of his family start to crumble. Katherine and Lillian helped Rebecca from the couch and took her for some fresh air, secretly snaking their way through the backyard of the neighbor and onto a wooded path they'd all walked together for decades. James stayed seated and wondered. When the rubble from this quake was removed, would anyone looking at the space be able to recognize that there had once been something whole there?

By the time the girls had made it home, he'd prepared himself mentally, understanding that the waiting conversation would be very difficult. Even so, he thought there would be residual feelings for him, and they would show him that despite everything, they would not be able to totally deny their love for him. He had been wrong. Not only didn't they show him love, they displayed, along with Rebecca, a deep disgust. He was revolting to them. He knew that his time with Lady Nymph, the resulting public abuse, and the permanent alteration of their lives meant he had to go. There was no other way around it.

James called his Uber driver, who met him in the driveway behind their house, leading to their garage. They put his bags in the trunk and the back seat of the car. He left home for the last time.

In a half hour, he walked into his and Rebecca's favorite suite in the Willard Hotel. He waited for the bellhop to set his bags down. He gave him a fifty-dollar tip and watched him leave. He walked across the beautiful room to a window overlooking Pennsylvania Avenue. He stood and wondered. He had been a good man. So how does a good man lose himself? How does he not see himself dimming and beginning to disappear like a candle's last flickers before drowning in its own residue. Before giving way to the darkness. How does he not see himself turning into someone that he would have routinely despised? How does he allow himself to drown in such selfishness, born of the slow burn of anger, resentment, and the fear of abandonment? How does he set aside his love for his family to appease that anger? To quiet that fear? What happens to the clarity of thought that has always been his saving grace? What happens when he can no longer see himself in the mirror his father spoke of from the pulpit? There but not there. Soulless.

THIRTEEN

You are a billionaire, damnit! Mr. Jimmy thought to himself. *You are an influencer!*

After all, he called the president of the United States friend. He supped with the giants of industry and world leaders. He was sought after for his intellect, intuition, and business acumen. He was a person of note. Yet here he sat in the waiting room of this small-town lawyer and chairman of the county Board of Supervisors, unsettled and nervous. He stared at the plaques and framed newspaper articles hanging on the walls. One of the headlines read *Welton Knox - Ham, Mississippi's Leader and Savior.*

Olivia Fey Carol was sitting beside him. She was into her phone, catching up with real estate clients and confirming appointments. Good. She might not notice his discomfort. She might not notice that he was just beginning to understand what she'd meant when she'd said, "Mr. Jimmy, Welton Knox is the king of the hill around here. He knows one thing for sure. You are a formidable man, but you are Black, and this is Mississippi. All of your money may not be as influential as his skin color. He's betting on that."

Mr. Jimmy had smiled and even attempted to laugh it off as he drove, but that was for Olivia. He was well aware of the inescapable truth, which now haunted him. All of his life, he had known that Whiteness provided an upper hand in the United States of America. All of his life, like so many African Americans, he had been told that he had to be twice as good just to measure up to average Whiteness. Of course, a southern White man would know this and understand his advantage. So Mr. Jimmy sat, feeling the weight of this man's race, and he hadn't even met him, though he understood what the feeling portended. Many, many times, as pastor and first lady, his parents had to fight battles with the White powers that be on behalf of their church members and other African American community members. On many occasions, they had to diminish themselves in order to broker good outcomes, even when they knew themselves to be the better people. This notion sat in Mr. Jimmy's chest and burned like a bad case of heartburn. He would have liked a moment to gather himself, a second to cool the heat of insecurity. But the secretary called to them, and Olivia looked to him, expecting James Henry Ferguson in the moment instead of Mr. Jimmy. He smiled back and nodded, hopefully expressing the confidence that they both needed.

Welton Knox didn't bother to get up. That was the first instance of gamesmanship. He was a fit, good-looking man. Piercing eyes, a short, professional, yet relaxed haircut. A big silver watch and a big ring on his right hand. As he reached out his hand, Mr. Jimmy could see that it was an SEC championship ring. He was the athletic story opposite of Fountain Hughes.

"Ya'll come on in and take a seat," he said turning to Olivia. "I'm surprised to see you here with this . . . gentleman. Your folks know what you're up to?"

"Mr. Knox," she replied. "I am a grown woman."

"Still somebody's child though," he said. He leaned back and nodded at a chair for Mr. Jimmy. "Still have a family's respectability to consider."

"Wow," Olivia responded. "I haven't settled in yet, and you're getting all passive-aggressive on me."

Mr. Jimmy smiled. Without knowing, Olivia was helping him find his way back.

Welton Knox sat forward and leaned on his desk. "Well, what can I help y'all with today?"

"You know why we are here," Olivia said.

"You," Welton said, pointing to Mr. Jimmy. "You want my hospital."

"Your hospital?" Mr. Jimmy replied, incredulous. "I don't believe I've seen your name on any related documents."

"You heard me right," he said evenly and softly, yet full of thunder.

"Mr. Knox, the hospital purchase is already underway," Olivia said.

"The Merrimack General Board was pleased to have an offer," Mr. Jimmy added.

Welton nodded. "All of that is as y'all say. However, we don't want you to have it."

"Why?" Mr. Jimmy asked.

"Because you're Black and arrogant. And you think that just because you got a little bit of money, that you can carpetbag yourself down here and create your own little kingdom. Shouldn't have fucked up the one you had in DC."

Mr. Jimmy and Olivia were momentarily stunned.

Welton laughed. "You see what I did there? Fucked up? Got a couple of different meanings going on there."

Mr. Jimmy and Olivia remained quiet, both considering their next statements. The fact that he didn't just fire back with the wrath of generations saddened him. It was best for him to take his time, he knew. It was best for him to think the situation through, gauging how the moment would affect his plan. At the same time, he knew he was diminishing himself as his parents had before him. Another generation. The same forced conflict resolution.

"You think you can come down here and toss your billions around, threaten the jobs of my fellow citizens. You think just because you got a little White girl hanging on your arm, calling around town for you—that's gonna make a difference for you."

"Welton Knox! How dare you speak to us that way!" Olivia snapped back.

Mr. Jimmy could not find any voice. It had been a very long time since he'd had to face anything like the racist, sexist gas that was now overtaking him.

"You both need to remind yourselves of your places in Ham, Mississippi. Now, here's what's going to happen. Merrimack is going to remain the owners in part because all the work you want to do, building a free clinic, et cetera, would take some reworking of roads around the hospital. I think I heard the planning commission report stated that might take years to work out. If ever. And by the way, that nice young Dr. Longford. Sadly, I heard he got suspended a couple of days ago."

"For what?" Mr. Jimmy snapped.

Knox hunched his shoulders. "Could be anything. All those years of studying to be in the emergency room. When he comes back, he'll never get out of Urgent Care, taking care of the lower level of our society."

"You can't do this," Mr. Jimmy said.

"I am already. And you know what else?"

Mr. Jimmy did not answer.

"I'm going to run you right out of Ham or make it damn painful for you to stay here. We know everything about you, and by the time you get home, most of Ham will too. We're gonna shame you back to where you came from."

Mr. Jimmy stood up to leave.

"If they will have you back," Welton Knox said, laughing.

As Olivia and Mr. Jimmy left his office, Welton Knox shouted that he might even have to get on Twitter so he could enjoy what he started.

In the car, Mr. Jimmy and Olivia sat quietly.

"I thought we had more of a chance than that," Olivia said. "I can't believe he spoke to me that way. He and my daddy are friends, and he out-and-out suggested that I was your little whore or something."

"I am really sorry about that. I was unprepared. Sometimes it sneaks up on you and takes your breath away," he said before falling quiet again. He drove away and remained silent for a while.

"What are you thinking?" Olivia finally asked.

"I'm hoping that I haven't messed things up for folks around the way. I had this grand plan. It's coming apart before I can even tell anyone."

Olivia nodded. She reached over and patted him on his arm.

"You still up for pizza and meeting my family?" She asked.

"I think so," he replied. "At this point, it feels like the kind of evening I need."

Yankee met them as Mr. Jimmy pulled into the circle driveway in front of Yankee and Olivia's house. It confirmed the image Mr. Jimmy had of them after seeing Olivia drive up to his house in a Honda Civic. It was a modest bungalow. On one side of the center porch steps, there was a hanging swing for two. The other side was like an outdoor family room with wicker furniture positioned around a coffee table. Even outside, in the burgeoning winter, his perceived character of the house made him feel warm inside, and he needed that. It made him conclude that a good family lived there.

Yankee looked to be about six feet tall, his brown hair a bit spontaneous for a lawyer, Mr. Jimmy thought. But from his face, a person could see that he was an affable fellow. Even kind. As they exited the car, their children, Bea and Walt, ran out to complete the welcoming party.

Inside, the children gave him a quick tour. They were quite pleasant and well raised in terms of their manner and deference to his elder status. He was offered a glass of wine.

"Eighteen bucks," Olivia said, laughing as she poured it. "I know you're used to a libation, which requires more funding."

"I am a connoisseur of all wine," he replied, smiling.

The kids got their Pepsi, and Olivia delivered a toast to new friends.

"Baby," she said to Bea. "Why don't you guys give us some adult time until the pizza arrives, and then you can get to know Mr. Jimmy."

In the interim, they retired to the cozy family room among stuffed animals, iPads, and video game controllers stranded between the couch cushions. This all made Mr. Jimmy smile. It made him think of Kathrine and Lillian.

Olivia filled Yankee in on their short and painful meeting. He nodded continually, keeping an eye on Mr. Jimmy, who again felt somewhat diminished.

"What is your next move?" Yankee asked.

"I don't quite know," Mr. Jimmy replied. "I have to call my best friend and my lawyer. We will brainstorm about what to do next."

"Mr. Jimmy," Olivia said, "maybe you should be worried about what his next move will be. His threat was pretty clear. You left everything to come here to escape exactly what he's planning to do to you. How will you respond to that? Do you even want to deal with that?"

Mr. Jimmy offered a sad and knowing smile. Olivia's face was covered in worry. He believed that she was deeply concerned for his mental well-being, and that touched him. He thought he would come clean, and he told them both everything about his fall from grace. Afterward, he looked down, noticing that his hands were tightly entwined and trembling. It hurt a little bit to separate them. It took a moment or two of awkward quiet to calm them. When he could finally look up, he asked for more wine. Yankee nodded. He went into the kitchen, and Olivia asked Mr. Jimmy to stand. He did, and she folded him into her arms. Though he desperately needed it, he somehow felt it was wrong to hold on too long, although the comfort he felt was a hard thing to let go of. Maybe she sensed it or maybe it was just from her heart, but Olivia squeezed tighter, and she didn't let go, even when Yankee came back into the room. Mr. Jimmy waited until she did, her eyes welling. There were tears in his eyes too.

"I don't understand how you can be so caring when you know what I did to my wife. To another woman."

"Have a seat, you two," Yankee said.

"I already told you," Olivia replied, as she sat, and Yankee passed out the wine. "You were wrong. No doubt. But people with good hearts do wrong things all the time. They don't deserve to wear a scarlet letter because of it. Certainly not for the rest of their lives."

"I agree," Yankee said. "And so do our kids."

Mr. Jimmy looked shocked.

"Look," Yankee continued. "They only know you were unfaithful for one night. They haven't seen much on social media. They are as worldly as any 13- and 10-year-old I've ever known, thanks to their mother. They understand a bit of the human experiment and how we all fail from time to time. And most importantly, they have complete trust in their mother's judgment. As do I."

Mr. Jimmy nodded. He offered a soft thank-you.

"How has it been?" Yankee asked. "The transition from Washington to Ham?"

"It's been shocking to say the least," he replied. "As you know, I had no idea that the house I was buying was in such a neighborhood. I can't believe I never asked you that," he said, looking to Olivia. "My neighbors. My friends. They are so poor. I have never personally seen such poverty. It's outrageous that it exists. Especially in this country."

"We agree," Olivia said. "Everybody there is extremely poor. Everybody there is in debt which they will never pay off."

"You know, they are Americans. There is so much wealth. It's hard to comprehend why this has to be."

"Mississippi," she continued, "has the highest rate of poverty in the nation. And we seem to be in a race to the bottom with several other southern states. Nothing at all to be proud of."

"That's for damn sure," Yankee added.

Olivia continued. "Second highest obesity rate. Second highest rate of uninsured. Forty-sixth out of fifty in education. A sad state of affairs, no doubt."

"My kids are examples of that poor educational effort by the state."

"Your kids went to Princeton," Olivia smiled.

"That, they did," Mr. Jimmy replied, chuckling. "I guess I've kind of adopted the kids from around the way."

"You have," she said. "And it's wonderful."

The time was getting away from them, and Yankee expected the kids were getting hungry. He ordered the pizza from his phone, and Mr. Jimmy laughed, expressing the fact that technology never ceased to amaze him.

He talked to them about how much joy it gave him to read with the kids, to watch football and movies with them and their families. He felt very much a part of the community except for his being a part of the haves while they remained firmly ensconced with the have-nots.

"So what's the big plan that Olivia has been telling me is on the way? I know the land has something to do with it."

"Well," Mr. Jimmy said. "The land could be their way out of poverty. I made my money in the restaurant business. I see them raising crops and selling them to restaurants and stores via my network. It's one hundred acres. That could sustain the twenty or so households around the way. I just need the land."

"What does the hospital have to do with it?" Yankee asked.

"Nothing really. Except I got pissed at the display of racism, and I let my ego get in the way, and now I may have ruined everything. I already had enough obstacles."

"Like what?" Olivia asked.

"Well, I don't want this to take years to get going. How they live," he said, slowly shaking his head. "I don't know how they continue from day to day."

"It's all they've ever known," Yankee replied. "Generation after generation."

Mr. Jimmy nodded. "Anyway, I had planned to buy the equivalent of FEMA trailers. Enough for all of the families. Put them on the land and have them live in them while their houses were torn down and rebuilt. But you see the problem. I am no architect or builder, but it seems that it might take years to build all of those houses. With the trailers on the land, we can't plant all of the land. I'm still thinking, but none of it matters if Welton Knox goes after me and causes trouble where I haven't noticed it."

"Well, he's only concerned with the hospital," Olivia said. "I believe we've got the owner of the land ready to sell."

"Why hasn't he sold it already?"

"No more small, Black farmers in Ham," Yankee answered. "Your neighborhood, around the way, is considered, I don't know, like being in the worse slums of India. No White farmer wants to come near it. It's like they're afraid of the runoff or something. The farmer who owns it, Crawford Alden, said a while back that he didn't want to farm it anymore for the same reason. He has two hundred acres of family land around his farmhouse. I guess that's enough for him and his to survive nicely. He's had it on the market now for five years."

"Five years!" Mr. Jimmy said, disbelievingly. "I would have thought a company might have purchased it."

"And build an office across from that poverty?" Olivia said, shaking her head. "I don't think so."

"Why haven't they just evicted the people and taken the land? Don't they rent them with their social security and welfare checks?"

"No," Olivia said. "They all belong to the church that Miss Septima attends."

"Christ Our Lord Church," he replied.

"Yes, and by the church, I mean the community. It was the only opportunity to acquire a loan big enough to purchase the homes to keep people in the houses."

Mr. Jimmy took a large gulp of wine and reached for the bottle that Yankee'd placed on the coffee table.

"Listen," Yankee said. "When you were running your corporation, were you a good delegator?"

Mr. Jimmy nodded. "I like to think I was."

"Then let us help. I already have an idea."

"Okay, shoot," Mr. Jimmy replied.

"My firm represents a man who owns several roadside motels. A very rich man might be able to rent those motels or even buy one to house his neighbors, keeping the field free of FEMA trailers."

Mr. Jimmy smiled and nodded.

"And," Olivia continued, "a very rich man would be able to contract with several different companies to put up prefab homes. It would be a much faster process."

Mr. Jimmy lay back his head and laughed. "Well, look at you two."

"If we contracted for the motels immediately, and got the land sold and into your possession, you could move folks just after Christmas and start planting the land this spring if you know what you want to grow."

"That all sounds reasonable to me," Mr. Jimmy said. "I should have come over here sooner."

"You could have," Olivia said. "If someone hadn't been hiding from me for the first month."

"Oh, I think you're not going to live that down," Yankee said.

"I guess not," Mr. Jimmy replied. "I think I deserve it."

Sweet mayhem overtook the bungalow when the children joined them at the kitchen table. Yankee had ordered three full-size pizzas, which they did devour. Mr. Jimmy enjoyed being in the middle of a family again. Loud, excited, overlapping conversations. Instructions to grab paper napkins and drinks. Paper plates for the pizza.

"Mama!" Bea said with embarrassment.

"Sweetie, I am sure Mr. Jimmy has eaten off paper plates at some point in his life."

"It's true," he said with a smile to Bea.

Overlapping hands and arms. A pizza slid halfway out of a tilted box and prompted near hysterical laughter. The kids seemed to forget he was there and began to talk about their friends and school. The movies they must see and how old Bea would have to be to get her learner's permit. Walt feigned uneasiness about his sister behind the wheel of a car, which brought out some good-natured sibling rivalry. Mr. Jimmy glanced at Olivia, smiling, and laughing, in love with her kids. He held himself back from participating, quietly nestling himself within their good cheer.

"Oh, Mr. Jimmy," Yankee said. "We apologize. We just get carried away sometimes."

He nodded. "I see that you do. In the best kind of way."

Like his girls, these children were being raised in love and with respect, and they reflected that. They were brilliant little minds like his girls. *Opportunity breeds success*, he thought as he watched them interact with each other. That's what he wanted to give Juba, Beech, and the rest of the kids from around the way.

When all of the pizza was gone, everyone sat back in their chairs, each claiming to be fuller than the other.

"I can barely move," Walt said.

"Excellent," Olivia said. "We'll give your dessert to Mr. Jimmy to take home."

"Oh nooooo," he replied.

Over dinner, the kids had become more comfortable with Mr. Jimmy, asking about his wealth and what a billion dollars looked like. He told them that he didn't know. He'd never seen one hundred thousand dollars, let alone a billion dollars. "Mr. Jimmy," Bea said. "Mama says that you have become a reading teacher."

"Of sorts. A tutor would be more appropriate," he replied.

"Are they okay with it? The kids, I mean? Do they treat it like homework?"

"I guess so. I made a deal with them. They could come to my house to watch football. And we would have movie nights and eat pizza. All they had to do was read with me."

"Why are you doing it?" Walt asked.

"Because I want them to know that reading leads to education and that education leads to opportunity. I want them to have the same options that you two have, and again, in my mind, that requires an education."

"What else are you doing for them? Mama said you had some sort of plan."

"Walt," Olivia said. "Let's wait on that one. Mr. Jimmy is still working things out."

"In the end, Walt," Mr. Jimmy said, placing a hand on the

boy's shoulder and focusing solely on him, "I want to show them that there is life beyond their lives. I look around your house, and it's full of books. I love books, and I know they open the world to you. The kids from around the way don't have books in their homes. They don't know the same world as you do. I would like them to."

"I'm sorry," he said.

"Oh, you're a nice young man. But I'm not asking you to be sorry for the blessing of your wonderful family. I will ask that when you grow up, that you'll be a little bit like your mom and get to know the world outside of your world. And help where and when you can."

Walt nodded. "I can do that."

Yankee smiled at his son and ran his hand through his hair.

"One thing bothers me though," Mr. Jimmy said. "It's one of many things that causes me to lose sleep these days. The kids from around the way have only traveled a few miles from their homes. Some, only as far as to school or church and back. They asked me once about the ocean. I told them about a little cottage I used to go to with my parents. I told them how special it was. They keep asking me about it. Sometimes, it makes me sad because I know most of them may never have the chance to see an ocean."

"That makes me sad also, Mr. Jimmy," Bea said. "We go to the ocean every year."

Mr. Jimmy nodded. "I have an interim plan though, Bea. It involves your mother. I might need your help convincing her though. You too, Walt."

"I'm feeling pretty nervous about now," Olivia said. "What's on your mind?"

"You know the wall opposite my television? The one that could use some pictures or a large painting?"

"Yes, it's a little bare. As is the rest of the house if you asked me . . . "

"Mama!" Bea called out, exasperated, and everyone laughed.

"I was hoping that I could pay you to paint an ocean on my wall."

"Oh!" Yankee shouted. "What a great idea."

"Of course, I will," Olivia said, smiling. "I would be honored. And how about this. We could make it educational."

"No, Mama. Please," Walt said. "Don't ruin a good thing."

Olivia held up her open palm to her son, signaling that she was not entertaining his impertinence. "I could paint things into the sand and change them up. You know different kinds of crabs. Different birds in the air."

"That would be awesome," Mr. Jimmy replied.

It was settled, and soon Mr. Jimmy declared that it was time for the old man to go home. The kids seemed disappointed. He thought they were putting on an act for him. But even that was nice.

Olivia walked him out to the car, and as he opened the door, he thanked her for the hug. "It was perfectly timed."

"It cements our friendship, Mr. Jimmy. We are all here for you."

He had nodded and moved to sit in the car when Yankee exited the house bearing a look that made plain to Mr. Jimmy that the night's good feelings were about to disappear.

"Look," he said, holding out his phone. "It's the local paper, *The Ham Gazette*, online."

Mr. Jimmy looked over Olivia's shoulder at the phone and the headline.

Sex Offender from Washington, DC
Takes Up Residence in Ham.

"I'm so sorry," Olivia said.

"No need. I was a fool to think I could escape it. Maybe if I hadn't taken that walk and hadn't heard Miss Septima in pain, I wouldn't be in this predicament. Maybe I would be a lonely but safe recluse in his little house around the way."

No good deed goes unpunished, he thought.

"I don't think so," Olivia said. "I don't think that's who you are."

"That's part of my problem. Since I left Rebecca, I haven't known who I am. And in this moment, I need her more than ever."

No one had the words. Mr. Jimmy slowly eased into the car. Olivia and Yankee stood arm in arm and watched as he drove away.

FOURTEEN

James Henry Ferguson was not surprised by the knock on his hotel suite door. It even made him smile a bit. He and Rebecca had been checking into this four-room suite for years. It was their in-town getaway. Not long after Katherine was born, James's parents offered them the gift of a long weekend, which was something special because his father had real trouble leaving his congregation in the hands of another minister. James and Rebecca accepted the rare opportunity and immediately booked a flight to Turks and Caicos, renting a villa along the extraordinary white-sand beaches of Grace Bay. But on the way to the airport, they became afraid to be so far away from little Katherine, so they called The Willard. The only space available was the four-room suite. A little pricey for the up-and-coming businessman and junior marketing executive, but they decided to splurge. Over the years, whenever they wanted a quick getaway, they checked into their favorite suite. James eventually negotiated a deal through his company to rent two other suites. Those were for the executives of other companies that James wanted to impress. So the folks at The Willard were, in turn, quite fond of James and Rebecca. They had been especially kind to him throughout his ordeal, bringing him fresh fruit and flowers and making sure his laundry was attended to. They brought his favorite meals to his suite. They made sure his favorite employees were at the ready, hotel workers that he and Rebecca had come to know by name. James was expecting to see one of them when he opened his door without looking through the peephole. He was preparing to give whoever showed up some pleasant grief for not leaving him in peace, but his smile turned to wonder when he found Rebecca standing before him.

She looked more like the old Rebecca. Her face wasn't swollen from crying. Her resting face didn't scream anger. In fact, she seemed calm and at peace.

"You look almost happy," she said. "You couldn't have been expecting me."

"No. I wasn't. I thought it was either Wesley or Kayden. They have been taking care of me."

"I'm sure," she replied. "How are they?"

"They are good. I will tell them you asked after them."

Then they stared at each other. For a moment, it was if they were again discovering each other for the first time.

"Rebecca," he finally said, still astonished by her presence.

She smiled. "May I come in?"

"Oh . . . oh, of course," he replied, clumsily stepping aside.

She walked in looking and assessing. They took a seat on the couch beneath the window overlooking the White House grounds.

"Everything is so neat," she said.

"You were expecting chaos?"

"More like tragedy."

"He was here for quite a while. We were pretty serious drinking partners. Mason came over, and we kicked him out together."

"Thank goodness for best friends."

"Amen," James replied, smiling. "Would you like a glass of our favorite?"

"No, I don't think so. I don't think I will have that again."

"Ever?"

She nodded.

Why are you here? James wondered. He stared at his most beautiful wife. He desperately wanted to ask her the question out loud, but he was afraid. If there was a chance she was there to ask him home, shouldn't he let her create the moment? If he pressed her by asking, would that put her on the spot and make her change her mind in an instant? As always, she read his mind.

"I am not here to ask you to come home, James."

Though he tried not to show it, his heart fell. He could feel the emotions rising, and he dropped his head in the hopes that she might not see how a chasm of hurt was growing inside of him.

"Why are you here then?" he asked softly, still looking at the floor.

"I came to offer a proper goodbye. Our years together. Everything that has gone between us requires that."

James nodded as he looked up. She had begun to cry.

"Why didn't you tell the girls the whole truth, Rebecca? Why didn't you explain, that although I did what I did, I was an emotional wreck because of what was going wrong between us. And that we couldn't or wouldn't talk about it, which just drove me crazy."

"What would it have changed?"

"There were extenuating circumstances. I am human. Maybe they would have understood. It's not like I ran out and did it right away. A year went by."

"Again, what would it have changed? You did what you did."

He nodded in agreement, but his face still asked the same question.

"Just because something happens and it makes you mad doesn't mean you're not responsible for your subsequent choices."

"Okay."

She pulled a handkerchief from her purse and dabbed at her eyes. She blew her nose. "It was the love of a lifetime, James."

"And you can walk away from it? Without fighting for it?"

"I don't trust you anymore. I can't get back to that feeling I had. I can't trust you not to hurt my heart like that again. And I cannot be associated with a man who the public now connects with rapists and pedophiles. And who pays for sex with little girls I tutored."

"To be fair," he said, "she's not a little girl now."

Rebecca handed James her phone. "Lillian sent this to me," she said.

He pulled it to him, looking at a screenshot of a Twitter post. Someone had done their research and found a picture of Rebecca years ago sitting with the little girl who would grow up to become Lady Nymph. They smiled at the camera, Rebecca's arm around the little girl's shoulder, a picture book on the table between them. The caption below the tweet read:

OMG! Some serious queasy disgusting when you sit and think about it.

James was glad that it was a screenshot because he couldn't be tempted to read the rest of the thread, which he knew would not be to his liking. He did the only thing he could do, nod acceptingly.

"Still," he said. "I would like it on the record that you hurt my heart too. A whole year of something that you kept away from me and then no discussion about what you were doing with your therapist. It made me ask myself multiple times a day, *Does she really still love me.* And those sad attempts at lovemaking that led to more nothing between us."

"I do know now that I hurt your heart, after talking about it with my therapist. But I still see you in my mind's eye with that girl—woman. I still feel the way people now stare at me. When they do, I feel like my whole world drops out from under me. It can leave me extremely hurt, and so many seem to be happy for my pain. Were we mean people?"

"No. Just wildly successful. And wildly in love, until, well, you know. Some people like to see others fall."

"You fell."

He stared.

"And you took us all with you."

"I know."

They sat. Outside, Washington bustled. Lives were being lived. The one they shared was coming to an end. It hurt so badly that, even though he was pleased to be looking at her in the moment, he wished she would leave. He couldn't take much more.

As always, she read his mind. She stood up, and they walked quietly and slowly to the door. Standing in the doorway, they again stared at each other. Rebecca placed a hand against his cheek, and he leaned his head into it . . . her touch.

"What do I do with all of our life together? Where do I put the memories so they don't hurt?"

She took her hand away, and they considered each other for a moment before she said it.

"Goodbye, my love. Goodbye."

She turned and walked away. As she began to turn the corner toward the elevator, he called out to her, and she stopped.

"I am so sorry," he said.

Rebecca Gale Harrell Ferguson offered a look of sad resignation before turning the corner and leaving his life.

FIFTEEN

The For Sale sign was gone. Mr. Jimmy stood on his front porch, morning coffee in hand, staring at the empty space where it once precariously hung, its surface ravaged by time, Mother Nature, and the lack of human attention. Though it was often a noisy nuisance, it had kept him company, banging and creaking its way through many of his darkest moments. Now that it was gone, he realized that it had been kind of a salve for his soul. He sat down in a rocker and sipped his coffee. He felt like he'd lost a friend and that something additionally nefarious was afoot.

It had been 12 days since the pizza dinner and the commencing of the war on James Henry Ferguson—Ham, Mississippi, style. Each day, the rumors and misinformation grew. The paper kept writing articles about his philandering ways. About how untrustworthy he was around women. Opinion pieces referred to him as a gang leader and drug dealer who dreamed up a story about being a legitimate billionaire. They pontificated about how the shady morals of urban Blacks had come to Ham. Luckily for Mr. Jimmy, folks around the way didn't get any newspapers. No one had computers, and although some of the rumors made their way into the neighborhood, it was not enough to outweigh the goodness they had already assigned to him.

"As if the truth wasn't bad enough," he told Mason.

Mason said he was sorry, which, of course, was all he could do. But he was someone whose word Mr. Jimmy could trust completely and take comfort in. Otherwise, he felt he was on shaky ground. He tried to stay active in the neighborhood to keep his mind off the building campaign of shame and to remind his new friends that despite what they might be hearing, he was there for them, that he was a good man.

Weeks had passed since his reconciliation with Fountain Hughes, and much had changed around the way. First off, he'd had to find a different kind of employment for the kids after the weather changed and the grass stopped growing. While contemplating his options, he remembered his Saturday afternoon job as a boy. His father had cut the brush off a broomstick. He hammered a large finishing nail into the bottom of the shaft and gave it to Jimmy, whose job it was to walk the church property picking up trash.

"Folks shall not have to walk through garbage to meet Jesus on Sunday mornings," his father had said.

Some Saturdays, there were only a handful of candy wrappers to be picked up, but the mission of tidiness had become a part of young Jimmy. To grow mentally and spiritually, it was best to have a clean and organized environment. Mr. Jimmy wanted his young neighbors, in particular, to believe that they were worthy of such an environment. So he, Juba, and Beech turned brooms into trash collecting tools. On the Monday after they were done, the kids gathered around the way. Mr. Jimmy helped them layout a plan to clean the neighborhood, which in comparison to his father's church property could be considered a trash dump. There were years' worth of waste.

"If you live in filth," his father had once preached, "you can begin to think of yourself as such."

Mr. Jimmy outfitted everyone with work gloves. They created

a grid and began to work. Typically, in an hour after school, they could fill up enough garbage bags to fill half his truck bed. Sometimes, he could see them tired and pointing at the large amounts of trash awaiting them, stretching the length of the neighborhood in spaces that their lawnmowers hadn't been able to go. And that was just the trash they could see. There was always more lurking at the edges of yards near the woods and tucked by the foundations of the houses. They were beginning to feel overwhelmed. Juba attempted to keep his team motivated, but after some time, he began to falter as well. *They are just children,* Mr. Jimmy thought as he watched them struggle one day. Still, he did not want them to give up on the job or more importantly, on themselves. So he began to step outside, delivering motivational speeches and hugs. Soon, he began to collect alongside them. Strangely, some of the adults who were home that time of day began standing outside to watch their children work. Mr. Jimmy found it to be a curious activity.

"Why are they just standing there," he asked Bess and Miss Septima one afternoon.

"Mr. Jimmy," Bess replied. "Everybody ain't on board with you. Lot of them think that the children working for nothing. Two, three dollars a day. You getting them all to think this mean something. They want to tell the children to put down the sticks and come on inside, because they know in the long run, this don't mean nothing. But they don't want to break their little hearts because they think they doing something."

Mr. Jimmy's face fell.

"I'm sorry," Bess said. "You asked."

"That, I did," he softly replied, refocusing on the children. "And I hear you, but this is about so much more than what they are getting paid. They can't see it, and I understand that. Life has never given them or you a reason to look beyond the horizon."

Bess looked quizzically at Mr. Jimmy.

Miss Septima softly nodded. "Artificial flowers," she said. She went into her house and returned with her head wrapped, wearing a fleece jacket that Mr. Jimmy had bought for her. She stood yards away from the mothers and fathers. She wanted more from them, and she told them so.

"Ya'll can do better now," she chided. "For and by these babies."

Then she asked the children to make her a staff for collecting, and she joined them with Mr. Jimmy at her side, making sure she didn't fall or overdo. With a cane in one hand and a trash staff in the other, she provided inspiration. Little by little other members of the small community made their own tools or Mr. Jimmy provided more. The children were pleased to have their parents with them. Their load seemed lighter. They began to joke around and laugh as they worked. Their parents joined in the fun. But as they began to work together, deeper into the neighborhood, Mr. Jimmy was not laughing. He thought he'd seen the worst of the poverty. Many of the homes had no bathrooms or the plumbing had been backed up for so long, they had to live as though there was no bathroom. Some had old outhouses, and others dug holes in the woods behind the houses, the older people using buckets in the houses adding to the already acrid air. Many had no running water. Beside their homes were big plastic barrels for catching rainwater. Trash and bugs floated in the water. They strained it and boiled it for drinking and cooking. They strained it and heated it for bathing. They took baths once a week, on Saturday, the night before church.

"It's not until you clean that you see how dirty it's really been," his father's sermon had continued. "That goes for your property and your soul."

Mr. Jimmy could see that the children were looking upon their poverty with new eyes. It made them sad, but they pushed forward. Juba needed little inspiration. If anyone had a desire to reach beyond the horizon, it was him. On Saturdays, he would come to the shed for a saw, a hammer, and nails. He began, in his own way, to fix the interior of his house. During the school day, he started asking fellow students if they knew of any houses being torn down. Eventually, he was told about one, and he walked miles to and from the site, bringing old insulation home. When he saw what was happening, Mr. Jimmy drove him to the site, and they put as much insulation in the truck as possible. Juba began to stuff the insulation into the gaps in the walls of his house. He ripped out broken pieces of wood, stuffed in the insulation and replaced the wood. It was a futile task, but Mr. Jimmy decided not to discourage him.

Less emotionally complicated was the time spent in his great room after the tools had been put away in the shed. The children looked forward to their time with the Bob Books. And they had gotten better quickly. They were more confident and even more supportive of each other. He so loved the applause everyone received after a reading.

"One day," he said to them. "Maybe you will read from the books you've written at libraries and literary societies."

"You just dream crazy sometimes, Mr. Jimmy," Marquetta replied to laughter from the room.

Mr. Jimmy scanned and printed pages of the books. He gave them to the children to read at home in their spare time. He was so pleased to see that they did their homework because each day they arrived having conquered the assignment and ready for the next challenge.

He leaned forward in the porch rocker, smiling about his kids, as he now thought of them. But thinking of them had amounted to only a brief distraction, pleasant though it was. The empty space where the sign had been still called to him. Somebody took it. It had to mean something. He sighed. The day now felt like two cups of coffee, rather than his usual single. So he got up and walked into the house and was immediately startled by the mural on his wall. It would take some getting used to. It was beautiful, and one felt a bit overwhelmed by the size of it.

The day after his pizza dinner at the Carol household, Olivia came over with Bea. Olivia painted, and Bea assisted. Yankee helped him install a ceiling light for special nighttime viewing.

"I didn't mean you had to do all of this right away," Mr. Jimmy said.

"It was such a good idea that I couldn't wait," Olivia had replied. "I didn't want one more day to go by without them seeing the ocean."

She worked all day each day, giving up her weekend and after hours the next week to get it done as quickly as possible. Mr. Jimmy gave the kids the week off from work and reading. They did not take the news well, which made him happy, but he managed to calm their rebellious notions by promising a big surprise for them on the next Monday. When that day came, he had Olivia hide in his bedroom.

"Just keep the door cracked," he'd said. "I want you to be able to see their reaction."

"Ya'll, look!" Reenie shouted as she walked into the room. The kids all gathered around her, staring in awe of the ocean mural. They giggled and laughed and pointed. "Mr. Jimmy," Reenie continued. "You brought us the ocean."

They cheered and jumped up and down. Olivia and Bea had painted shells, shovels and buckets, crabs, white sand, and crashing waves. Mr. Jimmy turned to look at Olivia peering out of the bedroom doorway. She was smiling, and he waved her out. She came out quietly, trying not to disturb their joy. He put an arm around her and called to the kids who turned to find another surprise.

"Bruh," Beech said, looking around. "How many surprises you got in this house?"

Everyone laughed.

"This is my friend," he said. "She painted the ocean for you. This is Ms. Olivia."

The kids were quiet, having been warned all their lives against being in the same vicinity as a White woman for more than a minute.

"Mr. Jimmy told me," Olivia said, "that you all wanted to go to the ocean. We thought this might do for now. Until you grow up and take yourselves. Every Monday, look for something to be taken away and something new to appear. Okay?"

Some of the kids nodded and some of them stared. Olivia took her leave, and Mr. Jimmy put aside reading for the day. They just wanted to ask questions about the mural and all of the items painted onto it. He had never seen all of them so happy at once. It warmed his heart.

He turned away from the memory and began to make another cup of coffee. While he waited for it, he called Olivia.

"The For Sale sign is gone," he said, when she answered.

"I know," she said. "I was just about to call you. Yankee and I are on our way over. We think we know what happened, just not why. See you shortly."

They waited patiently as Crawford Alden and his son, Coy, walked out of their massive barn and headed toward them. They took their time, assessing their guests along the way. Mr. Jimmy noticed the For Sale sign leaning against the barn. He couldn't help feeling somewhat violated, as if they had stolen it from inside his house or had kidnapped a family member. He reminded himself that it didn't belong to him, yet the longing persisted.

On the ride to the Alden farm, Yankee and Olivia had explained to him that the farmland had been taken off the market.

"The truth is," Yankee said, "Crawford Alden has so much land, I bet he even forgot he had the land around the way. Until Welton Knox got to him."

"Are you sure that's the case?" Mr. Jimmy had asked.

"We don't see any other reason for this to have happened," Olivia replied. "After you asked me to look into purchasing it, the office contacted him, and he seemed happy to be rid of it. Ecstatic even."

Crawford Alden was quite a tall man. To Mr. Jimmy, he seemed to be at least six feet seven and maybe fifty-five years old. He wore hiking boots and blue jeans. He had a couple of days' worth of stubble, and he wore a light blue shirt that stretched across a protuberant belly. He and Coy wore baseball caps with a logo—a silhouette of an old Farmall tractor above the words *Alden Farms*. Coy was almost as tall and looked like his father, except for being clean shaven. When they came to a stop, there was nothing ecstatic about either of them.

"Ya'll get on now," Crawford said, pointing to the car.

"Mr. Alden," Yankee replied in his lawyer voice. "We would like a moment of your time to discuss the land near Mr. Ferguson's place. Where you had that sign over there."

"I know where all my land is," Crawford replied testily.

Yankee nodded.

"Mr. Alden," Olivia said. "Our families have known each other for a long time. Out of respect for that, can we just have a minute or two to ask why you took it off the market? After it had been on for so many years. And after you told my colleague that you were happy to sell it."

"What colleague? From what I hear, you'll be standing in the unemployment line with your people of color friends."

Coy laughed along with his father.

Mr. Jimmy was caught by surprise, which didn't go unnoticed by Crawford.

"I guess you didn't tell your colored friend here that he got you fired."

The Alden men laughed, and Mr. Jimmy's mood went from

surprise to anger.

"Look here," Crawford said. "We got work to do. Ain't having no discussion about the land. It ain't going nowhere no time soon. So ya'll can get off my property."

As they turned to walk away, Crawford let Yankee and Olivia know that being associated with a man like Mr. Jimmy was going to cause more problems for them, their kids, and her parents. They should reassess their alliances.

In the car, Olivia apologized for not telling him that she had indeed been fired for associating with him.

"May I ask how they told you?"

"Loudly," she replied. "They wanted the office to hear. They said that they couldn't have their company's name associated with a wife-beater and serial philanderer. And just like Crawford Alden's parting advice, they said I should know better than to get entangled with a man like you. And especially a Black man like you. That's the worst, you know."

"I never hit Rebecca," he said quietly.

"We believe you," Yankee replied.

"We do," Olivia said. "But these White folks don't know you. And they believe everything Welton Knox says. This is what I meant about your money not being much help around here."

"I am sorry about your job," Mr. Jimmy said. "I forgot what southern hospitality was like after so many years away from it. But I will make up for your job loss. And for Dr. Longford's."

"I'll be okay, Mr. Jimmy. I'll just let my man take care of me for a bit."

"No need for any apologies, Mr. Jimmy," Yankee interrupted. "This is all Welton Knox, and it's wrong."

"Well, it can't be your battle anymore. You can't get fired too, Yankee."

"That wouldn't be so easy. I'm a very successful partner in the firm. But if they did, I can't say that I would be torn apart.

We were always going back to Austin at some point. If you're really into helping those folks around the way, then we're going to do our part."

"We've even spoken at length to the kids about this," Olivia said. "We're all in this together as a family."

"You all are very special, and I thank you, but right now there isn't much to be in together," he said sadly. "It's kind of falling apart before I've had a chance to really get started."

Silence overtook their drive back to around the way. Mr. Jimmy gave in, allowing the drone of the automobile and the fading early evening light to carry his mind elsewhere. He found himself staring blindly out of his window, lost in a quicksand of reflection. A painfully slow, muddy, vexing descent into failure. In the few months that he'd been a resident of Ham, he had begun to build strong relationships. Miss Septima, Juba, and the rest of the neighborhood had grown to accept that he believed in them. His actions showed that he was committed to their welfare. They were convinced he wanted to help them and trusted that a Black man who made billions of dollars had to have some kind of special juju up his sleeve. How would he explain that it had played out as it usually had? That in the end, it had come down to their common denominator: Blackness. Even his money could not overcome that in Ham.

He readjusted his position in the car seat, but it brought him little comfort. Maybe, he thought, Fountain Hughes would be the most disappointed in him. Mr. Jimmy knew that the pendulum had swung to the opposite extreme in terms of Fountain's respect for him. Maybe the same could be said for Mr. Jimmy's feelings for him and his family. He was particularly fond of little Essie. During his neighborhood walks, which he was becoming famous for, he would often stop at their house. He chatted in the front yard with Fountain and Bess while playing with Essie. Sometimes, he would take Essie with him, walking hand in hand

and other times carrying her on his shoulders. She inspired him to sing songs from Katherine's and Lillian's bedtime rituals. When Bess told him that Essie wanted him to be her granddaddy, he was touched. So he allowed her to begin calling him that, and it made their relationship almost as special as his and Juba's. It further endeared him to the neighborhood. He thought about how much he would be letting Fountain down if he failed to get the land and it all just fell apart.

He forgot himself and got out of the car without saying goodbye. The sound of the closing door broke his trance. He turned and leaned over, waving at them. He circled a finger by the side of his head, making an excuse for his forgetfulness and rude exit.

As he walked to his porch, he listened for Yankee driving away, but the car remained in place as he approached his house. He supposed they were waiting for the disappointed, scared, and sad old man to safely enter his house. By the time he stepped onto the porch and flipped on the light so they could see him successfully enter, Olivia was beside him.

"One for the road," she said, before wrapping him in a hug.

He accepted it with great emotion. Not because she seemed needy to deliver it, but for himself, because, in the moment, it felt lifesaving.

SIXTEEN

Hope transformed Fountain Hughes.

But expectations could ruin a man, Mr. Jimmy feared.

As he walked the road back toward his house, he waved at neighbors. He put on a smile. He pretended to be upbeat and happy. He concealed his worry and his fear as he picked up his pace, hoping beyond hope that he could just walk it all off.

He and Fountain had bonded on the road to what they hoped to be significant and positive change for the folks from around the way. He'd tapped into Fountain's strengths and made him believe that they were enough to get the job done, to bring the heart of his plan to fruition.

Fountain now had his own keys to the truck and the shed. He had Mr. Jimmy's trust. Even the neighbors saw how he carried himself differently. They were proud of him and happy for his family. One more little Black girl would have a father in her life.

"I pray, Mr. Jimmy. Every night I pray like . . . like ain't no man ever has. I was born for this. My daddy and my granddaddy, they smiling in their graves because farming is all they ever knew. Besides playing football, it's all I ever knew. You get me that land. I'll make them crops grow for sure. I'll even make them sing gospels. So you might think you hearing the old sharecroppers in song, bent over them seeds, watching over them as they grow."

Mr. Jimmy had nodded and smiled. He loved that image and

still found himself stopping now and then to conjure it up along with the emotion he'd attached to it.

Together, they traveled to farm equipment stores. Mr. Jimmy let Fountain take the lead wherever they went. He would smile as Fountain questioned salesmen about the specifics of tractors, planters, and other machinery. Mr. Jimmy was impressed. Fountain asked about costs, and Mr. Jimmy said not to worry. Fountain smiled. A lot.

They sat together with Mr. Jimmy's cell phone, a makeshift conference tool for conversations with some of Mr. Jimmy's colleagues in restaurants in which his company still held an interest. They discussed the kinds of crops that Fountain could grow for restaurants and stores. Fountain made a list of grandsons and granddaughters of sharecroppers. People with the knowledge but without the land. He handed Mr. Jimmy the list, and Mr. Jimmy pushed it back to him.

"This is going to be your show, Fountain. You have the responsibility of picking responsible employees who won't let you down."

"That's some responsibility, Mr. Jimmy," Fountain replied.

"That, it is. So you'll want to get it right."

Fountain nodded. "Yes, sir. You know I will."

They had many conference calls with Mason. Fountain listened and learned as they created a new company from nothing.

"I'm going to be the boss of a whole company?"

"Well, we are going to hire some people to help you with the finances, but yes, you will be the big boss."

"Bruh, I just got out the joint!"

Mr. Jimmy and Mason laughed. "Figure out what you learned in there that can make you better out on the farm," Mason said.

Fountain nodded and smiled. "Well, what we gone call this company?"

"I haven't decided yet," Mr. Jimmy replied. "I'll know when it comes to me. And I'll let you both know."

As he walked, he grew angry, knowing that Crawford Alden's refusal to sell the property to him put everything in jeopardy. What was he going to do now without that land? Sit on his porch and stare at it, disappointed and angry. How could he keep looking at Fountain's hopeful face and not tell him that he had only offered, at best, a dream deferred.

"Mr. Jimmy! Wait a minute! Why you walking so fast?"

Juba ran up alongside him.

"I'm getting my exercise," Mr. Jimmy responded. "Back in DC, I used to have an elliptical. I don't have the room for it here, so I have to walk."

"Maybe you can come to my school. They got one there. And a treadmill, but don't nobody use them. At least as far as I can tell."

Mr. Jimmy laughed, but his attention was pulled away by the screams of a child. He saw a girl named Shanice rolling in the road. He and Juba began running toward her.

"Mr. Jimmy!" she cried out as he got to her. She was in tears and holding her leg.

He and Juba knelt beside her.

"What happened?" Juba asked.

"I was running. I didn't jump right and didn't get over the ditch all the way. I hurt my leg bad. I think I broke my knee."

"Juba, go get Ms. Evie."

Juba ran off, yelling for Shanice's mother along the way. Mr. Jimmy sat her up and he straightened out her leg. She didn't yell, which was a good sign. He felt around her knee.

"Shanice, I am certainly not a doctor, but as a dad," he said, adding a big smile, which she returned in kind, "I don't think anything is broken. I'm feeling here around your knee, and everything feels normal to me."

Shanice didn't look convinced.

"Okay," he said. "I learned this a long time ago from watching a master of the healing arts."

He clapped his hands loudly one time. That startled Shanice, and she began to laugh as Mr. Jimmy started rubbing his hands together vigorously. Then, he placed a hand on either side of her knee and slowly rubbed her knee and leg while humming.

"Now you know what that did?"

"No," Shanice said.

"Nothing."

"Awww, Mr. Jimmy. You just silly."

By the time Juba arrived with Ms. Evie, Mr. Jimmy and Shanice were sitting face-to-face laughing.

"Girl, I thought you hurt yourself," Ms. Evie said with a smile.

"I did. Mr. Jimmy made it better though."

Ms. Evie smiled at Mr. Jimmy.

"Can you walk?" he asked Shanice.

She stood up and had some discomfort. But she could bend it. Still, she limped, so Mr. Jimmy scooped her up and carried her home.

"If for any reason you want to take her to the doctor or hospital, send someone to get me. I'll take you both."

"Thank you, Mr. Jimmy," Ms. Evie said.

"Anytime," he replied.

Mr. Jimmy and Juba resumed their walk. Soon they were talking football and placing bets with each other as to who was going to win each NFL division. It was almost Christmas, and the playoffs would happen just after the New Year.

"How you get to be a Dallas fan anyway if you didn't even live there?"

"It's a question I got all the time, living in Washington, DC. I got a lot of trash talk for being a Cowboys fan. Let's see. When I was about seven, I walked into our family room to find my daddy terribly angry. He was screaming at the television, and I couldn't figure out why. When he saw me, he got himself together and called me over to him. He told me that everything was okay. He just got carried away with football. He said that's why my mother went to her grandmother's house when he watched football. He sat me down and began to teach me the game. He was a Cowboys fan. I never asked him why. I fell in love with the game and the team. I was never any good at it. I tried out for junior varsity and was the first one cut."

"What is it like?" Juba asked.

"Oh, like I said. I got cut right away. I did get to wear a uniform for a few days, but I couldn't tell you what it's really like."

"No, Mr. Jimmy. I mean what is it like to have a daddy?"

"Oh, I see," Mr. Jimmy replied. He put his arm around Juba and pulled him close as they walked. "It's like the best kind of comfortable there is. You don't worry because you feel safe all the time. You know, someone with a big hand to hold your little hand. Someone strong enough, even at your size, to throw you on his back and carry you upstairs to bed. And when you kneel next to him to pray, you are comforted by that strength. You know that if you falter in life, he can put you on his back and carry you until you can walk again by yourself. Someone to throw dirt on your shoes to remind you that you are no better than anyone else. To help you keep life in perspective. Someone who loves you no matter what."

"Does he still love you since you a grown man?"

"Yes. And I am sure of that."

They stopped in front of Juba's house.

"I don't know my daddy," he said.

"I know. And I am so sorry about that."

"It's okay though. I don't know my daddy, but I know you."

Mr. Jimmy gave Juba a hug and kissed the top of his head.

"I'm not your daddy, Juba. But I plan on always being a part of your life. If you will have me."

Juba smiled. "I think so. You might have to fix my knee or something."

SEVENTEEN

James Henry Ferguson got drunk. He did so with the complete understanding that a full-on bout of inebriation had never solved a problem for him or set one aside for even a moment. But since there is a first time for everything, he started his third bottle of grocery store wine in an evening. *A desperate man can hope*, he thought.

Since the day that Rebecca's disclosure altered their lives, disorder and emotional distress had become the norm in his life. Even worse, always without intention, he carried his dysfunction into the lives of others. This fact pained him to no end.

The Ham Gazette, in its attempt to be as topical as the big city papers, put out an evening version of its morning paper online. The fuller stories would appear in the delivered paper. The early online version seemed to be just sensational headlines and teasing copy for the real thing. In his lap was his tablet, logged on to the paper's website. Yankee had called and told him that he might want to see what was being said about him and Olivia. The headline read:

Is James Ferguson, the Carpetbagging, Black,
Faux Billionaire Sex Offender Now after Ham Women?

This is an actual headline in a real newspaper!? he wondered, simply astounded by its non-objective salacious inclination. Welton Knox was indeed a powerful man.

Below the headline were two photos of Mr. Jimmy and Olivia. Each from the early evening they had visited Crawford Alden and Olivia had hugged him on his front porch. In the first picture, they were in a close embrace. In the second, they had just pulled apart, her hands on his arms and his under her elbows, the two of them seemingly caught in a lover's gaze.

He considered that the pictures had to have been taken from the field across the road from his house. Someone had been lying in wait with a nice zoom lens on their camera. That kind of surveillance was truly unsettling.

Yankee told him that one of Bea's school friends tipped them off. She called Bea to tell her that kids were texting about her mother being a Black man's whore.

"My mama was wondering what other kind of pictures they had of your mama and that Black man," Bea's friend had said. "Everybody's talking. They can't wait for the morning paper."

"Goddamnit," Mr. Jimmy growled.

"This particular game still gets ugly fast in Mississippi," Yankee said. "Olivia would have called you, but Bea is deeply upset and wanted her mother at her side."

"I'm so sorry," Mr. Jimmy said. "Please tell Bea."

"It also didn't help that Olivia's parents came over and laid into her about you as well. In front of the kids. It also got pretty ugly. Her dad was on the verge of getting physical with her. I've never seen him seriously call her out on anything. She's daddy's little girl, and he does nothing but dote on her. I had to grab him and escort him outside and demand that they leave."

"This is just horrible," Mr. Jimmy said.

"Yes, it absolutely is," Yankee replied, his voice a mixture of anger and heartbreak.

During the uncomfortable silence that followed, Mr. Jimmy tried to imagine the distress and hurt on his face. How he could have looked in Yankee's eyes to find them reflecting a frantic and unsure disposition. As his body grew taut to trembling with frustration, in his heart and mind, he accepted the responsibility for the Carol family pain. He grew angry with himself and prepared to accept the fallout he felt would be accompanying Yankee's next words.

"But," Yankee said, "we know it's not your fault. Any of it."

"It may not be my fault," he replied, thankful for Yankee's attempt to be the good guy and ease his pain, "but it is happening because of me."

Yankee was silent.

And there is the inescapable truth, he thought.

"I guess we should assume we are all being followed," Mr. Jimmy continued.

"I suppose so," Yankee softly offered. "This is a different world for us."

"For me too," Mr. Jimmy replied.

Yankee hung up, and the click of the phone sounded exceedingly harsh to Mr. Jimmy. He sat down and reclined into a morbid trance. Crawford Alden's refusal felt like a roadblock, terribly disappointing, but maybe not insurmountable. But this article added something. Something genuinely disheartening. Something uglier than ugly. Maybe the beginning of a permanent unwinding of his plan for around the way and for the reason he came to Ham in the first place.

That night, Mr. Jimmy hardly slept and when he did, it was a fitful sleep. On top of that, he woke to an upsetting early morning phone call from Olivia.

"I'm sorry to wake you," she said. "But I can't be with you for a bit. I'm sorry. I've got to get my family together again."

"I understand," Mr. Jimmy said. "Olivia, I am deeply, deeply sorry."

He grumbled and stumbled his way into the kitchen. He made his coffee. Immensely tired of being sorry, he decided to shut himself off from the world again before he could do more damage.

He sat at his table, looking out of the window as around the way was coming to life. The kids were on their way to school. Fountain was standing in front of Miss Septima's. She must have been in the doorway having a conversation with him. He was thankful that they didn't get a paper, but it would be hard to imagine this not getting back to her and everyone else.

He opened his tablet to read the full story. It made him sick to his stomach. Especially because Welton Knox had been quoted, claiming to have been looking out for Olivia's best interest.

"I told them when they came to see me about the hospital. You know, the idea that he was going to buy it because he claimed that the place was overrun with racists. I warned Ms. Carol that she was keeping bad company and that it would not be good for her if she continued with the relationship in public or behind closed doors."

"Behind closed doors?" the reporter had inquired.

"Well," Knox continued. "I don't want to speculate too much, but you saw those pictures on the porch. Leads one to the only possible conclusion. I told her that she had a respectable family. One that she was putting at risk."

The article also quoted Crawford Alden. "They came to my farm and tried to intimidate me out of some of my land. I sent 'em packing, I sure did."

Other Ham residents, who didn't know either Olivia or Mr. Jimmy, were given ample column space to criticize.

"I don't know how that girl can stand to look at herself in the mirror in the morning," one had said.

"And the poor children," said another.

"If I was the lawyer husband, I'd start them proceedings and get out of that mess. I bet he can't stand to be in the same room with her and her tainted self."

Mr. Jimmy went to Twitter, and there was some local traffic. It didn't seem to be on the road to going viral. Apparently, the world was now used to him being in sex scandals—nothing new or in any way impressive.

That afternoon he began to isolate himself from his community. When the kids arrived at the shed to get their tools, he called to them from the porch. He told them that he had some thinking to do, so they couldn't come in after work for reading.

"For how long this time?" Beech asked.

"Maybe until after Christmas."

They all began to groan and show their displeasure at the same time.

"But Mr. Jimmy," Juba said, "we were going to finish the Bob Books. We were going to have a party."

"Yeah," Reenie said. "And what about the Christmas movies you promised?"

"And the ocean," Shanice said. "We will miss all the new stuff Ms. Olivia paints on the ocean."

"Ms. Olivia won't be coming around for a bit either."

At this point, the children understood that something was very wrong.

"What's the deal, Mr. Jimmy?" Juba asked with concern.

"There are some things happening," he said. "I can't say right now, but they aren't nice. I just need some time to gather my thoughts."

"This was going to be the best Christmas year ever," Juba said.

"I know," Mr. Jimmy said.

"Well," Beech said. "If all the good stuff ain't happening, I ain't picking up no more trash."

The other kids agreed. Juba looked very hurt.

"I'm sorry," Mr. Jimmy said.

The kids began turning to leave, whispering disbelief, their shoulders slouched. Juba lingered, as did his stare. Mr. Jimmy met his stare until Juba blinked and turned away, dropping his head. He looked back one more time.

Mr. Jimmy understood that he had badly hurt the kids, especially Juba. He understood that this was a hurt Juba would always remember. Even if his life turned out to be a great success, when he paused to think about the melancholy moments, he would remember this one. Mr. Jimmy stepped inside and closed the door, hating the thought that Juba would ever carry a negative thought about him. It would be another pain and regret that Mr. Jimmy carried daily, alongside those for the most important children in his life, Katherine and Lillian.

EIGHTEEN

For how long this time?

Until Beech uttered the question, Mr. Jimmy had not understood that in his short four months in Ham, he was embarking upon his fourth self-imposed solitary confinement. His original bearded solitude, the recovery from his beating at the hands of Fountain Hughes, Thanksgiving, and now, his return to what he considered tabloid hell.

Sitting at his table looking across the land, Miss Septima's house seemingly growing smaller as dusk claimed the sky, he regretted telling her that he would have Christmas dinner at her house. He felt like it might take him several weeks or months to overcome what he'd done to Olivia and her family. And to overcome what he was becoming in the town where he was supposed to find absolute peace and quiet, far away from this kind of nonsense.

The week before Thanksgiving, Miss Septima had stood outside his house calling to him as she had many times. By now, he had a routine. He'd step outside the front door with two bottles of sweet tea. He'd set one by each of his rocking chairs, and then he'd help Miss Septima up on the porch, and they would sit, sip, and chat.

Comfortably seated, she asked him to share Thanksgiving with her and her church members.

"We all gone make dinner in the church kitchen. Gonna cook and have a big dinner in the fellowship hall. I want you to come and do some fellowshipping with the people."

He hadn't wanted to disappoint her, but his relationship with Thanksgiving was not at all pleasant. In fact, he held a near lifelong grudge against it, only coming to some resolution when Rebecca came into his life.

As a child, he would watch specials on television or read stories leading up to the holiday. Family dramas about the special day, the gathering of loved ones, and the family dynamics, which could sometimes be fraught with extreme emotional pain. But by the end of the show and at the turn of the last page, the problems had been sorted out. As the family gathered around the table to eat the Thanksgiving meal, the only thing in the air besides the smell of turkey was love. The kind of love that could only emanate from the intimacy and generational ties of blood relatives. At least that's how he saw it.

As the child of a pastor, young Jimmy would never experience this joy. After the morning services, his parents opened their home to members who were alone, who couldn't afford a Thanksgiving spread and to those whose troubles left them with nowhere to go. Not only did Jimmy lose his parents, who had little if any time for him during the day, he even lost control of his house. One year, he sat in his favorite chair in the family room preparing to watch a football game. A woman from church walked up to him.

"Child, I need that chair," she said.

Jimmy had stared back in disbelief. How could a person be so rude? His parents would never approve of his speaking to someone like that.

"I mean get up now," she continued. "Mind your elders. I need to sit down."

"This is my chair," Jimmy responded. "I'm not getting up. It's my special chair. It's where I sit when we watch TV."

"Not today. You got adult guests, and you need to show some respect."

"You need to show some respect," he fired back.

The woman was stunned, and her face was overcome with anger. She went away and returned with his father.

"James Henry Ferguson, you get out of that chair immediately and apologize to Sister Wilkins."

"But Daddy, this is my chair."

"I'm not arguing one second more. Up and apologize."

So Jimmy got out of his chair and grudgingly apologized. Sister Wilkins said his heart wasn't in it, so his father made him apologize again. He stood by and watched her sit in his chair until his father pulled him away by the collar of his shirt. Jimmy never sat in that chair again, and it was at the core of his long-standing discomfort with Thanksgiving. In the years that followed, he kept to himself. For the 18 years he lived at his childhood home, he never had a Thanksgiving dinner with his parents. He never once sat next to them at the table and heard family lore or felt that special love he'd read about and seen on television. His mother eventually gave the chair to a charitable organization in the hopes of ridding the house of the fog of discontent it created. For the most part, it did. Still, every Thanksgiving, he stayed in his bedroom and wished he belonged to another family.

That was why he reacted so strangely when his newfound love, Rebecca, asked him to accompany her to her family's house for Thanksgiving.

"I don't know them well enough," he'd said.

"And how do you expect to get to know them if you don't visit?"

"You know I have this thing about Thanksgiving."

"Yes, I do."

"I'll just stay here. I want to wait until I can have a family Thanksgiving."

"This is like waiting to get married before losing your virginity," she said smiling.

"Well, we broke that rule already."

Rebecca kissed him. "Indeed, we have. Look, here is my promise. Until we get married, I am going home for Thanksgiving. After we get married, I promise the first Thanksgiving will be spent with your family. Me, that is. And when we have kids, we will stay in our home, but we will invite our family. The relatives of our children. No strangers. How's that?"

"Who says we're getting married? We haven't been dating that long," James said.

"You don't fool me, Mr. Ferguson. I know what I see in your eyes."

On their first Thanksgiving as a married couple, they dined alone in their living room. Rebecca spent the two days before cooking. James acted as her sous-chef. That was the beginning of James learning to cook and the two of them creating meals together. That day, they had a romantic, candle-lit Thanksgiving dinner. They sat at the small kitchen table so that they could reach across it and hold hands. They told each other family stories and secrets of their own that they'd never shared before. It was the Thanksgiving he had dreamed of.

By the time Katherine and Lillian had come along, James had become more relaxed about the day. Rebecca still honored his feelings and though they would have her parents and her brother's family over to share the day, she never invited a non-family member. On occasion though, James would turn out the light and try to find a comfortable position to sleep in with his happily extended belly. And he would remember, whether he wanted to or not, that he never had a Thanksgiving dinner with his parents.

This year, he wondered where his family would be for Thanksgiving. Surely Rebecca and the girls wouldn't want to be in the house without him and the ugliness in the air that he left behind.

No, he pictured them gathered around a table with Rebecca's family. All of them, forcing smiles, determined to make a pleasant go of it. But they wouldn't be able to hide from the hole in their lives any more than he could.

Miss Septima had stopped rocking. She was holding her sweet tea in her lap, and she was staring at him, waiting patiently for him to come back to her and to give her an answer.

"Miss Septima," he said, finally. "I just can't. I'm not interested in spending Thanksgiving with a lot a people I don't know. Everyone should be with family."

"Well, you family enough, I think," she replied.

Mr. Jimmy smiled. "I thank you for saying that I am, and I do appreciate the offer. I really do. The thing is they are not family enough for me just yet. It's just that I have a complicated history with Thanksgiving, and I should just be at home."

"The only thing complicated I see around here is you," she replied.

"Well, that's unfortunately on point."

Miss Septima paused and assessed for a moment before asking, "What's going on inside that head of yours, son?"

"A lot more than I hoped."

"Like what? Lay it all out."

"I can't. Or I don't want to, just yet. The things I've been working on I hope will be good for all of us here around the way. But my plan hasn't come far enough to tell you about them. I had hoped to make them a Christmas present for everyone."

She nodded. "Okay, then here's what we gone do. You come to Christmas dinner at my house. I will cook at the church and bring the food to my place 'cause my kitchen ain't hitting on nothing. But you coming. You know that, don't you?" she asked with authority.

"Yes, ma'am. I do."

"And you can give me my gift at dinner."

"Yes, ma'am."

"And one more thing. You gone to take me shopping for the food."

"So I'm paying for the dinner you're asking me to attend?"

"You mister bigshot, ain't you? Put that money where your mouth is."

Mr. Jimmy laughed because she made him happy in his soul. There was far too little of that in his life.

Now, alone at his table, the sky having turned to night, he regretted accepting her invitation. He just wanted to be alone as he was on Thanksgiving. Just him and his football for as far into the future as he could see.

NINETEEN

Mr. Jimmy refused to shave. Even though it was Miss Septima who was asking him to do so.

"Boy, you can't be out and about with that scruffiness on your face. You Mr. Jimmy!"

"I'm not shaving, Miss Septima."

"It ain't even even though."

"Not shaving. It's enough that you got me out of the house, interrupting my solitude."

"You mean you hiding from life. That's what's real."

"I suppose I can't argue with that," he replied. "Still not doing it though."

"Lawd have mercy. Well, all right then. I guess I ain't got no choice, so I reckon I'll be seen with you then," she said.

As they pulled away from her house in his BMW, he considered that his scruffiness might actually be useful. Maybe, he thought, his three-day beard could be like Clark Kent's glasses. Not much, but enough to keep people from recognizing him. As he drove, he was mentally kicking himself for agreeing to take Miss Septima shopping. He didn't want to be seen and didn't want to see anyone, but it was tough to turn her down. It would be difficult for him to make a decision that might hurt her in any way. So he found himself taking her to the Piggly Wiggly to shop for Christmas dinner, which was just over two weeks away.

"I need to shop early so I can get what I need. Folks get crazy at the holidays. I hate going to the grocery store and they run out of what I need. I'll put it in the church freezer and refrigerator."

By the time they had made it from the car to the door of the supermarket, Mr. Jimmy knew that his beard was not living up to Clark Kent's glasses. People were giving him the side-eye. By the time they had a cart and had begun to shop, people had started a whispering campaign. Every turn they made down an aisle was met with angry glances that soon became sustained looks of contempt. Black shoppers looked concerned for them but turned their heads away. More and more White shoppers had begun to stop and stare, to briefly stand in place and block their cart. To come face-to-face with him, delivering a telepathic message that the carpetbagging, White woman–chasing, fake billionaire should vacate the premises if he knew what was good for him.

"Miss Septima," he whispered. "I'm sorry, but—"

"I know, son," she said before he could finish. "Best to be safe."

They left the cart in the middle of the aisle where they were about to grab some stuffing mix for the frozen turkey already in the cart. In the car, they were silent until Miss Septima summed up the moment nicely.

"Child, people are something."

She shook her head, and Mr. Jimmy just kept driving. That night, he told himself that he would have to disappoint Miss Septima. He couldn't do Christmas dinner. He wasn't so sure he could even stay in Ham much longer. It was taking a toll on him emotionally and physically. Welton Knox was tightening the screws, and it was working. He was beginning to bleed.

He was sitting in his Barcalounger, in complete darkness and halfway through a bottle of wine when his phone rang, lighting up like a spot of phosphorus on the ocean surface at night. It was Olivia Fey Carol calling. He hadn't spoken to her since the day after their pictures had been published. Now, given that it was almost midnight, he knew whatever she was calling about could not be good. The phone continued to ring as he considered whether to answer. On the last possible ring, he did.

"Hello, Olivia," he said. "While I would love to hear from you, I think this can't be good news."

"Hello, Mr. Jimmy," she said. "You're right. It's very bad news. It's . . . it's actually quite awful. You should look at *The Ham Gazette* online. And then if you want to call me back or if you need me to come over, I will. I am sorry for all of this."

"Before you go, how is your family?"

"Very upset. The kids especially. But we are making it through, coming back to life. We are going to be here for you. We just need another minute or two."

"Okay. I do understand," he answered. "I guess I better get the bad news."

"Please call me if you need me."

"Of course," he said, knowing full well that he wouldn't be calling her. In fact, depending on what he saw, he might just pack up and leave at first light without acknowledging a soul.

Mr. Jimmy's hands began to tremble, rolling up into his arms and causing spasms in his forearms. They trembled so much so that he had trouble opening the case for his tablet, which had an attached keyboard. He could feel his heart thumping, each beat a dull, thudding inside his chest, echoing inside his head. He mistyped the passcode twice before taking several deep breaths and finally getting it right. He found his way onto *The Ham Gazette*'s webpage, where he was once again front-page news.

A picture of him and little Shanice filled the screen. The caption read:

James Ferguson, seen here, caught in the act
of improperly touching a child.

Shanice was sitting on the ground, scared and in tears. He
was kneeling before her and the angle from which the picture
was taken made it seem as though he was reaching to touch her
inappropriately. His eyes widened in surprise. *I would never,* he
thought, even as he fought the unfair memory of Lady Nymph as
a child. The picture made it seem as though Shanice was crying
out of fear and shame. *I. Would. Never!* In his anger, he thought
someone must see that he had been followed. Reasonable people,
able to put together two and two, would realize that a person was
following him and photographing his life and making it look like
he was someone else. Or rather, *something* else.

Mr. Jimmy screamed.

There was more. An entire article, but he could not, would
not read it. He had seen enough. Now, his whole body shook.
The tablet slid off his lap as he tried to close it. He didn't pause to
wonder if he'd broken it. His mind was immediately elsewhere,
stolen by fear. It was one thing to be cheating with someone's wife.
Even a White wife in Mississippi. It was another thing entirely to
even be accused of molesting a child. This would follow him for
life, and there would be no redemption for him ever. The embarrassment. The shame. The public scrutiny that would never end.
He was overcome by an excruciating panic. Only once before
had he known such fear, the kind that left a person without any
ability to rein in his life, now careening out of control. The kind
that indicated an unfortunate ending was imminent and that it
looked to be unstoppable.

It happened back on the day when the rain came sideways.
He was seven years old and standing in front of the family room
window, mesmerized by this strange natural phenomenon. He
called for his mother to come and witness Mother Nature's show.

But when she arrived and saw the rain and the clouds racing and circling across the sky, her eyes widened. Jimmy thought she had the look of the bad guy in the movie who was falling after being thrown from the roof, reaching wildly back for the grace of a saving hand he knew was never coming. He absorbed her alarm. It rushed through him as she grabbed him and began to drag him through the house. As they passed the screen door to the backyard, he saw his father running. He'd never seen that before. His father sprinting like Gale Sayers. He came inside out of breath and pushed them toward the bathroom, yelling tornado! Jimmy had never been in a tornado, but he knew from the stories of his elders that they sounded like powerful locomotives. Amid his parents' desperation, he listened and waited, his concern growing. His father lifted him and dropped him in the claw-foot tub. It hurt when he fell against the cold, white porcelain, but he did not scream. Somehow, he knew his parents shouldn't be distracted by him. They came into bathroom with the mattress from his bed, the top sheet and blanket falling to the side. Reverend Ferguson leaned over him, scaring him as he implored him to stay under the mattress, to not come out until they told him to. Jimmy nodded, tears welling in his eyes.

He heard the door to the bathroom close and his parents on their knees. They were loudly reciting Psalms 23. *The Lord is my shepherd. I shall not want.* But he wanted. More than he'd ever wanted his parents and his life. But when the train came, he lost their voices and he wet himself. It was a rumble so violent that he curled up tighter and screamed at the top of his lungs even as he wondered if his parents had been blown away and killed. What would he do? Who had claim to him? What kind of life would be waiting for him? The uncertainty was devastating. He was drowning in absolute fear. But the train left almost as suddenly as it had arrived. And when his parents hurriedly removed the mattress, he felt he could breathe again. His mother pulled him out of the tub and down to the floor onto her lap as if he was an infant. She held him so tightly. She didn't even care if his pee got on her dress.

That old, absolute fear he'd felt that day was raging in him now. This time, he was lying on the floor in his house, a grown man in the fetal position, carrying the life-altering fear of a seven-year-old, crying as if he had lost his whole world. Hoping against hope that this storm would also pass.

Mr. Jimmy had only been truly drunk twice in his life. Neither of those hangovers could compare to what he was feeling when his phone rang the next morning. The light rushed into his great room and caused him to squint. He rubbed his head where it ached, and he felt nauseous. And there was still a bit of a tremble in his fingers as he reached for the phone. It was Mason calling.

"I have to call you back," he said. "I have to put the phone on a charger."

He hung up without waiting for a response from Mason. He stumbled into the bedroom to find his charger cable. He attached his phone and lay down on his bed. It felt good. Better to remember for a moment that his top-quality mattress was better for his body than the floor. He questioned whether he wanted to hear from Mason. It had to be more bad news. Instead, he could just lie back and close his eyes and shut out the world.

Mason was in a rush. "Listen, you are everywhere. All of the papers. Some online news organizations. Twitter, where no one that I can see is in your corner. Facebook, the same. You are all over cable news. They are talking about you like you have been molesting children all your life. They have psychologists on the air diagnosing you. It's crazy. They are saying things like once you had sex with what's her name, you somehow opened a door to this part of you that maybe you had been successfully blocking for a long time. This is nuts!"

Mr. Jimmy did not respond. *What does one say to that?* Now, his stomach was roiling again. He thought he might throw up at any moment. His head hurt so much he could barely think straight.

"Are you hearing me?" Mason asked. "James?"

"Of course, I hear you. But what in the hell am I supposed to say to that? I didn't do anything to Shanice. She fell and hurt her knee. I was taking care of her."

"I'm sorry to be so agitated. I should have calmed myself before making the call. But listen, I have sent you a link. You have to see this video."

"Why?"

"It's Rebecca, James. And know that she's not alone. Aubrey is at the house. Go watch the video and call me right afterward for more. Okay? You hear me? There is more."

"Yes, I do," Mr. Jimmy replied and hung up his phone.

The last thing he wanted to do was to pick up his tablet. Maybe he'd broken it and he wouldn't have to look. But there was his laptop. Whatever it was, he was doomed to see it.

Mr. Jimmy called up his email and clicked on the YouTube link Mason had forwarded. When it opened, it was his old house again. Reporters out front with microphones attached to a stand, waiting for . . . Rebecca? Hadn't he said it was Rebecca?

Mason had also said that Rebecca was not alone. That Aubrey was there. But when the door opened, only Rebecca stepped into the morning light. She looked stunning. She was dressed as she had been in her days as an executive. She wore a pantsuit and a blouse. A simple and clean look. Emphatically professional. As the camera people and reporters rushed to their positions, she started her walk to the microphones. When she arrived at her mark, she ignored all questions and began to speak her piece.

"My name is Rebecca Harrell Ferguson. I am the wife of James Henry Ferguson. We have been married for decades. We have raised two girls, who we treasure. The girls and I stand with

James regarding this outrageous claim. In the days to come, wait to see if anyone else comes forward with such nonsense as has been alleged by *The Ham Gazette* in Mississippi. I guarantee that there won't be anyone else because this is not my husband. I know him inside and out. I understand him at his core. At his soul, and he is not a child molester. He could never do that. And if he had, he'd be dead by now. He would have taken his own life because he would never be able to live with it. This is wrong. Whatever is going on is out of control."

A reporter broke in. "How are we supposed to believe you? How do you believe him? He cheated on you without your knowledge, didn't he?"

"Yes, he did," Rebecca replied. "And that was wrong. Because of it, we are headed for divorce, but we have reached an understanding about what happened. We will always love each other. But why you are here, what we are speaking of now is something deeper than a one-hour stand. Someone has to be truly lost at his center, I think. You know, to do what they are claiming James did. I am telling you that at his core, in his soul, he is too kind to hurt anyone in such a manner, and especially a child. There is nothing *off* about James Henry Ferguson. He's a good person, and no one who knows him would ever tell you that he could molest a child."

Another reporter responded. "But how can you be so sure?"

Rebecca stared at the reporter for a moment, until there was quiet between the question and her answer. A look of conviction steadied her eyes and formed the set of her face. Finally, without emotion, but with surety, she spoke. "Because his eye is on the sparrow."

The reporters yelled questions as she turned to walk away.

What!?

Mrs. Ferguson, what does that mean in this context?

Is that what you want to leave people with?

Rebecca softly closed her front door and Mr. Jimmy smiled. He had never thought of the sparrow story as a testimony to his character. He never suspected that throughout their years together, she had used it as a marker for who he was and who he was not. He whispered a soft thank-you. He turned off the tablet and called Mason.

"You saw what she did for me?" he asked.

"Yes. So no matter what happens, you can carry the knowledge that she does love you and probably always will. Even if she may never find the strength to forgive you. But there is more to the story, and it's going to hurt, brother."

"Okay. Let's just get it over with."

"Rebecca is selling the house."

"That's not particularly shocking. I have actually been expecting that."

"And she's dropping your surname. She's going back to Harrell. I don't think you were expecting that," he said. "I know I wasn't."

"No," Mr. Jimmy sadly responded. "That never occurred to me. Never in a million years."

Rebecca was busy editing the movie of her life, clipping and deleting, leaving their lives and their love on the cutting room floor, where they would eventually be swept up and thrown away, lost to history. She was symbolically eliminating him from her life. He understood in the months that had passed, he had been no good for her mental health. However, he thought that in time, she would heal. She had bounced back strongly from so many challenges in her life. But maybe the picture of him with Shanice was just too much to take, even if she was supporting him publicly. Maybe she felt the reporters, the tweets, and the general reaction to him had begun to put her in physical danger as well. Most disturbing though was the fact that she would no longer have the same last name as the girls. It would have been one thing if she'd never taken his name. But she had, and now it would separate her from her children. At least in his mind. This hurt much more than he might have expected.

"James," Mason called.

"Yes, I'm sorry. Do Katherine and Lillian know?"

"Yes."

"And they agree?"

"James, what are they going to say? Really? They still aren't happy with you."

Mr. Jimmy sighed. "I know they are unhappy. I have tried to reach them. I've sent emails and cards. I have texted. They don't respond."

"Listen, Aubrey is calling. I need to go, and I will call you back if there is anything significant about Rebecca."

After hanging up with Mason, he didn't know what to do with himself. There were so many emotions running through him, it was hard to concentrate on anything. He thought it best to go back to bed. If he could sleep, it might mean a few more hours of forgetting. When he woke up, maybe he would be stronger and better able to deal with everything. But that would not be the case, because when he was next awake, things just got worse.

The sirens woke him from a deep sleep where he had momentarily found the peace he had desired. He slept so deeply that he struggled to awaken. Yet, any benefits he might have gained were lost in his sighting of six police squad cars and two unmarked sedans slowly creeping through the neighborhood. He saw Miss Septima come out onto the porch. Fountain ran up to her and stood beside her. Other folks began to congregate as three of the squad cars and one sedan stopped among the houses of his neighbors. The others kept moving until they reached his house.

His hair was uncombed, and he hadn't brushed his teeth. But

to hell with it, he thought. He didn't think his cell mates were likely to care. Maybe they would put him on the other side of the table in that room. In the seat Fountain sat in on the day he promised himself that he would never enter a police station again.

Though he didn't show it, he felt some relief when the nice, young female officer from his first encounter with the Ham police stepped inside.

"Mr. Ferguson," she said, with an acknowledging nod of her head.

"Officer," he responded as she stepped to the side of the door and placed her hands in front of her.

But the next person through did not bring with him such a kind disposition. He was a little man. Wiry and particularly unfriendly. He was wearing an ill-fitting gray suit. His blond hair was in a buzz cut. He had bright and intensely dismissive blue eyes. He didn't offer a greeting or speak Mr. Jimmy's name. He got right to business.

"I'm Lt. Carlton. Are you aware of the claim made into today's paper?"

Mr. Jimmy stared back at him while trying to gather himself. He walked back into his bedroom and came back with his phone. He called Mason.

"Mason, the police are here about the picture with Shanice."

"Put me on speaker," he said, and Mr. Jimmy did.

"I am James Ferguson's attorney. My name is Mason Easton. I will speak for him."

"Well," the detective replied. "Mr. Ferguson is in a bit of trouble."

"For what?"

"Child molestation."

"Who is making that claim?"

"It's in the paper."

"You and I both know that's nothing. You need evidence.

Where's the evidence?"

"We have detectives with the girl's family right now. The girl is also being interviewed by herself at school."

"So your visit is just an attempt to scare and bully my client."

"Your client is in trouble."

"Not until you have some evidence. And until then, I suggest you take your leave. You've made your point. You have carried out Welton Knox's orders for the day."

This made the detective angry.

"Welton Knox is not my boss," he shouted at the phone.

"You and I both know better," Mason stated, undeterred by the change in the detective's tone.

The detective walked closer to Mr. Jimmy and suggested that he not try to leave Ham. Mr. Jimmy did not respond.

"We'll be back," the detective said as he turned to walk away. When he stepped onto the porch, the young officer followed. Mr. Jimmy watched them get into their cars and drive away. He went to the window to see what was happening in the neighborhood. The other cars were still there. He told Mason.

"They are probably interviewing the little girl's family."

"Her mother. She only has her mother."

"Well, her mother then. I am so happy you called me. Just stay around the house as much as you can. This is not my thing. Let me find an attorney for you."

"Don't worry. I have no place to go that won't cause me great pain. I'm staying right here."

But staying put was not pain free either. He made hot tea and sat in his chair by the window, envisioning his complete demise. He had planned for death in terms of preparing for his family. Prison certainly never crossed his mind. What did he have to change financially? How would he make sure the girls were going to be okay? Would they ever visit? Would he even want his two precious girls to even walk the grounds of a prison?

Mr. Jimmy never drank his tea. It got cold, sitting on the table while he stared out of the window. Eventually, those officers left as well. His neighbors gathered to talk for quite some time before finding their way home. Mr. Jimmy saw Fountain start walking to his house. Mr. Jimmy put on a coat and met him outside.

"I'm sorry about all that, Mr. Jimmy. But I was there with Evie. She tried to set them straight, but they said how could she know all what went on. They said that she won't in the picture, so how can she tell what you did or didn't do. She said Shanice told her that night what had happened. She told them you carried Shanice home, and that Shanice was so happy to be in your arms. She told them that Shanice loved you. But they said, 'we'll see' and left."

"The detective who was with me said they were interviewing Shanice at school. They could frighten a child into saying anything."

Fountain nodded. "Man, this is all something just crazy. I just don't know what to say, Mr. Jimmy. I know we all still behind you."

"But I came down here and brought some hell with me."

"Hell, the Devil been all up in our shit for all time. We used to it. But I know you ain't. But Miss Septima say you know the president. Can he speak for you?"

"No. I would never ask him, and it would not be good for him politically."

"Well, you know best, Mr. Jimmy."

Mr. Jimmy laughed. "How I wish that were true."

"Listen, Miss Septima also told me what happened at the grocery store. So I told her that I would walk down here and get the truck and some money to take her shopping."

"I don't think I can come to Christmas dinner."

"Well, you gone have to tell her that part for yourself. In the meantime, she still gonna want to have a dinner. Can I beg a few bucks off you?"

Mr. Jimmy smiled. "Of course, you can. I'll be right back."

He gave Fountain enough for Miss Septima and enough for Bess. He also sent money to Patrice to buy something for herself and the kids for Christmas dinner. Fountain gave him a hug and drove off in the truck. Mr. Jimmy watched the dust rise and settle behind him.

Mr. Jimmy reverted to his first days of living in his new house. Although his effort was earnest, he could not sleep through the night. So he put on jeans, a shirt, a sweater, and his winter coat. He made hot decaffeinated tea and sat on the porch, wrapped in a blanket. He rocked and rocked and rocked.

The breezy Mississippi night seemed to be as forlorn as he, each gust, in his mind, an earthly sigh in response to his plight. After a time, he longed for the For Sale sign. The dreadful clanging in the early days that had transitioned over time into a strange and comforting melody. A peaceful and heartwarming sound that reminded him of the truces he often established with himself while sitting by the ocean, his eyes closed, his soul fully open to the sound of bell buoys on the water. Without the song of the sign, there was no respite from his gloom. He sank deeper and deeper. He wanted to go home. Not back to Rebecca but all the way home because the way to her was closed. At this point, he felt it was the only thing that could save him. He dialed his parents' number.

He hadn't spoken to them since the story broke of his sexcapade with Lady Nymph. He didn't like to recall their strong disappointment in his actions. How could he betray such a woman? How could he betray the love of his daughters? How could he tell them that some of this belonged to Rebecca? How could he tell them that he stewed in his anger without an opportunity to discuss his feelings? How could he remind them that he was human? *Let he who is without sin cast the first stone, father preacher!*

It was three in the morning when he called his childhood home. He was surprised by how quickly his mother had answered the phone. He was shocked by how hard she was crying. She could barely say his name. His father took the phone.

"Hello, James," he said.

His mother's cries moved into the background as his father moved away from her.

Your mother has been crying like this off and on since we saw the picture of you and the little girl."

"Daddy," Mr. Jimmy said, his voice pleading for understanding. "I didn't do that. I could never do something like that."

"No, James. We didn't think that you could."

"I am so sorry that I have upset Mama so. I made a stupid choice months ago, and it just keeps developing into other tragedies. I know I have hurt you deeply, and I don't know what I can say or do about it."

"You can do better from now on."

"I am trying."

"It doesn't look that way to folks."

"What folks are you talking about?"

Mr. Jimmy could tell that his father had returned to his mother's side. Her crying was softer, and he heard his father tell her that he loved her and that things would work out as God would have them.

"What folks?" Mr. Jimmy asked again. "And what things have to work out?"

"I'm going to put you on speaker so your mother can join in if she so desires."

"Okay. Hi, Mama. I'm so sorry for everything. I did not harm that little girl. She had fallen and hurt her knee. I was helping her. Her mother arrived shortly after that picture was taken and

I carried the girl home. I did a good thing, which got turned into something else."

"Why would it get turned into something else?" Reverend Ferguson asked.

"I have been trying to help the people in my neighborhood, Daddy. The poverty is astounding. I ran into some racism at the local hospital, and I responded by threatening to buy it. And I actually started the process. It turns out that a powerful man here doesn't like how I went about it, and he is behind the picture of the girl and the one with the woman, if you've seen that one."

"We have."

"She's a friend. A lovely person and her husband was maybe twenty feet away at the time. He is my friend also. This is just evil at work."

"The Devil is powerful indeed."

"Daddy, why are you two up so late, and why has Mama been crying off and on all day?"

"When you first got into trouble, it started a rumble in the church. Folks didn't like what you did. They held us accountable because our family brought shame on the church. They quickly forgot how much you have given to the church and its mission. If we failed so badly at raising a child, who were we to tell the church members to get their act together. There was a backlash against us. The congregation split. Some for us. Many against us. Your mother and I worked hard to keep their confidence, and we thought we had it under control until yesterday morning when the picture of you and the little girl came out. The Deacon Board took a vote, and by dinner time they were asking us to temporarily step down while they figured out what to do next. I think it will be more than temporary soon. I have been preaching in the tradition of the Baptist church. That is, preach until you die. But I know that some people have thought I was too old a long time ago. This is convenient for them. Reverend Keith, my assistant pastor, will take over until they decide if they will let us rejoin the church family. They said that you are bringing a lot of negative attention to the church, and although they love us, we are somehow the faces of your sins. We couldn't give direction to the community while this was going on. So we have been either temporarily or permanently removed from our church community. It has hit us hard. I have shed many tears today as well. You mother was crying so hard because she just got off the phone with Katherine."

"Katherine?"

"Yes, she has been calling all day. Lillian called twice as well. But your mother needed to hear her voice, and so she called in the middle of the night, and Katherine talked with her for an hour. Then she was calm until the phone rang and it was you."

"Has Rebecca called?"

"We haven't heard from your dear wife since the first issue you had."

Mr. Jimmy took a moment, his mind spinning, working so hard in the moment to find a way to help his parents. But it had been so long since he left his hometown and his church. He didn't know half the congregation and had forgotten many others. He had no influence. He didn't know what he could do.

"I wish I could help you both. This is all my fault."

"At this point, the fault doesn't matter anymore. Whatever happens is in the Lord's hands, and we must abide. Listen, your mother and I are tired. She's already up and moving to the bedroom."

"She didn't talk to me."

"No, she didn't. She's deeply hurt, and she is trying to separate her love for you from the pain you have caused us, your wife, and your girls. It will take some time."

"I'll call her in the morning then."

"No, don't do that. We need some time. What you should

do is call Katherine and Lillian. They want to know about the sparrow. I told them it was your story to tell. We do love you. We will always love you, but you have created a mess for us. As I have said, it will take us some time."

Mr. Jimmy questioned whether or not it was smart for him to have another volatile conversation on what had already been a full day of serious discontent. On the other hand, maybe it would be good to get it all over with and whenever he woke up, he could just sit quietly in his home. If he could concentrate, he might try to get lost in a good book. If not, he could vegetate on the NFL and college football. He could remain secluded until he knew what his legal fate would be. He decided that he should make the call but that it had to be to Lillian. She might be angry, but it would be nothing like the immediate fire that Katherine would bring.

When she answered the phone, Lillian also understood why he'd chosen her.

"Daddy. I was expecting a call from you but in the next few days. Pops said that he would call you and tell you that you could call us."

"As it turns out, I surprised them with a call a few minutes ago. I couldn't sleep. Your grandmother was very upset."

"Yes, she was all day. Can you blame her?"

"No. Not at all. Anyway, I thought it best to call you."

"Because Katherine might bite your head off?"

"In a word, yes."

"Well, we are all afraid of a wound-up Katherine. That's for sure," she said, chuckling. "Why don't you let me call her, and I will add you to our call. Sound good?"

"Okay."

Mr. Jimmy decided that he would not give Katherine's fire a chance to ignite when they connected him. He would just launch into his story, and maybe it would cool her down and lessen their frustration with him. Particularly with regard to Shanice. When Lillian called and asked if he could hear them, he just started talking.

He told them that it had been a stunningly beautiful day. It was June 10th and he had been out behind their large shed at the edge of their property, which backed up against the land of a neighboring farmer. The sky was a deeper blue than most days, he'd thought. And the edges of the clouds were clean and crisp against it. For a while, he lay on the grass and watched the fluffy white shapes move gently across the sky, their shadows falling on the field, which was covered in rows of that year's soybean crop. At some point, he sat up and stared at the dirt spaces between the rows. He was hoping that a groundhog might cross over them. The rodent would make excellent target practice.

On May 15, he had turned eight years old. At that age, it was a rite of passage for many boys in his hometown to receive a BB rifle for their birthdays. Young Jimmy considered his to be the best present of his life. His parents had to take it away from him at night because otherwise, he would just sit and hold it while reading or watching television. During the days that followed his birthday, he spent hours outside, shooting tin cans off fence posts. He tried to hit walnuts on the tree in his backyard. He hunted groundhogs, and he tried to shoot birds. He could hit the cans and sometimes a walnut. The groundhogs never showed, and the birds moved too fast, and that frustrated him.

But on that June day of his eighth year, several sparrows crossed his line of vision. He forgot about the groundhogs and began to wildly shoot into the sky, trying his level best to hit one of the birds. But he failed, and it made him angry. He reloaded and quickly, without thinking too much and without aiming, he shot into the sky. The sparrow rolled over in the air and thudded into the field. Jimmy could not believe it. He let out a cheer and ran to see his conquest. But when he arrived, he did not feel what he had expected to feel. The sparrow was tiny. He nudged it with his rifle, but it did not move. Finally, he worked up the nerve to brush its wing with a finger and it surprised him when his tear landed by his finger on the sparrow's wing. Its eyes were open, its face so sweet and even kind. And it was a beautiful thing. And it was *innocent*. And he had taken away its life. And for nothing.

Jimmy dropped the rifle and fell to his knees in the field. He continued to cry. This bird would never fly again, and it was his fault. He had taken the joy of flight away. Was it a baby or a small mother? Would her children die in her nest? He had done something so unspeakable. He had taken another life, and there it lay, judging him as evil, unkind, and inhumane. He hated himself.

Jimmy got a shovel from the shed. In the field, at the spot of the kill, he tearfully dug a grave for the tiny sparrow. After laying it to rest, he knelt in the dirt and asked for forgiveness for the life he took. He gave the BB rifle to his parents after telling them what he had done. He didn't want to hold that gun or any other gun again, he told them.

"What you feel in your heart right now should speak to you," his father had said. "It is telling you about your character. The little sparrow has shown you who you are. For that, you should be thankful."

Every day for a year, Jimmy visited the grave site. Even after the earth was turned, he knew the spot he needed to kneel by and pray. Years later, as an adult, James still had moments of deep regret for that action. And each time he felt the regret, he prayed for forgiveness and went out into the world searching for lives that he could help better.

His daughters were silent after he finished the story. There were tears in his eyes, as always when he thought of the sparrow. There had been real sorrow in his voice.

"Thank you, Daddy," Katherine eventually said. "I believe you."

"So do I," Lillian said. "So do I."

"Daddy," Katherine continued. "I know you were expecting me to give you a bit of hell when Lillian brought you into the call."

"Yes, I was.

"Well, most days you would have been right. But today has taught us both a lot. We've had several phone calls between the two of us. And we've both talked to Pops and Gran several times. But most importantly, Daddy, we talked to Mom. Or maybe I should say, she talked to us."

"Yes," Lillian said. "She wanted us to know that you would never hurt a child and especially a little girl. She told us stories, Daddy. Stories that we'd never heard about you and your gentle love for us. That's what she called it. A gentle love."

"And, Daddy," Katherine continued. "She said that she wanted us to remember that you were all around a very good man. She said that there has been so much trauma surrounding your breakup. She has been hurting so much that it's been hard to speak to your virtues but seeing the accusation of child molestation in the paper made her realize that she had to speak up. Especially to us. Because she didn't want a lifelong estrangement between us. And I think we can all agree that we were heading in that direction."

"What did she say?" Mr. Jimmy asked.

"She told us, Daddy," Lillian said. "She told us about her inability to find the love in your lovemaking. She told us it was a year before you broke down and ended up with that woman. She told us you were still wrong to do it. Of course, we all know that."

"But it wasn't as heartless a process as we thought," Katherine said. "Even so, I know I still need time. I'm not ready to be in your presence just yet. But I will respond to your emails and take your calls. We can build it back slowly."

"Or into something a little different," Lillian added.

He was sure they could hear him trying to gather himself, and after a bit, they had to have realized that he was failing in that effort.

"It's okay, Daddy. I love you," Lillian said.

"Me too," Katherine added, softly.

"I love you both," he struggled to get out.

Hearing them express their love for him for the first time since he'd broken their trust heartened him. He felt hope, faint but tangible, rising in his heart. And he wondered if their offering of love was hinting at the possibility of reconciliation for the family. Had Rebecca handed them her proxy in a vote to end his exile from the family?

"Do you think," he started, breaking the emotion-laden silence, "that Mom might take me back? Do you think we could be a whole family again?"

"You shouldn't go there, Daddy," Lillian said. "If you're searching for redemption, that's not where you will find it."

"I agree, Daddy," Katherine added. "That's just not happening. Mom said she could never go back. Neither can we. Like Lillian said, it will be something different. But the something different for Mom is a new life. Away from you."

"She's changing her name," Mr. Jimmy said sadly.

"We support her," Katherine replied.

"Okay. Good to know. Thank you for giving it to me straight."

"I'm sorry, Daddy," Lillian said. "But like you used to say to us. You made your own bed. Now you have to sleep in it."

Indeed, he did, he thought. Alone, alone, and alone.

Mr. Jimmy said goodbye and ended the call. He came into the house and shed his layers of clothing. He pulled down the room darkening shades because the morning sun would be arriving soon. He climbed into bed. It took him quite a while to gather himself after the conversation with his daughters. He took deep breaths, trying to slow his heartbeat. He counted backwards from one hundred. For some time, nothing worked. He tossed and turned until finally he found comfort on his side, staring into the deep darkness. He eventually nodded off to sleep, feeling tremendously foolish for daring to hope.

TWENTY

The truth is that James Henry Ferguson loved his family more than anything else in the world. Long ago, his mother had told him it would be so. She said that it would start with his wife.

"One day," his mother said, "I will be replaced as the most important woman in your heart."

At first, Jimmy, at age 16, had laughed at the notion. Then, he argued forcefully against such a thing. Certainly, he planned to marry. But could that love overcome the special connection with the woman who carried him and delivered him into the blessing of his life? He didn't see how that could be possible, but she sat across from him and held his hands. She told him that he would always have room for her, but one day another woman would stand front and center and that was as it should be. It was what she wanted for him. And if he were completely open and honest with himself about his love for this woman, whoever she might be, then their relationship would be the most important blessing in his life.

This was his thought as he sat in his car, across from his house in the middle of the night, one year after his tryst with Lady Nymph, one year after Rebecca had come to the hotel to touch him one final time and then turn a corner, walking out of his life for good. He had been taught that a true blessing never ends, but this one had.

All of the lights were out, except for the under the cabinet fluorescent lights in the kitchen. Some things had not changed. James sighed and began to think about the 8 x 10 photo of Rebecca probably still on his desk at work and on the wall in his home office, which he knew she hadn't touched. Mason said she'd just locked the door. It was his favorite picture of her. He had taken it at a county fair before Katherine was born. Behind Rebecca had been a moon bounce and crepe paper. Playful signs and energetic clowns on unicycles. They were all far enough away from his camera that they fell into soft focus, fashioning a beautiful, edgeless blending of color. On top of that, Rebecca's image was crisp, clear, and beautiful, looking as if she'd just walked out of Najee Dorsey's painting "Love Is in the Air." He snapped the photo, and she became playful.

"Sir, did I give you permission to take my picture?"

"Why, no, ma'am. And I apologize. But if you had seen how beautiful you looked, you wouldn't have taken the time to ask either, because you would have missed the moment. And I don't think moments like that come along all the time."

Her playfulness turned into her beautiful smile. *The* smile. He took it in and the love it represented.

As he sat out front of his house, he realized that smile—the smile that he absolutely adored—was gone forever. If it was always meant just for him, and she no longer saw him that way, it had to be so. It made him sad. He had cost the world something truly beautiful.

On the left side of the house, on the second floor was Katherine's room. One night when she was a toddler, he stood in the hallway outside of her room. He considered his upcoming role in her life. People kept telling him how important fathers were in the lives of their daughters. He made a pledge never to let her down. He made a pledge to be present in her life. But as she grew, he didn't understand how any parent, much less a father, would not want to be a part of raising a child like Katherine. Who needed a pledge? Their relationship began with long "daddy walks" as Rebecca called them. He would carry her all around the neighborhood, pointing out birds and flowers. He loved the playful bath times and braiding her hair afterward. He loved the arts and crafts projects. He loved just snuggling and telling stories. He loved putting her to bed at night and staying in the room until she fell asleep on the nights that she was sick. They developed such a tight bond that when Rebecca became pregnant with Lillian, Aubrey said to her, "Well, good for you, girl. It's about time you had a child too."

Then one day, everything changed. Katherine and Rebecca were sitting in the car talking. The conversation went on for some time.

"What was that all about?" he'd asked Katherine when she walked into the house. For the first time, she was obviously uncomfortable with him. She dropped her head and ran by him, upstairs to her room. Rebecca could see the confusion and pain growing in his eyes.

"We went shopping. To pick up some things. Katherine got her period this morning."

James started up the stairs to speak to her. He didn't know what he would say, but it felt like he should acknowledge such an important moment in her life.

"No, sweetie," Rebecca said to him, grabbing his arm. "She asked me to tell you."

"She can tell me anything," James said.

"She was uncomfortable telling you. Don't be angry with her. It's the beginning of so many changes for her. Let her come to you."

But she didn't come to him. At least not in the way she had before. Things changed. She and Rebecca giggled behind closed doors about boys. Although Rebecca would fill him in later, he still felt left out. Little by little, he played a smaller role in Katherine's life. He existed on the periphery. Most of the time, she seemed bothered by him hovering and wondering. She offered him no solace. There was a time when he felt he knew everything about her. Now, though he felt she still loved him, he felt a bit like a stranger. Stranger still was Rebecca telling him that everything was as it should be.

Luckily for him, he had two daughters and he had doted on Lillian just as much as he had Katherine. She took up the empty spaces, and in truth, maybe Rebecca was right. It had to be this way, that Katherine did not need either of them so much, because Lillian did. She was a brilliant little girl with a heart of glass. It was beautifully decorated artisan glass, but it was thin, and it easily suffered cracks. And there were many. Where Katherine was strong and independent, Lillian was tender, fearful, and needy. Perfect, because he needed her.

By the time Katherine was 16, life was busy in the Ferguson household. Mornings sometimes seemed out of control. When the girls were finally off to school and he sat down at work, he really had no idea how everyone had gotten to be where they needed to be. It made him smile to think of it.

One morning, he had been laughing at Rebecca and Lillian's breakfast conversation. Katherine, behind schedule as usual, burst into the kitchen.

"I'm so late," she said. "Jules and her mom are going to be here soon."

"Sit down and eat something," Rebecca said.

"Okay. Just the eggs though."

But before she sat down, she stuck a Post-it note to the refrigerator. Rebecca and James waited expectantly as Lillian ran to read the quote on the note. She read aloud.

"Today is a good day to die."

When the mood struck her, since she was 15, Katherine would

grace the morning with a quote for them all to live by. In the beginning, it was a cute thing that served to make them laugh at her outlook on life. But she continued, and it became a bit of family tradition, which soon became a moment they looked forward to. Often, her messages were very thoughtful and instructive as she, more times than not, tied them to something going on in the life of a family member. But this one came from somewhere unexplained.

"Who said that?" Lillian asked, sitting back down at the table.

Katherine smiled because she had them. "Chief Crazy Horse, of course. Lakota warrior of the Oglala Sioux. Just before the battle of Little Big Horn."

"That might just be kind of morbid," Lillian said.

"It's a simple thought to live by," Katherine responded.

"You're telling me to live by a saying that tells me I should be happy to die today."

Katherine shook her head, feigning disgust. "You're sooooooo eleven," she said.

They all laughed.

"You have to think of the context, Lillian, to get what he's saying. For you, right now, this morning, at this very moment, what in your life is so important to you that you would be willing to die for?"

"Can I just get through middle school first before I have to think about that kind of stuff?"

More family laughter.

"If you place it in context with our lives, I think it's asking what is so important that you would want to put yourself in a difficult situation to force others to see the truth. What are you willing to march for? You know, like the March on Washington in the sixties. What are you willing to speak out for even if you know it will make things difficult for you? What kind of trouble are you willing to face to make a difference? Get it?"

Lillian and Katherine continued the conversation, and James watched Rebecca, her chin resting on folded hands, smiling at her children. When she glanced up at him, he was waiting to share the moment with her. They spoke without speaking, their expressions asking, *Baby, aren't you so proud?*

A car horn broke their glance, and the conversation stopped.

"I gotta go. Jules is here," Katherine said. She picked up her backpack and ran around the table kissing everyone on top of their head.

"Have a good day, family," she said as she ran out of the door.

"Thank you, sweetie," Rebecca yelled.

It was just a regular morning, and he had gone to work thinking that family dynamic would always be in place. Now, he was leaving Washington, DC. It had taken a year to find the city, the little house, and to complete its renovation. He started his new BMW and took one more long look at the home he'd shared with Rebecca and family for over 20 years. He pulled away slowly, looking over his shoulder until the house was out of sight. He drove through the night, until he had arrived in Ham, Mississippi.

TWENTY-ONE

Hope was a storm cloud. It had hovered over Mr. Jimmy since the first time he'd begged Rebecca for forgiveness. It had stayed with him every moment of every day, a misty cold, dark mass, blinding him to the acceptance of his fate and the path to a modicum of closure. It was counterintuitive. Why would he want to escape hope? Why would he want to let it go? It was the only thing keeping him near his family, dark though it was. So he held onto it because it was, well, hope after all. And he ignored the thunder that kept pounding and pounding, keeping him unsettled at his core. He ignored the bolts of lightning, the shocking surges of pain from Rebecca and the girls that stunned him constantly and spread through him like an electrical fire. Sometimes, he thought he felt his flesh burn, but still, he would not step away from the fire. For an entire year, he had lingered beneath his hope. Now though, he realized that it had been pointless. Hope had been a fool's paradise. When the girls finally shut the door on reconciliation ever becoming a reality, he understood he had been that fool. And though it hurt him deeply to begin the process, he did wake up the next day and force himself to take the first step into the light, standing just outside the shadow's edge, leaving the storm cloud to dissipate without his neediness to act as fuel for its existence. Katherine and Lillian had said they needed more time. Well, now, so did he. So that he could take the first steps into his future.

So he was not angered by the knock on his door. In fact, he was ready for it. He was done with his fourth self-imposed exile. There would be no more of that, he thought as he walked to the door. It was time to move forward. To not give up on himself. He found motivation in the girls' belief in him. In Rebecca's public declaration. So he began to feel that he could and should fight for what was left of his reputation. He felt, if they would let him, he should continue to fight for the people of around the way. Even though he knew he would fall short of his original intentions.

Miss Septima stood on the other side of the screen door and looked him up and down.

"Lawd, child. Now don't you be looking a mess. And I'm bringing folk to meet this upstanding Black man, and you look like you spent the night in the ditch with some moonshine."

The young woman who stood beside Miss Septima had not been able to contain her smile.

"And that's exactly what I feel like," Mr. Jimmy said. "Would you both like to come in despite that?"

"Maybe we should stay out here in the cold breeze. Cold air keeps the smells down," Miss Septima said playfully as he escorted her into the house. They took a seat in the great room.

"I'm James Ferguson," he said, reaching out for the young woman's hand.

"It's Mr. Jimmy," Miss Septima said.

He smiled and nodded. "My mistake."

"It's nice to finally meet you. My name is Mary Ford," the young woman replied.

"Would you both like some tea? The water is already hot. Lipton decaf is the only tea that I have though."

"Good enough for me," Miss Septima said.

"Me too," Mary answered.

The young Ms. Ford unnerved him a bit. She reminded him too much of Lady Nymph. Same coffee-colored skin. Same cascading braids. He was thankful for her eyeglasses that set them apart. But he began to wonder if Miss Septima had fallen for some kind of prank, and then brought it to his house. He leaned over and looked out of the window as he walked back to them. He didn't see anyone or anything out of the ordinary, but still he was concerned. He poured their tea, took a seat in his lounge chair, and projected skepticism into the moment.

"What can I do for you, Ms. Ford?"

"You've already done it. I'm just here to thank you for it."

Not falling for whatever this is, he thought. "I'm sorry," he said a bit coldly. "I don't understand."

She smiled. "I'm the one Juba and Beech told you about. The young teacher who had them selling chocolate. You know, the one with her Teach for America self, who they predicted would run away like their previous four teachers."

Mr. Jimmy relaxed and softly smiled. Then he laughed out loud. "Well, well, well. I guess you beat the odds."

"I did, but I didn't do it alone. I'm here to thank you because you helped. Really. More than you will ever know."

"We've never met. I'm not sure how I could have helped you."

"Mr. Jimmy, I got into teaching because I believed children, and particularly Black children, need to be literate in order to have any chance of success in this world. I don't think everyone is college material, but what can you do well without being able to read? If nothing else, you learn about the world and you learn to reason. That's more important than people think, you know? I've seen this failure in literacy at the schools I worked in while I was in college. I see it here, and it breaks my heart. Day after day, I would go home and cry. These kids, Juba and his contemporaries, they are so far behind. I can't teach them history unless I become the griot around the fire and just tell stories. I can't teach them science. I can't teach them math. They wouldn't try, and I couldn't figure out how to change things. I had no idea how to attack a problem of this magnitude. I had so many plans that had to be set aside. I didn't really know how to begin. I couldn't get them to focus. They came at the beginning of the year, expecting me not to care and to fail. It was really difficult, and then gradually they began to behave without me asking them to. They began to try to understand the lessons. They began to care. I was stunned. Even the kids who don't know you began to fall in line. I told a fellow teacher who I trust, and she didn't have any idea what was happening either. Finally, I had to ask and hope that someone would actually tell me the truth. Juba, Beech, and a few others laid it out for me. I began to hear about afterschool jobs, Bob Books, and a guy they called Mr. Jimmy from around the way. They said that 'bruh was special.'"

Miss Septima and Mr. Jimmy smiled.

"I knew I had to meet you," Mary continued. "I wanted to tell you that even though we've never met, you taught me through them that I couldn't look too broadly at their needs because it could seem too massive a task. For me and for them. The Bob Books taught me that I had to start small across the board. I've been doing that in math, history, science, et cetera. I have created lesson books. Little books written in the simplest language about historical events and about science. It's working, Mr. Jimmy. It really is. Now, I go home, and there are no tears. In fact, I just sit down and laugh with wonder. I wanted to come here and thank you."

So many awful events had been filling Mr. Jimmy's recent days. For a moment, it seemed difficult to know what to do with good news. Miss Septima leaned forward and touched his knee. She smiled as she sat back. She offered him a proud nod.

"No," he finally said. "Thank you, Ms. Ford. Thank you for being a teacher. Thank you for caring about our kids. Thank you for wanting to do right by them. I only hope they can find more teachers like you along the way. It isn't going to be easy for them."

"You're right," she replied. "It is going to be difficult, but you have proven, Mr. Jimmy, that love and unconditional support can make the journey easier for them. But there is another side to this."

"Oh."

"Yes. In the past few days, all of the positive momentum just stopped. Or maybe I should say crashed since it happened in an instant. One day they show up and no one wants to do any work. They were as uncooperative as they were the first day of classes. But there was something different. On the first day, they were just indifferent. Now, on top of not wanting to do anything, they were angry. I could tell that they were hurt by something, but they wouldn't talk to me, so I couldn't figure out what went wrong. So one afternoon I followed their school bus to the neighborhood. Thankfully, the first door I knocked on was Miss Septima's. She brought me to you. She said you were the source of the break-through and the source of the recent issues. I'm here also because I need your help."

"I never imagined," Mr. Jimmy said. "Truthfully, Ms. Ford, I have had my own setbacks recently. I didn't give or maybe I should say, I wasn't able to spend time thinking about my kids. I didn't have the emotional capital."

She nodded. "I understand. I read the papers. I did my online research. Notwithstanding, I still needed to find you. The school and its administration are not invested in the students the way some of us believe they should be. There is little money for the things that matter."

"But Juba was bragging about the exercise equipment," Mr. Jimmy interrupted. "It made me think the school was doing all right."

"It's true. That's at the high school though. The middle school is across the street from the high school. It's really one big campus. People will give money for football players to build muscles but not so much when it comes to building brains for Black children."

"That's heartbreaking," he replied.

"Lawd, have mercy," Miss Septima added.

Mary Ford continued. "The thing that really bothers me is that so many teachers and administrators didn't believe in the kids. Probably because it was happening just in my class. They were not into giving a Teach for America kid any credit. And, of course, I shouldn't have had all of the credit. Several very vocal teachers never believed what was happening. They claimed I was making things up. When I invited them into the class, they passed on the offer. They just stayed outside and took shots at us. They said the kids just didn't have what it took to be real students and productive people. They said it was some sort of fad."

Ms. Ford reached into her purse for some tissue. She wiped her eyes and blew her nose before continuing.

"I need you," she said. "The kids. Your kids, as you called them. They need you. They have a writing project due on the day before Christmas break. They had to write a two-page book about their lives so far this school year. A very simple two pages. But I would love for you to hear some read aloud. After the reading, we had planned to have pizza, but they are refusing to read now. They come; they sit. They look out of the window or sleep. Will you come to school and hear their words? Will you help me bring back the hope?"

Mr. Jimmy stiffened when he heard the word hope, but he worked to stop the rush of negative emotions he had associated with it.

"Ms. Ford, you've seen the papers. No one will allow me to come to a school of all places."

"Mr. Jimmy, these people don't care enough about the kids to worry about you. Besides, I made it plain that Shanice told the police the truth about what happened with you two."

"How did you do that?"

"Well, she's not in my class. She's a year behind my kids, but Juba had introduced me to her because she also did the Bob Books here at your place. So I befriended her, and I helped her with her reading when I could. We would often meet during lunch. When they couldn't get her to say anything, she told them she would talk if I was in the room. So I sat next to her. I must say, you came out of that looking pretty good. She said you were the best grown man she ever met. She loves you, Mr. Jimmy. They all do. Won't you come?"

"Of course, I'll come. I'm beginning to think I might run through a wall for you, Ms. Ford."

"Oh, you got him now, girl," Miss Septima said to Ms. Ford as they all shared a laugh.

"Where are you from, Ms. Ford? And where did you go to college?"

"I grew up in Chicago, Mr. Jimmy. I know your daughters are Princeton. I hate to disappoint you, but I went to Yale."

Mr. Jimmy laughed out loud, and it felt good. "You remind me of my daughters. University alliances notwithstanding."

As Ms. Ford and Miss Septima stepped onto the porch, Miss Septima turned back to him.

"And boy," she said waving her hand at him. "You get that mess off your face before you step in that classroom."

"Yes, ma'am," he said to Miss Septima. "I will do that."

He stepped onto the porch and wrapped her in a hug that she pretended to resist.

TWENTY-TWO

Despite his good feelings about meeting Ms. Ford and his freedom from hope, Mr. Jimmy still had trouble sleeping. So he put on his layers. He made his decaf tea and grabbed a blanket. He sat on the porch again, stared into the darkness and found himself engaged in some existential cogitation.

Who was he at this new starting point in his life? Rebecca would always be in his heart and mind, but he knew now that part of his journey was over. Completely over. Still, he couldn't see clearly which steps to take into his future. He was happy and optimistic one moment, drenched in melancholy the next. He sought the steadier emotional middle ground. The sweet spot where life was nothing special but nothing horrible either. Just a good life.

His tea was good. It went down well, warming him throughout. He kept rocking and thinking, trying to reorient himself, the way his parents had one Christmas when they saw that he had begun to think only of himself and what pleased him. He was becoming a taker rather than the giver they had hoped he would aspire to be. He had been 12 years old and blessed, yet he didn't understand his blessing and had not been treating it with respect. That morning, he received the usual number of gifts under the tree, but he was upset and confused when he opened them. There were little kid puzzles. There were paint-by-the-numbers kits. There were coloring books and picture books. With each unwrapping, he became angrier. He questioned his parents. Where were his gifts? They pointed to everything he had opened. Jimmy sat and pouted. His parents made no attempt to make him feel better.

Later in the morning, he and his father packed up his gifts and put them in the back of the station wagon. The three of them drove out of their small town, past the wide-open fields and their life of patience and grace. They drove across the bridge that connected them to the only city he knew. They went there occasionally to have dinner at a restaurant or to go to the movies. That morning, they drove past all of that into a world that was vastly different than his. They ended up in a community center, full of children and their families. There was Santa, who should have been back at the North Pole by that time of the afternoon. But he was there passing out gifts. Reverend and Mrs. Ferguson led Jimmy into a big kitchen. All gleaming metal, it was full of people preparing meals.

"Jimmy," his mother said, "sit here for a moment."

He sat down next to his mother, his eyes still taking in the scene around him.

"You see the children, Jimmy?"

"Yes, ma'am."

"You can tell that their clothes aren't as nice as yours. Theirs come from The Salvation Army, kind folks who are better off and from churches like ours. This is the only time of the year that many of these children get anything new. But I want you to look at them. They really aren't playing with their gifts so much. They're just so happy to be in this environment where it seems like they have a life as advantageous as yours. You, my son, are so blessed and in so many ways. Today, we want you to earn that blessing."

"That's why I got the gifts I did?"

"Yes."

"Okay, Mama," Jimmy said. "I think I understand."

Jimmy got his gifts from the car, and he gathered a group of the kids. They played the game Twister. Afterward, Jimmy stepped outside to throw a football. Inside, he gathered some of the smaller kids, and they ate candy and made use of his coloring books. He painted and did puzzles one-on-one. He read from his picture books to a circle of children. By the time Christmas dinner was served on big folding event tables, he had a group of kids following him around. He ate dinner with them instead of his parents.

That night, the Reverend knocked on his bedroom door, and his mother followed him into his bedroom.

"We didn't come in to preach at you," his father said.

"Good," he replied. "I got the message already."

His mother smiled and handed him an envelope. She hugged him and said, "Merry Christmas, my love."

"Merry Christmas to you both," Jimmy said. "I think this might be the best Christmas I've ever had."

"I am not surprised," his father said with a knowing smile.

"Can we go back," Jimmy asked.

His parents looked at each other and grinned.

"Of course," his mother said. "It would do us all good to return often. To keep perspectives intact and to make a difference in this world."

After his parents left his room, Jimmy settled into bed. By the light of his bedside lamp, he opened the envelope. He was surprised to find that it wasn't a Christmas card. It was plain and white, folded horizontally. He flipped it up to find just a quote inside.

"The place in which I'll fit will not exist until I make it."

James Baldwin

Mr. Jimmy rocked until the sun rose above the horizon. He thought more about the quote in his Christmas card and glanced down the dirt road to Miss Septima's and beyond. He went inside and set his laptop on the table by the window. As the morning light softly claimed the sky, he smiled, remembering a saying the old folks in his hometown used when it was time to work.

The Lord helps those who help themselves.

TWENTY-THREE

Mr. Jimmy shaved.

He attempted to close the door on his pain as best he could. He got busy. Even though he had no sleep, he showered, made breakfast, and returned to his laptop to put what was left of his plans in motion. He woke up Mason and asked about suing *The Ham Gazette*. He told him that he was going to Yankee's firm to talk about buying the motel and to discuss prefab homes for his neighbors. He hung up before he was sure Mason was awake enough to grasp everything, but he would figure it out.

By 10 a.m., he was waiting outside Yankee's office. To his surprise Olivia Fey Carol opened the door to her husband's office and invited him inside. He and Olivia gave each other a warm hug.

"Careful," Yankee said. "I think I just heard a camera shutter somewhere."

They laughed, and Mr. Jimmy noted how good it felt to do so. Yankee delivered his own hug, which Mr. Jimmy delighted in receiving.

"We are so happy to see you," Olivia said. "I wanted to come by, but Yankee thought you might need some space."

"He was right, and I thank you for that. I had some things to work through. How have you guys been?"

"We are good," Yankee said. "Olivia can't find work, but luckily, I'm still working."

"Just as well," Olivia said. "The kids needed me around. But
they have bounced back. And they are even more feisty and supportive of you."

"That's nice to hear," Mr. Jimmy said. "Maybe you guys
would come to dinner one night over the holidays?"

"We'd be happy to," Olivia replied.

They took seats to discuss their plans. Mr. Jimmy was surprised
and happy to find out that his friends had never given up on
his dream. In fact, Yankee had secured a motel. All he needed
was a signature and money. Mr. Jimmy signed the papers and
referred him to Mason for payment. Then, Olivia showed him a
list of eleven prefab companies. They were planning to have each
company simultaneously build two homes in the neighborhood.
That would speed up the timeline and everyone could move in
at or around the same time. Mr. Jimmy liked the idea, thinking
a community move-in day would be special. He asked what he
could do.

"We need your mind. Keep dreaming of what you would like
to happen, and let us help figure out how to put things in motion,"
Olivia said. "Oh, and you could write some checks."

"I can do that," Mr. Jimmy said, laughing. "Also, if you are
willing to accept it, Olivia, I think you can consider yourself
hired as a consultant on this project. You can write your ticket
on salary."

Olivia smiled. "Thank you very much. That would help us
tremendously. I would take my last full year income from the real
estate agency. What would you say to sixty thousand?"

"I would ask the question, why does everyone around here
sell themselves short?"

"I don't understand," Olivia said.

"Never mind. How about one hundred sixty thousand? To start, I mean. And with a year-end bonus."

"You're serious?"

"Indeed, I am."

"Well," she said, holding out her hand. "I accept."

TWENTY-FOUR

Mr. Jimmy worked to tidy up his mind.

Hope had exploded there. And stayed. In defiance of the good feelings from Ms. Ford, Miss Septima, Olivia, and Yankee. In defiance of other efforts to move past it, its residue still hung in the air of his consciousness. Hung like the smoke from an artillery blast, blanketing his beachhead, carrying with it shrapnel and the haunting cries of needless and shortsighted loss. The smell of things fading and taking their sweet, damn time dying away. The odor of things lost forever. But there are those who are lucky enough to live through the salvos. He knew he was one of them. Those lucky enough to be shocked back into their senses after the blasting concluded, physically unwinding from their impromptu holes on the beach as their sergeants yelled. *Get up! Move it! You want to see your Mamas again? Get off the damn beach!*

Mr. Jimmy was struggling to get off his beach. He wanted to live. He had stepped forward, feeling that things were moving in the right direction only to find himself again sitting on the porch in the middle of the night, longing for the comfort of his For Sale sign. But as the days passed, he recognized that he had to be like the soldiers who described surviving battle. He had to perform surgery of the mind, shifting his emotional scar tissue, using it to build walls against feelings that might distract him from the mission of living. The problem with moving scar tissue is that it creates more of the same. However painful, he knew he had to push forward. He kept repeating the words of the old folks, *The Lord helps those who help themselves.*

He whispered the words before he called Mason. He explained that he was having good days and bad days. Swings from the highs of positive anticipation to the lows of present reality. Mason wasn't surprised.

"It's been a year of you hoping that Rebecca would come around. Now that's gone. Give yourself some time."

"I keep telling myself that."

"Keep doing it. You have things to do. Plans to carry out. Keep your head in that game. Every time you feel yourself falling backward, think about Juba and the twenty-two houses on that dirt lane. You can make a difference. You can and should remember this part of your past world. The part that brought you incredible joy and peace of mind when you helped others. I think that has to be your ticket out of the funk, yes?"

"You should be right, but that's not going so well either. The hospital is gone, and the main plan of creating a farm is gone because we can't get the land."

"Let the negatives go if you can, brother. The positives are that you are going to put them all in new homes. I have no doubt you can help to guide them to lives better than the ones they are leading right now. I wish I could come down there and help you. It kills me that I can't. I thought time would ease things for Aubrey, but not so much."

"You know I understand?"

"Of course."

"And now is not a good time anyway. You never know who is following me around. You might end up with your picture in the paper."

"But it's well known that I'm your lawyer."

"True, but it will look different if they see you next to me. You'll trend alongside the molester on Twitter. That would bring it all home to Aubrey again. Maybe in a worse way."

"None of that is going to be a problem going forward. The opportunity just appeared right in front of Knox with the picture, and he ran with it hoping to force you to leave Ham. But there is nothing there. They know it. The police interviewed the girl, the mother, and your friend, Juba. They all told the same story. You've weathered that storm."

"Yes, I know," Mr. Jimmy replied. "I had a visit from Juba's teacher who was in the room with Shanice during the interview."

"And so that's going nowhere, but I guess you're right. I could get caught up in nonsense, and Aubrey wouldn't be too happy about that."

"I can't imagine she would be."

"Listen, you just keep your head up. Put all the bad stuff away somewhere."

Mr. Jimmy chuckled. "I know just the place. Back in the corner of the kitchen cabinet, right alongside the 2009 Lafite-Rothschild that Olivia gave me."

"I miss you, brother," Mason said.

"I miss you too," Mr. Jimmy replied.

Mr. Jimmy was thankful to Mason for reminding him of the good he could still accomplish and of how he had felt in the past when helping to change lives for the better. Truly one good thing he could hold onto through his transition. With that in mind, he met with Fountain midway between his house and Miss Septima's. They stood side-by-side, quietly in the cold winter breeze, facing Crawford Alden's one hundred acres. Mr. Jimmy controlled his anger, thinking of the day he, Olivia, and Yankee had tried to make a sincere and good offer to the man for land he had not used for years.

"I have bad news," Mr. Jimmy said.

Fountain turned to him, his face immediately indicating he understood that things had fallen apart. It was the way Mr. Jimmy had said it. The sadness in his voice.

"I knew this shit was too good to be true," Fountain said.

"We can't get the land. Alden, the owner, won't sell it to me. It's because of a man named Welton Knox, who got upset that I threatened to buy the hospital."

"Mr. Ham, Mississippi," Fountain said, laughing sarcastically. "Every Black man, woman, and child know him. Dude is the devil in the flesh. Been down on us forever. Now, he got down on you too."

Mr. Jimmy nodded. "Yes, I angered him, and he's successfully putting me in my place. Along with that, he's killing the wonderful idea of the farm. I even thought," he continued waving toward the land, "that we would build a park for the kids. Playground equipment, benches for the parents, and picnic tables for community barbeques. It was going to be the buffer between the farm and the community. But that's gone now along with all of the work you did researching equipment and finding labor. It seems it was for nothing. I am so sorry."

Fountain turned back to the fading dream. His eyes panned the soft rises and falls of the land. He had seen himself running the farm, growing the food, happily and confidently earning his family's keep. He saw himself, for once, doing something positive for his people. He dropped his head. Staring down at the road, he kicked the dirt.

"I do have something else in mind for you if you find it agreeable. If you'll come with me."

"Why not," Fountain said. "Look like ain't nothing else calling my name."

They walked to Mr. Jimmy's and took the pickup. Mr. Jimmy drove a few miles out onto the highway and pulled into the parking lot of the Wayside Motel. They got out and stood looking at the facility that Fountain knew well. It had been there all his life. An L-shaped building, two stories tall. The short end of the L was obviously the office area. Attached to it were forty rooms. Twenty on the first floor and twenty on the second floor.

"I know this place," Fountain said. "Why're we here?"

"I bought it."

"Why you do that? Don't you like your own house?"

Mr. Jimmy smiled. "I do, and I don't plan to leave it, but if you agree to my plan, you will be leaving yours."

Fountain turned away from him. "Bruh, I don't know. I ain't got no more room in me for some more pie in the sky dream shit."

"I assure you, Fountain. This will work. It's all already underway."

"How's that supposed to work, then? That I'm gonna leave my house?"

Mr. Jimmy looked up at Fountain. "I want to get all of the families from around the way out of those homes. Your house, back in DC, would be condemned. You wouldn't be allowed to live in it. None of the homes are safe. So my plan is that I will move you, Bess, and Essie along with everyone else into this motel. We will tear down those houses around the way. Build new houses for each family and move you all into them when they're done. What do you think?"

Fountain slowly shook his head. "Man, I don't know. Ain't nobody gone believe that's for real. How you expect people to believe that can happen when you can't even get some land that's been up for sale for as long as I can remember? And you a billionaire."

"It can work. I mean, it is working. I can give you this much. I am truly, truly sorry about the farm, but that's gone. This is right here."

Fountain thought for a moment. "So that's a lot to ask a man. Seems like a lot more than the farm somehow."

"I want to do this for you all," Mr. Jimmy said. "Other people get help all the time. Especially, the privileged folks who often don't need it. Allow some luck to fall your way for a change."

Fountain turned to Mr. Jimmy who understood that Fountain was taking his measure. Much like the day he had attacked Mr. Jimmy. But on this day, instead of showing anger, his eyes relented.

"I reckon," he said softly.

"And since I can't offer you the farm, I can offer you the job of running this place. What do you think?"

"Aw, Mr. Jimmy, I know what farming takes. I don't know nothing about this. I can't be taking care of nobody's books. It'll take me a week to figure out what fifteen times five is."

"I thought you might say that, so what about you become the head of maintenance here. You keep the place up, and I know you told a couple of friends that they could work on the farm. They can work here if you want them to. But I will ask you all to keep it a secret from the neighborhood for a bit."

Fountain's eyes began to shine. He smiled. After a moment or two, he nodded. "It ain't like the love I got for farming, but it's good work, Mr. Jimmy. I'll take it, and my family thanks you. I can make Essie proud of me here with this."

Mr. Jimmy smiled. "I like the sound of a daughter who is proud of her father. Never take it for granted. Ever."

Fountain turned to Mr. Jimmy. "I hear you."

"Great. You can start tomorrow. You know, there is a whole diner behind the office. Hasn't been used in years. Maybe we can start a little restaurant. In the meantime, we'll buy a green pickup for you to go with the green building."

Fountain held out his hand to Mr. Jimmy who took it firmly.

"One more thing," Mr. Jimmy said. "You and Juba have a lot in common."

"How you figure?"

"You will accept a job without asking about the money."

"Bruh," Fountain said, laughing. "I'm just glad to have a job."

"Well, I researched the pay of a director of maintenance, which will be your title. They average forty-six thousand dollars a year."

Mr. Jimmy watched Fountain's eyes grow wide.

"But that's not it. You have to make more than the men you hire, so I am going to start you at eighty thousand a year. Plus, year-end bonuses and if we ever get a farm going, you will earn, much, much more."

"Nooooo, bruh?" Fountain asked, bending over in disbelief, holding his head in his hands.

"Yessss, bruh!" Mr. Jimmy replied, laughing. "Here's the thing though. There is an art to handling your money. So at the risk of having you beat me up again, and I don't mean to insult you, but I am going to suggest that I help you set up your budget and I have asked a friend of mine, a financial planner, to help you out with long-range goals. So you will have money when you retire and maybe some to leave for Essie when you depart this lovely world."

"Mr. Jimmy, I don't know what to say, Bruh. But I am thankful down to my soul."

Mr. Jimmy smiled. He felt a bit of wholeness returning.

Mr. Jimmy was embarrassed. Not because everyone in the urgent care waiting area seemed to recognize him but because he had let the good Dr. Longford down. He'd pitted him against his ER chief in the moment he had threatened to buy Merrimack General. He knew then that he had created a serious problem for Dr. Longford. It's why he had promised him a better job if the hospital purchase didn't go through. Then he promptly left him to face a workplace political firestorm. Still, the young doctor came to his aid after Fountain had attacked him. When he heard that the doctor had been suspended and demoted to urgent care, he should have been there for him. He had not, and that failure had been a part of the collection of issues keeping him up at night. He was sitting in the dingy waiting area hoping to make things right.

He had been told that Dr. Longford had a busy daily schedule. They would tell him that a Mr. Jimmy was waiting. There was little time in the day for breaks, the receptionist told Mr. Jimmy. Dr. Longford was under siege for a good part of each day. Mr. Jimmy told the receptionist that he would wait. In the meantime, people stared, pointed, and whispered, but thankfully no one said anything to him.

Mr. Jimmy had been in the waiting area for four and a half hours when Dr. Longford walked out of the doors leading to the exam rooms, looking as if he was on his way home. He stopped in place, shocked to see Mr. Jimmy. They hadn't told Dr. Longford that he was waiting. They both looked at the receptionist and she stared back, unmoved and proud.

"Could you spare time for an apology?" Mr. Jimmy asked.

Dr. Longford offered a tired smile but nodded. They sat in the BMW. Mr. Jimmy asked for the doctor's discretion before telling him the plan surrounding the Wayside Motel and the neighborhood around the way. Dr. Longford was intrigued. He told Mr. Jimmy that he had had dreams of a similar nature when he entered medical school. He had wanted to get in the trenches to help people who didn't get a fair shake at life, especially the proper medical care. The working underclass that was just as human as the upper classes who had access to the hospitals and the best doctors.

"What changed your mind?"

Dr. Longford laughed. "Debt! And I am not alone. You get into medical school to help save the world. Literally. And you don't think, at least I didn't, about the weight of the school bills. I was just so freaking idealistic. But I had to set all of that aside and get a job that would pay back my tuition. That's why I'm in a hospital and not doing what I dreamed of. Why are you smiling?"

"Because," Mr. Jimmy said. "I have a plan that you might be interested in."

"Okay."

"What if I offered to pay off all of your debt, tuition and otherwise, for five years of running a top-notch community clinic for those folks you just spoke of?"

"Are you really serious?"

"Absolutely, and I will pay you well above your salary at the hospital. You might be the best paid physician in Ham."

"But I like to treat patients. I'm not so sure about administration."

"Why can't you do both? Hire the best possible people to support the things you want to do. I am here because of how you treated Miss Septima and me. I am here for your humanity if you are willing to share it."

Dr. Longford sat up. "I am definitely willing to share it. And not only that, but I can easily find a like-minded staff if you are willing to pay them. There are more people like me than you know."

"I want a truly diverse staff."

"Done, and you sign off on it when you are satisfied."

Mr. Jimmy offered his hand, and Dr. Longford took it.

"One question though."

"Okay."

"I know you have many billions, but it's still a finite amount of money."

"I see where you are going but not to worry. I am not in this alone. My best friend, Mason, who is also my lawyer is working with my old company. Your clinic will be an investment and a public service. It doesn't have to make huge amounts of money, but I am told we can get to a place where it sustains itself. We are looking to help our fellow citizens. Not make a profit. If I had been able to buy the hospital, I would have made it a part of that plan. I am spending some of my money, of course. I am buying the motel, but it is successful now. No reason that it can't continue to be. I will subsidize it until folks can move into their new homes. I am paying for the homes too."

"That's amazing. It will be quite a shock for them, I think."

"Probably. But I can't wait to see them walk into homes befitting human beings. No one should have to live like they live."

"I saw the neighborhood when I came to your house. I agree. No one should have to live like that."

"I'm glad that we agree and happy that you are willing to put your trust and your career in my hands at this moment."

Dr. Longford offered his hand, and Mr. Jimmy took it.

"When can I start?" Dr. Longford asked.

"When do you want to start?"

"How about two weeks' notice for the hospital, then two weeks of vacation, and then I start helping you plan the facility. I have thought about this for years, and I have some good ideas, I think."

"I trust you do, and that's why I am going to let you lead all of that. My friend Olivia is a former real estate person in this area. She's now working for my new company, and she has her eyes on a couple of pieces of land owned by people not beholden to Welton Knox. We will build it and your dreams from the ground up. In the meantime, you can also plan a staff. Work out a salary with Mason. And one final question. Do you know the man who was mopping up the floor on the day I brought in Miss Septima?"

"Sure. His name is Arthur Thompson. He has a wife, Sarah, and three kids. I can put you in touch."

"No need. I'd like you to hire him. Make him Head of Maintenance at the clinic. And thank you for agreeing to do this for the people."

"No," Dr. Longford said. "Thank you, Mr. Ferguson."

"It's Mr. Jimmy."

It was the last day of school before Christmas vacation. Mr. Jimmy sat in his car, outside of the middle school. To say the building was weathered would be kind. He could see that the foundation was uneven. The windows were old and wooden. The paint was peeling away from them and the door frames. The brick walls needed to be repointed. Yet, there was a weight room with ellipticals across the street, somewhere in the high school. He frowned.

Soon, Ms. Ford appeared at the main entrance, and he got out to meet her. She was excited, and he couldn't help absorbing some of it. She shook his hand and thanked him for coming.

"The kids will be so surprised," she told him.

They passed the school office, turning down a long hall of classrooms.

"Don't I need to check in?" he asked.

"No, I got permission from the principal. She just wanted me to keep it all quiet."

The hallway was dark as much of the overhead lighting was broken. The walls were dingy. It smelled liked mold.

"This is a shame," he said.

Ms. Ford turned to him and nodded. "Can't let that get in my way though," she said.

She sounded like his mother, he thought. He remembered being upset about his middle school as well. At the time he thought it had problems, but it was nothing compared to this school. Still, he had complained about the building, and his mother promptly sat him down for a lecture on focus.

"That school is what we have. Folks are doing their best to maintain it with the funds we have. What you have to understand is this. No brick ever educated a child. So don't you worry about the holes in the wall or the doors that won't shut. You keep your eyes on your teachers and your head in the books. That's what's going to get you where you need to be. It's not about the building."

Ms. Ford had him stand outside the classroom. She went in, pretending that everything was normal. Or maybe she knew that he would stand in a way so as not to be seen by the kids, but with a view into the room. And he would see that while the kids were not troublesome, they were certainly disinterested in anything she had to say. Several kids had their heads on their desks, asleep. Others quietly looked outside as she talked. She walked around the class putting little blue books on their desks. For the most part, they ignored her.

"Okay class," she said after she'd finished passing out the little books. "Today is the last day before our Christmas break. So I have a surprise present for you all."

Mr. Jimmy walked into the classroom. The kids from around the way looked stunned. The kids who didn't know him understood that something special had happened because of the reaction of Juba, Beech, and some other kids who stared at the situation in disbelief. Ms. Ford took her cell phone out of her desk and typed something into the phone.

Mr. Jimmy smiled at Juba and walked to the center of the classroom.

"Some of you know this gentleman," Ms. Ford said to the class. "All of you have had your lives affected by him. I don't have to tell you how. You will understand. It's why I had you write about what was special the first half of your school year. Most of the good things that have happened in this classroom, academically speaking, were because of him. For those of you who don't know, this is Mr. Jimmy. The man you have heard about. The man that started teaching from the Bob Books."

All of the kids were now paying strict attention. Many had

smiles on their faces. Mr. Jimmy was looking over the classroom, meeting the eyes of students when the door to the classroom opened. Shanice walked into the room followed by another teacher who held up her phone acknowledging her receipt of Ms. Ford's text. When Shanice saw Mr. Jimmy, she ran to him and hugged him. The room changed in that moment. Everyone felt something. Mr. Jimmy could tell in the set of the kids' faces. Ms. Ford gave him her seat at her desk. She set another chair beside him so Shanice would not have to leave his side. Mr. Jimmy could feel the emotion rising in his chest.

Ms. Ford told Mr. Jimmy about the little blue books on each child's desk. But she had picked one to be read to him because it spoke to why she wanted him to visit the class. She asked Juba to come to the front of the class to read his essay. Juba was not happy about this. His happiness turned quickly to fear.

"It's okay," Ms. Ford said to him. "What you wrote comes from the heart. Mr. Jimmy will understand."

That was an indication that Juba had written something questionable about him. Maybe, Mr. Jimmy thought, Juba had scolded him for abandoning him and the rest of the kids.

When Juba got to the front of the class, the other students clapped for him as if he had been introduced at a speech before a corporate audience.

"That's all you," Ms. Ford mouthed to Mr. Jimmy.

Juba stood frozen after the applause had died down. Ms. Ford gently adjusted his position so that he would speak to the class and to Mr. Jimmy, who otherwise would have been behind Juba.

"Really," Ms. Ford said to Juba. "It's going to be okay. You have to trust me."

Juba looked at Mr. Jimmy, who sat with his arm around Shanice. Mr. Jimmy smiled and nodded. Juba began to address the classroom.

He opened the booklet to the first page and held it up before the class. It was a stick figure of a man standing beside a basic house. Mr. Jimmy noticed that it was an artistic nod to the drawings in the Bob Books. Juba flipped the page and read the title to the class.

The Big Man in the Little House

The man in the little house is Mr. Jimmy. Miss Septima said his name. Beech and I went to his house. He gave us the candy that was his. But we did not think he was real. Not yet. He worked on Miss Septima's house. I worked on it with him. He gave my Mama money. But he was not real. Then, Mr. Jimmy got beat up. It was bad. I saw Mr. Jimmy mess his pants. I saw him crawl. I sat on the porch. I saw Mr. Jimmy cry. He gave my Mama more money for food anyway. He still loved Miss Septima. He carried Shanice all the way home when she got hurt. After these things, I knew Mr. Jimmy was real.

Juba looked down at the floor when he finished. The class was quiet. Shanice looked up at Mr. Jimmy. He knew she was wondering how he would respond to hearing some of his worse moments shared with the class. He understood why Juba had not wanted to read his essay in his presence, but he gave Shanice a squeeze and smile. He got up and walked over to Juba. He took hold of his shoulders and leaned to the side a little, to try to meet Juba's eyes. Juba gradually looked up to him. Mr. Jimmy gave him a hug and held onto it. The classroom erupted in applause. Beech came up for his hug and handed Mr. Jimmy his blue book. Rube followed and gave Mr. Jimmy his book as well.

"I am so happy to be in your classroom today. When we started reading at my house, I had no idea that you could be so bold with your words so soon. Juba wrote with heart and with passion. I felt it, and I know that you did. Some of the things he wrote about, I am ashamed of. I feel badly that they happened to me. But I am most, and I mean most proud of being declared real. I think it will be my best Christmas present this year. Juba, I think you will write a very fine memoir one day. That's a story that you write about your life. I thank you all for welcoming me."

"It's pizza time," Ms. Ford shouted. "Let's celebrate your hard work."

The kids cheered. Ms. Ford came over to Mr. Jimmy.

"May I give you a hug?" she asked.

"I would be honored."

TWENTY-FIVE

Mr. Jimmy stood looking in the bathroom mirror. The sun was setting on Christmas day, and he was getting ready for dinner at Miss Septima's. He woke early, as he had since he was old enough to believe in Santa Claus, even though he knew the morning would find him alone and greet him with silence. It was the second Christmas without his family. But at least for this one, there were presents to be opened from his parents, Mason, Katherine and Lillian, and the entire Carol family. He felt badly because he hadn't thought to give anything to Olivia, although she reminded him that he had given her one hundred sixty thousand reasons to be happy over the holidays. They had shared a good laugh.

He had paid for Christmas dinners at all 22 homes around the way. So he felt good about families having full meals and even some toys for the kids if they used their money wisely. This at least kept his spirits up, and he kept reminding himself of that after the joy of opening his presents had dissipated and the loss of Rebecca had seeped into and through the cracks in the partition in his heart.

On their first Christmas as a married couple, both sets of parents vied for a visit from the newlyweds. But they chose to stay at home, creating holiday traditions of their own. When Katherine was born, they invited both sets of grandparents to visit with them on any Christmas, because they would never be traveling for the holiday. Their new daughter and any kids to follow would attach all of the love and joy associated with Christmas with their family home. The one that Rebecca had recently sold. Because of him, those traditions had died hard.

He flipped up the collar of his freshly starched dress shirt. He buttoned the top button and placed his tie around his neck. He tied it, thinking how appropriate that he wear his favorite suit to Miss Septima's. She had fought so hard to get him to relent and come to her house for dinner that he thought she deserved his best appearance. He slipped the knot up to his neck and adjusted the fit for comfort. Then, he turned out the light, left the house, and began his walk.

Down the row of homes, all was quiet. In the darkness, with the soft glow of the interior lights, the homes looked like those of a normal neighborhood. With the ragged exteriors hidden, the houses appeared whole and safe. He hoped the kids had experienced a beautiful day. If so, it would have been a wonderful culmination of one celebration after another since school had closed for the holidays.

After his visit to class, he had invited the kids and families to his house again. Luckily for him, the weather was mild for late December, so they spilled out of his home into his front yard. They drank hot cider. They ate pizza night after night. At one point, Mr. Jimmy had had enough. So he rented two buses and took everyone who wanted to go to Five Guys.

"Five Guys?" Olivia questioned, with laughter, during a phone call.

"The children were happy," he replied.

On nights at his house, they played games that he'd shipped in overnight. They watched some of his favorite childhood Christmas shows. *A Charlie Brown Christmas, Rudolph the Red Nose Reindeer, How the Grinch Stole Christmas,* and *Frosty the Snowman.* He tried to give them his best, and they had responded in kind. Even the weight of Rebecca's loss had taken a back seat to their thanks and their joy.

When he walked into the door of her house, he was surprised to see Miss Septima's three friends from the Missionary Circle. He had expected it to be just the two of them.

"I can see it in your eyes," Miss Septima said. "This is tradition, now. Since our men went on to glory, we get together for Christmas. We never use my house though," she said as she took his arm and led him to the kitchen. "Because it's the worse house. It's cold. Juba over here half of Christmas Eve stuffing rags in my holey walls. Cause I wanted you to come to my house. Fountain got the space heater for us."

Like the view of the houses from outside, her interior looked better at night, with just lamps around the table. He had not paid a lot of attention to her kitchen, the tiny room off the back of her tiny house. He smiled when he saw the signature picture wall that was in the home of many Black people in the South. Three pictures, all in a row. Martin Luther King, Jr., Jesus Christ, and John F. Kennedy.

The Missionary Circle women were smiling at him and winking at each other as he unbuttoned his suit coat and took a seat. All of them, with their thin silver hair. The three friends with narrow faces and wide smiles, dressed in their Sunday best. They all wore glasses, the frames well-worn and a bit misshapen. They wore their imitation pearl earrings and necklaces. They wore their good natures. He was surprised that they didn't have on their Easter hats.

"Ooooooh, Mr. Jimmy. Septima is right. You sho'nuff is a fine looking young man."

Mr. Jimmy smiled awkwardly.

"Yes, indeed," she continued, looking to the other women. "If I won't so old and dried up, I'd have me some of that."

The other women nodded agreeably.

Mr. Jimmy was stunned. He couldn't believe this woman, who had to be in her late 80s or early 90s, said that.

"I'm shocked," he said. "I thought you were all churchgoing women."

"Oh, we all Christians here," one of the other women said. "We just know how to find the Holy Ghost in everything we do."

Mr. Jimmy could only smile and shake his head. The women laughed boldly. Miss Septima took a moment after the amusement to introduce her friends by name. There was Miss Frances, Miss DiDee, and Miss Mae Rose. He reached across the table and shook each of their hands, and Miss Frances offered a wink after he shook hers.

They began to make comfortable small talk. They chatted about the weather and if the Reverend was speaking at church the next Sunday or were they having a substitute. Miss Frances did not like substitute preachers and spoke to that fact with great passion. The others chuckled at her being so bothered. Then, the ladies were interested to hear more about how he got the kids to want to learn. Miss Septima busied herself taking the meal out of plastic bags and placing the plastic plates full of food on the table. Mr. Jimmy asked if he could help, and she told him to move the turkey to the table. As he did that and took his seat again, he saw that the center piece was made up of artificial flowers. Also on the table was the bucket of buttons that he'd knocked over while trying to lift her on the day he took her to the hospital. He wondered why it was taking up room where some food should be.

When Miss Septima was through transferring, she took her seat and they looked at the food, admiring the dishes. It was a homemade abundance of southern soul food. Turkey with gravy and dressing. Candied yams, collard greens, and string beans, seasoned with country ham. A small dish of homemade mac and cheese. Sweet potato casserole, small plate of seasoned cabbage especially for Miss Septima, and warm dinner rolls. They made iced tea especially for him.

"Ain't this something?" she asked.

"It's a good-looking spread for sure," Miss DiDee said.

"We'll never eat all of this, you know," Mr. Jimmy said.

"Child, there is dessert too!"

They laughed.

"No need to worry," Miss Septima said. "You take some home and folks round here will finish it up. We don't normally eat this good around the way no more."

They asked Mr. Jimmy to say the blessing and he repeated his father's words from his childhood. Amens followed around the table.

"You worked hard on this," Mr. Jimmy said to Miss Septima. "Did Fountain bring all of this from the church for you?"

"Yes, he did. But I didn't make none of this, child. No sireee. Patrice made everything for us."

"I didn't know she could cook like this."

"That girl can make a tire taste like your Mama's best meat-loaf. Her food'll make you praise the Lord every time you take a bite, honey. I kid you not. Just like her mother, she is," Miss Mae Rose replied.

"Where is her mother?" Mr. Jimmy asked.

"Child, who knows?" Miss DiDee answered. "That woman took a life's worth of beatings from her man. I reckon, Patrice was round seventeen when her mother up and left that situation. Father died in jail and left Patrice in the house. She had a hard life, that girl."

"Ummmm," Miss Frances said, after taking a bite of her dinner roll. "This is so good. And we gone talk tonight, Mr. Jimmy. You gone see that a lot folks from around the way just didn't have the heart to keep on living. There's some things that have happened on this lane, child."

"But first things first," Miss Septima said. "We gotta deal with you first."

"In what way," Mr. Jimmy said.

"We want you to tell us your story, son," Miss Frances said. "Septima thinks you need to get some stuff off your chest."

He looked at Miss Septima and offered a soft smile. She had taken it upon herself to act as his psychiatrist and created a group therapy session. He didn't know these three women who, along with Miss Septima, were now quietly and expectantly gazing at him. He believed that Miss Septima wanted to help him, and he fondly remembered the wisdom of the old folks from his hometown. He figured that it couldn't hurt. After all, everything was already out in the open.

"Okay," he said, slowly nodding. "I don't see that it can do much more damage to my reputation."

So they ate, and he talked. Often, they would tell him to catch up on his plate, and he would stop talking and eat something. Their faces softened, and they smiled when he spoke of his love for Rebecca. He explained that she had been everything to him. He told them some of his favorite stories about her. He told them about her special smile. He explained their issue and their year of emotional struggle. He even explained what he did to himself in the darkness of his basement office as he grew angrier and angrier. He explained that ultimately, he had been tremendously foolish and had made a supremely bad choice. He explained that he was still paying for it and that, in his heart, he believed he would never be free of it. It lived within him and followed him online and in the press. Maybe it had left his reputation permanently stained. Certainly, it left him crawling out of long periods of seemingly inconsolable despair.

When he was finished, true sorrow and regret lingered in his eyes. He looked down to find one of Miss Septima's hands resting on top of his. She looked at him with warmth and great tenderness.

"Thank you for your truth, Mr. Jimmy," Miss Frances said. "All of it will stay in our hearts. Nobody will hear nothing from us. But any time you need to talk, we will be here for you. Old as we is, one of us might drop off on any day. Tonight, we make sure that all of us will know what's what so that somebody can be here for you."

"Thank you," Mr. Jimmy said, sincerely.

"But, I'm gone lighten this up," Miss Frances continued. "'Cause there are some things about your lifestyle that we gotta know. Only way we gone know what it is to be rich."

"Whatever you want to know," Mr. Jimmy said.

"Me first," Miss Septima said. "You have a big house?"

Mr. Jimmy took out his phone and showed them pictures.

"Lord, have mercy. That's something," Miss DiDee said.

"How many cleaning women you have?" Miss Mae Rose asked.

"None," Mr. Jimmy answered. "We did it ourselves."

"Boy, you gone sit there and tell us you a billionaire and you cleaned your own toilet." Miss Frances replied in disbelief.

"Rebecca and I did. You see, we both had family members who cleaned houses for a number of White families. We remembered that it wasn't something they were proud of. They took that work out of necessity because society didn't provide many alternatives. We remembered them talking about those families. We remembered their faces as they talked about cleaning up somebody else's shit. Excuse my French, but it is what they said. A lot of the times they were angry. The rest of the time sad about what they did."

"Yes, Lord," Miss Frances said.

"I can even remember some of the White families saying that my great-aunts and aunts were like family to them. They said it proudly. But is that all you offer a family member? Poor pay to clean your toilet and, in many cases, raise your kids. The White people never knew what our aunts said to us about them. Rebecca and I knew that we might be taking work off the table for someone, but we could not be like the White folks. So we cleaned our own house."

"Did you have a driver?" Miss Septima said.

"No and pretty much for the same reason. I did have the same driver as much as possible when I was in Washington, DC, but he was private contractor. He has his own business that I felt I was helping to support. And the business itself didn't degrade him."

"Let me see your girl," Miss DiDee said.

Mr. Jimmy pulled up his best picture of Rebecca and passed the phone around the table.

"My, my, my," Miss Frances said. "Girl hold herself like a queen, I do say."

"I never needed to see her picture," Miss Septima said. "I could see what she was in your face. Yes indeed, I could all this time."

"We are sorry for what you lost," Miss Mae Rose said.

The other ladies offered more amens as their support.

"Look here now," Miss Septima said, and Mr. Jimmy turned to her. "Now we know the sins you come here to get away from. And let us say, child, you ain't the first one to make a mistake. No matter how bad. But listen. You see all the biggies in the Bible, from Adam to Moses to the Apostle Peter and them in between. All of them failed the Lawd and their own selves. But in the end, they wind up sitting right next to the throne of the Lawd. Cause he know who they really were. We can see who you are. The truth is, Mr. Jimmy, we knew everything when you came in that door. Word about you all over Ham. And just because we ain't got no computers don't mean all Black folk don't. People found out this stuff, and we heard it too. But we wanted you to open up to us so we can be here for you, like we said. We want to help you get back to you because the other thing we learned is that you was such a good man. You helped so many people and didn't ask for nothing back. You doing the same thing here, and there just ain't so many like you. When it is all said and done, I believe my Jesus will see you like we see you."

"Yeah, child. I do agree," Miss Frances said. "You got a good heart in you for sure. How did you come by it?"

"My heart?"

"Yes, your heart?"

"Oh, I am sure it's my parents," Mr. Jimmy replied. "They believed that the Holy Grail was not some cup that Jesus drank out of, gold or otherwise. They believe that the Holy Grail was a gift to your fellow human being, asking for nothing in return. Inside that deed was the greatest description of what it meant to be a good person. Inside that deed was the closest you got to God and the best way to make the world a better place."

The women smiled.

"I think we getting what we came for tonight. All of us," Miss Septima said.

"No, not everybody. Not yet anyway," Mr. Jimmy said. "There are things I need to know as well. About you, Miss Septima. About my neighborhood."

The ladies looked at each other and nodded. Miss Septima got up and went to a cabinet. She gently opened the crooked door to keep it from falling off. She pulled out a bottle of whiskey.

"This is quite a leap from iced tea," Mr. Jimmy said.

"I keep it for the winter. I take a nip or two before I get to bed. Well, all right, a glass or two. Enough to help me pretend that I'm warm."

"What are we going to pretend right now?"

"Nothing, baby. We just gone take the edge off the real. Pass me the bucket of buttons now," she said to Mr. Jimmy when she sat down. "In here. These buttons. They tell my life and the story of the people on this dirt road to nowhere. All of the buttons have a story. They belong to family and friends. And some just belong to people who passed through, and this is how I remember them. Over the years, the children. They play with them. Use them for checkers and such, not knowing that they jumping the great-aunt that watched her child be hung. Or the great, great-uncle coming out of slavery that had seen so much hard labor that when he come to freedom and found himself sharecropping in the same old field, he just lay down and died. They some good stories in there too. Like my grandmama, Tilly, who had a love as big as the sky. I ain't never felt nothing like it. When I touch the button I took off her housecoat, the love comes over me such that I have to sit down and cry for joy. Her button is in here. Ain't no games played with it either."

She held up a little drawstring bag that had been resting on top of the buttons. Her hands started to shake as she tried to open it. Her eyes welled, and she took a deep breath to calm herself.

"It's all right, girl," Miss DiDee said. "Take it slow now."

"In this bag," Miss Septima said, "I keep my most important buttons. The people that mean the most, bad, and good. She pulled out one. This is Tilly's. The one from her housecoat. This one is hers too. I took it from her dress just before they took it to the undertaker. I don't think she woulda minded. This one, big and black. It was my granddaddy's. He came out of slavery too with them big dreams but ended up like everybody else, sharecropping. It was all they knew. Now this one, the faded blue. This from my daddy's overalls. He dreamed too. But like his daddy, he got so in debt to the man, look like a thousand years his family be trying to pay it back. He went hunting one day. Somebody heard a shot echo. It was deer season, but that wasn't no deer. It was him. Blowed his damn head off. Mama and me had to get down hard in them damn fields to stay in this house. Don't, the man would have kicked us out. I married Ad Ruffin, and we had a boy. All of us worked the fields. My boy grew up and got hitched. Had a daughter. She got pregnant and had Fountain. Then she married the father who gave Fountain his name."

Miss Septima paused for a moment and took a drink of whiskey. Seeing the sudden tiredness in her friend's eyes, Miss Mae Rose reached over and rubbed her back.

"I'm sorry, Miss Septima," Mr. Jimmy said. "Here I am complaining and feeling sorry for myself. It's nothing compared to what you speak of. I don't know how you made it through those times. I don't know how you seem so strong today. I don't know how you keep going."

"Son," she replied. "I just wake up and take inventory. Do I have air pressure, blood pressure and water pressure? If I got all of that, I walk step by step into whatever the new day brings, and I try to drop that day off in my sleep so I can wake up clean the next day and do it again. Check that air pressure, blood pressure, and water pressure. Then I'm good to go again until the day the good Lawd takes me."

Mr. Jimmy nodded as he tried to remember her recipe for getting through each day. The Missionary Circle ladies looked concerned.

"You ain't got to go no further tonight," Miss Mae Rose said, seeking to stop Miss Septima's growing sadness. "Let's just say that from then on, life happened."

Miss Septima nodded. "I just say I outlived everyone but Fountain for reasons I won't speak on tonight, but I will say later for you. In what years I got left. You won't be surprised. Just folks that could not rise above, you know? They all got buried with artificial flowers on their graves."

"Let's all take a drink and have some dessert," Miss Frances said.

Mr. Jimmy asked the ladies to stay in their seats. He cleared the table and set the desserts out on the table. Patrice had outdone herself again. He placed an apple spice cake and a lemon meringue pie on the table. He cut everyone a slice of each before taking a seat.

"Would you have the energy to tell me more about Patrice?" he asked the group.

Again, the women all looked to each other. They took bites of their desserts with their heads down, quietly considering his request. They all drank some whiskey.

"I can tell you this," Miss Frances said. "I remember a time that girl could talk. As good as anybody sitting at this table."

Mr. Jimmy was surprised to hear that.

"Uh huh," Miss DiDee said. "She telling you the truth."

"What happened?" Mr. Jimmy asked.

"Just like her mama, only worse. She got used and abused, child," Miss DiDee said, slowly shaking her head.

Miss Septima started to speak, but Miss Mae Rose gently cut her off. "You have had enough trouble to speak about on this Christmas, let me tell this story."

Miss Septima nodded.

"Goes like this," Miss Mae Rose said. "Just remember all the people around the way, they so poor. All the family that come before them just the same. It's Mississippi, you know? Ain't nobody to speak up for poor Black folks. When the kids are young and just getting a feel for what they don't have and they see what other folks do have, they start dreaming. They tell the old folks that they going to be different. They tell the old folks that they gone grow up and make a lot of money and they gone take care of us. Generations of young folks been saying that. None of it come to pass. People ain't even got a bank account. No reason. Ain't nobody got enough money.

"But let me tell you about Patrice. She was as sweet as this cake she baked. And pretty too. Her husband knocked out her teeth because she was complaining that she was hungry. Both of them working all day long, sharecropping just to keep up with the bills. Never getting ahead. He got some bad ideas in his head, he did. Somehow, he talked that child into giving up her body to get money to pay the rent. All these men having their way. No telling what they did to that poor girl in the wee hours. She didn't stutter one bit before all of that started happening and them babies started showing up. Nobody know who their daddies are. Some of these neighbors know what was going down. People say her husband gave them a piece of change now and then to shut up. When Patrice's brother found out what was going down was when everybody found out. He went after the husband, but that fool had skipped town. Then, not too long after that her brother showed up dead. Found his body over yonder, cross the road in the field you tried to buy. He was shot dead, they said, but his body was beat up something bad. Now she ain't got no family but them children.

"Anyway, Patrice got back on her back. Girl had to make some money, or she was gone lose her house. Finally, after way too much time, we had a meeting at church. We couldn't let this mess carry on. Nobody know what the children know or what they seen. Folks say she sent them out to friends' houses on the nights she made her money. Well, Mr. Jimmy, she won't the only one struggling. All of us was. Miss Septima got a piece of money from the government, but that won't nearly enough. So you know the only Black group that can get a loan around here is the church. So the church did that and bought all the houses around the way. Yeah, the church own all these houses. That's why the church look a mess. Near about falling down now. And that's why we driving around in that beat up, rusty van. The church is barely keeping above water, but we had to do what was needed. The Missionary Circle came up with the idea. You see, we responsible for getting Patrice off her back, but we also put the church in trouble. It's all a mess."

Miss Mae Rose took her paper napkin and wiped her face of both tears and sweat. Mr. Jimmy took her hand.

"I am so sorry to hear all of this," he said. "But let me tell you that I can do what generations of dreaming children could not. I have a plan to help fix some of these problems, and I can help the church too if you all will let me."

"What is the plan?" Miss DiDee asked.

"Well, wait a minute now," Miss Septima said. "Just so we don't get things wrong, why don't you come to church on Sunday and tell everybody the plan. Let everybody hear it from the horse's mouth. Will that work?"

"If that's what you want, Miss Septima."

"It is."

"Then, that's how it will be."

They all milled around the kitchen, packing up the food and putting the trash away. Mr. Jimmy said he would pick up the trash in the morning. Because they had stayed so late, the church van was no longer available to them, so Mr. Jimmy drove Miss Septima's friends home in his BMW, which they all appreciated. Miss Frances had him blow the horn so that everyone in the nearby houses would come outside to witness her being assisted out of the beautiful car and escorted to her door by a handsome man in a suit.

When he was back around the way, he parked his car in front of Miss Septima's. He had forgotten his portion of the desserts and he felt like some pie with his wine. He quietly let himself in. He used the light on his phone to get to the kitchen, and as he picked up the plate wrapped in aluminum foil, she called to him.

"I hear you in there," she said.

Mr. Jimmy smiled and walked to her bedroom.

"May I come in," he asked.

"Yes, you can."

She lay on her back, and he turned the phone's light away so that it wouldn't hurt her eyes but would still allow him to see her.

"Came to give your best girl a kiss goodnight?"

"Yes, I did."

"Ha! You men telling them lies. I know you came back for the food."

They both laughed.

"Thank you for tonight," he said. "I feel more attached to you and to everything after our conversations."

She nodded and smiled.

"There was one thing still on my mind though, if you don't mind."

She leaned over and turned on the lamp by her bed. It was a child's lamp, the base chipped and cracked, covered in faded, little Thomas the Tank Engine illustrations.

"Ummmm," she said. "The flowers?"

"Yes, ma'am. You read my mind."

"I saw it on your face at the table. What do you need to know?"

"When I met you, you said that the only thing you were afraid of was artificial flowers on your grave. Tonight, you told me about your ancestors, who were buried with those flowers on their graves. What is it about your people's predicaments and the fake flowers?"

"Artificial flowers was the first flowers I can remember paying any attention to. It was easier than growing real flowers. Ain't nobody have time for that after being in them fields all day. So we went to the cheap stores and got the fake flowers. When people died, we put them on the graves. They stayed there until they got disgusting looking. I used to look at the situation and try to figure out what I was feeling about it, you know? When the babies were born, people put artificial flowers by the boxes that the babies was in. Babies grow up and die. People put them same looking flowers on the grave. And I started to think that the flowers represent the whole life, you know? Round here, you get them when you born, and they mark your forever resting place. The flowers show that there ain't no change in your life. You ain't been nowhere, and you really ain't grown as a person.

"Sometimes, I get so scared, even though I know my Jesus in my heart. Sometimes I get afraid that maybe there ain't really no heaven. That all there is is black after you die. And I get to thinking that I had one chance at this life. I got one chance to get out of this kind of life. To see something else. To do something else. What if I can just do something that means something? You know we just so tired living, we ain't got the energy to make a difference. My house is damn musty. Got these torn up walls. It's beat up like me and my life. If I die and they put artificial flowers on my grave, it will be the stamp on my life that says, I stayed in the same place, lived the same poor life, never did nothing. Never was nobody. I am afraid of my one chance at life ending up in a big nothing. Them flowers on my grave will say that."

Mr. Jimmy thought, *What can I say to that?* He looked at her and offered a smile, which she returned. He leaned over and kissed her on the forehead, and she patted his cheek.

"Do something for me before you leave."

"Of course."

"Go in the kitchen and bring me the button bucket."

Mr. Jimmy found the bucket. He carefully carried it to her, setting it beside her on the bed. She was sitting up with a pair of fingernail scissors in her hand. She patted the bed beside her. When he sat down, she reached for his suit coat. She took one of its buttons in her hand, and she looked at him. He smiled and nodded. She cut the button from his coat. She opened the drawstring bag and put his button inside. She pulled the drawstring closed, shook the bag, and placed it back in the bucket.

"There now," she said. "You see what you mean."

He slowly nodded. "I love you, Miss Septima."

"I know you do, baby. I have grown to love you too."

He turned out her light and tucked her in. He left the button bucket on the kitchen table, picked up his pie, and closed the front door softly behind him.

2O18

Ham, Mississippi

TWENTY-SIX

Mr. Jimmy zipped up his winter coat and put on his hat. He felt like a good long walk. He'd been taking lots of them during the holidays. He had become such a fixture along the dirt road, folks around the way stopped taking notice as he strolled by. He liked it that way. A smile and a nod here and there, but mostly he was allowed the freedom to just walk and breathe in the crisp winter air. Just after the New Year, his celebrity had grown and to his mind, had gotten in the way of him living the simple moments of life.

As he stepped down off the porch and turned toward the houses, he thought he would walk past them, almost into town. About four miles in total. As he got started, he noticed that there wasn't one speck of blue in the sky. Just the kind of grayness that made a person feel colder than the air around him. He so disliked the dark days of winter. On this day, even the clouds were gray, and they inspired in him a deep feeling of foreboding. Looking back, he should have taken the sky at its word and prepared himself. But there was no way he could have ever imagined what was to come.

Just after the New Year, he had honored Miss Septima's wish, and had gone to Christ Our Lord's Church. Most of the congregation did not live around the way, but they had sacrificed so much to help the residents there. He wanted to give them all some hope for the new year.

When the sermon was over, the minister welcomed him to the pulpit. Mr. Jimmy looked out over the sanctuary, trying to get a feel for what people might be thinking about him. When his eyes met Miss Septima's, she smiled and nodded. She gave him permission.

I am here today because I believe in all of you. Especially, the children. And because Miss Septima told me to be here. When I was a boy, the grown-ups used to say that they wanted better lives for their children. The generation to come should do better than the one before it. I grew up believing that, and luckily for me, it played out that way. I would like to give your children the same kind of chances. Those chances began with the ability to read. My thinking is that childhood literacy is supremely important. I don't believe that any Black child in this country can succeed without being at least proficient at reading. Of course, I know it won't and can't solve everything. But it is a fundamental building block. I know that it's responsible for me standing before you today. Yes, the world is unfair. Yes, your government, federal, state, and local have failed your children. Many people feel there still isn't equal education here in Mississippi today. The Southern Poverty Law Center has filed a lawsuit against the state because it does not give your children the same educational start it provides for other children. But we do not have to wait for lawsuits to play out. We do not have to wait for the government to come to our aid even though they should. We can get up each morning and step up to the task of helping ourselves. Because to do anything less leaves our children at risk of failing to experience the best life has to offer them. I know that this is not as easy as it sounds. I know that some of you are single parents with a couple of jobs. For others, there are different struggles, and reading can't always be your priority. This is why I would like to establish a reading committee in the church. I would like to be on this committee. You have already shown the power of a church when you bought the homes around the way. You saved a community. Now let's be a village and save the children. Every time a child is born in this church community, the committee will meet with the parents and offer to read to the child. So that no day goes by without the child being read to several times. And this continues until the child can read for him- or herself. You will be amazed how much better your children will do in school. How much less they will need you academically. For those who are planning to have children and have trouble reading, well, many of you know Ms. Ford from school. She's here today. There, she's raising her hand. She's a great teacher, and she's going to start a reading class for adults. Learn to read so that you can give the gift to your children. In the summer, she and I will continue to work with the kids. I am happy to say that she will return next year as a teacher. We all need to be her support so that she can help guide others in the care of our children. But it cannot just be Ms. Ford. We have to be that village. This is just a start. A way to get the church community in position to help give its children a better beginning. Secondly, I have big news for the church. I am going to pay off the debt you incurred in order to save the homes of my neighbors from around the way. I will pay to make repairs to the church building. I will buy four new church vans. As far as my neighbors around the way, if you are willing, here is a dream I have had for you since I took my first walk through the neighborhood. I have purchased the Wayside Motel. I want to move all of you into motel rooms. It will be tight, no doubt, but everyone will have running water, electricity, heat, air-conditioning, and bathrooms. All the things so many folks take for granted. When you move in, we will tear down the homes you have now. And those homes will be replaced by beau- tiful prefab homes. On the way out of the church, there are brochures with many different types of homes. Twenty-two are already under construction. I hope you don't mind that I planned on you saying yes to my proposal. I hope you won't mind that I have assigned homes, in terms of styles to each family. If you get together with another family and switch, that's fine. We hope to move you into the new homes just before the kids go to school next year. In the meantime, you will all live together in the motel. I have also purchased three vans that can take the kids to school and deliver folks to work if need be. Fountain has said that he will drive some and will look for others who would like to help. You will be paid. I wanted to be able to tell you that I had bought the land across from the houses. Fountain and I wanted to start a farm. We would grow crops that would serve restaurant groups that my company owns. I had envisioned a company right here in Ham that could grow with and support the community, putting a lot of folks to work in good paying jobs with health care. I had even planned a park just across the road from the new houses. But I made a bad mistake, and now I can't buy the land. They won't sell it to me. I am truly sorry about that. So this is what I came to tell you this Sunday morning.

As first there was quiet in the church, and Mr. Jimmy scanned his audience for a reaction. Would they find his plan helpful, or would they resent him for looking down on them as some poor incapable souls who could not make a life for themselves without his money and his time? He felt it could go either way. Patiently, he waited. Soon, he began to see people wiping their eyes. He began to see others, closing their eyes and tilting their heads upward, quietly sending up prayers. Miss Septima got out of her pew and began to walk to the front of the church. Miss Frances walked beside her. Others began to follow them. When she stopped, Mr. Jimmy understood that he was to meet her halfway, so he stepped down from the pulpit and walked over to her, the minister following. She looked up at Mr. Jimmy and smiled as others gathered around them. She opened his coat jacket, stepped closer to him. She leaned in, gently kissing his heart. As she pulled back from him, she patted him there. Her eyes were overflowing. The rest of the congregation stood.

One might have expected them to break into song, but they did not. They just stood in recognition of the moment. Mr. Jimmy understood that when those close to him began to reach out to touch him, he was about to receive the traditional laying on of the hands. They put their hands on his back, his shoulders, his chest, his head, and about his neck. They began to hum a spiritual, and above that moving sound, the minister began to pray. He walked out of the church a new and favored son of the community. He could not go anywhere without receiving hugs and prayers. But now that part was thankfully over. He and his team were quietly changing their lives while they allowed him to walk in peace.

In the distance, he could see that Juba was sitting, legs crossed, at the ditch bordering his yard. He was rocking back and forth. As Mr. Jimmy got closer, he recognized that Juba was only in a shirt in the cold weather. As he got closer still, he recognized that Juba was in great emotional pain because the boy's cries were the screams of enormous loss. Mr. Jimmy began to run. He ran hard and as fast as he could, like his father had run to him before the tornado. When he reached Juba, he knelt before him. Juba's eyes were lost in pools of tears. His nose was running, over his lip and into his mouth, still open, still making those deep and painful cries. At first, he didn't see that Mr. Jimmy had arrived. Mr. Jimmy looked around and saw Juba's siblings standing in their front doorway. He pulled his shirttails out and used them to wipe Juba's face. He then cupped his face in his hands and forced Juba to look at him and to take some solace in the fact that he was there to take care of him. But Juba screamed on until his little body, wracked with grief for something, could make no more sounds. He just hiccoughed as if he was about to throw up. Mr. Jimmy leaned over and began to hug him. Soon, he recognized that Juba had a metal box in his lap. Mr. Jimmy slowly took it away from him and opened it. It took his breath away and made him fall backward onto his rear. He looked back at Juba and immediately understood his pain.

The metal box was home to old pictures. Lots of them. And each one was a record of Juba's mother, Patrice, being raped by men. Many men. The pictures had to represent some kind of sick sex parties for the men, because she was not happy or safe. *Just sick,* he thought. All of these men and Patrice, nude in some pictures and partially clothed in others. Every sex act you could imagine was represented. Juba saw his mother, completely helpless, being abused by these men. And he had been devastated to his core. Mr. Jimmy had not seen Fountain arrive or recognized that Miss Septima was making her way to them. When she arrived, he was hugging Juba and telling him that he was loved and that he, Mr. Jimmy, would not leave him. He handed the metal box to Fountain. He opened it for himself and Miss Septima.

"I'll be goddamned," Fountain said. "This is some shit. Where is you mama?"

Juba still couldn't speak but he turned his head and far down the road toward town was a speck of a person.

"I'll get the truck and go get her," Fountain said, before running off.

As Fountain drove by them, Miss Septima handed the box back to Mr. Jimmy.

"I will take Patrice when he gets her back. We can get other folks to take in the children for a bit."

"Okay," Mr. Jimmy said, still hugging Juba. "I'll take Juba home with me."

Minutes later, Fountain returned. He parked the truck in front of Patrice's house and helped her out. They directed him to Miss Septima's house and Mr. Jimmy stood to see her pass by, escorted by Fountain. She was somewhere else in her mind. She was catatonic. Mr. Jimmy felt a wave of sadness roll over him, and he shook his head in despair. He put Juba in the truck and put the box of pictures on his lap as he drove the two of them to his house.

The grayness was now giving way to darkness in the sky and in their hearts. Mr. Jimmy had no idea what he should do in the moment. He sat Juba in the Barcalounger, and he called Dr. Longford.

"I know you're not a psychiatrist," he said, after explaining what had happened. "But maybe you can find someone for this family. They have to have some help if they are to survive, don't you think?"

"I am so sad to hear about this situation. It's horrible," Dr. Longford said. "I have contacts. Let me reach out. In the meantime, just love him the best way you know how."

Mr. Jimmy turned to look at Juba, now quiet and staring into space. How do you console a child who has now seen men at their worst? How do you console a child who now has visions of his mother that no child should carry? He will never be able to unsee them. *What can I do or say to begin to assuage this kind of pain?*

Mr. Jimmy sat at his table and looked back at Juba as the fullness of night took over. The boy was now like his mother, catatonic. Mr. Jimmy was now afraid. Could Juba be lost inside his mind or, rather, outside of it somewhere? He flipped on the light next to his table. Juba didn't react, but a glance around the room gave Mr. Jimmy an idea. He went to his tablet and downloaded sounds of the ocean and made a playlist in his iTunes account. He hooked his tablet to his sound system via Bluetooth. He turned off the light next to the table and turned on the lights Yankee had especially installed for the mural. He adjusted those lights as best he could to mimic the gloaming, his favorite time of day at the beach. He picked Juba up and laid him on the floor in front of the ocean mural. He sat down and pulled Juba up into his lap and against his chest. He turned on the ocean sounds, and for a while they sat like that. He asked Juba to look at the mural.

"Try to block everything out except the ocean and its sounds."

They sat like that for some time until Mr. Jimmy thought that Juba had actually moved a bit away from his pain and into the moment.

"I have never had to feel what you are feeling inside right now," Mr. Jimmy said. "But I have also suffered loss and felt great pain. When I was a boy, as you know, my family used to go to the beach. To the ocean. And I used it to get away from my pain. I want to show you how I did it. So take a deep, deep breath for me. Now, let it all out. Now let the sounds of the ocean replace everything in your head. See the ocean and let it be the only thing you see right now. Just breathe, Juba. Just breathe."

Then he asked Juba to sit beside him and to stretch out his arms. Mr. Jimmy did the same.

"So you stretch out your arms, close your eyes, and lay back your head and feel yourself becoming so light that you roll in and out with the waves. You do not care in this moment about anything except the ocean. You keep your arms out, and now you are floating. The waves come one at a time. They roll in and flatten out on the beach, they take sand, shells, and your pain away, back out to sea. Over and over, they do that for you. When I was a boy, sometimes the freedom in the sounds of the ocean was so great that I just had to scream. And after each scream, I would just get lighter and lighter."

For some time, the sound of oceans crashed against the mural. Soon Juba's chest began to rise and fall. First slowly, then growing more rapid until finally, he began to yell. And then he began to scream at the top of his lungs. Mr. Jimmy dropped his arms and got behind Juba, cradling him as the screams continued. Mr. Jimmy leaned over and turned up the sound of the waves as high as possible. Juba screamed and screamed and screamed until finally, his body went limp, and his crying became softer and softer. He turned around as best he could and began to hug Mr. Jimmy.

"You go on and cry now," Mr. Jimmy said. "I got you."

TWENTY-SEVEN

That night, Mr. Jimmy put Juba to sleep in his bed. He laid on the floor next to him until he fell asleep, and for a time afterward as Juba thrashed about and shouted in his sleep. Eventually, Mr. Jimmy left him for a full glass of wine. He fell asleep in the lounge chair and woke up to the rising sun. Juba would sleep for fourteen hours.

In the late morning, Fountain and Miss Septima arrived. They left Patrice, also still asleep, in the care of Bess. They had pieced together the events of the previous afternoon. Juba had worked on Miss Septima's house to get it ready for her Christmas dinner. He stuffed holes with cloth, but he also ripped out some boards and replaced them with wood that he had gathered. He had been proud of his carpentry skills. So much so that he started doing the same thing in his house. Patrice had mentioned to Bess that he had been doing a fine job. Even after they knew that Mr. Jimmy was going to give everyone new houses, he kept at work.

"Might as well be warm as can be until it happens," he had said.

So he ripped out boards and he replaced them. Fountain helped him get more wood and nails. Fountain thought he was becoming quite the little man.

The day before, he was ripping out a part of the floor in his and his siblings' bedroom. It had become sunken and was rotting in some places. For some time, Juba was afraid his siblings would step into it, break through the boards, and hurt themselves. When he ripped out the broken boards, he found the metal box. Juba opened it and his world came undone. He showed it to Patrice, who started to cry and to walk away. Juba followed her, asking her what these pictures were all about. He wanted to know who took them and where they came from. She refused to answer him and ran out of the house. Juba ran after her, but still she refused to discuss it and started running away from him. She yelled at him, trying to order him to stay at home, and that was when he sat down in the dirt and began to cry.

In the days to come, there would be so many more tears. The folks from around the way rallied. They all chipped in their time to take care of the little ones while Juba stayed with Mr. Jimmy and Patrice with Miss Septima.

Mr. Jimmy chose not to ask questions. He knew enough already. He just stayed near Juba, not even speaking unless Juba spoke to him. Often, Juba would walk up to him in tears and hug him, holding on for long periods of time. Often, they would take blankets and sit quietly side by side in the rockers on the porch, drinking hot tea or cider. This went on for days, until one morning Juba woke up needing more.

"Can I see my mama?" he said.

"You don't have to ask for that. She's your mama. If you're ready now, I am sure she is."

They got dressed and walked down to Miss Septima's. She and Patrice were sitting in housecoats and fleece jackets that Mr. Jimmy had given them. When Patrice saw Juba, she looked around quickly, as if she was searching for a place to hide from her son's searching eyes.

"It's okay, Mama," Juba said. "We ain't gotta talk about it."

Patrice, now in quiet tears, nodded. Miss Septima took her hand. Later, they walked outside with the idea of gathering the other children and moving back into their home, but neither Juba nor Patrice could even start up their short dirt path. It was too emotional. Too much pain. What else might be inside that house?

"It's okay," Mr. Jimmy said. "We can just keep doing what we're doing for a while."

Patrice shook her head. "No," she replied. And she worked hard to tell him what she wanted, but eventually had to rely on Juba to let them know that she wanted to be with her children.

"She needs to be with her babies," he said.

Patrice nodded.

"Okay," Mr. Jimmy said, wanting to give her everything she needed, but if they couldn't enter the home, he didn't see how it would work out.

Miss Septima looked to him. "Mr. Jimmy," she said.

"Yes, ma'am."

"I think it might be time for that motel of yours."

It was much earlier than he planned, but that night he and Fountain went house to house to tell everyone about the updated plans. They would move Patrice and family, Miss Septima, and Fountain and family first. Then one house per day until everyone was settled in the Wayside Motel, their new community home.

The Wayside had been empty for about a month, since no one else had been allowed to check in. Fountain and his crew had been cleaning rooms and making repairs. They rented a U-Haul truck and moved the families in. In the excitement of moving into a room with heat and television, the kids were distracted from their pain. Mr. Jimmy had Fountain clean out the kitchen in the diner behind the office so that Patrice and Bess could cook. As they got settled, Fountain and crew began to move other families.

Mr. Jimmy was saddened to sit at his table around the way and look out of the window, knowing that Miss Septima was gone. His walks were now too lonely. At nighttime, on his drive home from a day at the motel, he hated passing the dark, empty houses, and the loss of the daily lives of his friends.

Dr. Longford came through for Mr. Jimmy. He found an African American psychologist to meet with Patrice and her family. She also met with Juba and Patrice together. Mr. Jimmy paid extra to get the therapist to come to them. He gave up his office at the motel for their sessions.

A month had gone by since Juba found the photos. Mr. Jimmy had scanned and saved each one on his computer and on Dropbox so he could access them on his phone. In the days just after the discovery, he had called Olivia and Yankee to fill them in. Now, they stood in his office at the motel with Miss Septima and Fountain.

Mr. Jimmy showed them the pictures on his computer. Mr. Jimmy watched them and imagined the looks they had on their faces to be akin to what Juba had seen on his.

"Oh my God," Olivia said. "This is . . . is . . . I don't know what to say."

"This is inhumane," Yankee said.

"That's putting it mildly," Mr. Jimmy said.

Everyone nodded, and Mr. Jimmy pointed at one of the photos. "Look at that face."

"Well, I'll be damned," Yankee responded as Olivia looked over his shoulder. "It's Crawford Alden."

"The farmer that owns the land around the way?" Miss Septima asked.

"Yes, ma'am," Yankee responded.

"I recognize all of the White men," Olivia said. "Some of them went to my church when I was growing up. Two of them are still teachers at the school Juba goes to."

"And I recognize the Black ones," Fountain said. "Every last one of them. I could kill 'em dead."

"You know," Yankee said. "This is the ticket to getting the farm. I know it's a horrible thing to say in this moment when we should just be caring for Juba and his family, but we can put pressure on Alden and get the farm so that you can create the business and the jobs you want for the community."

"Shouldn't we call the police first?" Olivia asked.

"What will they do for a poor, abused Black girl in Ham, Mississippi?" Miss Septima asked.

"I hear you, ma'am," Olivia replied.

"We will have to tell them at some point," Yankee said. "But think about what I said. Patrice deserves justice. I hate to have her wait one moment more while these men go unchallenged. There would at the very least be the charge of solicitation."

Mr. Jimmy flinched, and everyone saw it, so he thought he might as well say it out loud. "I, unfortunately, have some experience with the threat of solicitation myself. Seems kind of ironic."

"Mr. Jimmy," Yankee said. "This is apples and oranges, really. The woman you were with was a businesswoman. It was an illegal business, but she was in charge of herself and her choices. What happened with Patrice is a solar system away from that. She had no choice in the matter, and what happened to her, well, let's just say it's something beyond your experience."

"Thank you, Yankee," Mr. Jimmy said. "And I do agree with your thoughts on the matter, but Patrice might not want us to do anything. I could imagine all kinds of trauma involved in that decision process. We shouldn't be making that decision for her."

"Let me talk to her," Miss Septima said. "It will be that child's pain, but it will also be her one chance to get some payback. That ain't a small thing. That can bring a whole lotta peace of mind."

The next morning, Patrice made breakfast for the kids before the buses took them to school. She scrambled eggs and fried sausages. She topped it off with biscuits and honey. She told Mr. Jimmy, via

Juba's translation, that she liked it that the kids were losing their hollow cheeks. She said the kids looked healthy.

Fountain and crew had cleaned up the diner. Many of the kids liked to eat at the counter and others picked a table or booth for breakfast and dinner for themselves and their families. Patrice, now with the help of other mothers, even made Sunday brunch.

Mr. Jimmy and Miss Septima buttered their biscuits at the counter after the children were gone.

"Girl, you just in motion. Come over here and lean across this counter so we can talk to you."

She arrived at the counter with a grin. Mr. Jimmy and Miss Septima turned to each other and smiled.

"That doctor. What they say, your therapist?" Miss Septima asked.

Patrice nodded.

"Seem like she doing all right by you."

Patrice nodded and smiled.

"That's good. We need to talk to you about something. You remember from the church that Mr. Jimmy can't buy the land around the way because the man won't sell it to him."

Patrice nodded.

"That man is in some of them pictures with you."

Patrice's face hardened and her body stiffened.

"We want that land so Mr. Jimmy can start that farm and help all of us out. And we think we should call the police too. But first we want to let that man know that we have his picture doing something so bad, that if we tell about it, he gonna have some real trouble in his life. We might be stirring up a hornet's nest though. Raise up a lot of feelings for you and Juba. Do you want us to do nothing?"

Patrice was quiet for a while. Mr. Jimmy and Miss Septima busied themselves with eating their breakfast until she decided she was ready to answer.

"You want us to do nothing?" Miss Septima asked again.

Patrice shook her head.

"You want us to go get the land and get after that man?"

Patrice nodded passionately, and she took Mr. Jimmy's hand. She struggled to speak but she wanted the words to come from her lips.

"I . . . t . . . tru . . . trust you," She said to him as tears came to her eyes.

Mr. Jimmy called Mason. If ever he needed him by his side, it was in the moment they challenged Crawford Alden. But Mason would not come. He couldn't. Rebecca had moved away. She bought a home on the water in her hometown hours away. As girlfriends go, she and Aubrey had been at the top of the list in closeness. Though she understood Rebecca's need to leave, losing her friend had been traumatic for Aubrey. There was no way he could even mention leaving her side to help the man who cost her her closest friend.

So Mr. Jimmy took Fountain for protection and the intimidation factor. Fountain was pleased and ready to play the part. They drove up to the farm and they got out of Fountain's new, green pickup with the name of the Wayside Motel stenciled on both doors.

"Nice truck," Olivia said, smiling. She and Yankee were already there and had gotten out of their car to greet them.

"Thanks," Fountain said. "It rides nice."

"You have the photos?" Mr. Jimmy asked Yankee.

"Yes," he replied. "Holding up a large envelope. I'm also going to secretly record this meeting."

"Can we do that?"

"Mississippi is a one-party consent state."

"Works for me then."

Mr. Jimmy noticed his old friend, the For Sale sign, as they approached the porch. It brought him some comfort as he loudly and aggressively knocked on the door. He wanted Crawford Alden to come to the door pissed off, annoyed by the noise and brimming with anger so that he could watch him deflate and beg. He wanted to see fear in the man's eyes. He wanted to see in his face the acknowledgment that his deeds had come back to haunt him. He wanted the pictures to be branded on his brain, causing him pain for life. The door opened, but it wasn't Crawford.

"Lacey," Olivia said.

Lacey Alden looked at the White woman and man and the two Black men. At first it was surprise, but it turned quickly to ugly.

"You need to get your Black behinds off my land. And you," she said jabbing her finger into Olivia's face, "you should be ashamed of yourself. You got a husband right here, and you still hanging around with these monkeys."

"The only animal here," Olivia said. "Is your pig of a husband."

Lacey Alden's face reddened with anger. She kept her eyes on Olivia as she yelled for her husband.

Crawford Alden came to the door. When he saw who it was, he left. He came back with his son and carrying a shotgun. Mr. Jimmy, Fountain, Olivia, and Yankee, stepped backward on the porch, putting some space between them and the angry man with a shotgun.

"You can leave now," Crawford said. "Or I am going to shoot me a Black billionaire and his White whore, her stupid husband, and this monkey criminal."

"The only gun going off here," Yankee said. "Is the one inside this envelope."

Yankee pulled out a picture and handed it to Crawford who immediately tore it up.

"Oh, you didn't think we came without copies, did you?" Mr. Jimmy said.

Fountain reached out and snatched the shotgun away from Crawford and threw it into the yard. Coy Alden, the son, made a move as if he was going to run around Fountain for the gun, but Fountain shifted his massive frame, blocking Coy's path. Coy did not try to get by him.

Yankee held up another copy of the photo so the Alden family could see it.

"Here is your husband raping a Black woman with his buddies." He pulled out another picture. "Here he is another time, doing the same thing. We have four pictures of you raping this woman."

"It was not rape!" Crawford shouted.

"I don't think she gave you permission," Olivia said.

"Her husband did. I paid him like everybody else. I didn't have to ask her."

"Like I said," Olivia replied. "She didn't give you permission, and I cannot believe you are that ignorant."

"Whatever it is, it doesn't look good for you," Mr. Jimmy said. "By tomorrow, this could well be all over the internet. It could be in the papers, on local TV. National cable could pick it up. You could feel the fire that I have been feeling."

Lacey Alden looked at her husband and back at the four of them. She gave her son a look as if to ask him how much he knew. He dropped his head, and she turned back to them; her face now drenched in embarrassment. Her superiority and bravado were gone. She turned and went back into the house, letting the door slam behind her.

"What do you want to end all of this right here? To make it go away?" Crawford asked.

"The land," Mr. Jimmy said.

"I can't do that," he replied.

"Why not?" Olivia asked. "Don't you own it?"

"I do, but Welton Knox got the squeeze on me. He told me not to sell it."

"Well, I don't think his squeeze is bigger than this," Yankee said.

"But he got the pictures too, don't he?" Fountain asked.

Crawford nodded and Mr. Jimmy smiled. "It seems you're between a rock and a hard place."

"How does he have the pictures and how did he get involved in the first place?" Yankee asked.

"That boy was whoring out his wife. We began to hear about it in the whispering from men who had paid to be with her. I wasn't interested until Welton decided to make a guy's night of it. He invited a select few of us. He was even there at the beginning, but he snuck out before the action started. It turns out that he made a deal with that boy. He would pay for the first night of fun and he would pay him a lot extra to take pictures that night and beyond. He promised the boy that the pictures would never be seen other than him flashing a couple around so that people would know he had something on them for sure. We heard tell that the girl's brother, who ain't from Ham, found out by accident. Came by late on a wrong night and caught things in action. He and the husband had a big fight, I heard."

"That's right," Fountain said. "Didn't nobody know what that was all about. After that Patrice's husband booked it out of town. But then they found her brother dead about a week after that."

Crawford nodded. "Her brother got a hold of the camera and the film the night of the fight. He took it somewhere and got it processed. Nobody knows how he found out Welton was at the top of this mess, but he did. Maybe the girl knew and told him. Anyway, he went to him, gave him copies of the pictures and threatened to blackmail him, knowing he was behind everything. Next thing we heard that boy was found dead on my land. I don't know anything about who killed him, but I am sure Welton was behind it."

"That's murder," Yankee said. "Knox is too smart for that."

"He knows that ain't nobody gonna give a good goddamn about a troubling Black buck."

"This is some fucked up shit," Fountain said, angrily staring at Crawford.

"You continued going to these nights after Knox invited you?" Yankee continued.

"I did."

"Welton always paid?"

"Only twice. The rest of the time, we all paid ourselves."

"Why did you do it?" Olivia asked. "Didn't you have any respect for Patrice?"

"It was between them. I thought she was in on it. Those share-croppers do anything for money."

"But you knew he was in charge. He was making the decision for his wife."

"Maybe so. There was some talk about him beating her up pretty bad if she wanted to stop. But she could have left if she didn't want it. That's how some of us saw it. So we figured she was into the money. And we were into the fun. Welton, he was trying to get some things done in the county that didn't nobody really want. It was just for him and his cronies. All of us that had some pull in the county ended up invited to this party. It was good fun. Get a buzz on. Get drunk even and get some . . . well, you know. Then after a while, we all start getting these letters. And we knew we was had by him. And not a damn thing we could do about it."

"My God," Olivia said, slowly shaking her head, staring at Crawford with disbelief. "I just feel sooooo sorry for you."

Crawford frowned at her response. He seemed to be tiring of the question-and-answer process.

"I'll be back," he said. "Come on in the house," he called to his son, who followed. Crawford returned with an envelope and handed it to Yankee. Yankee took out the handwritten note and read it.

I suspect you will fall in line now,

W. Knox

"Every White man in that photo and probably some more got one of these notes. That's where the power comes from. That's how he runs the county. He gets stuff on people. He got this on a lot of us." Crawford said.

"Did he ever rape her?" Olivia asked.

"I said it was not rape! And not that I know of. Like I said, the one time he was there but he was gone by the time all of that started."

"How were the pictures taken?" Mr. Jimmy asked. "Did you see a camera?"

"The house had all kinda holes in it. It's just a damn shack. We figure he was standing outside the bedroom with the camera."

"And he hid the picture copies under the floor in the children's bedroom," Fountain said angrily. "For that child to find."

"He did or Patrice's brother did. We may never know the truth about that," Olivia replied.

Mr. Jimmy shook his head. "Well," he said. "This is a lot to digest."

"I'll say," Yankee replied.

"We got a deal?" Crawford asked.

"If you sell me the land. We will take care of Knox," Mr. Jimmy said.

Crawford Alden nodded.

"And I want the For Sale sign too," Mr. Jimmy added.

Crawford Alden nodded.

"I used to have respect for you," Olivia said, before spitting on the porch floor at his feet.

They all drove away, leaving Crawford Alden standing outside his front door, looking as if he was trying to decide if it might be safe to go inside.

TWENTY-EIGHT

Olivia Fey Carol's bright red hair bounced about her head as she painted because she was painting angry. She had not been able to release much of her anger about the years of abuse absorbed by Patrice. Despite her mood, Mr. Jimmy noted to himself that she still painted well as she put the final touches on a red crab, half covered in sand, one claw reaching to the sky. The children would love this addition. There were a few others. A blue shovel close to the water's edge. A circle of burnt wood and half a hot dog not too far from it. Mr. Jimmy was curious if Juba would ever regard the mural as fun again.

Olivia, Yankee, Fountain, Miss Septima, and Mr. Jimmy met many times after Crawford Alden had been confronted. Over many days and long hours, they discussed their strategy to bring down Welton Knox. Olivia had dreamed of confronting him face-to-face. After his malicious and callous use of Patrice's tragic situation and after he had treated her with such disrespect in his office, he deserved to have his door kicked in by her, she felt. But Mr. Jimmy wondered what good would that do. Wouldn't it be enough to see him fall from a distance if they could make that happen? Possibly, Olivia thought. But at some time, he was going to have to face her, she told them.

In the end, Mr. Jimmy thought that Welton Knox might deserve a surprise pain. Like the one he received when the young reporter and cameraman met him as he left work for what would be his last time at his office. They just had to figure out the best way to make that happen.

After a phone conversation with Mason, Mr. Jimmy decided to reach out to *The Washington Ledger* reporter.

"Why not the television reporter?" Yankee asked. "People like visuals, yes?"

"Yes, but the truth is that I was hurt more by the detail of what appeared in the paper. I want to invite the reporter down here, to watch the end of this. Maybe we do confront Knox with the reporter in tow."

"Now, you're talking," Olivia said.

So Mr. Jimmy got out his tablet and searched for the front-page article written, he felt, as an obituary to the life he led before his fall from grace. He had not been able to read the full article on the day it came out, but he had carried it with him to the Willard Hotel, where he read it over and over and over again. Funny, though, that he did not remember the byline. Maybe it didn't really matter in the moment. Or maybe he didn't want to believe that another human being could be so cruelly detailed about another human life already in distress. But when he opened the online version of the paper, the article was still there for the world to see. The byline read, Claire Simpson.

Mason reached out to Ms. Simpson. When she and her boss heard about Mr. Jimmy's flight to Mississippi, his battle with Welton Knox, and the photographs of Patrice, she found herself on the next plane. It had been a year and a half since his fall, but they seemed to find his continued story to be sensational enough to be covered by a national paper. She arrived the following day, and although Mr. Jimmy offered her a room at the Wayside Motel, she stayed elsewhere.

Ms. Simpson met Mr. Jimmy at his little home around the way. He was standing at the door when she drove up in her rental. He took note of the way she sat in the car for a few minutes, gazing at his house. *Yes*, he thought, acknowledging his agreement with her expression. *I have come down a peg or two.*

Just outside of the car, she stopped to take a picture of the house with him in the doorway. They shook hands and exchanged greetings. He was casual, wearing jeans and a sweatshirt. She was taller than him, a very fit, medium build from which she transferred a significant aura of strength. She wore black slacks and a black turtleneck under a brown blazer, which matched her eyes. She was intense, and he felt it. They took measure of each other. She held back any inkling of friendliness, clearly sending him vibes that she would be keeping her distance. She was not there for him. She was there for the story. In fact, she seemed to be somewhat repulsed by him. So Mr. Jimmy readjusted his attitude, treating her from that point on as if she were a new business partner who he did not yet trust. She refused any refreshments, and they sat across the table from each other.

"How did you get here?" She asked. "Were you running away from what you'd done? Did you think you could hide here?"

"I drove. Yes, and yes," he replied.

He explained that he couldn't go outside in Washington, DC. without being noticed. People either made fun of him or treated him as human sleaze. Both responses were hurtful. In time, he found himself in his hotel suite scanning the internet for homes in rural parts of southern states. When he saw this little home, dilapidated though it was, he fell in love. He no longer needed a large home, and he didn't care for the trappings that came along with it. He just needed a place to sit and stare and think. He found a local real estate agent online and called her. He told her he wanted to buy the house and asked if she could put him in touch with a contractor. She offered to represent him in purchasing the house and for an extra sum, she would act as a manager of the construction. She'd keep an eye on things and make sure everything stayed on schedule. After moving, she and her family had become his friends.

"She did that for the kids in the neighborhood," he said pointing to the ocean mural.

Ms. Simpson stared at the painting. "It's really very good. Why are kids spending time in your house? Especially after that photo of you and the girl. What parents would allow their kids to be around you?"

"Am I that horrible?" he asked.

She ignored his question. "I'll come back to that. What happened after you moved in?"

Mr. Jimmy told her about meeting Miss Septima, and about Juba, Beech, and their candy. He told her about everything leading up the moment that found them sitting together. He told her why he needed her.

"I'm not here to be your detective, cop, or lawyer. This is a follow-up piece in my mind. As distasteful as the whole thing was, people are curious as to what happened to you. My editor, most importantly."

"Okay then," he said. "Let's take a walk."

She took a picture of Mr. Jimmy at his table before they began a walking tour through around the way. They stopped first at Miss Septima's. He pointed out the holes in the thin walls, some of them patched by Juba, others now stuffed with cloth and foam. He explained the new porch he'd built and how it hadn't made a real difference. But it had been worse than the house, and he thought she would hurt herself eventually as she tried to navigate the warped floorboards and the brittle steps. She took pictures before they continued. Next, they walked into Fountain and Bess's house. The smell of mildew and mold was overwhelming. He couldn't believe the family wasn't sick all the time. He was happy little Essie was free of it now and hopefully would have no long-term health concerns or memories from her time living there. In Patrice's house, the reality of the life around the way came to the fore. By the time Claire Simpson stood for a few minutes in the black-walled kitchen, the sticky smell of grease and butane hanging in the air, her hard demeanor began to soften. Even without the people in it, this kind of poverty was eye-opening and staggering. The bathroom sent her briskly walking out into the open air. She had been holding her breath. She bent over as she gulped in the fresh air. Mr. Jimmy took her camera, went back inside, and took pictures of the bathroom.

"Would you like to see more?" he asked.

"No, thank you," she said, taking back her camera. "I'm going back to my hotel to make notes on what I've seen. Can we visit the motel tomorrow?"

"Of course. Be there by six-thirty in the morning to catch the kids before they go to school."

When Claire Simpson arrived the next morning, she did so with a photographer, who had flown in overnight. From the look of him as he got out of the car, he was as intense as she, and Mr. Jimmy imagined that they both would be better off in a war zone. He stood in the office with Olivia and Yankee, watching her and her colleague through a window. She stood, quietly taking in the morning scene as the photographer took pictures of the children who were up, dressed and working. Fountain had found jobs for all who wanted work. From trash duty to exterior building care to kitchen duty at breakfast and dinner.

"Nothing like some good child labor in the morning," Ms. Simpson said as she entered the office. "This is Derrick. A photographer with the paper."

Further introductions were made, and Olivia responded to the reporter's comments. "The children want to work. They've asked for it, and it's good for them. And the motel pays them at just above the federal minimum wage. My children do the same kind of work at my house for free. Would you accuse me of some sort of child abuse?"

"That's in your home," Ms. Simpson responded.

"And for now, this is their home," Olivia responded. "Until Mr. Jimmy came along, these kids were living in abject poverty, growing up with no responsibility to themselves or their families. No hope. No realistic dreams and no money in their pockets. They are learning to be responsible. To show up on time. To recognize how their portion of the work keeps the whole operation here going. They are being prepared to operate in a world they only knew tangentially. There is no child labor issue here. There are life lessons being learned and appreciated."

Ms. Simpson stood quietly for a moment, realizing that not everyone felt the need to be cautious in their tone around her. She nodded respectfully to Olivia.

In the kitchen, there were more photos to be taken. The children, now accustomed to the routine of their morning jobs, moved without instruction in the preparation of the community breakfast. Patrice or Bess could be seen making minute adjustments in their responsibilities, leaning over to whisper a change in orders, followed by a kiss on the head or a quick hug.

In the diner area, families came in and filled their plates, ate, and left for work or school. Those adults who didn't have jobs, cleaned up afterward. The operation, put together by Fountain, was quite impressive. Mr. Jimmy was proud of them all.

After they ate, Mr. Jimmy, Olivia, Yankee, Fountain, Ms. Simpson, and Derrick went to visit another influential White man from Ham who had appeared in the photos. He owned the two top restaurants in Ham and was a significant landowner. He was from a family with deep Mississippi roots. He was from extremely old money.

"What would someone in this area want with a woman from your neighborhood?" Ms. Simpson asked Mr. Jimmy.

He shrugged his shoulders. "Old slave owner dreams of acting as if you can own someone else's body and do with it what you please. Especially that of a Black woman whose physical and emotional well-being is insignificant in his mind."

Ms. Simpson took notes but did not respond.

Olivia knocked on the door of the very impressive Victorian mansion. A Black woman answered to the door.

"Good morning, ma'am," she said. "May I help you?"

"We're here to see Sidney Corbin. Has he left for the restaurant?"

"No, ma'am."

"Would you tell him that Olivia and Yankee Carol are here to see him?"

"Yes, ma'am. Ya'll step in out of the cold and wait in the parlor there."

Within minutes a man in his late 50s came into the room where they all sat. Olivia stood as he walked in with a big smile on his face. The smile seemed forced and insincere to Mr. Jimmy.

"Well now," he said to her. "To what do I owe the pleasure of this visit."

Olivia was in no mood for pleasantries, real or fake. She opened the folder and handed him a blowup of one of the pictures from the metal box. Yankee, Mr. Jimmy, and Fountain now stood behind her as reinforcements. Ms. Simpson and Derrick remained seated.

"Mr. Corbin," Yankee said. "I don't have to tell you where this picture is from. I do have to tell you now that it's been found, you're in a bit of trouble. Solicitation is just the beginning I suspect."

The cultured and polished Mr. Corbin turned white with embarrassment and fear. After all, he was completely naked in this picture. On top of that, it seemed as if he had just finished assaulting Patrice or was just about to. Either way, it was clear he understood what was happening. There was a reckoning in the set of his face. Mr. Jimmy stepped forward.

"I'm the neighborhood Black, fake billionaire, carpetbagger. This young woman you assaulted is a friend of mine."

Corbin nodded.

"We know that this was originally orchestrated by this woman's . . . do you even know her name?"

Corbin looked down at the picture in his hands and then slowly shook his head.

"Well, her name is Patrice. Her husband forced her into these attacks on her body and mind. You happily participated on multiple occasions. Happily, at least, until you were blackmailed by Welton Knox."

Olivia handed him a copy of the Knox note to Crawford Alden.

"Did you get one of these?" she asked.

"Yes, I did," he replied.

"Why would he choose to blackmail you?" Mr. Jimmy asked.

"Because I carry a significant amount of weight in this town. My word can make some things happen. He was trying to get some business done, political and otherwise. In doing so, he would become the most influential man in the town and the surrounding county. He wanted the chair of the Board of Supervisors. He always had political ambitions for local office. He always wanted to be the biggest fish in this small pond."

"He got what he wanted from you, then?" he asked.

"Yes. That and more. I'm not the only prominent man to get caught up in this."

"We know," Yankee said. "We have all of the photos."

"Do you have your letter from Mr. Knox?" Mr. Jimmy asked.

Corbin turned his attention to the woman walking up to him. Derrick followed and began to take pictures.

"Who are you?" he asked.

"Claire Simpson. I'm from *The Washington Ledger*."

"All the way from DC?" Corbin asked, surprised.

"Because of Mr. Ferguson, it's a national story."

Sidney Corbin was overcome by the realization that this was a much larger problem than he had considered. He was frightened.

"I heard from Crawford Alden," he said. "I had thought we might be able to work something out quietly like you did with him. What can we do to make that happen?"

"There is going to be a story," Ms. Simpson responded. "There's nothing to stop that now."

"You'll look better if you help us focus this on Knox," Yankee said.

So Corbin left them for a moment, returning with his note from Welton Knox. The wording was the same.

"Thank you," Yankee said.

Olivia reached out for the photo, but Corbin pulled it away from her.

"I'll keep it," he said. "I have to explain this to my wife. She might as well see the cold, hard truth. Though it may be the end of things."

No one offered any sympathies.

"Mr. Corbin," Ms. Simpson said. "You seemed a bit stunned when you saw the photo. But now you seem, dare I say, relieved or resigned."

"Ever since I received the letter from Welton, I knew something like this day would come. And I suppose you are going to visit others."

"We are," Mr. Jimmy replied.

"Well, they all know you are coming. As I said, I spoke to Crawford."

Over the next week, they visited more men and sometimes with their wives. Most were quiet meetings, but they left several of the families in raging arguments. When they arrived at the last house, no one was home but the note from Welton Knox was tacked to the front door. Derrick took a picture. Now, they had the recorded stories of nine men and had acquired 10 letters from Knox. They were also sure that if these men had been talking to each other, at least one of them had been talking to Knox. Olivia was happy. Mr. Jimmy's desire to surprise him with a story in the paper wasn't possible now. If he knew it was coming, they might as well bring it to him.

When Mr. Jimmy and Olivia Fey Carol walked into the meeting room of the county Board of Supervisors, Claire Simpson was already seated among that night's audience of concerned citizens. Derrick, the photographer, was at her side, his camera on his lap, at the ready. It caused enough of a stir that Mr. Jimmy had appeared, but he was also holding the hand of the woman he was rumored to be having an affair with. He and Olivia walked hand-in-hand down the aisle and up to the audience lectern. By the time they arrived, the quiet gawking and whispers had morphed into shouting. They told him to go back to Africa. They told Olivia that she should be ashamed of herself. They asked how she could do this to her husband and her children. They called him a carpetbagger and a child molester. They reminded him that his wife left him for his womanizing. They asked him if he hadn't learned anything. They told him that they didn't want him in their town, their county, or their state. Mr. Jimmy remained calm and displayed no fear because he understood that he and Olivia would soon be in charge of the room.

Welton Knox sat center stage upon his extorted throne. His name plaque identified him as the chairman of the Board of Supervisors. His face identified him as a man overtaken by an unexpected concern. He slammed his gavel down so hard that it sounded like a shot from a gun, and it quieted the audience.

"I don't know what you think you are doing here," Knox said, pointing to Mr. Jimmy and Olivia. "Whatever you are here for is not on tonight's agenda. You can either leave peacefully or I will have you removed."

"Before you toss us out," Olivia responded, raising hers and Mr. Jimmy's hand, "we want you to understand that we are here in solidarity with the people of the neighborhood often referred to as around the way. Ham's poorest citizens. As I look around, none of them is here."

"No one is stopping them," one of the other board members said.

"No one has ever invited them from what I understand," Mr. Jimmy said. "And you have left your fellow citizens to wallow in such poverty that it stuns the mind and shatters the heart. You provide little to no services. Nothing compared to what you give these folks. And you would not welcome them if they came here. You and I both know that."

"That's enough," Knox said. "Officers, please clear these people from the room."

"Just one more thing," Olivia said. "Before you do what you do. You know, shut down any dissenting voices. Maybe the good people want to know how you extorted political favors, and the influence of prominent citizens of this community to take that chair you're sitting in. Maybe the people want to know how you invited prominent men to sexual assault parties where you purchased a woman's body for them to rape. Maybe they want to know how you had photos taken of these acts and later blackmailed the men for their support of your political ambitions. So you could become as the paper called you, *Ham, Mississippi's Leader, and Savior*."

"Officers, please!"

As the officers moved toward them, Claire Simpson stood and forcefully announced herself as a reporter for *The Washington*

Ledger. The officers stopped and turned to Knox for directions as to who they should escort out first. In the meantime, Ms. Simpson unleashed a barrage of accusations.

"Mr. Knox, I have the recorded confessions of nine members of this community who say you did invite them to a party where they sexually assaulted a woman. You paid for access on behalf of these men. They all say you blackmailed them using their presence at these sexual assaults. Here is a note that you sent to one of the men. It reads, *I suspect you will fall in line now*. It's signed by you. Do you deny anything I have stated or that Mr. Ferguson or Ms. Carol have stated?"

Welton Knox slammed his gavel down again. He called for order, but there was no need for that because the people had already quieted. Everyone, including the other board members, were focused on him now, awaiting an answer.

"Your response please," Ms. Simpson said.

Welton Knox did not answer. He was shivering with anger. The silence in the room was broken by the quick shutters of Derrick's camera and then the last words of Mr. Jimmy.

"You broke the law, and you used a young woman, causing her great physical and emotional pain. And you used the men from the pictures to pull the wool over the eyes of the Ham voting public. You have abused the trust of the citizenry to put yourself in a position of power to create personal wealth. The truth is that you're just a small-town mob boss."

"You know what," Olivia said, her eyes full of rage. "You're just a horrible human being."

They were escorted from the room and as the large, wooden, double doors closed behind them, they heard mayhem break out in the meeting room. They all took a moment to look at each other and smile.

"Savior, my ass," Olivia said.

TWENTY-NINE

The Ham Gazette

Early Online Edition – January 25, 2018
By Harper Birdie

"You're just a horrible human being."

Last night's Board of Supervisors meeting ended abruptly when Chairman Knox walked out of the meeting room before any county business could be attended to. Just as he was about to open the meeting, disgraced African American businessman James Henry Ferguson and recently fired real estate agent Olivia Fey Carol approached the public lectern holding hands. They claimed to be supporting Ham citizens from a neighborhood commonly referred to as "around the way," located at the edge of the Jackson Cove section of Ham. They also, without presenting evidence, accused Chairman Knox of purchasing a local woman for sex and inviting other prominent Ham male citizens to take part. They then accused the Chairman of blackmailing those unnamed citizens into helping him create the political environment that has allowed him to rise to the Chair of the Board of Supervisors and become, as many local citizens believe, the most powerful person in Ham.

At the moment, these are merely accusations, but The Ham Gazette, reached out to Deputy District Attorney, Walker Tuck. Mr. Tuck indicated that, if true, these accusations could result in the charges of human trafficking, sexual assault and extortion.

Before being escorted out of the meeting room, Ms. Carol shouted at Chairman Knox, who is a friend of her parents. "You're just a horrible human being."

Chairman Knox then left the room before officially calling the meeting to order.

This is a developing story. Stay with The Ham Gazette for the latest updates.

THIRTY

In the early spring, Mr. Jimmy took a rocking chair off his porch. He set it on the ground, angled a bit to the right so that he could see the farm to his left and the empty spaces that used to be the homes of his friends to his right. He opened his bottle of Pure Leaf extra sweet tea and took a long swallow. It was sweet and refreshing. He closed his eyes for a moment, allowing himself to acknowledge his satisfaction. *It's the little things*, he said to himself.

In the distance, Fountain Hughes and colleagues sat on their tractors, silhouettes against the rising morning sun. They were breaking up the land in preparation for planting the first crops that would be sold to restaurants all over the United States. And not just those attached to the former businesses of Mr. Jimmy. When Claire Simpson's article, four pages long, appeared in *The Washington Ledger*, restaurant owners immediately reached out to become clients of this new and unique agricultural company. Mr. Jimmy had even come up with a name for it—The For Sale Company, after his much beloved sign. He glanced at it, hung affectionately by Fountain in the same crooked fashion in the same lonely place in the field where Mr. Jimmy first saw it. Sometimes, he set an alarm in the middle of the night so that he could get up, sit on the porch in complete darkness, and listen to it flap in the wind.

At a distance, he could see that a white car from the Mississippi State Farm Service Agency was pulling away from the area of the farm populated by several very large metal buildings that Fountain had installed. Inside were his offices, storage areas, packaging areas, and garage areas for trucks and large farm equipment. After Claire Simpson's article and follow-ups in *The Ham Gazette*, the farm agency offered to be of assistance to Fountain, particularly in guiding his decisions about which crops the company could plant for harvest as late as December. In the next year, a greenhouse was to be built so that there would be no stoppage in growing appropriate crops. Fountain had blossomed, and had come of age. He was doing a spectacular job of running the operation and preparing the land. He was fond of saying that he just laid back one night and called on the wisdom of the sharecroppers and slaves who had come before him. Mr. Jimmy endearingly called him Boss.

To his right, he saw shadows in his mind. Faint and fading images of so many small homes, all in a row. The images of generations of suffering erased, at least in terms of the structures that had housed the pain. It had been a great day, though a bittersweet one when the neighborhood came together to pay tribute to what had come before and what was to be. Miss Septima hollered and wept when the bulldozer plowed into the side of her home, which had been occupied by her family since the end of slavery. At the end of that day, when Mr. Jimmy went by her motel room to say goodnight, she was still sad, sitting at the table going through her bucket of buttons.

"Don't you let my messy head get in the way now. Part of me just went away with that house and it hurt. Had to be though. I knelt down and called on my Jesus to set me straight. I know what's to come is his blessing."

Each of the families stood quietly as their homes were destroyed. Patrice looked on in tears for all that had gone on inside of her home. The children, excepting Juba, stood next to her, holding on about her waist. Juba stood alone, his eyes full of tears and anger. Juba was one not at all sad to see the walls come crashing down. It was an all-day affair, with everyone standing by to watch each other's home demolished. Now, construction was ahead of schedule getting everything ready for the beautiful prefab homes to come. All of it, everything that was occurring in their lives, was bringing them closer as a community.

Mr. Jimmy looked back at his For Sale sign and thought of Crawford Alden and the other nine men who had assaulted Patrice. He also thought of Welton Knox. Two days after *The Ham Gazette* wrote about Knox walking out on the Board of Supervisors' meeting, Claire Simpson's story ran in *The Washington Ledger* and was quickly picked up by national cable television. Soon after, the fabric of Ham began to unravel. People picked sides and argued in the streets. Fights broke out over evening meals and night after night, the moon rose over an increasingly divided population. There were emergency meetings of the town council and Board of Supervisors minus Welton Knox, who was locked away in the sheriff's jail. He had, indeed, been charged with human trafficking and extortion. The other 10 men, also in the same jail, had been charged with sexual assault and solicitation. They found themselves in cells with the Black men who had also appeared in the photos. White families broke apart. Some threatened the families from around the way. Mason advised Mr. Jimmy to hire some security for the motel for a few weeks. He flew in security officers from a company that had provided protection for many of his properties throughout his business days.

As a way to calm the near riotous state of much of the White community, all of the White men were let out on their own recognizance, but they had to give up any positions of influence within the community. Welton Knox had to part ways with his treasured position as chairman. Within a few days, his law firm would force him to resign. His wife and family supported him without question as did many others in the town and the larger county.

Mr. Jimmy called a community meeting. Everyone met in the diner. He pulled up a chair in front of the group and lifted Essie into his lap when she ran up to him.

"Grandaddy, pick me up."

So he sat with her and looked at the faces of his friends. He told them that the men may ultimately get away with their crimes, but at least they could take solace in that there was enough of the community upset with these men that they could never wield the power they had before. The folks from around the way didn't have to be afraid of Welton Knox anymore. He could not use them anymore. He could not keep them down.

"And because of Patrice," he said to everyone, "who allowed us to go after these men, even if it meant suffering through the pain of public exposure, the doors have opened for us to do the things we need to do to change the life of everyone in this room. This is the moment in your life when you can decide to break the circle so that no one who follows you, your children, your grandchildren, or your great grandchildren, will ever live with holes in the walls of their homes or worse. We are beginning to build some generational wealth here, just like many of the White families around you have always had."

Mr. Jimmy continued to sip his tea and watch the dust rise from behind the tractors. Although he didn't compare his suffering to Patrice's, she was not alone in harboring an unsettling anxiety about the release of personal information. Even though he willingly opened up to Claire Simpson, he worried about the world knowing so much about his life after his fall. After all, he had run away to protect himself from the world. But there was nothing left to protect now. She had revealed it all. She wrote the story of his attempt to hide from his poor decision that had cost him his family life. She wrote about his fleeing his city, hoping to hide somewhere in the rural south, in a place that reminded him of his childhood days. She wrote about his meeting Miss Septima, Juba, Beech, and Olivia Fey Carol, who was as fiery as her bright red hair. She wrote about the reading classes in his home after school, the jobs, and the overall plan to bring around the way out of the shadows of poverty and lost hope. She wrote about Patrice's black kitchen and about the day her son found pictures of her sexual abuse. She wrote about the ocean mural on the wall of his little house at the edge of the neighborhood. She wrote about the Wayside Motel and Mr. Jimmy's plans for the neighborhood. She wrote about his fight for the land so that Fountain could lead his community into financial stability, providing jobs with decent pay and benefits. She wrote about his nights alone on the porch, longing for his wife and daughters with only the For Sale sign to bring him comfort.

Shortly after the article came out, Mr. Jimmy, for the second time, began trending on Twitter. It was painful, because he had been hoping that people would see the true him and allow him to be redeemed in the eyes of the public. But each tweet spoke of or hinted at his moral failure. They retweeted Lady Nymph's tweet in which she recalled his *desperate, frantic fuck.* They reminded him that he left his daughters and his wife to face the press and the public without him, although he argued to himself that he was the first of his family to face the media over the affair. Some said he was doing what all of these filthy rich, no good, bougie sons-of-bitches do. They ride off into the sunset with their money, laughing at the world.

"Sorry, man," Mason had said. "I guess you need more time to pass."

In others, the article fostered a much different reaction. Mason began to receive calls from chefs whose careers had started with a handshake from the restaurant tycoon, James Henry Ferguson. When they offered to help, word got around, and more restaurants joined in. The For Sale Company got started with almost too many clients to please.

THIRTY-ONE

By the time the Fourth of July came around, a park had been built for the children of around the way. It was across from the now asphalt-covered street and the new sidewalks. It was across the street from the prefab homes, which were almost finished. Mr. Jimmy spent hours watching the progress and imagining the families living in a way that never occurred to them was possible. Each night, work lights were left on in the mostly finished homes. He would walk the street looking at them, sometimes stepping up and peering inside. Just before Miss Septima's house there was a street sign. *Around The Way.*

"You know we are somebody, child, when we got our own street sign. And numbers on my house," she continued. "Look there. I'm 1604 Around The Way. Lawd, ain't that something."

By the end of the month, they all would be moving into their new homes, and Mr. Jimmy could not wait. The neighborhood had been painfully quiet.

But on this day, the Fourth of July, they all gathered in the parking lot of the Wayside Motel. Music blanketed the area. It was an old-fashioned country fish fry, and everyone had been invited. Olivia and Yankee sat with him at a picnic table overlooking the festivities. He was looking at Ms. Ford, who was standing next to a group of kids but was lost in her phone. He wondered if something was wrong. It was not like her to be next to the kids and not engaged. He hoped there were no problems.

"I would have never believed that this is where I would be," Olivia said, dragging him away from his worry. "Some strange man did this to all of us."

They laughed.

"Well, it won't be long for you. Didn't you say you guys were planning to move back to Austin?"

"I don't think that's happening," Yankee said, nodding toward Olivia.

She laughed. "Mr. Jimmy, I told you that after I left the Peace Corps all I wanted to do was to help create hope and make positive change for people I grew up near and didn't do my part to help. You've given me that opportunity to live that dream. We're staying. And not just for us," she said nodding to a group of kids playing. "Look at them. Maybe this is how we make change a couple of people at a time."

Mr. Jimmy nodded as he watched Olivia and Yankee's children, Bea, and Walt, lost in play with the children from around the way. It was indeed a beautiful sight. Mr. Jimmy turned to Olivia and smiled.

"How are the plans for the clinic going?" Yankee asked.

"They are going well. It's good to see the building going up. I get briefed by Dr. Longford every week. I think he's going to be great, and the staff he's put together looks a lot like the community it will serve."

"That's excellent," Yankee replied.

"And I am so happy about the diner becoming a restaurant," Olivia said.

"Miss Septima wanted it to happen," Mr. Jimmy said. "She said we were wasting all of Patrice's talent just cooking for the kids. So The For Sale Company diversified and opened a restaurant. She has Bess to be her voice and to run things. We've hired a company to do the books and payroll. Other neighbors have signed up as employees. In time, the business will split. The motel will be separate from the restaurant. Patrice will own the restaurant. This week they had their first clients. The African American community is being very supportive. And we've opened up the motel to guests now. They are eating there as well. I'm not sure yet who will own the motel. And, of course, Fountain will own the farm business."

"That's quite a leap and a lot to put on them, don't you think?" Yankee asked.

"Well, it doesn't have to happen right away," Mr. Jimmy replied. "But I didn't start this with the idea of creating more minimum wage jobs. I'm planting the seed of ownership. I want the kids to grow up knowing they can choose to work for or to run a company. And I'm not going anywhere. My roots here are already quite deep."

"Music to my ears," Olivia said with a smile.

Their conversation came to a halt when a black, executive sedan came to a stop in the parking lot. It drew everyone's attention. The doors opened, and two tall, beautiful Black women got out. Mr. Jimmy's eyes welled, and he didn't know if he should move because it might be a dream and he did not want to wake up. Katherine looked around the parking lot and found Ms. Ford who was walking toward them. She gave Katherine and Lillian hugs and pointed them toward his picnic table. He didn't dare move.

The children were entranced. Ms. Ford had begun to spread the word that Mr. Jimmy's daughters had arrived. Juba and Beech stood frozen in place, already in love.

The hug was unlike anything Mr. Jimmy had felt in such a long time. He stood among his new family; each arm wrapped around a daughter. They whispered how much they loved him. How proud they were of him. People cheered and clapped. Mr. Jimmy looked to Ms. Ford.

"Thank you," he said.

"You deserved this," she replied.

Mr. Jimmy only had them briefly as everyone wanted to meet them. Katherine and Lillian were gracious and spoke with everyone. They ate burgers and drank soda with the kids. They curtsied when they met Miss Septima, and she loved it.

Just before sunset, Mr. Jimmy took them to visit around the way. First, he took them to his house and showed them big pictures of the old neighborhood and of the inside of some of the homes.

"Look at the ocean," Lillian said, pointing to seashells recently painted by Bea. "This part of the story, from the paper, of you sitting with Juba after he found the pictures. It was heartrending. I see why you did it though. This is beautiful, Daddy."

He took them on a tour of the almost finished, new around the way. They were astonished at everything that had been accomplished up to that point. They were happy for him. Afterward, they went back to the motel to a special dinner prepared by Patrice, and then they slept in his bed as he sat in his lounge chair, beyond thankful and full of love.

They stayed for two days, and when they left, the children were heartbroken. Especially Juba and Beech, whose dedication to Katherine's and Lillian's every need constantly left Mr. Jimmy laughing. As the car drove away, their hands waving from each side and his steadily waving in return, he felt sad. Not once had they mentioned Rebecca. Not once had he found the nerve to mention her either.

EPILOGUE

Mr. Jimmy had just finished hanging the new pictures in Miss Septima's new living room. Martin Luther King, Jr., Jesus, and John F. Kennedy.

"That don't look like my Jesus," she said.

"Well, Miss Septima, this is more like what Jesus would have really looked like. It's more historically accurate."

"More historically ugly if you ask me. My Jesus is handsome."

"He's good-looking."

"Hmmmm. You say. I'll see what the Missionary Circle say about it."

Mr. Jimmy laughed as he reached out to level the pictures just a bit more.

"You talk to your mama and daddy today?"

"Yes, ma'am."

"Good, good. How they doing?"

"They are good. They are proud of me, and that makes me happy. Just like I was still a little kid or something."

"Ain't no shame in that," she said. "Everybody wants somebody to be proud of them."

"Yes, ma'am. That's true, I agree. For me, especially after my father was told to step down from the pulpit. And they both were set aside and I think treated poorly considering all that they had done for the church and the community. But they seem to be happy with the way things worked out. They are just happy to be members of the church now. Daddy said that they probably should have retired a long time before the trouble started anyway."

"I agree with that," Miss Septima said. "A Baptist minister is harder to get rid of than the deepest, dug-in tick."

Mr. Jimmy roared. "Maybe I should tell him that."

She shrugged her shoulders. "A man of the cloth ought to appreciate the straight truth now and then."

Mr. Jimmy continued to laugh as he took two bottles of tea out of her refrigerator. They took them out onto her front porch and stood watching the neighborhood, alive in a way it had never been.

"To better days," Mr. Jimmy said, and they tapped their bottle necks together and drank.

"Today was something else," she said, smiling as she watched the kids playing in the park across the street.

Mr. Jimmy nodded his head, thinking back on the afternoon. Just after church, buses went by the Wayside Motel, picked up its residents, and brought them to around the way. All of the families were asked to line up across the street from their new homes. They had been urged not to enter until Miss Septima had crossed the threshold of her house. It was an absolutely beautiful scene, he thought. He had helped Miss Septima up her new steps and onto her new porch where she took a moment to look at the new furniture. She had squeezed his hand, looked up at him, and smiled. Mr. Jimmy handed her the key, and her hand shook as she used it to unlock the door. The smell of newness rushed out, over and around them both. She took a deep breath, and she began to cry.

"Oh, my Jesus," she said, softly. "Oh, my Lawd."

When she stepped into the house, the folks from around the way broke out in a cheer, and they ran to their homes like children running to great expectations on Christmas morning. He imagined them all doing what Miss Septima was doing, touching things, and lightly brushing their hands across things, and sitting on their new furniture. He imagined the joy of the kids, all of whom had their own bedrooms. And each house had two bathrooms. No more holes in the ground or outhouses around the way.

Now, he stood alongside Miss Septima in the fading light of day. He would be taking his leave shortly as the Missionary Circle Ladies were coming to have dinner at her new dining room table. Everyone would eat in their own homes that night. But it was hard to step away from the scene they watched across the street. Kids playing, as they should, without a worry. Up and down on their new playground equipment. Throwing footballs and playing basketball. Older girls and boys performed feats of skill with their hula hoops and jump ropes. Was his mind playing tricks on him? Could this be the same place that he walked into a black kitchen with the residue of butane on the walls?

"Oh, look at that now," Miss Septima said, pointing to Patrice, who had just joined her kids in the park. She still was not speaking well, but she was laughing just fine as the kids danced around her. She laid back her head and stretched out her arms. She twirled and twirled, and the kids began to do the same.

"Look now," Miss Septima said to Mr. Jimmy once again.

He turned to pay particular attention to Patrice, sporting her dental implants, her face alive with glee.

"That," Miss Septima said. "All of that is on you, son. That is your doing! And I thank you. I truly do."

Mr. Jimmy nodded, his eyes glistening, brimming with tears.

"And me," Miss Septima said. "I ain't afraid of no artificial flowers on my grave no more."

"Oh, Miss Septima," he replied. "You know I wouldn't allow that to happen."

She nodded. "Still, I want you to know. I ain't been nowhere, but at the same time, since you come around, I feel like I have traveled a lot. I feel like I been a part of something important and life changing in a good way. You see, Mr. Jimmy, I feel things that I didn't know I had inside of me. That's how I know I been somewhere. That's how I know I am changed. Because of that, I don't really give a hoot what goes on my grave. I'll be looking the other way anyhow, running to my Jesus to say *Lawd, I got something to tell you.*"

Miss Septima hugged Mr. Jimmy. She held on, he decided later, for a good five minutes. They did not say a word. Just held each other, and he knew when she stepped away, he would never forget it. He stepped off her porch and took a moment to stomp into place some sod that seemed to be coming up in her front yard. Then, as he started home, she called out to him.

"I know this is hard on you. I know you ain't found all that you been looking for. But we gone be here for you like you been here for us. Tomorrow morning, you know what to do, right?"

Mr. Jimmy softly smiled. "I do," he said. "Check for air pressure, blood pressure, and water pressure. Then put one foot in front of the other."

She nodded. "Amen, now," she said.

Mr. Jimmy entered his little house, now the oldest in the neighborhood. He went straight to his kitchen cabinet and shoved aside five-pound bags of sugar and flour. He pulled out the box that greeted him on his first day. The gift from his friend Olivia Fey Carol. He carefully slid the blue ribbon off the box and opened it. He knew he should decant a wine this special, but he didn't want to wait. He pulled out the 2009 Lafite-Rothschild, opened it, and poured a healthy glass. He sat in his lounge chair, reclined, and crossed his feet. In doing so, he saw that his shoes had been dusted and he smiled. Then he stared into the blackness of his television as the sun continued its decline. He drank his wine, and it tasted good. He made a mental note to order more before he nuzzled deeper into the softness of his chair and closed his eyes. He thought to clear his mind of everything and then wait to see what entered.

He was eight years old, and it was an absolutely perfect summer day. He was riding his bike. Riding as fast as he possibly could. He did not want to be late because his mother had promised him her special pound cake and French vanilla ice cream. He was riding so hard on the dirt road, his shirt flapping in the wind. He felt so incredibly alive. He thought of his mother waiting for him, and he felt so loved. In that moment, everything was right with his world. He started to smile as he peddled and then to laugh and then to shout with unabashed enthusiasm. He could feel a unique peace deep inside of him, and he knew that it was not an everyday thing.

His mother greeted him at the back door as he arrived just in time. The residue of his joy still on his face.

"What are you so happy about?" she asked, smiling back at him. "You look like we just let you stay up to watch Johnny Carson or something."

"I don't know why, Mama," he said. "It . . . it just came over me."

"Well don't question it," she suggested. "It's not every day we experience what's in your heart right now." She lovingly placed a hand on his back, directing him to the kitchen, where she sat him down in front of his large slice of cake. He started eating as she opened the freezer to get the ice cream. It was every bit as good as he had expected.

And then Mr. Jimmy imagined himself young again and outside the Post Office. He stood with her, this time right in front of her and he handed her one thousand dollars. She took it and said, *Thank you, child.* And this time, she smiled at him and touched him gently on his arm. As she turned to leave, she looked back one more time before fading away.

Mr. Jimmy opened his eyes to find the sun completely gone, his feelings of happiness tempered by the lonesome darkness in which he sat. And he felt it coming, rising up inside of him, taking over his body like a chill from a fever. He knew that it was futile to fight it. It would always be so. So, he gave in and let it take over until it controlled him, forcing him to say it out loud. *Rebecca.*

Air pressure, water pressure, blood pressure, he thought. *One step at a time . . .*

ACKNOWLEDGEMENTS

While writing a novel is a solitary endeavor, I never feel that I am completely alone in the process. By the time I've brought the story to its proper conclusion, family, friends, and colleagues have provided truly invaluable support. Sometimes, it's the space and time to write. Sometimes it is advice concerning a character's legal or medical situation. Sometimes, it's patiently listening to me as I babble on about where I am in the book's journey. I love this part of the journey because I get to say thank you.

To my wife, Jeanne Meserve. Every book I write is a journey for you as well. Thank you for your never-ending unconditional love and support for my literary dreams and the missions behind them. You are my greatest blessing and the keeper of my heart.

To my children, Julia and Jake, and my son-in-law, Jeffrey Kenny. Thank you for your encouragement and your cheers. I certainly needed them along the way. You are my heart.

To my father, R. Edward Blount. Thank you for continuing to be my north star. I would have never found my way without you.

To my brother from another mother, my oldest friend and my chosen family, Perry Nick Bell. Air pressure, water pressure, blood pressure. You know.

To Marly Rusoff, my agent and my dear friend. Thank you for

believing in me and the reason I write. Thank you for navigating the maze and finding a home for *Mr. Jimmy.* You are forevermore a part of each of my books. Thank you for being my dream maker.

To Kathie Bennett, my publicist and my dear friend. Your belief in me and my mission continually warms my heart. As I say often, if I give my work life, you give it the world. My literary blessing has been the impact my novels have had—the lives they have touched and changed. None of that would have happened without you. Thank you.

To Eric Kampmann, Publisher of Beaufort Books. Thank you for believing in *Mr. Jimmy*. Thank you for welcoming me into the Beaufort family.

To Editorial Director, Megan Trank, and Publicity and Editorial Associate, Emma St. John. Thank you for the enthusiasm. Thank you for your patient guidance. Thank you for all the hard work you put into this book and its author. It will be forever appreciated.

To Susan McBeth, Founder & CEO of Adventures by the Book. Thank you for your support of *The Emancipation of Evan Walls* and its mission through the five-part discussion series *Conversations in Race* on Firesidechat.com.

To my friends and fellow authors who gave advice and so much moral support. Rebecca Dwight Bruff, Mary O'Donohue Olen, Steve Majors, Jonathan Odell, S.A. Borders-Shoemaker, Christina Kovac, Kimmery Martin, Karen White, Marie Bostwick, Johnnie Bernhard, Susan Zurenda, and Susan Cushman.

Thank you to VCU (Virginia Commonwealth University) Libraries. Thank you, Kelly Gotschalk, Teresa Knott, and Irene Herold.

Thank you to those of you who provided advice. Thank you to those of you who have through friendship and the kindness of your book-loving hearts, supported my writing dream. Lauren Silberman, Joe and Dabney Cortina, John and Lynn Sachs,

Elan Blutinger, Alex Paluch, Jonathan and Emily Meserve, Jennifer Sisk, Kevin Barr and Mary Houghton, Lois and Michael Fingerhut, Samuel "Skip" Halpern, Dianne Delk, Richard and Marty Meserve, Steve and Emily Henn, Abigail Smith and Mike Zamore, Mary Batten, John and Anne Edwards, Timothy Lane Smith, Linda Lipsett, Susan Nelson, Frank Sesno, David and Margaret Hensler, Marquetta Brown-Cagg, Stephanie Brown-Valderrama, Valerie Cofer Butler, Rebecca Mercer, Pamela Meserve, Valerie Leuchter, Linda Meserve Gonzalez, Deb Meserve Beckwith, Tom Gehring, Jonathan Edelstein, and Robin Roulette.

Thank you to the real Fountain Hughes. Your stories continue to influence how I see the world and my place in it. I have attempted to pay tribute to you with the character named in your honor. I hope you would have been proud of my attempt.

On June 10, 2022, my mother, Doris Delk Blount, passed away. A lifelong educator, she loved and vigorously supported my literary dreams. Because of her long battle with dementia, she never knew that I was writing *Mr. Jimmy from Around the Way.* That fact deeply saddens me. I suspect it always will. On the night she died, I had an opportunity to be alone with her. By this time, she was non-responsive, but we had all continued to talk to her. I held her hand, just admiring her and thinking about the many life lessons she had offered as a guide to living a good and decent life. The notion of humility was at the top of her lesson plan. When I thought of that, I smiled remembering Reverend Ferguson's lesson for young Jimmy—throwing dirt on his shoes. So I pulled out my phone and called up my manuscript. The last thing I did with my mother was to read that section of the manuscript to her before kissing her and leaving. An hour or so later, on my way home, my brother called to say that she had gone. *But I remember, Mama. I always will.*

ABOUT THE AUTHOR

JEFFREY BLOUNT is the award-winning author of three novels—*Almost Snow White*, winner of the 2013 USA Best Book Awards; *Hating Heidi Foster*, winner of the 2013 Readers Favorite Book Award for young adult literature; *The Emancipation of Evan Walls*, winner of the 2020 National Indie Excellence Award for African American fiction, winner of the 2019 Readers Favorite Book Award, winner of the 2019 American Bookfest Best Book Award, and a Shelf Unbound 2019 Notable Book.

He is also an Emmy award-winning television director and a 2016 inductee to the Virginia Communications Hall of Fame. During a 34-year career at NBC News, Jeffrey directed a decade of *Meet the Press*, *The Today Show*, *NBC Nightly News*, and major special events.

He was a contributor for HuffPost and has been published in *The Washington Post*, The Grio.com, and other publications, commenting on issues of race, social justice, and writing.

Jeffrey grew up in Smithfield, Virginia. He and his wife, journalist Jeanne Meserve, live in Washington, DC.